MORE P

TH:

LOOKING THROUGH THE SHADOWS

I S.P.I.

SHORT STORIES & MORE

Michelle Lee on the Web

Michelle on Facebook at
tiny.cc/MichelleLeeWrites

or write to
MichelleLeeWrites@gmail.com

THE RAVEN'S JOURNEY
BOOK SIX

HAWK

Michelle Lee

BLUE FORGE PRESS
Port Orchard, Washington

Blue Forge Press is the print division of the volunteer-run, federal 501(c)3 nonprofit company, Blue Forge Group, founded in 1989 and dedicated to bringing light to the shadows and voice to the silence. We strive to empower storytellers across all walks of life with our four divisions: Blue Forge Press, Blue Forge Films, Blue Forge Gaming, and Blue Forge Records. Find out more at www.BlueForgeGroup.org

Blue Forge Press
7419 Ebbert Drive Southeast
Port Orchard, Washington 98367
blueforgepress@gmail.com
360-550-2071 ph.txt

For Melissa
and your never-ending support.
You are priceless.

HAWK

Michelle Lee

Chapter One

When will you settle down and start a family?" Chief Tyee walked into the exam room and studied Onida.

"Chief. What brings you by other than that intrusive question?" Onida leaned against the counter and looked over her clipboard of supplies she needed to restock the room.

"You used to call me Dad." He settled back in a chair and looked at his daughter, a pensive look on his face.

"And you used to be a lot less invasive," she shot back at him.

"I'm your father. I worry about you." His steady gaze on her was unnerving. Sometimes he saw things she didn't want him to see, which felt like one of those times.

"Why are you here? Do you not feel well?" Onida went back over her list of supplies trying to think of anything Tama may need to get through her pregnancy that Onida didn't already have on hand.

"I simply wanted to see you and was nearby talking with Taklishim. Thought I'd stop by since you've been a bit reclusive lately."

"Lately? I'm always reclusive; this isn't anything new." Onida shrugged and set the clipboard down. "I like my privacy."

"You've been spending a lot of time with Taklishim's angel," he remarked casually.

So that was it. "You are worried about who I am spending my time with now? You know she doesn't belong to Taklishim."

Chief Tyee sighed. "No, I'm not worried about who you are spending your time with now. The last three months have changed you. I'm your father, I'm worried. It's my right. I'm aware Airiella doesn't belong to Taklishim; she doesn't belong to anyone. It was more of a snide comment than anything else. I've not seen that man that protective of someone other than your sister and you."

"Tak isn't protective of me," Onida argued, suddenly very uncomfortable.

"Oh, my daughter, he is. Maybe not as much as he is with Tama or Airiella, but he is. Who do you think demanded that Airiella get told when you were missing? It's beside the point. My point was I'm worried, you haven't been the same since the demon. I've also noticed Degataga is still around."

Onida stiffened, there was the other shoe dropping. "We are helping Airiella learn. She hasn't had all that many chances to test or practice the abilities she has developed other than under literal fire of demons. Stop worrying; there is nothing wrong with me."

"You still seem to be under the impression that I can't tell when you are lying to me." Chief Tyee scrubbed his hands over his face. Maybe a change of subject would take the steel out of her spine. "Are you going to be the one caring for Tama's pregnancy?"

"Who else would she trust?" Onida knew what her father was up to, and she wasn't falling for it.

"Right you are. Naturally, you will be taking care of Tama. Silly question. I still don't understand how after years of failed pregnancies and countless doctors saying she couldn't conceive, she now has. I'm grateful for it, though."

This conversation was what Onida had been hoping to avoid. She shifted her weight from foot to foot in a nervous gesture. "Yes, well, the Great Spirit shone his blessing down on her."

"Ah, my child, some things never change with you. Still guarding the secrets, you don't think I know about or see you hiding. You will be attending the wedding, right?" Chief Tyee smiled softly at his daughter.

"Why do you always make me feel like a child?" Onida resisted the impulse to stomp her feet in frustration. "Yes, I am going to Airiella's wedding. If you think I am keeping secrets that you should know about, then come straight out and ask me. Stop trying to trick me into it."

"Tell me how she did it, then." He stood up and hugged his daughter to him, dropping a kiss on her head.

"I don't know," Onida admitted in a whisper. "I only know it's because of her. The same thing happened with Mags."

"Not knowing doesn't make you a failure, Onida. Remember that. Airiella is a rarity, and you studying her like you are doing isn't going to provide the answers you seek. Let the poor girl alone. Teach her what she needs to know and stop picking her apart. Taklishim said you recommended her for the council," he said as he changed the subject again.

"Seems to me the world's only angel should be on the council." Onida gave in and rested her head on her dad's chest. "I'm not picking Airiella apart," she told him, her voice soft in the quiet room. "I know how much Tama wanted this, and I'm worried something will happen."

"Have faith, my dear. You have the world's most talented people among you. Tama will be well looked after. Science isn't always the answer. Sometimes love can create miracles on its own. Airiella should be proof enough of that."

"Love and I don't always see eye to eye," she said so softly that the Chief wasn't sure he heard her right.

"Try letting it in every once in a while. See what happens." Chief Tyee released Onida and headed out of the room. "See you later, daughter of mine."

"Bye, Dad." Onida thudded the clipboard against her head. She hated it when he used that dad sight of his. Onida stood there waiting, knowing the spectacle wasn't quite over yet. "I know you are out there Tama, let's get this over with," she called out.

"How'd you know I was out there?" Tama sidled cat-like into the room.

"Twins, remember? I can feel you. If you are going to harp on me too, spit it out. Then get out."

"Dad has a point. You've been different in the past three months. Every time we try to bring it up, you shut us down. No, that's not why I'm here. I wanted to see if you wanted to get lunch with me. I can pry information out of you then."

Onida let out a bark of a laugh. "No ulterior motives

12

there, then."

"We do need to get wedding outfits. At least I do. My clothes aren't fitting that well, and I think leggings might not be exactly appropriate. Though in my defense, Airiella would probably rather wear those than a dress." Tama sat down on the chair her father had deserted.

"If Airiella were choosing, she would wear one of Ronnie's t-shirts with the leggings," Onida added. "Even still, it's not an entirely formal wear type of wedding. Didn't she tell you that?"

"She did. Come on, feed me. Miracle baby is hungry." Tama stood up and waited for Onida to give in. "Listen to your elders, especially the pregnant ones."

Onida let out another laugh. "Three minutes hardly counts as an elder."

"Shall I invite Dad?" Tama shot her a malicious look.

"Fine, I'm coming." Onida stuffed her wallet in her pocket and followed her twin out of the office. "Pregnancy has made you mean."

"Funny how the roles reversed, isn't it?" Tama joked getting in the car. "I want a big, fat, greasy burger. We are going to the diner."

"Love the healthy choices you are making, my dear sister."

"Perfect segue. Let's talk about healthy choices, my dear sister," Tama mocked.

"That felt like a setup." Onida closed her eyes.

"It was one you created, not me. Degataga's still here, Onida. He hasn't left." Tama took a chance and brought up the subject that had the potential to send Onida over the edge of insanity.

"He's working with Airiella, of course, he's still here. Getting her well versed in her skills is more important than anything else," Onida pointed out hotly.

Tama parked, "Is that what you are telling yourself?" She got out and looked at Onida over the top of the car. "He's here for you. Don't be an oblivious bird."

"An oblivious bird? Maybe I should scan your brain if that's the best insult you can come up with." Onida ducked as the keys came hurtling over the top of the car at her. "See? Mean."

"If you don't talk to him, you will force my hand," Tama warned.

"Force you to do what? Tama, he left me. He made the choice to go back and stay away. He's here now because of Airiella, not me."

"He may have come because of her. He's not still here because of her. For someone so smart you can be completely dense. Talk to him," Tama hissed at her as they walked in.

"Mind your own business," Onida fired back, her voice taking on a bitter edge.

"You *are* my business, sister." Tama sat down, pulling a menu out and looking it over, ignoring the pissed off look she knew her sister had on her face.

They placed their orders, and Tama leaned back in the booth. "Now, why have you been even more distant that normal?"

"Why does everyone keep saying that?" Onida threw her hands up in the air, accidentally knocking the water the waitress had been bringing them out of her hands, drenching them both.

Tama tipped her head back and howled in laughter.

"See? Even the universe thinks you are out of balance."

Onida said nothing. Using the napkins, she soaked up the water from her clothes and tried to formulate something to respond with that would end this conversation. All her snappy comebacks fled as she saw the confused look on Tama's face. "What's wrong?"

"You're crying."

"What? No, I'm not. It's from the spilled water." Onida wiped her face quickly.

"Stop lying. I can tell the difference between tears coming from your eyes and water dripping from other parts of your face. What is going on?"

"Nothing," Onida muttered, flushing with embarrassment. She never cried.

"You've been like this since Bael died. Taklishim said you disappeared so fast when Stolas showed up the other day to work with them on plants, that he thought you had turned to your Hawk and flew off. I know isn't true because you haven't given over once to your animal, or you wouldn't be so cagey right now."

"What's wrong with not wanting to be around a demon?" Onida looked down at her lap as she said it, unable to meet Tama's eyes.

"If Dad came to talk to you, then this is something worth worrying about, he doesn't interfere usually. Talk to me, please?"

"I froze."

"What?" Tama looked confused.

"When Airiella got injured, I froze. I didn't help her or Jax."

"That's what this is about?" Tama's expression was pure shock.

"If Stolas hadn't shown up, we'd have lost them both. I couldn't do anything. My brain went numb. She got disemboweled, and I froze."

"I'm aware of what happened to her," Tama remarked acidly.

"All the rest of you stepped up, except me. I took the easy route and helped Mags."

"Are you forgetting your help at the hospital?"

"Tama, all I kept thinking was I was so happy it wasn't you, Tak or Dega."

"This is guilt?" Tama shook her head. "This is something I would never have thought would come out of *your* mouth. You were right when you said there wasn't anything we could do for her."

"Tak and Dega still tried."

"Taklishim damn near lost his mind when Bael gutted her. I've never seen him so furious, scared, and overcome with emotions like he was that day. He *cried.* She could have gotten decapitated, and he would have tried to sew her head back on."

"How is that helping?" Shame started seeping through her pores.

"You stepped up at the hospital. You even worked with Degataga to help bring her back when she died on the table a second time. Why has this shaken you so much?" Tama was genuinely confused.

"Because I didn't want her to die. Because I'm not used to feeling things like this."

Light dawned on Tama's face. "She broke through those walls of yours."

"Like a wrecking ball."

"And now that she has, your feelings for Degataga

are close to the surface, and you can't hide from them," Tama guessed.

Onida touched her nose in response and looked out the window of the diner. Nothing was ever easy; that was a lesson she had learned long ago. Matters of the heart were even messier, and Onida hated dealing with them after Degataga had left. It was far less trouble for her to erect walls to keep people out and think her cold and unemotional.

Chapter Two

Taklishim pinched the bridge of his nose and tipped his head back, frustration evident on his face. "Why do you think this meeting is necessary?"

Degataga looked between the two men, another local tribe leader that wanted a meeting with Airiella. Word had spread among the scattered tribes along the area that an angel was in their midst, and they had gotten it into their heads that she could solve their problems for them. An utterly ridiculous notion since their issues were political.

"She can help us," the leader tried to argue.

"Seek counseling, that would be more helpful. Or vote in new leaders. An angel can't help you with political strife amongst your people. Besides, what makes you think I have any sway with such a being if one even exists?" Taklishim had taken the line that he wasn't aware of her and was sticking to it.

"That's what the others are all saying."

"I'm not a leader. You shouldn't fall prey to the gossip mill," he told them as he tried to make his point.

Degataga stood before the warrior lost his cool. "Taklishim has had this conversation at least three times today. Enough. We have work we are doing, please excuse us." Degataga held the door open for the man who finally got the hint and left.

"Thanks, Dega."

"Did you find out who it was that leaked the info?" Degataga sat back down, then thought twice about it and stood to lock the door before retaking his seat.

"It had to have been one of the people the Chief brought to help Smitty and Aedan pack up. I don't know which one though. It doesn't matter who. I just need to stem it, stop it from bleeding. The Chief is holding a meeting with his people tomorrow night to try and stop it."

"Does she know?" Degataga wondered if that is what had been bothering Airiella.

"I don't think so. I've tried keeping it from Airiella." The gray warrior sighed. "Have you talked with Onida yet?" He changed the subject.

"Not yet. I approached Onida a couple of times, and she took off the other direction. Let me ask you this if I moved here, would I be accepted?"

"What do you mean?" Taklishim crossed his ankle over his knee.

"You have three medicine people already within the tribe. I don't want to step on any toes, nor do I want there to be a conflict between tribal knowledge."

"You think the other leaders would protest having you here?" Taklishim thought about it before shaking his head. "They accepted me."

"You are married to a chief's daughter," Degataga pointed out. "Makes not accepting you a little harder."

"Possibly, but they aren't like that here like they are in some of the other tribes across the nation. It's small and personal. Most of the people here in this area are ones that weren't happy with their current situations and migrated. I don't see a problem among the general population. A problem with Onida is a different matter."

"One, I am not sure how to address either," Degataga admitted.

"I want to be clear on the reason you would consider moving here, so care to enlighten me?"

Degataga huffed at him. "You know exactly why."

"You two need to talk." Taklishim repeated the same words Tama had told Onida. "Trust me. I know how daunting that task is. She's not romantically seen anyone since you left. Dega, that's going to be a big wall to scale. She shut down after that."

"I know," he said as he gritted his teeth at the memory. "I never stopped loving Onida, and I repeatedly reached out."

"Have you thought about involving Airiella?"

"Doesn't that go against everything that you have been talking about to these people?" Degataga was flabbergasted. "She can't make Onida listen any more than Tama can."

"I don't mean involving her in that way. The next time you two are working with her on honing her skills, ask Airiella to touch both of you at the same time."

"I'm sure that won't come across as weird or anything like that at all." Degataga snorted.

"Just trust me. It's not something Onida can ignore. If you want to get through to her, start there."

"No wonder Airiella is always calling us cryptic

bastards if that's all you can tell me."

Tak leaned back in his chair, stretching out his long sinewy frame. "She has this way of seeing the bonds people have. When they touch her at the same time, and she pours a little energy into it, you can see future scenes, if there is one."

"Perfect. So Airiella can confirm for me that Onida hates me. What every man in love wants to hear." Degataga leaned forward and rested his forehead on the desk.

"She doesn't hate you, Dega. I can guarantee you that. She might be hurt still, but there is no hate in that woman's heart. That indifference she shows everyone is only an act. She freaked out just as much as I did when Airiella was hurt."

"Are you talking about me, Gandalf?" Degataga and Taklishim jumped, both being caught off guard by the angel they were just talking about using.

"Caught red-handed. You are getting better at that sneaking around stuff. What are you doing here, Raven?" Taklishim got up and hugged her.

"A hug? You must be feeling guilty about something. Or are you trying to bribe me into doing something I don't want to do?" Airiella smiled happily.

"I hug you every time I see you now." Taklishim grunted.

"Chill, Gandalf, I know. You make it so easy for me to pick on you. Something told me I needed to be here, so here I am. What's going on?" She leaned over and hugged Degataga and sat in the chair next to him.

"Well, Onida recommended you be on the council, Tama and I both agree. I haven't had a chance to ask Dega yet. I can now that he's on the spot so you can make *him* uncomfortable instead of me for once."

"Do I get a say in this? Have you talked to Jax? He might have an opinion as well." Airiella looked a little nervous at the thought.

"Where is Jax? Usually, you two are always around each other." Degataga looked out in the hallway.

"He's out in the car. He was on the phone, and I'm in no danger from you two. At least that's what I thought. Do you seriously want me in a political position? I'm kind of blunt. The two don't always mix."

Taklishim laughed. "You do have a point. You still should have a say in what happens on that side of things. You are probably the most powerful person on earth."

"This is a Jax discussion. I won't decide this without his input. He's way better at that crap than I am."

"I'll give you that. Jax knows how to play the game well. We can talk about it later. I need to get a vote from the others first before I can offer you a position. I do have a favor since you are here. Tell Dega about what happens when you touch two people who have a bond they don't know about."

"That's an oddly specific request." She crossed her legs and looked at them both with a curious expression. Before they knew it, she had both of their hands in hers and was doing something with energy that Degataga couldn't define. "You two are not a love connection."

Taklishim howled in laughter. It was strange seeing him this free and unrestrained for Degataga. He knew it had everything to do with the magnificent creature that was with them. Degataga himself was different around her. She brought out the softer sides of people. Ah, now he got it.

"May I ask a favor instead?" Degataga asked of her.

"Of course. You guys don't have to ask with the expectation that I will turn you down. How can I help you?"

"Our next training session, can you touch Onida and me at the same time?" He flushed.

"Are you propositioning my future wife?" Jax grinned as he walked in and leaned against the wall.

Degataga felt all the words flee his brain at the question. Of all the times for Jax to walk in, that hadn't been the best time. He wasn't worried that Jax was offended, but he didn't want all his business with Onida to come to the surface. It would make her uncomfortable, and he was trying to avoid that.

"They do need to talk to you, but can you give me a few minutes alone with them?" Airiella stood and kissed him on the cheek, whispering something in his ear.

"Sure. I'll go back out to the car." He handed her a couple of envelopes and walked back out.

Airiella gave each man an envelope. "Okay, Degataga. I will do as you ask, but you need to tell me why. If this is going to upset Onida, I want to prepare for that."

"Raven, can you do it without the explanation?" Taklishim asked gently. "It might upset her, but it would be for a good cause."

"I love her, Airiella. I always have," Degataga implored her.

"Is it not reciprocated?" She shifted uncomfortably.

"It used to be. If there is nothing there, nothing will happen, right?" Degataga asked.

"It used to be like that. I am not sure now. The last thing I want is to hurt Onida. She's been a little different since I killed Bael. She tries to hide it from me, but when I'm with you two, I have to keep my senses open, and she's got a storm going on inside. It's kind of painful."

"Can I ask a bold question?" Degataga glanced at Taklishim, who narrowed his eyes, ready to jump in and protect Airiella from any perceived slight.

"Ask away. Fair warning, this falls back on the blunt statement I made earlier. I'll either answer it or tell you to stuff it."

"Was it you that helped make Tama pregnant?" As a medicine man, he'd been trying to figure it out. As a friend, he was happy for the couple. As a man in love, he was hopeful that the deep well she had inside would help open Onida's heart.

She glanced at Taklishim, who simply nodded at her. "After Taklishim got me released from the hospital, and after the engagement party, they both touched me at the same time. The first time I hadn't fed any power into it and saw them both with a child. When I had repeated what I'd seen, it had hurt Tama pretty badly. I hadn't known that doctors had told her that she wouldn't be able to have children. Having known that pain for myself, I understood it. The next time, still at the party, I fed it power and saw the same vision, so I knew it had to be a future. I can't explain how it works because it was different for Mags. This time I simply asked the universe to make it real while I was touching them. Honestly, can you think of two people who would be better parents than Gandalf and the Catwoman?"

Taklishim was full of surprises for Degataga today; the warrior had tears in his eyes as he gazed at Airiella. "Raven, you've given me and my soulmate the best gift in the world. We can only hope that we will be worthy of it."

"Oh, Gandalf, you are." She blew him a kiss and looked back at Degataga. "I'm sure I'll see something. If you'd rather me not say it out loud in case it's possibly a painful subject, then let me know now. I have a blood link with Onida, so the chances are, she will see the same thing that I do. Probably you too since you are both powerful on your own."

Degataga sighed. She was his soul mate, he knew it with every fiber of his being, not to mention Onida had told him he was years ago. "It's not my intent to bring her pain. I only want the door open for personal communication with her again. I hope that if she sees a future with me in it, that door will open on her end. If that door opens, I can work on repairing the damage I did. Try to explain my reasoning."

"I'll do what I can, Dega. I'm calling Jax in now so that *you*," she pointed at Taklishim, "can tell him of your plans with the council regarding me. On this, I will defer to him. Might be the only time, who knows."

Taklishim chuckled, "How are things with Ronnie?"

"He's the second love of my life, and it's a little slower for him to separate. He said that Jax had to share until the wedding. I've never said that I wouldn't still be with him if that is what he wanted. Jax never said he wouldn't share either." She shrugged. "He's slowly starting to get to know Chrissie and spending a lot of time with her. He's totally in love with those boys. And with her, but he hasn't admitted it yet. They do indeed have a future together; he's just overly cautious. I don't mind. I'm still stealing his t-shirts in the meantime."

"She's right, he's a part of us, and he doesn't have to stop because I am marrying her," Jax said as he walked in. "We've made that clear to him."

"For the record, Airiella said with both Dega and me here as witnesses, that she defers to you on something. I just wanted you to hear that, for the first time, probably," Taklishim said with a grin. "Dega, he might have a heart attack, get ready to help."

Chapter Three

"Will you please just try?" Onida spat out in a frustrated tone. This time spent training Airiella with Degataga was getting harder to deal with every day.

"What do you think I've been doing?" Airiella yelled back at her.

"Arguing. That's what you've been doing. Why do you think you have wings?" Onida tried again.

"As armor. Stolas told me they'd protect me and anyone behind them. I don't see how they would protect me from impacting the ground, though."

Degataga tried to smother his laughter with a cough, but Airiella caught on and glared at him. "I don't have wings; I can't help you with this."

"She doesn't have wings right now, either!" Airiella pointed out.

"You have elemental powers! You aren't going to fall to your death!" Onida paced, trying to reign in her temper. "For someone who runs head first at demons that have said they would kill you, you are inexplicably terrified to lift yourself five feet off the ground with your gigantic wings."

"Fish, bugs, snakes, and heights are my fears," Airiella stated for the third time.

"So, if I threw a snake at your feet, you'd fly?" Onida challenged.

Airiella paled and shot a look at Degataga, who was not about to involve himself in this battle. "The best way to conquer it is to face it. What's worse, a snake or flying?"

"Damn you both!" She was shaking, and Degataga heard the pounding of feet as Ronnie burst into the clearing.

"Angel, you are sending some pretty loud distress signals."

"I'm trying to get her to fly!" Onida shouted at the end of her rope.

Ronnie laughed, kissed her, and silently left. "I see he's aware of the fear," Degataga said calmly.

"Fuck. Fine. But first, let me shake her a bit," Airiella whispered to Degataga. "Onida, come over here, please. I'll try, but hold my hand for a minute, let me feel the strength in you, it will help calm my mind."

"Sneaky." Degataga moved closer to her and took her hand.

"If you zap me, we will have big issues, Raven." Onida reverted to Taklishim's name for the angel. She walked over and grabbed her hand. Onida was immediately thrust into a vision of herself and Degataga blissfully happy and very much together. Shocked, she dropped Airiella's hand.

"What the hell was that?" She accused Airiella.

"How do I know? It happened when *you* touched *me!*" Airiella had a smug smile on her face, and Onida felt the wind surge and lift the black-winged girl off the ground.

Onida felt the stab of panic that shot through Airiella but couldn't bring herself to smile. She was stuck on the vision she had just seen. Onida was terrified to look anywhere other than the scared angel that hovered ten feet above her. She felt Degataga's intense stare boring into her.

Shaken and trying to hide it, she directed Airiella, "Try moving forward with your wings, not the air. Only use the element as a net if you feel like you are falling. Allow the air to be the ground to your wings. Catch the currents and glide."

"Uh-huh, right. Easier said than done," came the frightened voice from above.

"Your wings instinctively know what to do, allow them to function," Onida shouted, unable to hide the tremor in her voice as Degataga walked closer to her. Thankfully the piercing scream that came from Airiella as she dropped distracted them both.

They raised their arms to catch her, and again at the contact, Onida was sent right into another vision. This time she was pregnant, and her mind was screaming at her that Degataga was her mate. Onida stumbled, dropping to the ground in a tangle of limbs with Airiella as she struggled to get away from the angel.

"Whatever you are doing, stop," Onida gasped, her heart pounding with the knowledge that she had been right all along. He was her mate. She had known it back then but refused to admit it again since he had left.

"I'm not doing anything other than trying to not die from falling from the sky that you made me be in!" Airiella shot back at her.

"You wouldn't have died from ten feet in the air,

Airiella," Degataga said, his voice calm as he lifted Airiella to her feet while Onida put distance between them.

She looked at him then; she couldn't help it. His voice might have been calm, but his eyes were anything but calm. The panic that took over Onida far surpassed the fear Airiella had felt in the air, and she couldn't stop it. She couldn't breathe, couldn't move, couldn't speak.

Airiella was at her side in an instant, and Onida felt the calm, soothing energy of the angel wash over her, pulling the panic away as sweet air filled her lungs, and her legs wobbled under her. "I've got you; breathe slowly," Airiella was whispering to her.

"What was that?" Onida snapped at her quietly.

"Sometimes, I get visions when two people who are supposed to be together, touch me at the same time," she said apologetically. "I didn't know that would happen with you."

The words didn't get lost on Onida; she just couldn't face them right now. "Is that how Tama is pregnant?"

"Not because she touched me, but I saw a vision of her pregnant as well," Airiella admitted.

"Next time, don't use the wind to lift you. Do it yourself; you're done for the day," Onida announced, needing to be alone.

"Onida, maybe you should talk to him. I'm not going to interfere, and I won't touch you both again at the same time unless you ask me to. I do think you guys should talk. That mate thing is no joke. When Jax left after Bael, it almost broke me."

Onida nodded, trying to numb herself against the power of the visions over her heart. It had broken her when Degataga had left last time. "Airiella, can you please not mention this?"

"You don't even have to ask. It's no one's business but the two of you. I, um, well, you know I've been through a lot. If you need to talk, you can always use me as a sounding board," she offered Onida.

"Thanks, Raven. I may take you up on that." Onida slipped, and let the soft side she tried to keep out of sight, show.

"You might want to, um, wipe your face before you see anyone else," she struggled to get out.

"What?" Onida wasn't following.

"You're crying," Airiella said bluntly.

Onida swiped her face madly; this was not acceptable. She needed to get a better handle on herself. "I'm fine. Go back to Ronnie. I won't threaten you with a snake anymore."

She watched as Airiella walked away, stopping briefly to speak with Degataga before heading back out. It was inevitable she'd have to talk to him like Airiella and Tama had both suggested. She didn't want to cry while doing it, though. That needed to stop. She'd shed enough tears over that infuriating man already. Professional and distant, she could do.

The visions replayed through her mind. The feeling of love emanating from them, warming her cold heart. She'd never stopped loving him. That wasn't the problem. She was hurting that he'd chosen to leave instead of exploring what they'd had, even after she told him about the mate bond. She wasn't sure she could trust him with her heart.

The pain from being away from your mate was awful. Pieces of her heart just hardening up without the bond to feed it, the empty void feeling it left inside her that nothing else could fill. She'd shut down emotionally. Being around him again with Airiella coming into the mix had been hard. He brought things back to life in her she had no right to expect from him. He'd made his choice, and it hadn't been her.

Then there had been the night when they had worked on Airiella to stem the bleeding in her brain. She'd fallen right into bed with him as if it was the most natural thing to do on earth. If she was honest with herself, she hadn't been the same since then. She changed *before* the standoff with Bael.

"Please don't turn away from me." She heard the subject of her thoughts say as he walked upon her silently.

"We need to talk, I know." Her voice came out wooden. It wasn't what she intended, but it was better than tears. She couldn't look at Degataga yet. The urge to throw herself at him was too strong, and one look at those eyes of his, and she'd be lost. "I'm sorry I forced that on you."

"You didn't force it on me, and I'm not sorry in the least that it happened. What I saw was a beautiful confirmation of the way I feel." His words were soft, and he sat down on the ground. "Sit with me, please."

Chapter Four

Do you even know why I left?" Degataga stared straight ahead, resisting the need to touch her.

"I wasn't enough," she said simply, moving to at least sit on the ground near him.

"I can't believe you of all people would think that." He looked at her then, wishing he hadn't. Her face was carefully blank, but her eyes were a storm of pain and mistrust.

"What was I supposed to think? All you said was that you had to go. I had hoped you would come back. That you'd understand what I had told you was the truth. But you didn't. The distance grew; you didn't reach out to even talk to me. You were there, and then you were gone." The truth of her words hit him hard.

"You are right. I didn't tell you why I left. I was confused, worried and not thinking straight. I had told Tak. I had thought he would have said something. No matter now, I should have been the one to tell you. Nothing I can say now will alter the outcome or change anything. I can only explain and hope that you can find it in yourself to forgive me. I can hold on to hope that we can start again, because there is nothing that I want more than what those visions showed me." Degataga wished she would look at him.

"Dega, there's nothing to forgive. Did you lie?" She looked down at her lap. The confident woman he had fallen in love with lost under the insecurity he had brought down on her.

"No. I never lied, not about how I felt, or about needing to leave," he admitted cautiously.

"Forgiveness isn't the issue. Trust is. I don't hate you, Dega. I never could. The trust isn't there. Mate bonds are powerful and not to be taken lightly. Even though you never agreed to the bond, it killed me to be away from you. My heart withered up and just died." The words were said so softly and in a tone that made him need to scream out. "I have a black hole inside me."

"I don't believe your heart died. I can feel it every time we are near each other. I do believe that it probably felt like it died. It felt like it to me, too. A crushing heaviness whenever your name came up, or when I closed my eyes and didn't feel you next to me. I know the damage I caused, and I can't apologize enough." He sighed heavily. "Sorry won't fix it; I know that too. Again, I can only offer an explanation and an opportunity to start again. *Gvyageyuso'I*," he spoke in his native Cherokee language, telling her he always loved her.

"If you have to leave and go back to your people, what is the point of starting over again? The results will be the same." She still refused to look at him.

"I asked Taklishim what he thought about me moving here." Degataga laid all his cards out.

She looked up and over at him, a gasp of shock on her lips. Her eyes held hope, and Degataga grasped on to it with all he had. Despite how hard he knew it was going to be to win her over, he wanted that future with her. He believed she wanted it, too.

"What would you think about it? This is *your* choice, Onida. If you don't want me here, I will leave. I don't wish to cause you any problems, nor am I trying to force you into something."

"Explaining why you left doesn't change anything," she pointed out, unsure how to react to his statement about moving here.

"No, it doesn't," he agreed. "It only gives you a broader picture of the reasons behind it and allows you to see that it was *never* because you weren't enough. It might help start to heal the trust issue."

"How honest do you want me to be right now?" Her question caught him off guard.

"No matter how much I might not like what you say, I always want complete honesty," he said, longing to touch her again.

"I don't know how any of this makes me feel. There's hope, pain, confusion, desire, anger, and love. I'm not the same person as I was when you left; it was the very act of you leaving that changed me. I doubt that you are the same person either. I will admit that the deep feelings haven't gone away, and love doesn't change at the root of it all. I don't know if you can still love the person I am now, and vice versa. How do I know you won't do the same thing as last time and just up and leave if you decide you can't love me?"

"There's no question about how I feel in my heart.

As for leaving, I'd have to go back to move. Or if there was an emergency in my family. But what makes you think you couldn't come with me?" Degataga made his voice as gentle as possible.

"You didn't give me the option last time, you just left. Why would I think it would be different now?"

"As you said, we are different people now, both older and wiser. Onida, I had to go. My father was dying and they were trying to force me to be a leader. My priority was my father, and my family. I walked into a mess I wasn't prepared for, one that took up all my time and energy." He looked down at his hands. "My heart and my thoughts, however, those were with you. They were trying to force me into a marriage of alliance with the daughter of another local tribe to unite us. I worked tirelessly with the plants, herbs and skills I had at my disposal trying to heal him. In the end, I only bought him a year."

"Why wouldn't you have been able to tell me that before you left?" Her tone was slightly accusatory, but there was something underneath it.

"Time. My brother's call was urgent, and I'm the only medicine man allowed near the leaders. The timing of it all was awful, it happening so soon after you told me about the bond. I know it looked like I ran from you. I didn't. I also couldn't turn away from my father when he needed me. Without him, I would have been married off to someone I never had a hope of loving."

"If you had time to tell Taklishim, why didn't you have time to tell me?"

"He was with me when I got the call. I literally told him while packing my bags and getting a flight home," Degataga explained, fervently wishing that he could wipe the hurt look from her face.

"Why would they want to marry you off? Our country doesn't follow the tribal traditions, there is nothing to gain from a couple of tribes banding together. We live in a modern world." Onida looked down and was picking at the grass.

"That was my argument and the one of my father. It was his brother who was convincing my mother that it would benefit us. The other tribe wanted unfettered access to me. My knowledge, my skills, my humanity. Nothing more than that."

"How did you get out of it?"

"Airiella came into the picture. With her presence in my life it was easy to walk away from it all. Please understand, I can't turn my back on my family. If they need me, I will go. They are my family." He dared to reach out for her hand and held it gently between his own. "I'd be honored if you came with me if that becomes an issue."

"Why would you want to move away from them?" Onida so badly wanted to believe there was a chance for them. The longer he was around her, the more that hole inside her filled.

"For you, I'd move anywhere. There isn't much I wouldn't brave for a chance to have what I saw in those visions. Onida, it's your choice. I will honor my word, and if you decide that you don't want me to be a part of your life, I will walk away. If you give me another chance, I'll do everything I can to prove to you that what's in my heart is real."

"Does Tama know of all this?" She was going to have heated words with her sister if she did.

"No. I don't believe she does." Degataga took

another chance and kissed the back of her hand. "Do you need time to think?"

She pulled it back reluctantly, the bond within her responding to his touch. "I do. I'm not sure how I feel about another woman being in the picture."

"There was never anything between us. There's been no one for me other than you. It's been a long three years." He laughed dryly.

"I'm sorry about your father. I can't imagine losing my dad. Or Tama."

"Hawk-eye..." He used the old nickname he'd had for her. "If I don't give you space to think right now, I don't think I'm going to be able to stop touching you."

Her heart stuttered a crazy beat at hearing the name he'd used in their most intimate moments. Heat pooled in her core at the thought of his hands on her again. "Maybe I need a reminder of what I've been missing," she said boldly.

"So much for taking it slow." He groaned and yanked her closer, settling his lips on hers gently until passion curled through him at the stroke of her tongue on his. She pulled back too fast for his taste.

"My name is Onida, local doctor, fabled medicine woman, spirit walker, and hawk. Nice to meet you." She stuck out her hand for him to shake.

Trying to put the brakes on his smoking libido he shook her hand. "I'm Degataga. Cherokee medicine man, and used to be an energy guru until an angel usurped me."

Chapter Five

A couple of local parents found their cub, murdered," Taklishim repeated to the group the Chief had called together to put to rest the angel rumors. "Anyone know anything about this?"

Onida jolted. "Who was it?"

Tama put her hand on Onida's arm. "Calvin."

"He was six years old! When did this happen?" Onida stood, fury tearing through her ordinarily calm and detached demeanor.

"Sit." Tama tugged her down, her face sad. "Let Tak finish."

"I'm his doctor! Someone should have told me. Maybe I could have helped him," Onida hissed at her sister.

"No, Oni, no one could have helped him." Tama's face was stoic, but Onida saw how much the words hurt her.

She slumped in her chair. She'd just seen the boy a few days ago. His spirit animal was healthy, a bear, like her father. Her heart broke for the child's parents, and her hand involuntarily clutched tightly at her sisters.

"Ease up, unless you want to heal my broken bones," Tama said in her ear.

"No one saw anything at all?" Taklishim demanded, the anger evident in not only his voice but the stance of his body.

"Maybe the angel can help," said one of the town people.

"There is no angel. Put your gossip mill to better use to find out information about who would harm a child," Taklishim thundered, making Tama go rigid under Onida's hand.

"She might be able to help," Onida whispered to her sister.

"He knows that, but he doesn't want them to know about her."

"He's still overprotective?" Onida watched the warrior closely. He knew something he wasn't saying.

"They have a unique relationship, those two. Sometimes Tak acts like a father to her, other times like a big brother would act. Their closeness doesn't bother me if that's what you are thinking. I know how he feels for her and how he feels for me is drastically different."

"Do I need to listen to what he's saying?"

"No. He'll have a separate conversation when we get home. He invited Degataga over. Dad as well," Tama warned.

"There's danger again, isn't there?" Onida understood Taklishim's fury now. He hadn't known the child; she was sure of that.

"I think so," Tama hedged.

"What aren't you telling me? Why am I finding out like this?" Onida demanded an answer from her twin.

"You just got here. When it happened, you were with patients that needed you. There was nothing you could have done for the boy. He was decapitated."

Revulsion washed through her. "Oh, no. Kathy found him?" The sight would have been bad enough without it being her son. She needed to talk to Degataga about something that would help Kathy get through this.

"She did. Taklishim happened to be nearby when he heard her scream. Dad is currently with Kathy until her family arrives, hopefully soon. That's why he's not here."

"We don't get much murder here," Onida mused. "Why is he questioning them like that? Does he Truly think one of them decapitated an innocent child?"

"No. Tak doesn't want to tell them to watch out for demons, though," Tama said bluntly, shocking Onida.

"He thinks demons are back?"

"Something not of this world, for sure. The cut was way too clean, that's what Tak said."

"You are extremely blasé for a pregnant lady, talking about a child's murder," Onida remarked, looking carefully at her sister and noting the dilated pupils. "Are you drugged?"

She nodded, "Dega gave him something for me. Right now, I'm just numb."

"Does that mean you lost it earlier?"

"Sure does. I had an Airiella moment, and all sorts of emotions burst out of me in a scary display. I went from animal to back about four times before Tak called Dega."

Onida put her hand on Tama's slightly rounded belly and scanned. She didn't feel anything wrong and felt mollified. "Good thing this little sprout is resilient. I'm surprised he didn't call Airiella."

"Oh, he did. Then he found himself dealing with two hysterical women. She'll be here tomorrow."

"I'm going to go to the other side then. I've got an odd feeling about this. I'll see you back at the house." Onida stepped away with a look at Taklishim, who understood what she was doing and gave a little nod.

She walked out into the cooling night and let her anxious hawk take over and swooped into the sky, sailing right into the spirit world. She sought out Winnie, Jax's girlfriend, from his early life who died tragically in a car accident.

She spotted Marco, Airiella's ancestor, and now Winnie's boyfriend, first. "I need Winnie," Onida said to him, forgoing the niceties.

"I'm here, long time no see." She beamed at Onida, coming into sight.

"There's been a death in my town, a six-year-old boy. It wasn't natural causes. Tama thinks Taklishim believes its demons. Have you heard anything rumbling?" Onida got right to the point.

"That's awful! No, I haven't. I'll start asking around though. Have you reached out to Stolas?" Winnie looked horrified.

"No, this was my first move. I'd appreciate any help you can lend. I'm out of hiding now; you should be able to get a hold of me." Onida retook flight before Winnie could ask questions and flipped back to the living world and used her sight to look around.

She used the time to stretch her wings and let her animal do what it needed to do after being confined for so long. With one eye in the living world, the other in the spirit world she flew high, circling and taking in all the details below her, looking for things out of place.

It took her a few minutes, but she finally spotted something off and dove down for a closer look. It was a shrouded woman hiding among the trees. She was no one Onida had ever seen before, and she tripped Onida's spirit senses. She couldn't see her in the spirit world. Her hawk sensed danger and would only allow Onida to fly within a certain distance.

She perched on a branch and observed the woman's movements and came to the conclusion that she appeared elderly, even though Onida couldn't see her face. She was starting to doubt that this woman was a spirit until she moved. She sounded like thunder when in motion.

The woman wasn't a demon; she didn't know what it was. Not human was a safe bet. She sat as still as possible, not wanting to alert the creature that she was there watching. Something in the spirit world was moving towards the woman creature. Onida kept an eye on each plane, wondering what was happening.

Behind the creature, appeared a wispy form of a woman; it almost looked like she was submerged in water, the way everything floated around her. Her silver hair was drifting around her head, and she wore a long silver gown that billowed around her though the air was still. Her eyes looked like she'd been crying for days, her face was beautiful and filled with anguish.

She opened her mouth and the sounds that came out, almost sounded like the saddest song she had ever heard, but it wasn't words. Onida shook her head, trying to clear her thoughts. The creature didn't see the spirit, but it looked like the spirit saw the woman creature. Was the spirit warning her?

The creature moved again, and Onida saw her right hand, or what she thought was a hand. Well, it was a hand, but the pointer finger was a blade, and at the moment, it looked like that blade had an organ of some sort impaled on it that she was eating.

That could be what killed Calvin; as she took off for home, her hawk heard Winnie screaming for her, and she dove back into the spirit world at the frantic sound. "Winnie? What's wrong?"

"That's a banshee! A banshee!" Winnie cried frantically.

"Don't banshee's make awful screaming noises? That spirit is singing a wordless sad song," Onida pointed out, trying to calm her spirit friend down.

"She's not a bad banshee; she's trying to tell you death is coming! Heed her warning is what she is saying."

"How sure are you about this?" Onida asked curiously.

"I'm Irish. We all know about banshees."

"Okay, thanks, Winnie. I'm going to back and see what is happening. Oh, wait. How soon will death be arriving, and do they know who?" Onida thought to ask before going back.

"No, I don't know who, just that her song is a warning of death. My best guess is that it's going to happen soon, and if she appeared to you, then it's someone you know."

Onida didn't understand why the banshee was appearing to her; she wasn't Irish, and certainly not on Irish land. No matter what, she needed to get back. Should Onida go back to the creature or get home? If death was coming via that woman creature, she should probably go there, maybe head it off if she could.

She crossed back into the living world and went back to that location she had seen the creature, who was still there, only now she looked exactly like an older lady. Nothing sinister about her at all, except she was hiding her right hand from sight. Onida didn't see anyone else around.

She glided onto one of the branches high up on a tree that gave her a proper angle of the surrounding area and watched; the banshee's haunting song was echoing in her mind. The forested area was still empty as far as she could see. That didn't stop her from scanning for movement. Her hawk's eyes missed nothing down to the blades of grass that moved with the breeze.

She was about to give up when she saw the creature suddenly change course and move much faster than someone else her age would, the sound of her movements like thousands of flapping wings. Onida had no idea what this creature was, and she went from branch to branch following behind it, her eyes not once stopped scanning.

Then she saw the child, and her heart clenched painfully in her chest. Death was *not* coming for this child today. Onida swooped down without a care as to who saw her or what they would think. Her dad could deal with that, a small price to save the life of an innocent child, another one of her patients, no less.

She shifted back into her human form and placed herself between the creature posing as an older woman and the child that was her patient. "Sarah, run home. You shouldn't be out in the woods. Does your mom know you are here?"

Not knowing where the doctor had come from, the sweet girl shook her head at Onida in confusion. "I was

HAWK

chasing the butterfly," she explained. "Where're your clothes?"

"I see. Go home now. Don't talk to anyone other than your mom. Tell her you saw me and I said to go inside and stay there. Can you do that for me, please?"

"Okay." Sarah smiled that trusting sweet smile that kids her age so often wore, and she scampered off in the direction of her home.

"Who are you, and why are you targeting children?" Onida demanded an answer from the woman who was now glaring openly at her.

"I will just feed on you instead." The creature ignored Onida's question and pulled the cloak from her right hand, the blade of her finger swinging out and missing Onida's belly by inches.

Onida shifted back to her hawk and let out the cry she knew would carry on the breeze to Taklishim, alerting him of the danger. She tucked her wings and dove for the woman's face, her talons retracting painfully at contact, feeling almost as if they'd been cracked and broken by the woman's skin. Impossible.

"You can't kill me, bird. It doesn't matter what form you are in; I'll eat your liver from either." The creature lunged again, the blade missing the hawk's body but slicing neatly through her wing.

Onida plummeted to the ground and rolled. Shifting back to her human form, she got painfully to her feet. Her arm bleeding freely, the muscle exposed. "What are you?"

"Hungry." The creature grinned at Onida.

She heard the eagle's call and glanced up her head dizzy with pain. "Tak, don't attack!" Onida shouted barely in time for Tak to pull his talons back, no sense in him

48

getting hurt as well.

Tak shifted out of reach of the creature, "Can you fly?"

"No. Walking isn't easy either. Her skin is impenetrable." Onida filled him in, her eyes not moving from the creature.

"Leave now," Taklishim barked out as a giant bear and cougar burst through the forest, a wolf the size of the dire wolf not far behind.

The creature cackled an inhuman sound that made Onida's ears feel like they were bleeding. "I'm not done eating yet."

The wolf approached Onida and down, Onida gratefully climbed on its back, holding the fur with her uninjured hand. "Thanks, Mom. Dad, put the town on lockdown," Onida said quietly enough that the creature didn't hear her, but her dad would.

The bear loped off, his speed wonderous given the size of the bear. "You won't find easy prey here, I suggest you leave," Onida growled, trying to keep the pain from her voice.

Tama's protective growl let her know she wasn't successful in it. She didn't have time for an injury right now. They were at an impasse; there was no one for the creature to prey on, and there was no way the animals were letting her through.

The woman's eyes were eerie, giving Onida chills across the back of her neck. She was losing a lot of blood and knew she'd succumb to it soon. "I need to get to the James's house, Mom."

"No, Onida. Your father will take care of it, you need to go home now," Taklishim broke in.

"This is over," the creature sneered. "I will feed." She turned, once again looking sinister and stalked back into the thicker part of the forest.

"Tak, you can boss my sister around, but not me. Mom, take me to the James's, please. Sarah was about to become a meal for whatever that was." Onida's voice was firm. "If you don't take me, I'll just walk."

The wolf begrudgingly carried her to the house she wanted, where Onida knocked weakly at the door. "It's me, Onida," she called out, her voice sounding reedy.

"Onida, why do I need to keep Sarah in, and where are your clothes?" her longtime friend Molly answered.

"Some sort of creature out there. Calvin was killed by it. Stay inside. Please." Onida swayed on her feet.

"You're hurt!" Molly cried, catching her right before she fell, the extra weight dropping them both to the floor.

Chapter Six

Degataga flew out the front door of Onida's house, Tama hot on his heels directing him to the house where Onida was. "Why do all you women have to be so damn stubborn?"

"Me? That was all her." Tama huffed in frustration. "She probably would have gone home first if Tak hadn't barked at her. Who knows? Molly, Sarah's mom, is a good friend of Onida's. If Sarah got threatened, I'm not sure that Onida would have listened to anyone."

"How bad was the injury?" Degataga asked quietly, his insides a mess of nerves at the thought of Onida hurt.

"Not good. I can't lie. It looked like Oni was cut right through to the bone."

Degataga bit back a curse; it wasn't Tama's fault. He didn't need to take it out on her. It wasn't Onida's fault either. "What was it? Another demon?"

"That was no demon. I don't know what it was. It kept talking about feeding."

Degataga was out of the car before Tama even finished parking, and pounding on the front door. A bloody mess of a woman opened the door after Tama announced herself and Degataga practically fell inside he was in such a hurry to get to Onida.

"She's lost a lot of blood," the woman said to Tama.

"I know, thanks, Molly. Do you have her in the kitchen?"

Molly nodded and pointed the way. Degataga ran in the direction and halted at the bloody scene before him that could easily pass for the sight of a grisly murder; there was so much blood. "I'll take care of her, keep them out of here," he told a startled Tama.

The giant wolf sat back near the back door, softly whining as Degataga kneeled before the woman he loved. "Let's see what we have going on, shall we?" He placed his hands on the injured arm and closed his eyes, swallowing the gasp that came up as the vision formed in his mind.

"Tama?" Degataga called out. "I need Tak for this."

She popped her head in the kitchen, "It's that bad?"

"It's almost severed," Degataga whispered.

"He's on his way," she replied, looking down at her sister. "I'll help too if you need it."

"Her toes are all broken too, every one of them." He was surprised by that.

"I think she's more stubborn than Airiella," Tama said wistfully.

"It's a close tie. I'm surprised Onida didn't pass out long before she did," Degataga remarked. "She might need blood; she's lost a lot. Feel up to donating?"

"I will if it's needed," Tama said quietly. "Tak's here. I'll go let him in."

Taklishim walked in with a grim look on his face. "Let me scan, and then we'll split it."

Degataga waited, somewhat impatiently while Taklishim scanned. "Can you start with the bones while I fix the bleeding?"

Tak nodded and got to work, his face breaking out in a sheen of sweat as he started repairing her toes and mending the clean slice through her humerus. Degataga couldn't see any signs of poison or infection from whatever cut her, and once he had the bleeding stemmed, he started stitching the muscles back together. Taklishim joined his efforts after the bone had healed.

"She's dangerously low on blood," Degataga announced.

"I saw that. Onida keeps two bags back at her office in case she or Tama needs it. Her blood. Let's get her back there and you can hook her up." Taklishim stood and looked around at the blood coated kitchen. "I'm guessing Molly tried to help."

"That was my guess too." Degataga sat back on his heels, exhaustion rolling through him. "Help me get her up," he requested.

Taklishim helped lift Onida, and they got her to Tama's car. Tama stayed behind to clean up the kitchen for Molly, promising to stay put until Taklishim came back for her. "Do you need my help anymore?"

"No, I've got it from here, thanks, Tak." Degataga got an IV going and got her hooked up for a blood transfusion. He sat back and closed his eyes, letting the fatigue carry him under as he wondered what could slice so cleanly through bone like that.

He woke to a rustling sound, and when he opened his eyes, the hawk was sitting there on the table watching him. "Hello, Hawk-eye. How does it feel? Can you extend your wing?"

She extended both wings out with some difficulty and bobbed her head. Degataga stretched his hand out and ran a finger down her feathers. "You are beautiful. Maybe don't try flying just yet. Give it a few days of rest; it was almost severed."

She shifted back into human form and sat there naked on the table, staring at him. "You used my extra blood? Or did Tama donate?"

"I used what you had here. How are you feeling?" Degataga looked her over, his body warming.

"Tired and a little sore, but nothing too bad. I will do as you said and wait to fly. Did Tama help you?" Onida gave him a curious look.

"No, Taklishim did. Tama stayed with your friend and her daughter." Degataga stood and stripped off his shirt, handing it to her. "I don't want you to get cold."

Her brows furrowed, but she put it on, her eyes landing on his chest, and his body warmed again. He sat down next to her and gently put an arm around her. "Thanks for fixing me." She gave in and leaned her head on his shoulder; his warm skin soothed the pain inside her.

"I can now say I understand why Jax and Ronnie don't leave Airiella's side when she's injured. I don't want you out of my sight, and yes, I know how unreasonable that sounds." Degataga didn't think he could ever forget the sight of her lying there covered in blood.

"Why did you cover me up?" she asked him quietly.

"Your blood isn't all replenished yet, and I don't want you to get cold. Why do you think?" Degataga was confused.

"Well, I thought I was visually unappealing to you."

Her blunt words shook him. "Oni, that's a thought you should *never* entertain." He gently took her hand and placed it on his chest. "That beats for you. And it's beating fast because of what's under that shirt." His breath stilled as she slid her hand down his chest and settled it on his crotch. He was rock hard under her hand. "That's for you too."

"Are the doors locked?" Her voice was husky.

"No, and as much as I want to take this as far as you possibly will let me, you still need to finish recovering. Can you tell me what happened?" Degataga didn't move her hand. He didn't want her to think he didn't want her.

She moved her hand away on her own and looked down at her bare legs, her shoulders slumping a little. Degataga groaned; he pulled her face towards him, settling his lips on hers. Sliding off the table mid-kiss, Degataga moved to stand in front of her, between her legs. "I'm not rejecting you, Hawk-eye. I'm trying to take care of you. Seeing you like that scared me stupid."

Onida had no idea why she felt so insecure all of a sudden. These emotions were making her soft. "You want me?"

"So badly that it's all I think about; I want you in every way that I can have you. Every way that you will allow me to have you. I want nothing *but* you. In my bed, in my life, by my side." He kissed her again, deeply and slowly, his tongue leaving a scorching trail everywhere it touched.

"Then take me, Dega," she breathed into his mouth, longing to feel him inside her again.

"Not like this," he growled into her ear. "You deserve so much better than this." He felt her try to pull away, and he wasn't having any of it. He pulled her hips closer to the edge of the exam table and knelt in front of her. "I will taste you, though," he purred as he licked along her folds.

She tasted so sweet he almost lost control of himself. He spread her lips apart and flicked his tongue over the swollen bud that had her mewling above him. He lapped up her juices and focused all his concentration on making her shatter under his tongue. It didn't take long, and his name on her lips was the most beautiful sound he'd ever heard.

When he rose to kiss her again, she wrapped her legs around him. "What about you?"

"Hawk-eye, the sound of my name on your lips was all I needed right now. Later, we will finish this, because there is no that was enough, I need more of you." He wrapped his arms around her and felt the trembles still rolling through her. "Let's get you dressed and see if we can figure out what is happening."

"You make me soft," she whispered.

"You make me hard," he chuckled, pulling her hips more tightly to his. He had every intention of fulfilling his promise of later; he'd been too long without her.

Chapter Seven

Tama rushed forward and crushed her in a hug. "Damn it, sister! You scared the hell out of me. Tak was so pissed you didn't go home when he told you to."

"I'm fine," Onida argued.

"Because I went back and got Degataga and Taklishim came to help him. That's why you are fine." Tama smacked her on the back of the head. "Stop being such a stubborn bird."

"Thanks for bringing Dega." She kissed Tama's cheek.

Stunned, Tama looked at her twin, "Did you just say something nice?"

"Girls, stop it and come sit down please." Chief Tyee grinned at the siblings.

"Where's Mom?" Onida looked around. "I'd like to thank her for helping me."

"She's still in wolf form. She rarely comes out of it these days," her dad said sadly.

"Have you given her a reason to?" Tama quipped.

"Tama, we aren't here to talk about your mother. We gathered to try and figure out what we are dealing with, zip it, please. I'd like Onida to tell us what she saw."

Onida took a deep breath in, drawing strength from Degataga, who hadn't left her side. "I left the meeting and checked in on the other side with Winnie. I asked her to keep an eye out for me because I suspected demons like the rest of you. I came back and was circling overhead about to give up when I caught something that didn't quite look right. The closer I got, I was more sure this was what I was looking for, and I watched the creature for a bit and got visited by a spirit that I learned was a banshee."

"Did you just say a banshee? As in the wailing Irish woman?" Tama broke in.

"The very one. Winnie told me. She did say that this banshee didn't wish us harm; she was warning me of death. It was strange. The spirit was beautiful and silver, and the song she sang was heartbreaking but captivating." Onida shook her head to clear her mind. "Anyway, shortly after that, I saw Sarah coming into the woods, and the creature morphed into this elderly woman who appeared normal and innocent. She went for Sarah, and I swooped down to claw her, and when my talons hit, it felt like they all crushed. Like she was cement."

Degataga shifted a bit, "Is that why all your toes had broken?"

"Yes, her skin was impenetrable. That's also why I warned you off Tak. I shifted and got between the creature and Sarah, telling Sarah to go home. To tell her mother for them to stay together and inside. That's when the creature started rambling to me about feeding. She had been eating what looked like an organ when I first spotted her, and I wondered if it had been from Calvin. Somewhere in all that, she cut me, but she didn't have a knife from what I could see. She *was* the knife. More specifically, her right hand, the first finger is a knife. She keeps it hidden. It's damn sharp."

"I know what she is!" Degataga said, his tone frightening. "Cherokee, call her *U'tlun'ta*, Spearfinger."

"You've encountered her before?" Chief Tyee looked intrigued.

"No, not myself. I'd always believed it to be a myth, one the adults used to tell us, so we didn't wander off alone. I didn't know that it was true." Degataga shook his head. "I thought it was just a Cherokee legend. I have no idea what she would be doing out here. There's also a male version like her, but no knife for a finger. Supposedly they are enemies."

"There are some transplanted Cherokee's out here. But not enough to call a tribe, maybe five of them. Six if you join us," Chief Tyee explained.

"Why can't we penetrate her skin?" Onida asked.

"Let me see if I can get my mom on the phone," Degataga said, pulling his phone out. "She's the one who told the story; she'd know a lot more than I do. I only remember the part about the knife for a finger and eating livers. That's what you saw her eating, probably. A pretty effective way to scare the heck out of a kid to keep them wandering off in the woods."

"Yeah, that would do it," Tama agreed, running her hand over her little belly.

Onida felt her father observing her carefully and refused to meet his eye. Instead, she looked down at her lap. Only half-listening as Degataga spoke rapidly to who Onida assumed was his mother in the Cherokee language. She sensed his agitation and stole a glance at him out of the corner of her eye, and his body was rigid with tension. She placed her hand on his arm and felt him relax. The mate bond at work, even though they hadn't sealed that deal.

"I'm going to put you on speakerphone, mother," he switched to English. "Everyone, this is my mother, Asgasga. Please, share what you know with the group," he asked her, his voice harder than it typically was.

"In Cherokee, Spearfinger is called *U'tlun'ta*, or sometimes *Nûñ'yunu'ï*, which means a stone dress. She is very deceptive. She can shift to look like the family of her victim, or she can appear to look like the victim. She can't change back if anyone is looking at her, though. She is very powerful, sounds like thunder when she walks and can crush rocks into the ground. She can stack them, break them, and form a large rock, or build stone bridges to get to where she wants to go."

Asgasga switched back to Cherokee and spoke in a rapid-fire manner that made Degataga stiffen up again, and his face went hard. Onida cocked her head sideways but didn't say anything. She just ran her thumb along the skin of his arm. "Mother, speak English, you are acting rude."

"You want me to speak your private business to everyone in there? You want me to tell the chief how you left your family?"

"Mother, everyone in this room is also my family. They know why I am here. I have no secrets from them. If you feel like you must continue this conversation, then do it. I'll wait here patiently until you are ready to continue with the legend of *U'tlun'ta*."

There was a huff of indignation, then she continued. "Spearfinger was killed by my people many years ago. I don't know why she is there now. What are you expecting me to say?"

"Tell us what you know of her," Degataga said calmly, though his face was still hard. It was because he was here with her that he was having issues with his mother. Onida started to pull her hand away, but Degataga set his hand over hers, keeping it in place.

"*U'tlun'ta* preys on children mostly. She eats their livers. It's what sustains her. The legends say that her finger leaves no mark, and the victims didn't know their livers had gotten stolen until they suddenly died. I have heard tales of her being more violent than that. She gets lured to villages by smoke. She follows it and waits unseen until she picks her victim; then, she either appears as a member of the family to lure the child to her or as an old woman who looks harmless."

"She was an old woman this time," Onida said carefully. "She kept her right hand hidden beneath a cloak."

"That is part of her deception. The Cherokee tried to trap her to kill her. They lured her in with large fires and dug a pit they filled with stakes for her to land on, and when she approached, she fell in the trap, but nothing killed her. The stakes shattered, the knives thrown were shattered, arrows were useless. Her skin is like a stone."

"Then how did your people kill her?" Chief Tyee broke in.

"Her heart is in her right hand. When you see her, you will see her fist is always closed. That is her weak spot. Pierce her palm, or where the blade meets the wrist. It isn't easy; she protects it well. She is incredibly strong and dangerous."

"I thank you for this information, Asgasga," Chief Tyee spoke. "It means a great deal to me to know how to take this creature down and keep my people safe."

"There is a relative of hers that may be nearby if she is there. We call him a stone man. He is like her, though much stronger, and carries a staff with him. Be wary of them," Asgasga warned. "It is only the medicine men that can kill them."

"Thank you, Mother. I will talk to you soon," Degataga said, hanging up before she could say anything else.

"Chief, that means you can put the word out to keep people away from the woods. And no fires inside or outside. An adult must accompany children at all times until we can take care of her. Or them if the other one is here as well. Between the four of us, we should be able to kill it. I'll ask Airiella if she can help us locate it as well," Taklishim said, his hand propped under his chin.

"Didn't she say only medicine men can kill it?" Chief Tyee asked, confused.

"She did," Degataga agreed, "though, with Airiella, it's hard to say what she can or can't do. Lightning may be able to penetrate through to her hand. It's worth a shot, and if it keeps us out of her reach, even better."

"All right. I'll activate Onida's phone tree and make a trip out to the woods for the few that live out there with no phones. Degataga, I'd like to talk to you before you guys head off. Why don't the three of you try and get a plan together? Girls, please, for one, listen to Taklishim. For once, he is a warrior after all."

"Yes, Father," the twins answered in unison with

matching mischievous smiles on their faces while Taklishim groaned.

"That pretty much guarantees they won't listen to me," he grumbled.

Chapter Eight

Son, I understand some Cherokee." Chief Tyee started in as soon as they were out of earshot from the others.

"I'm sorry, sir."

"Why does she think you abandoned your family and your tribe?"

"Because I want to move here and marry your daughter." Degataga answered him truthfully and bluntly. This conversation wasn't how he would have liked to ask for Chief Tyee's blessing, but his mother had to purposely interfere and paint a bad picture of Degataga's actions like he was a disobedient child. Not a powerful man.

"You'd leave your home to come here?" Chief Tyee was surprised. "You don't want to take her there?"

"I'd go anywhere for the chance to be with her. I know she doesn't want to leave here or be away from her sister. Where I live doesn't matter to me. I was honest with her and told her that I would have to leave before moving here to finish up a few things back home and make sure my family was okay. I also told her that if they got sick, I would need to go back and help and that she is welcome to come along. I would love to share my home with her, have her meet my family."

"What did she say to this?"

"Not a whole lot. She didn't turn me away, either. I'm letting her set the pace. I explained why I had to leave the first time and asked her if we could start over, she at least agreed to that. Sir," Degataga took a deep breath in, "I love her more than anything."

"I know, son. I may not be a medicine man, but I *am* a man in love with an impossible woman. I know the signs. It'd be an honor to have you as a part of my family."

"I don't think Onida is an impossible woman," Degataga said cagily. "She is a stubborn one, though."

"Thank you for healing her. I trust you'll do your best to keep her safe?"

"It goes without saying." Degataga smiled. "I'll be as successful as Tak at that."

Chief Tyee laughed. "Not at all then? I know my daughters, son. Onida is a formidable opponent in her own right. I'm more worried about her heart getting broken. It crushed her last time when you left. She hasn't been the same since then."

"I'm doing all I can to make up for that."

"I believe you. Have patience with her." Chief Tyee patted him on the back. "Now go back before she comes out here and yells at me for butting in again."

"You remind me so much of my father, sir. Thank you." Degataga bowed slightly and headed back in the home. He found Tak leaning against the wall with his arms crossed across his chest, and the twins glaring at him.

"Uh oh," Degataga said, spying the standoff.

"What's going on?"

"He thinks he can keep us from fighting against this Spearfinger thing." Tama spun around, furious.

"Taklishim is under the impression that the almighty and powerful men will take care of it while the weak females stay home and do their hair," Onida snapped. "Please tell me you don't see it that way."

"Would I rather not see either of you in the line of fire? Yes. Do I think you women are weak? Absolutely not. Do I believe we all have a part to play in bringing this creature down? Yes. How's that?"

"Better than Taklishim's answer," Tama bit off, smoke practically coming out of her ears.

Onida walked up to Degataga, "What was that about with my father?"

"He was asking me about the things my mother was saying. It's fine, don't worry. I was truthful with him about my intentions for you." Degataga brushed some hair from her face.

"What was your mother saying?" Onida took a step back and studied him.

"Yes, Dega. Let's talk about that," Taklishim added, happy to be out of the line of fire.

"It's between Onida and me," Degataga fired back. "Fix your mess."

"You seriously are going to let Onida go back out there and face that thing after it damn near severed her arm off?" Taklishim shouted.

"I can't stop her, nor do I want to. If Onida agrees to a relationship with me, I can guarantee you it won't be a dictatorship. Your relationship with Tama isn't that way, so I'm not sure where this attitude is coming from," Degataga blew out. Between his mother and Taklishim's outburst, he'd had enough.

"It's because she's pregnant," Onida said quietly. "He does the same thing with Airiella, too. Tries to boss her around."

"I won't do that, Onida." Degataga glanced up at the fuming warrior. "I don't have to like it, Taklishim, but I refuse to tell her she can't do something because I don't like it."

The large man deflated, "I'm sorry, Tama."

"You better be!" She walked away from Taklishim, still angry. "I'm tempted to tell Airiella to zap you with lightning."

Degataga tried to hide a grin, but it came out anyway. "She'd probably do it too if you told her why. She's coming up tomorrow?"

Taklishim nodded. "I don't know what she can do if anything. But with that sight that she has that she can see souls with, she might be able to at least locate it for us."

"Will she need to ask permission from Jax first?" Tama was unwilling to let the slight go.

"Do you honestly think she will show up here without Jax or Ronnie? Or both of them with her?" Taklishim shot back. "They know her penchant for danger."

"Jax doesn't tell her what to do," Onida butted in. "Enough. Tak, apologize to your wife again, so she calms down." She looked over at Degataga, "We might need to warn her of that hornets' nest."

"She *will* zap him if you do. Let it be. He'll calm down." Degataga took her hand. "Do you have any ideas?"

"No, not really. We have to find some way to get her hand open. I seriously don't think it will be easy, and there's only so long we'll be able to keep people indoors before someone gets bored and goes out anyway."

"Even with your father warning them all of the danger?" Degataga didn't want any more children to die. "Oh, we should look at the body of the one to see if he still has a liver."

"I thought of that, too; my guess is he doesn't. We can go do that and leave these two alone before they give us a headache with their bickering."

"Hey," Tama said, her voice weak.

"Well, it's true. Kiss and make up. Tak, pull your head out of your ass." Onida turned and walked out of the room. Degataga followed her out, and as soon as they were out of earshot, she swung around. "Tell me what your mother was saying."

"She accused me of abandoning my family for a fling," Degataga admitted. "Only she said it about five different ways."

"She doesn't like me? Why? She doesn't know me," Onida said, hurt coloring her tone.

"It doesn't have anything to do with you. It's more about me doing what makes me happy instead of what my mother and uncle think is best. I'd like you to come back with me to get my stuff packed up and help me move here." He retook her hand and kissed the back of it. "Even the thought of going back there without you makes my heart feel like someone is ripping it out. Plus, if she meets you, she will love you. Even if she doesn't, my brothers will, and I'd like you to meet them."

"You are serious about moving here, then?" Onida held her breath.

"Dead serious. My future is with you, Oni. I asked

your dad if he was okay with me following this path, and he had no objections."

"He doesn't get a say." Onida turned hard in an instant.

"He knows that and said as much. I don't think just because he had no objections that you wouldn't, my goal was to make sure that your father had no issues with me. I'm aware that you don't trust me yet, Oni."

"I trust you with my life, just not my heart yet," she amended. "I'm hungry."

"Then let's eat, what sounds good to you?" He put his arm around her, hoping she wouldn't push him away.

"You." Her simple answer stopped him in his tracks. "Food-wise, anything right now. I need energy."

His heart thumping in his chest, he looked at the gorgeous woman, "After that statement, I'd eat a log and wouldn't know the difference."

"For some reason my animal trusts you, I'm not going to argue with her right now. She wants to finish what you started earlier, and I want that too. If you want to stay with me tonight, I'll cook us up something."

Degataga was not about to let the opportunity slip from his fingers. "Sounds perfect to me. Can we swing by the hotel so I can grab my bag?"

Hesitating for only a moment, she nodded briefly. "Let's go before I change my mind."

Degataga dragged her to the car as fast as he could.

Chapter Nine

Every logical reason Onida could think of as to why Degataga being there was a bad idea her animal shot down with a single word in her mind, "Mate."

The very touch of his skin on hers sent resounding waves through her body of rightness. The years away hadn't changed that, nor had it changed the way she felt around him. He peeled away those protective layers she'd built like they were nothing and saw her as she was. She both loved it and hated it. She felt treasured yet exposed.

"Why do you make me feel so off balance?" she blurted out, regretting it instantly.

Degataga was leaning against her kitchen counter, watching her as she moved around, trying to keep her hands busy, so she didn't strip him right then and there. "What do you mean?"

"Around you, I feel so much."

"Did you not feel that way before?" He made a movement towards her, and she backed away.

"I did to an extent. It seems extra," Onida tried to explain, the words failing her.

"Maybe because you are trying to hide from me."

His words echoed inside, ringing true. "Even when I hide, you still see me." Onida whispered the truth, hoping he wouldn't hear it but knowing he would.

"Because I know the truth in your heart, I can feel it in my own." He stood up straight his body like a magnet for her, and before she knew what was happening, she was in his arms.

"Damn it. Why does that keep happening?" Onida pushed away, frustrated with herself.

"Because you belong there," he answered with a quiet smile.

"Whether that's true or not—" She knew it was. "—it doesn't mean I have to make it easy for you."

Degataga laughed. "Oni, you are anything but easy."

"I don't need a man to save me." She bristled, whisking two plates out of the cupboard and dishing up the simple stir fry she'd made.

"I've never thought you did. Maybe I need you to save me." Degataga came up behind her, wrapping his arms around her waist. "I'm not ashamed to admit I need you, probably more than you need me."

"Dega, you don't need me." She struggled with the sentence. He was wrong; she did need him as much as she needed oxygen to breathe. She wasn't ready to admit that.

"You're wrong, Oni. For once in your life, you are wrong. I've never needed anything as much as I need you. Believe me when I say that. It's humbling for me, and as soon as I realized it, my life changed."

She swallowed the lump in her throat and moved away to set the plates on the table, placing herself across the table from him, so she didn't do something to embarrass herself. "Let's eat."

He sat down across from her and locked gazes with her. "I mean it, Oni."

"I know," she admitted. She was struggling with taking it all in, and she felt a little guilty for wanting to skip past all the emotions and just have Degataga's body sink into hers. It wasn't that the feelings weren't there for her, they were. She'd just gotten used to denying them and ignoring them for so long that now that they were surfacing, she didn't know what to do with them.

"You look like you have something on your mind," Degataga said gently.

"Too much, truthfully. You know how I told you that you make me soft?" He nodded. "It's true. You are bringing out all these emotions in me, and I don't know what to do with them. I've never cried as much as I have recently. I didn't even cry after you left. It was more of a wither up and die sensation than tears. I started to hide my feelings and shoved them all in a little box and locked it away. Now it's like someone disassembled that box, and all those emotions are just running around loose and wreaking havoc on me."

"Hawk-eye, to me, you've always been soft with hard edges, not afraid to confront hard truths and freely admitting questions that most wouldn't ask. That doesn't seem different to me. There might be a few more hard edges now, and the hard truth I have to accept is I put them there. The tears are different, I'll give you that, but you still seem like the same Hawk-eye I've always loved."

"I don't feel like the same one."

"Give yourself a break. The past year has been a lot to deal with; we've been through some pretty big things with Airiella. She, herself, is still adjusting, why should it be any different for you?"

Onida conceded that point. "I am trying, at least." She decided to take a chance, "I am happy you are here and that you want to try to work things out. I've missed you."

Degataga pushed back from the table and came around to kneel before her, "Thank you, Oni." He had tears in his eyes, and something inside her melted. "I know that wasn't easy for you to say, and you just gave me the best gift by saying it." He laid his head on her knees and let the tears to soak into her pants while she ran her hands through his hair.

She pushed her plate of half-eaten food away, she needed him more than she needed food right now, and this vulnerable man before her was tugging on those emotions running through her with a ferocity that unsettled her stomach. "I need you too, Dega," she whispered, "more than I want to admit."

He surged to his feet, pulling her with him and buried his face in her neck, holding her tight. She pulled back and led him to her room, comforted by how he was still completely open and honest with her about everything. There was no deception between them; there had never had. No shyness either, just truth.

She stripped off her clothes, leaving them in a pile on the floor while he stood there watching her, heat in his gaze. "You are the most beautiful woman I've ever laid eyes on, Oni."

"Then don't let me stand here and get cold, lay your hands on me, not just your eyes," she told him, reaching for the button of his jeans. He let her undress him, gave her the control to set the pace, but was a full participant in the actions.

She took the opportunity to run her hands over every inch of his body, remembering the places that made him moan, go weak, tremble, and arch into her. She tasted him, letting her tongue stroke his length until he was desperate for more. She glanced up at his face and saw tears streaming from his eyes.

"Dega, am I doing it wrong?" She slid her thumb under his eye and across his cheek.

"No, my heart, I'm so happy right now. I didn't think I would ever be here again with you, and it's so precious to me that I couldn't hold back."

Onida wrapped her arms around his neck and pulled him down into a kiss, backing them up to her bed and tumbling them down on to it. He was giving her everything, holding nothing back from her, and it made her eyes pool. "Touch me," she whispered hoarsely against his lips.

He needed no more encouragement and hit the spots on her body that had her crying out his name over and over, with his fingers, tongue, and lips. Not once had he touched her where she wanted it most. He saved it for last, and when his tongue finally settled on the bundle of nerves, she exploded, and he lapped it up gently, savoring her taste.

Her hands pulled at him, desperate to have him inside her, his own need bordering on the edge of losing control. She hitched her legs up, their bodies aligning perfectly, and he eased in slowly, gritting his teeth against the urge to slam in hard, her tight heat an unbearable pleasure he didn't want to end. She took matters into her own hands, and flipped them over sinking onto him fast, burying him deep inside her with a gasp and a moan.

She swiveled her hips on him, grinding into him, her head thrown back, exposing the elegant lines of her body. He slid his fingers up over her. Tracing the contours and making her shiver and convulse around him. He arched up, brought his hand back down to where their bodies joined and slid the pad of his finger against her.

"Don't stop," she pleaded and rode him with wild abandon, the rhythm hard and fast. He stroked his fingers over her, bringing her to a blinding orgasm that had her crying out, clenching around him and dropping her to his chest, where he flipped them both over to slow it down. He wasn't ready for it to be over yet.

He pumped in and out slowly, letting her come down from the high the she was on, and she locked her legs over his hips, drawing him into a passionate kiss that had him twitching inside her. He drew her legs up and hooked her feet over his shoulders and buried himself to the hilt, her eyes losing focus as he drove into her, alternating the pace until he felt her tightening around him again, and then let go his control. His hips were hammering her fast and deep until they both screamed out in release.

He held still until their bodies came down, and he eased himself gently away and grabbed a washcloth from the bathroom and cleaned them up. "Did I hurt you?" he quietly asked, as Onida molded herself to his side, her head on his chest.

"Not at all. It was beautiful, Dega." She traced her fingers over his chest, unable to stop touching him. "I want to say the words you want to hear, I want to say them so badly, but I'm afraid."

"It's okay, Oni. What you just gave me was enough, and I'm not afraid to say them. I love you, Hawk-eye. I've never stopped."

"You'll stay here, with me, tonight?" She didn't want him to leave.

"For as long as you will have me, I'll be right here," he promised.

"One of the things I missed the most was hearing your heartbeat under my ear," she said in a moment of complete vulnerability.

"What I missed most was the reason it was beating." He kissed her head. He stroked her skin until her breathing evened out, and she settled into a deep sleep. He didn't move until she shifted and rolled to her side, then he slipped from the bed and quietly closed the door behind him.

He went back to the kitchen and cleaned up the mess from the dinner she'd made, reheating his and finishing it up. Then he checked all the doors to make sure they were locked and grabbed his bag before heading back to the bedroom, closing the door behind him.

Her hair spread out on the pillow, and her bronzed skin a contrast to the white sheets was so beautiful he wanted it etched in his memory forever. He picked up their clothes from the floor, put them in her laundry basket, and brushed his teeth before getting back in the bed. Their bodies molded together as if they were magnetized.

There was no doubt in his mind; he belonged with this woman. There was no other choice for him. He just had to work on getting her to see that. He didn't need the words she couldn't say, her body spoke them for her whether she realized it or not. He was smiling as he drifted off to sleep.

Chapter Ten

Onida woke to the sound of voices coming from outside her bedroom. The bed next to her was empty, and she remembered that Degataga was an early riser. She saw he'd placed a bottle of the herb mixture that he made Airiella drink to help ease the pain, and she drank it down, grateful for it.

She slowly climbed out of bed and stretched, her body tingling in places it hadn't tingled in a long time, and she felt herself smiling at the memory of last night. As much as she didn't want to admit it, having him here was fantastic. A sense of rightness filled her.

She wondered who was out there talking, she wasn't expecting patients today, and the voice wasn't Tama's. She climbed in the shower and got herself ready, wrapping her hair up wet into a bun and dressing in her old worn-out favorite pair of jeans and a hot pink t-shirt.

She made the bed and smiled again as she noticed that Degataga had cleaned up their clothes. She pulled open the curtains and gazed out to the woods behind her house, wondering if that creature was out there watching them. She was going to find a way to destroy it; she refused to lose any more children to Spearfinger.

As she stepped out of her room, she pulled the door closed behind her; she smelled fresh coffee and cinnamon. She came out to the kitchen and stopped short at the sight of her kitchen filled with bodies. She didn't think she'd ever had that many people in her home at once before.

Degataga was at her side in a second and kissing her deeply, in front of everyone. She wasn't shy, and they'd all seen her naked after a shift. But they hadn't ever seen her in a romantic situation before. Degataga's kiss was magic, and she fell into it without another thought, only coming back to her senses at the whoop of joy that came from her twin's mouth.

"So you *are* here," Onida said, her eyes glazed. "Why didn't I hear you?"

"I was busy with a little one," Tama said, her voice soft. Onida glanced through the group of The Shadow Seekers and saw Tama holding baby Jackson. Mags was behind her with baby Angel, and Aedan had baby Ronan.

"What brings all of you to my little house?" Onida made her way to the coffee pot and poured herself a cup.

"Taklishim said he needed Airiella, and once she told us what was going on, we all decided to come and see if we could help," Jax spoke up, Airiella on his lap.

"I see, and you are here instead of over there, why?" Onida sipped the coffee, waiting for the caffeine to hit.

"It was time for the babies to have a checkup, and I wanted you to do it," Mags clarified.

"You want me to be their doctor?" Onida was a little surprised. "I'm an hour away from you."

"You brought them into the world, and I can't think

of a better person to make sure they stay healthy," Aedan added.

"You honor me," Onida said, humbled.

"So, out of all of you, who is the best medicine man or woman?" Ronnie asked.

"Depends on what needs work." Degataga supplied more coffee to Onida's almost empty cup. "I made French toast, go grab some." He propelled her back to the kitchen. "You'll need to eat; you didn't have much last night."

"You made French toast?" Onida repeated. He'd made her favorite breakfast food. He remembered.

"Better hurry before Ronnie eats it all." He smiled at her.

"He's a keeper, Onida. He makes a damn good French toast," Ronnie said around a bite of food.

"Nice to know I have your support." Onida felt her walls going up. "If only I had some peace to go along with it."

Onida grabbed a plate and noticed that Degataga had cleaned up after the dinner as well. She loaded up her plate with French toast and sat on the counter to eat. Tama came up with a gurgling and happy Jackson. "Everything okay?" she asked quietly.

Onida nodded and continued to eat, knowing Dega was right; she needed the energy. She looked down at the adorable baby Tama was coddling and felt a smile form. "You'll be a great a mother." She leaned her head down to Tama's.

"So will you," Tama responded without looking up at Onida. She knew it was a question about what was going on with Degataga, but Onida wasn't ready to talk about it yet.

HAWK

Onida finished up her breakfast and set the plate in the sink next to her. "Why is everyone here?"

"I thought it would be easier for you to check the babies here in your office. I called. Degataga said you were still sleeping but that he would make breakfast. Ronnie was all for that. So here we are. Did we wake you up? How's your arm?"

"A little residual soreness, but otherwise okay. No, you didn't wake me up. And no, I don't want to talk about it yet. Let me adjust slowly."

"Okay," Tama agreed, looking her over carefully. "The just laid look is a good one on you."

"Tama," Onida warned, blushing.

"Just pointing out the obvious. Dega can't keep his eyes off you," Tama kept pushing.

"Pregnancy has made your mouth too loose." Onida jumped down and put the last pieces of French toast on Ronnie's plate and started to clean up. "Have Mags and Aedan meet me back in the office with the babies. I'll be there shortly."

Smitty came up behind her, "I'll clean up for you. It's the least we can do since we crashed your place."

Onida gave him a cautious look, but let him take over. She walked over to Dega, "Thanks for breakfast. And cleaning up."

"You're welcome, go be Dr. Hawk-eye. I'll keep these guys out of trouble. Taklishim and your dad are on their way over," he warned.

"Great." Onida rolled her eyes and headed to her office. With Tama's help, she got patient files started for the babies, got them weighed and checked out, gave any shots needed, and then scanned both parents.

"Everything looks great, though you two look a little tired. Make those guys out there babysit and take a nap. Three babies at once is a lot to take on. You've got to make sure to take care of yourselves too," Onida cautioned them.

Mags flushed. "Am I safe, to uh, be intimate?"

"Yes, you are." Onida gave her a gentle smile and picked up Angel to carry her back out. The sweet baby cooed and smiled, her hands smacking into Onida's cheeks as she babbled her secret baby talk.

Tama followed closely behind, the other two babies in her arms, and she settled into the chair in the living room, talking to both of them as Taklishim walked in and paused. Onida stood back to watch the warrior take in the sight of his wife and the babies. His soft expression one that others rarely saw. He knelt in front of her and took Ronan from her. Standing back up, the warrior instantly transformed into a lovesick puppy.

"Amazing what babies can do to the hardest men, isn't it?" Degataga whispered from behind her.

"He only wants people to think he's hard," Onida answered, passing Angel to Degataga, who looked rapturously at the infant. "She's beautiful, isn't she?"

"She is. Does it make you want one?" He asked so quietly that Onida had to strain to hear him.

She sighed because it did make her want one. She wasn't sure how to feel about that. "Let me adjust to you being here with me first."

"You want me to stay?" Hope bloomed on his face, and Onida felt her walls crumble.

"I do. I'll also go back with you to meet your family," she whispered, fighting the fear that came crashing through her. She saw Dega blink back tears as she felt Airiella pulling on her arm.

"Come talk with me, please." Airiella's gaze raked over Onida's face.

Onida led Airiella back to her office, where there was a semblance of peace of quiet. "What can I do for you?"

"I didn't want to talk to you about me. I wanted to talk to you about you. Things are kind of a mess inside, aren't they?"

"Are you reading me?" Onida demanded to know.

"No, you are broadcasting pretty loudly. Loud enough that you got through my walls actually." Airiella sat down in the chair and leaned forward on her knees. "I understand what you are going through. God knows I've been through enough shit of my own to know where you are coming from with this. I think things like this are one of the reasons I exist. To make sure that others know you aren't alone, and you have an outlet in me."

Onida hopped up on the exam table, once again vulnerable. "I'm afraid."

"I know. That came through pretty clear. What I don't know is what you are afraid of."

"That he'll leave again."

Airiella's face mirrored the way Onida was feeling. "I understand now. That's a pain and a fear that isn't easy to get over."

"How did you get over it?" Onida knew when Jax had left to move in secret, that Airiella had become like Onida had been when Degataga left. An empty shell, devoid of life.

"I haven't really. It's still there. The fear is easier to accept because Jax is always with me. The times we aren't together, he checks in up here—" She tapped on her head.

"—and he texts. It just takes time. When Michael left me, it destroyed me in a way I never really expected. It tore me down to pieces and undermined all positive feelings I had about myself. It wasn't until meeting those guys, and you, that things started to click for me. Piece by piece, those guys out there built me back up. We talked it out when they felt me withdraw. They confronted the fears with me. Jax, especially."

"He told me he wanted to move here, I want to believe him so bad," Onida admitted.

"Like you told me, sometimes you need to take a leap of faith. He has no walls up around him, I can feel everything that is coming off that man, and it's nothing but love. Maybe knowing that will help you?"

"Are those visions you saw, are they real?" Onida wanted to know.

"Destiny can be changed by the choices you make. If you follow your heart, I believe those exact visions will come to pass."

"I need to confess to you that when all that happened with Bael, I froze. My fear took over, and I didn't know how to help you."

"Onida, that's not the way I see it. From my perspective, I saw you become more human that day. I saw your emotions come to the surface, I saw the love and worry you had for me, for Jax, for Mags and the others. You helped Mags, and it was precisely what you should have done. With your guidance, I have come farther than I ever thought I would. Please don't think that you've let me down; it's the farthest thing from the truth there is."

Onida felt tears slipping from her eyes again. "Why does this keep happening?" She pointed to her eyes.

"Annoying, right? I said the same thing so many times. It's what happens when you allow yourself to feel all those things you try to hide. They don't make you weak, Onida." Airiella took hold of Onida's hand and pushed love into her. "Love is a terrible beauty. Death is a terrible beauty. Life is a terrible beauty. But they are still beautiful, and it's okay to see both sides of them."

"When did you get so wise?" Onida smiled through her tears.

"These damn medicine people I know kept beating me over the head with their wisdom, and I guess some of it stuck," she teased Onida.

"Thank you, Airiella."

"Anytime, Doc. Now get your shit together. We got another monster to slay." She handed a tissue to Onida.

Onida stood up, drying her face off. "How did Jax handle that news?"

"The monster bit?" Onida nodded. "Well, since it wasn't after me directly, a lot better than I expected. But my willingness to dive in made him pause. He won't stand in my way, that's more Ronnie than Jax."

"How do I look?" Onida tossed the tissue in the garbage can.

"The tears are obvious, but no one will question you. At least none of my group, I already gave them the heads up that if one of them were mean to you, I'd zap them."

Onida laughed at that. "Tama threatened Taklishim with that. Said she would tell you to zap him."

"Oh? Was he a jerk?" Airiella asked over her shoulder as they walked out of the office.

"Yeah. In Tak's usual way," Onida said with a smile.

"So overbearing and bossy?" Airiella asked, shooting the warrior a look as she walked into the room.

"You got it."

"Hmmm. It would be a good test to see how much I can control it," Airiella said thoughtfully. "Not while he's holding a baby, though."

"Tama may kiss you, just a warning," Onida quipped.

"Gives a different meaning to the word cougar," Airiella fired back.

"Airiella, thank you again. You've helped immensely," Onida told her quietly so that no one else could hear.

"My pleasure. I'm well versed in pain." Airiella hugged her. "Hey Gandalf, give up that baby." She started towards him. He looked at Airiella in surprise. "Let's give the old man some practice before his grandkids get here."

Onida laughed then paused at Airiella's wording. She'd said grandkids, plural. She looked over at Tama who was absorbed in the baby in her arms. Were there twins in there? She had missed the third baby in Mags, just as the doctor had who confirmed the pregnancy. She got lost in her thoughts about how to scan without giving her hope that there was two when she heard Taklishim yelp in pain.

Onida couldn't help the roar of laughter that burst through her. She'd seriously done it, Airiella zapped him. His thunderous look was as priceless as the innocent one on Airiella's face. "I'd heard that you needed to get zapped for being an ass to your pregnant wife," she said with a smile.

Tama threw her head back and let out a laugh just as loud as the one that came from Onida. Degataga coughed to hide his laughter, and the rest of the guys were sitting quietly, stunned at their angel. Onida smothered another laugh as Jax tried to pull her away from Taklishim, discretely.

"I apologized to her," came Tak's gruff reply as he rubbed his arm.

"Let that be a lesson to you," Tama told him. "I've got the angel on my side."

"It's called vagina power," Airiella told him smugly. Tama snorted, and Onida turned around so they couldn't see her hiding the laughter that threatened to bubble up again.

"Well, now that I know she can safely do that, you all better watch out," Mags warned the guys around her. Smitty and Ronnie groaned.

"The level of control is impressive," Degataga commented. "You've come a long way."

"Yes, I'm so glad to see all those lessons have been put to good use, Raven." Taklishim glared at her.

"Right? One more skill under my belt. Now, let's talk about this monster." She sat securely on Jax's lap again, tucking her shoeless feet under Ronnie's legs.

Onida longed for that level of comfort with Degataga. *It'll come, give it time,* Airiella said in her head. It would only happen if Onida invited it. With that thought, she moved closer to Degataga and leaned against him, his arm settling over her shoulders with an ease that surprised her.

Taklishim led them in the discussion about Spearfinger while Ronnie and Smitty broke out their computers and took notes. After getting the Wi-Fi password, Ronnie started researching while Jax talked about ways to find the creature using their gear and Airiella.

They got a plan of action in place and worked on ways the guys could collect evidence to use in a future episode Jax wanted to do about the possibility of mythical creatures being real. Ronnie and Smitty moved to the kitchen table to continue researching, and Airiella approached Onida again.

"Back to who is the best medicine person here, who is it?" She looked at Onida and Degataga curiously.

"Well, Onida is the only one medically trained as a doctor, so I would say she is," Degataga said.

"That's not true. If you are talking about healing, the two best are going to be Taklishim and Degataga. Finding out what is wrong would probably be me. Tama is best when it comes to mental issues and healing things like that. Degataga is best with delicate issues like when we had to work on your brain, and what he did with stopping the bleeding in me. Taklishim is overall the strongest. We all specialize in certain areas. Why do you ask?" Onida tried to explain, feeling like there was an issue Airiella was attempting to address.

Airiella pulled them to the side farther away from the others, looking back to make sure they were busy. "You did miss the second baby, I can feel it, and see it when I look with soul sight. But it's weak, and I don't know if it will survive without some intervention."

Both Degataga and Onida snapped to attention. "What kind of intervention?"

"I don't know. Its glow is very faint, but it's still there. Degataga, if I fed her energy, would it help?" Airiella looked a little distressed.

"I'd need to scan her. Airiella, this is something she would need to be a part of."

"I was hoping we could do it without telling them, in case it didn't work. That's a pain I'd like to avoid Tama feeling," Airiella said quietly.

"I understand your reasoning," Onida interjected. "She'd want to know. Tak will find out the second she knows. What if the five of us went to my office and addressed it together?"

"Actually, can I talk to Taklishim separately?" Airiella suggested. "If nothing else, he will understand what I am trying to accomplish, and as a last resort, we can always see if my blood will help."

"Okay." Onida hesitated. "He's territorial about her."

"I know, that's why I think he will understand where I am coming from on my reasons. Just don't tell Tama yet, let me talk to Taklishim."

"I'm going to come with you to talk to him. I've had years with him, and I know his reactions," Degataga said. "You can do the talking, and I'm just backup. Please let me scan Tama first for confirmation that it's there. He will need that."

Airiella nodded faintly. Onida looked between the two of them, scared for her sister. "I'll do everything I can to help her." Airiella put her hand gently on Onida's.

Chapter Eleven

Degataga walked up to where Tama sat with Jackson; the baby cradled between her legs and its little feet resting on the start of her belly. "Do you think he knows there's a little one inside you?" he asked her.

"I think they can sense the security of it," Tama agreed.

"Would you allow me to touch you? I want to feel it, you know, practice. I'm hoping your sister will want one with me," Degataga spoke softly.

"She loves you," Tama whispered. "Yes, go ahead and feel my little miracle."

Degataga had only spoken the truth to her, though he felt awful about not telling her all of it. He focused his energy on seeking out the life inside her, and it took longer than he was comfortable with, but he eventually found it precisely as Airiella had said. It's life force very faint.

"Amazing. Thank you, Tama." He stood. "Now, I'm going to steal your husband for a moment with Airiella."

"Have her zap him again if he gets bossy." She smiled as Onida sat on the arm of the chair next to her sister, her face paler than it had been.

Degataga gave her a little nod and went to pull Taklishim from Jax. "Hey, come outside with me for a moment." Degataga gestured to the door where Airiella had just gone through.

Taklishim stepped outside, and Airiella patted the stair next to her. "Take a seat, Gandalf, and buckle up for a bumpy ride."

He sat down, leaning against the pillar and faced the angel, Degataga took up a position behind him. "Spill it, Raven."

"You trust me, right?" She looked at him, and for a moment, Degataga thought she looked like a child, her purity shining through her eyes.

"You know that I do. What's going on?" Taklishim's posture had stiffened. Degataga knew Taklishim would never hurt Airiella, but he also knew his friend's reaction was going to be straight fear.

"I'm giving it to you straight, Gandalf. So, you need to listen to me carefully and trust me." Tak nodded at her, and she continued. "Tama is pregnant with twins. I can see the second baby when I use my soul sight, but its glow is incredibly faint. It needs help. I think it needs all of us. We can use my blood if we need to," she offered.

Taklishim sat upright, his posture rigid, and Airiella took his hand. "She's okay?"

"Tama is fine," Degataga confirmed. "I checked before we came out here. Airiella is right, the second baby is hard to find, but it's there. Airiella suggested she feed it her energy, and if the three of us scan while she's doing it, we might be able to find why it's weak and fix it."

"Does Tama know?" Taklishim's voice was harsh,

but he hadn't pulled his hand from Airiella's yet, and Degataga figured she was calming him.

"If she's listening to you, she does," Airiella said. "I didn't tell her yet."

Taklishim's eyes filled with tears, "Twins?"

"Yes, Gandalf. Twins. One of which needs our help. Can you stay calm enough to do this?"

"If you help me. I'm feeling a little rough at the moment," Taklishim admitted, shocking Degataga.

"You never need to ask for my help; you always have it," she told him.

"How are you going to feed it energy?" Degataga squatted down next to them.

"I'll pick out its strand of energy and put my own into it. I don't know what you guys do, but I am assuming the way Onida scans the baby that's visible for issues you can do for the other one if its energy is stronger."

"You are correct," Taklishim confirmed. "I'll only use your blood if there is no other option, Raven. You mean more to me than that."

"It's an option I am willing to give, Gandalf. I'm out of my element here, with this stuff, so please don't let go of my hand. I'll be stronger with the bond of Tama and you flowing through me."

"You're full of it, Raven. We all know you make us stronger. I'm brave enough to admit that holding on to your hand will make me feel better when the life of my child is on the line."

"Come on, then, let's go fix that little bean." She stood up, and Degataga was amazed at how she handled the warrior with ease.

"She knows; Onida just told her," Taklishim's voice

was quiet.

"She'll have my other hand, Tak. I'll keep her calm the same as I'm doing for you." Airiella confirmed what Degataga had expected. "Shut out everything else."

Degataga led them in the house and back to the office where Onida already had Tama stretched out on the exam table and was hooking up monitors to her belly. "I think the blood flow is restricted," she told them as they took up positions around Tama.

Degataga placed his hands on the side of Tama's belly, Onida put one on the lower part, Taklishim had his on the top, and Airiella slid between them and put her hand right on the center. "Give me a second while I ground myself, not used to dividing myself this many ways," she muttered. "Okay, got it."

Degataga felt Tama relax, and suddenly the little life he'd had a hard time finding shone brightly. The gasps from the others around him told him they could see it too. "Tama, do I have your permission to work on these veins?" he asked softly.

"Yes. Do what you need to do," Tama answered him, her voice calm.

"Tak, I might need help." He glanced over at the warrior.

"Degataga, slide your hand up to mine, and I'll give you what you need." Airiella gazed at him.

"Raven, be careful. You are splitting yourself too much," Taklishim cautioned.

"Trust me, Gandalf," she responded.

Degataga trusted that she knew what she was doing and slid his hand up and sucked in a breath at the contact. Energy flew through him, and soon he was glowing blue, alive with Airiella's power flowing through him. He felt like he could lift the house. It was far more energy than she had given him when he worked on her.

He got to work, strengthening the veins that fed the little life, unwinding the others that restricted the blood flow going to it, and moved the cord that was wrapped around it while he could feel Onida checking over the life for signs of sickness or abnormalities.

He didn't know how much time had passed, but he was sweating and shaky by the time Taklishim declared a job well done after he scanned again, and the monitor clearly showed both babies well and healthy. Onida left the monitor hooked up, and guided Airiella and him out of the room while Taklishim climbed on the bed with Tama, both crying.

"Dega, you did some incredible work back there," Onida told him softly, wrapping her arms around him.

"I couldn't have done it without you or Airiella." He hugged her back.

"I need to check on her. She drained herself pretty significantly, and if I'm right, Tak is going to be bursting through here shortly to bark at her, then hug her."

"Give her a minute, Oni. She's in good hands," Degataga replied with a smile in his voice. Jax cradled Airiella in his arms, with each of her group touching her. "That little one would have died if she hadn't noticed."

"I know." He heard the pain in her voice. "I can't believe I missed it."

"Don't blame yourself, Oni. I barely caught it and would have missed it myself if she hadn't pointed it out to me. Not even Taklishim knew. His hands are always on her, scanning her. There is no blame to be placed in this."

"Here they come." Onida tried to shift away, but he tightened his arms around her, holding her to him.

"Don't move. I still need you." Degataga kissed the top of Onida's head.

"Too bad, that's my sister, and I need her more than you do." Tama burst into the room, throwing herself at Onida.

The twins clung to each other, and Taklishim fought to control his emotions. "Where is she?"

"With Jax, where else would she be?" Degataga noted the tone was stiff, and he wasn't sure what to make of it.

Taklishim edged around the women and barreled towards the angel who saw him coming. She wasn't afraid, she simply turned and opened her arms. Taklishim wrapped her up and stood, dangling her off the ground, and Onida's prediction was spot-on accurate. He lit into her for draining herself and hugged her both at the same time as he lost control of his emotions.

Degataga saw how alarmed Jax was and shook his head at the man signaling that it was okay. He moved to sit down in a kitchen chair, exhausted down to his bones. Taklishim was his best friend, and Degataga would do it again if it were needed. He knew Airiella would too.

He closed his eyes and felt Taklishim come up to him. "Thank you for doing what I couldn't have done, even with Airiella powering me. I was in no way calm enough, and I couldn't be more grateful that you stepped up."

"Tak, you don't need to thank me. I'd do it all over again as many times as I needed to. Besides, you deserve sleepless nights changing twice the amount of dirty diapers," Degataga said without opening his eyes.

He laughed weakly. "You've done a great job of working with Airiella. She split her focus on calming me, calming Tama, giving energy to both babies, and powering you up, and she's still standing."

"I can't take credit for that. It's all Airiella. Love is a powerful tool, Tak. You know that."

Chief Tyee sauntered into the kitchen. "Your angel told me what you accomplished, thank you."

"She's Tak's angel, not mine," Degataga answered him. "Technically, she's their angel." He gestured back at the group once again huddled around her. "Tak just likes to boss her around. And you're welcome. It was an honor to be able to help."

Taklishim grunted, "That stubborn woman belongs to no one but herself."

"Be that as it may, I am in debt to that stubborn woman," the chief said with a glance at his daughters still clinging together. "As I am to you, Degataga."

Chapter Twelve

How does it work?" Jax asked Onida as she sat down near Airiella, wanting to look her over.

"What?" She reached out a hand and did a quick scan.

"The healing."

"Oh. For me, it's like I am talking to the cells in the body. I direct them what to do and where to go to repair, or fight what's needed."

"She's okay, Onida. Just tired," Jax told her at the look of concern on her face.

"I see that. Would you like to use my guest room?"

"No, your father offered us the use of his house for the night."

"That was nice of him. Kind of unheard of, too." Onida was surprised at the gesture.

"I think it shocked him too, when he said it." Jax chuckled softly. "Is Tama okay?"

"She is now, and both babies are too. Thanks to this one." Onida nodded at the sleeping Airiella.

"She credits you and Degataga with that."

"She would." Onida smiled softly. "It was a group effort. Wake her up soon and make her eat. It will help replenish her energy. Something with carbs."

"I will. We keep charging Airiella with the connection too."

"Good. Airiella was close to burn out, Jax. I'm not acting overly concerned like Taklishim, either."

"Is he okay? I've never seen him like that before."

Onida checked on the giant warrior hovering over her sister. "Neither have I. Seeing Airiella recover will help him now that he knows the babies are okay."

"I think she's the little sister he never had," Jax commented wryly.

"It goes back and forth, sometimes he acts like he's her father, and other times like a big brother. I don't think he knows. Being attached to someone outside of his family is new for him. Tama figured it out right off the bat; she teases him about it all the time. She's family to all of us now. Tak *had* a sister, though, and it may be that Airiella's taken her place, figuratively speaking."

"I know that's how she feels about all of you, that you are family," Jax confirmed.

"Don't be surprised if he hovers," she warned with a smile. Degataga walked up, looking like he hadn't slept for a week.

"Have her drink this when she eats." He handed Jax a bottle with yellow-colored water in it, then gave one to Onida. "You too."

She took it and drank a long pull. "What about you?"

"I drank two already," he admitted to her.

"Onida said the cells talk to her and she directs

them what to do, is it like that for you too?" Jax was curious.

"I don't have the medical training she does. When I scan, I can see spots that don't appear like the rest; they sort of have a different color. My energy takes over and talks to the body, asking what it needs to make it right, and I use the energy to manipulate the matter until it's fixed. It's similar, but she knows or suspects what the issue is already, I don't."

"You know that you aren't supposed to know this information, right?" Tama said as she walked up quietly. "Now, we'll have to swear a blood oath that binds you on pain of death to keep our secrets." Onida bit her lip to keep from laughing at the look on Jax's face.

"I'll sign whatever you want. I'm not out to share your secrets. I was just curious," Jax mumbled.

"She's right about you not knowing, but not the rest." Degataga eased his fears.

"I've seen her in action, she's scary," Jax admitted. "I wasn't about to question her."

"You think *I'm* scary? Tak puts us all to shame in that department," Tama scoffed.

"Oh, I didn't say he wasn't. He's downright terrifying when he's pissed, even more so when he's pissed and glowing blue from her energy. You, on the other hand, are a cougar whose size is a small horse with claws and teeth that are nightmare inducing."

Onida burst out laughing, making Airiella stir in Jax's arms. She quieted her voice, "He's got you there, sister."

"I concur with Jax," Degataga added. "That night in Franklin was the first time I saw you pissed off in cougar form."

"Remember that if you decide to hurt my sister," Tama warned.

"By far, the scariest couple I've ever met." Jax shuddered.

Tama reached out and touched Airiella softly, "She's okay."

Onida nodded. "Of course, she is. She's got more lives than your cougar."

"I'd rather not test that theory," Jax broke in, tightening his hold on her. "Ronnie might argue that too."

Tama snorted. "Like Taklishim wouldn't as well." Tama stroked her hand down Airiella's cheek. "She's grown so much in such a short time. I'm so proud of her."

Onida clutched at her sister's hand; she was too. In her eyes, they were all in debt to Airiella. "My dad offered to cook a feast for dinner if you all are interested."

"A feast?" Jax questioned.

"He offered to cook up some salmon on cedar planks, make Indian fry bread and roast vegetables," Tama explained.

"Sounds good to me, she won't eat fish though. She doesn't do seafood and is allergic to shellfish."

"I'll have him do chicken for her." Tama stood and went to talk to their father.

"Take her to his house and let her rest for another couple hours. Wake her and make her eat something light and drink this. Taklishim will force food down her throat at dinner," Onida directed him.

Jax shifted to stand, and Taklishim appeared before him and lifted the angel gently from his arms. "Go, I'll follow." Slowly the group filed out to head to her father's house, which was large enough to fit them all.

Onida held her hand out to Degataga. "How about we rest up as well?"

"I could use it." He stood and followed her to her room. He had little doubt that Taklishim and Tama would lock up after themselves and succumbed to sleep almost instantly when his head hit the pillow.

Onida watched him for a few minutes, scanning him carefully to make sure he hadn't overextending himself. Satisfied, she settled down next to him, her heart overflowing when he pulled her to him even in his sleep. She went over her talk with Airiella earlier and decided to just go with it, giving in to her emotions of the past couple of hours.

She acknowledged the fear and anger and let them wash out of her with the tears. She allowed the love that had been present in the house since she had woken up that morning to fill its place. Airiella had healing magic all of her own that none of them could ever replicate, no matter how skilled they were. Onida found herself continually learning from Airiella, even though it was supposed to be her training Airiella.

Chapter Thirteen

W e are seeking the creature out, not engaging it," Taklishim reminded them sternly.

Degataga looked over the assembled group of himself, Onida, Jax, Ronnie, and Airiella. Tama had chosen to stay behind of her own free will, Taklishim was overly pleased with that fact. Onida would take to the skies, putting herself out of harm's reach, which made Degataga happy.

He was less happy about Airiella being on the ground crew with them. He also knew that she was the main reason they were there. She'd be using her soul sight as she called it, while Taklishim walked in and out of both worlds. Jax and Ronnie were there because they weren't about to let her out of view with the threat of danger being present.

They also had gear with them to help try and detect what energy they could, and Ronnie also had a small camera with him he'd turn on if they got lucky and caught sight of the creature. Degataga felt somewhat useless, but he was there to be a healer in case things became out of hand. He'd also try to manipulate the creature's energy if he could.

He could feel the thin ledge Taklishim was on with Airiella being put out there again, in the line of fire so to speak. She hadn't given him a choice really, which wasn't surprising in and of itself. She was their best chance at finding this creature instead of using a child as bait.

"Weapons won't work against her," Tak reminded them again. "Well, at least blades or guns."

"Do you think Stolas could help?" Airiella asked.

"We aren't going to ask. I'd rather leave demons out of this." Taklishim winced at the thought.

She shrugged it off, and Degataga saw her eyes glow with an amber light he'd never seen before. "Why are your eyes glowing?"

"Angel eyes," Jax replied with a little smile. "That's what I call them anyway."

An apt enough description, Degataga thought, noticing Taklishim watched her every move. "Back off a little. She's not helpless," Degataga told him quietly. He saw Onida stripping out of her clothes, placing them in a neat little pile, and then her magnificent hawk took shape. "Work your magic Hawk-eye," he told her.

"Ooohhh! Hawk-eye! I love it!" Airiella crowed with delight. "I called her that once."

Taklishim cringed, "She's going to make you pay for that."

Degataga whispered an apology to the sky. "I realized it after I said it, Gandalf."

Jax laughed. "Yeah, Airiella's not going to let that one go. If you have others, you might want to keep them quiet."

"I remember Taklishim's face the first time she called him Gandalf." Ronnie cracked up. Degataga smiled too, remembering the mighty warriors face. He saw Airiella pulling out a set of earbuds and start to put them in when they all jumped at Taklishim's booming voice.

"Raven! What in the hell do you think you are doing?!" he bellowed at her.

Jax, recovering first at seeing that she wasn't in danger, sidled over to Degataga. "If you want to see Taklishim lose an argument fast, pay attention to what's about to happen," Jax whispered at him.

"What the fuck is your problem now?" She spun to face him. Degataga was silently grateful he never drew that look from Airiella.

"How do you expect to watch for danger by distracting yourself with what you call music?" Taklishim was furious. Degataga thought he had a point, but with Jax's prediction, he assumed that he'd had this argument with her before.

"Here it comes," Ronnie warned, coming up on the other side of Degataga.

The ground rolled under Taklishim, throwing him off balance. "Seriously, Tak? The earth talks to me; the air talks to me. They talk to me." She pointed at Ronnie and Jax. "I can sense things before you can. Nature is *my* territory." She blasted a gust of wind at him, forcing him to step back. "I don't need to hear danger to sense it coming."

"I'm not letting you walk out there with your ears plugged!" he yelled.

"You can't stop me," she told him.

Degataga howled in laughter when Taklishim found himself unable to move. He'd immediately seen what she'd done, and while he could free his friend, he saw no reason to. Taklishim glared at him as Airiella put her earbuds in and started for the woods.

He hadn't expected Onida to come swooping down in attack mode like she was out to prove Taklishim's point. Airiella didn't even flinch as she smoothly dropped to a squat and send a gust of wind up, knocking the mighty hawk off course. She hadn't even looked. Point made.

Degataga looked at Jax, "Did you tell her Onida was coming at her?"

"No, I didn't know. I wasn't expecting an attack from above," Jax stated. "Ronnie has had this argument with her before. Smitty was playing the part of Onida, and she took them both down."

"She's got an amazing connection with the earth. It's like it tells her when something is near," Ronnie admitted happily.

Taklishim staggered suddenly, and Degataga figured she'd let him go. He was still pissed, but he stopped arguing with her. "You're right; he lost that fast. And it was funny." He glanced up to make sure Onida was okay.

"I didn't hurt her," Airiella called back, sensing his thoughts. "I just blew her away from me."

"She's certainly not helpless." Ronnie clapped him on his back. "One of these days, Taklishim will believe it."

"I don't think he believes she is helpless; he just wants to protect her, the same as we all do. Look at the both of you," Degataga defended his friend.

"I'm here to watch the fireworks," Ronnie joked.

"Liar," Jax called him out. "We know she doesn't need us; she likes us close, and we like to be close. More of a mental thing."

"He's right." Ronnie stopped kidding around. "She's still human and can die. I'd rather be close by to carry her off if she falls, then to have her fall, and no one is around. Though she is a little scarier now that she carried through with the zapping threat."

Degataga saw how close they were, how their bonds united them, and how much Jax had changed due to it. "You guys are lucky. Hold on to that closeness."

Jax stiffened and called out to Taklishim quietly. "She said, stop. There's something in the tree line ahead of her to the left."

Degataga glanced up and saw Onida glide silently down to a branch above Airiella. Taklishim halted as requested, his gaze locked on the direction Jax had indicated. Ronnie had stopped and moved closer to Degataga and in front of him as if he were protecting him. He might not be a warrior like Tak, but he wasn't helpless.

He felt for the energy she was feeling and found it exactly where she said. There wasn't anything he could do to it as she could, but it was an intriguing energy. He didn't think it was the same energy he'd felt from the creature before.

"What the fuck is that?" Ronnie whispered as he fumbled with the camera and got it recording.

"Banshee," Jax answered. "She said Onida called it the banshee."

At that, Degataga moved forward to stand next to Airiella and underneath Onida. "Who is it here for?" he asked quietly.

"Onida said she is singing to her again. I can't see her, but I can feel her. It's incredibly sad," Airiella whispered to him. "I can't hear it either. Can you?"

"Obviously, you can't hear it with music blasting in your ears," Degataga shot back. "But no, I can't hear it. I can see her."

"What does she look like?" Airiella was intrigued.

"Silver. She's silver, and beautiful in an ethereal way." Degataga glanced back and saw Taklishim had stepped into the spirit world, the warrior in him plainly evident. "Jax, Ronnie, back up," Degataga warned.

The earth under their feet shifted, and what sounded like thunder boomed. "Something is coming from straight ahead," she said. "Malevolent. The earth doesn't like it."

"Back up," Degataga said more forcefully, and the guys backed up. "Tak, come back."

"I'm here."

Floored, they watched as a duplicate of Airiella walked out towards them. "It's after Jax or Ronnie," she said quietly. Degataga looked back as a ring of blue fire appeared around them. "I don't know if that will stop it or not, but she isn't getting past me."

"Don't engage, Raven," Taklishim growled out.

"I'll engage if it goes after them," she bit back.

Degataga watched the imposter Airiella get close; the right hand stuck in the pocket of her pants. "Remember the skin is impenetrable," Degataga told her softly. The creature stopped twenty feet away and started stacking rocks. "She has earth power."

Airiella did something with the earth's energy, and the rocks fell over, making the imposter cock her head and look at Airiella curiously. "I'm hungry," the creature called out.

"Eat the berries." Airiella pointed to the bush

behind the creature. "They are less fatty than livers."

"I'll take one of theirs." She pointed with her left hand at Degataga and Taklishim. Airiella pushed Degataga back into the circle with Jax and Ronnie with a gust of air, and another blue ring popped up around Taklishim.

"I don't think so. Dega, can you feed energy into that?" Airiella asked sweetly. Her voice a warning of danger.

Degataga couldn't duplicate whatever she had done to create the ring of fire, but it was easy enough for him to find the energy signatures and divert energy to them both. Airiella's hair was floating slightly; it was the only sign she was up to something unless you were able to feel the power she was drawing into her as he could.

"She said make Tak's stronger, keep him in," Ronnie muttered.

Degataga manipulated the energy a little more, and the flames around Taklishim grew brighter. He knew the warrior was pissed, but she was trying to keep him safe, keep them all safe. He didn't dare look up and draw attention to Onida. The creature wasn't aware of her, and he wanted to keep it that way, remembering her almost severed arm.

"Raven," Taklishim warned.

"Raven, is that your name, little girl?" the creature taunted Airiella. "I don't know what you are, but I'll take your liver instead of theirs."

"You aren't taking any livers. Go eat the berries," Airiella repeated and expelled a gust of air so strong the massive old-growth trees behind the creature bowed under the pressure as Spearfinger flew backward, landing with a boom that sounded like boulders dropping from a cliff.

A tremor tore through the earth, knocking them all to the ground, except Airiella; she hovered a foot off the field on a current of air. It became apparent she'd been holding back during their training sessions. Degataga saw that her focus was laser-sharp, and her command of the elements far surpassed his abilities.

"What are you, little Raven?" the creature moved with a speed that caught Degataga off guard as suddenly he found the two Airiella's circling each other.

"Which one is which?" Jax sounded worried.

The sudden appearance of wings and a glowing blue Airiella answered that question. "I'm not going to tell you what I am. We'll leave this chapter a mystery in your little murder book you're writing."

Degataga noticed that Airiella's wind burst had gotten the creature's right hand out, and he guessed that was why she was glowing blue and drawing insane amounts of energy to her. She was going to blast the creature. He had no idea if it would affect it or not, and he looked over at Taklishim, who was trying to figure out how to get out of his fiery ring.

"Raven. It's not your name; it's what you are," the creature puzzled out, staring with interest at Airiella's wings.

"Jax, tell her that thing almost severed Onida's wing off," Degataga said quietly, not wanting the same to happen to her. He didn't think he'd be able to fix that.

"She knows." If his tone was anything to go by, Jax was certainly afraid. "She wants to know if this thing knows anything about Ravens."

"I don't know," he answered honestly. "I'd assume it does to be safe."

"She told me that Onida said she wouldn't move, so stop worrying, it's distracting her." Jax gave a weak smile.

Thankful for that bit of information, Degataga decided to watch when he felt a large draw of energy drain from the area, the earth willing to help the angel. With an earsplitting boom, a bolt of lightning shot out, striking the creature in several spots. Most importantly, close to the right hand. He saw that the creature's skin was scorched and smoking. Spearfinger's howl of pain gave him hope.

Even Taklishim stopped his hopeless struggle to get out and stared open-mouthed in shock as the creature retreated from Airiella, injured and scared. "You aren't just a raven."

"Still going to remain a mystery, sorry to disappoint. I can strike you again if you'd like," Airiella offered sweetly, energy pouring into her again, though the first strike had forced the creature to hide her hand again.

A blast of wind and the earth trembling knocked the creature to the ground again, but she didn't draw her hand back out. More booms followed it as weaker strikes rained down on the stone beast. Degataga wasn't sure if it was because she was losing energy or calculated it to make Spearfinger believe she was.

The right arm was visibly injured close to the wrist. Degataga could see the skin there was pure black and scorched enough to be smoking. He didn't know what made Airiella flinch and swivel her head to the right, but she did.

The stone creature lunged at her while Onida took flight in the same direction Airiella had looked. Taklishim roared as the black knife sliced at Airiella way too close for comfort. "Food is coming to me, despite your efforts."

"Fuck this." Airiella got angry. Wildly angry.

Degataga felt the energy drain from the fires around them as she pulled.

The grass withered and died, branches on trees overhead creaked, and groaned. The ground shook with an earthquake force. Trees uprooted, and a funnel cloud settled over Spearfinger holding it in place. Degataga couldn't see through the haze. He couldn't even hear anymore between the roar of the earth and the force of the wind. The sonic boom of lightning that she blasted down bathed the area in a blinding light.

The explosive blowback of energy flung the angel directly back into Taklishim bowling them both other, her wings automatically going around him to protect him. Degataga's senses were reeling, and he felt several cuts on his body bleeding. He tried to stand but couldn't; his equilibrium wholly thrown off.

As the world around him slowly stopped spinning, he saw nothing but devastation and a large crater in the earth. Trees down all around them, the forest now a brownfield for fifty meters in all directions.

Degataga reached for Ronnie and Jax, scanning for injuries and finding only bruises. He woke them back up, and his vision filled with black feathers as Airiella knelt in front of him, his ears still ringing he couldn't hear what she was saying.

He ignored her waving him off and latched on to her hand, scanning her for injuries. He found some broken bones in her wings, which explained why she hadn't put them back in. Her face was bruising, and she had several cuts over the exposed skin of her arms. Otherwise, all he could find was her energy was weak.

She helped them stand up, all of them leaning

against each other for support as they waited for their balance to return. Degataga saw Airiella jogging off in the direction Onida had flown, and panic hit him at the thought that she might be hurt. His legs buckled as he tried to follow, Jax and Ronnie catching his weight.

Taklishim came up behind him, and he felt the healing warmth come over him as his senses returned to normal. "Go, Onida needs help," he heard Taklishim tell him.

Chapter Fourteen

Onida spotted the curious teenager trying to get closer to the commotion he'd heard. Hoping to scare him off, she swooped down, thankful that Airiella had felt his approach before the creature could kill him.

Unfortunately, she wasted her efforts. All she managed to do was startle the boy, not deter him. The sudden earth rolling under his feet halted him, and terror flashed across his face as a tree uprooted next to him and crashed to the ground.

Before Onida could turn back, a surge of energy following a blinding explosion sent her careening wildly into a tree breaking her wing, and she fell to the ground in a painful thud. The now scared witless teenager went flying backward, narrowly missing a tree but landing in a crunch that hopefully didn't break any bones. Onida didn't see him moving.

She managed to shift back to human form and take three staggering steps forward when a chilling sound stopped her in her tracks instead of propelling her forward as it should have. A huge tree came crashing down, a limb knocking her off her feet only to have the tree crush her beneath it. Branches punctured her skin, her legs breaking with a sound she hoped she didn't remember.

She floated in and out of consciousness, the crushing pain too much to bear. She thought she had seen Airiella, but she might have been hallucinating. She regretted not telling Dega that she loved him, now Onida didn't know if she would get a chance. She was dying.

"You aren't dying." She heard Airiella's voice. "This will hurt. I'm sorry, Onida."

"Tell him I love him," she whispered.

"You just told him yourself." Airiella appeared in her line of vision. "I'm going to lift the tree with the air, Jax and Ronnie are going to pull you out, and it will hurt."

"Airiella, are you crying?" Onida didn't know what was happening; she only knew that her body broke, and the pain was making her crazy.

"Yes. I'm crying. So are you," the angel said, softly. "Get ready."

Onida felt the pressure on her body shift and couldn't hold back the scream that ripped through her when she moved. Agony tore through her body, and then she wanted to die to escape the pain.

"We need Tama," Degataga said.

"She's coming." Taklishim was there too. Why couldn't she see them?

"Your eyes are closed, that's why," Airiella whispered in her ear. "Keep them closed."

"The boy," she cried out, her voice weak.

"He's fine, Jax is taking him home. Tak, I'm calling Stolas."

"Do it," Onida heard him order.

She must have blacked out again, because when her eyes opened she wasn't feeling any pain, and she saw her sister staring down at her. "Tama?"

"I'm here, Oni. We're almost done, just hold still a little while longer." She felt fingers on her face.

"Am I paralyzed?"

"I don't think so. Hush now."

Onida closed her eyes again, and when she woke this time, she was in her bed, and Degataga was beside her looking awful. She went to move and heard, "Don't move, Onida."

"Airiella?"

"Yes, it's me. Stay still. There might still be nerve damage. The others are all out of energy, and I have none left to give them. Here, rub this on your gums." A small container appeared in front of Onida.

"What's this?"

"Herbs to take the pain away," she answered sadly. "I'm so sorry you were hurt."

It all came back to her in a rush. "Is it dead?"

"Yes."

"Then I'll deal with it. No more kids getting killed is worth it," Onida muttered. "Did they all exhaust themselves trying to heal me?"

"Taklishim stopped them before it got dangerous for them," she reassured Onida.

"What about you?"

"Don't worry about me. I'm the reason you are like this." Onida closed her eyes at the remorse in Airiella's voice.

"Raven, don't do this to yourself. None of us knew

what would happen. You didn't hurt me on purpose, and I don't blame you. I am sure none of the others do either."

"I don't know. Taklishim is pretty angry," she said softly.

"You are still here, that tells me his anger is more geared towards you taking risks he thought you shouldn't. If he were mad at you or blamed you, you wouldn't be here. Aren't you the one who found me and got the tree off me?"

Her silence was the only answer except for the slight sound of sniffling. Onida chanced movement and shifted her legs, pain searing along her nerves. Indeed, there was nerve damage. If it was fixable, the only one able to do it was unconscious next to her.

"Stop moving and rub that shit on your gums," Airiella ordered.

"Only if you stop blaming yourself," Onida snapped back. "Otherwise, shut up and let me suffer how I feel fit." Onida blinked back the tears. "How drained are you?"

"Jax and Ronnie are sleeping in the hallway outside your door, and Taklishim and Tama are in your guest room."

"That's not what I asked." Onida thought about the answer she got. "How long have I been out?"

"As long as me," came her answer. "Your thoughts brought me out of it."

"No wonder Taklishim is pissed." Onida figured out that meant she had utterly drained herself. "What did you do?"

"We're not talking about this," Airiella answered woodenly. "Put that on your gums and go back to sleep."

"Sleep won't take the pain away, and my energy is fine." Onida thought briefly about moving to check on her.

"You have no walls around your thoughts right now. I know what you are thinking and if I have to, I'll yell and wake Taklishim and Tama up, and they can be the ones to scream at you."

"Don't yell, let Dega sleep." Onida stopped arguing. She reached for his hand and scanned him, seeing exactly how drained he was. "Did he eat?"

"He did. And drank a ton of his magic juice."

Onida tried to heal his energy reserve, but she didn't have the power with energy that Airiella had. She kept hold of his hand anyway; it made her feel better. "Airiella, you need sleep."

"I do. I know."

"Why didn't we know you could do all that?" Onida remembered what she had seen.

"Why would I display that kind of power during training sessions designed to help me focus on those skills? It would have hurt you guys."

She had been taking it easy on them. "You didn't need our help, did you?"

"Without your help, I wouldn't have been able to do that. Not with the level of control I had. It would have been wild and unpredictable before."

"What was the explosion?"

"Jax called it the death blow. Whatever that was exploded into dust and released weird energy that collided with mine. Leveled the forest in that area."

"Were you hurt?" Onida was trying to piece together the pieces of what happened after she flew after the boy.

"Nothing more than scrapes and bruises. It tossed me around a little."

Onida sensed hesitation and knew she was holding

something back. "What else? I can feel underneath that statement."

"A few broken bones in my wings."

That explained the rustling sound she'd heard. "They are still out, aren't they?"

"Yes. Can you stop talking now so I can go back to sleep?"

"Let me heal you," Onida said gently.

"Are you crazy? You haven't healed yet."

"I don't need to be healed to do my job, Airiella. My energy is fine. All you have to do is touch me. Let me do this for you, please." Onida hated to beg, and she was at the angel's mercy at the moment.

"No. I can deal with it, just like you are dealing with it."

Onida exploded in frustration. "Damn it! Listen to me, you stubborn girl, let me feel useful!"

Degataga shifted, "Oni, are you okay?"

"No. Airiella is still hurt and won't let me heal her." Onida felt awful for waking him up. "Go back to sleep, Dega."

He leaned over her and looked at her with those deep eyes of his. "She made us work on you. One of us will heal her when they wake up."

"I can do it. There is nothing wrong with my healing abilities."

"Let her do it, Airiella," Degataga gave in. He kissed her gently, and laid back down falling asleep immediately.

Onida felt like cheering in victory, though she held it in until she felt Airiella's hand in her own. "I'm only doing this to shut you up."

"Of course, you are." Onida let a smile color her

voice. "It still counts as a win. By the way, the argument with Taklishim was brilliant, and I'm sorry for testing you, but it was effective."

"It does feel good to win against him." Airiella chuckled weakly.

Onida scanned Airiella and found several broken bones in her wings as well as some torn muscles. It wasn't anything she couldn't handle, but she felt a flare of frustration with her at holding back. She got to work on healing, handing the container back when the pain got too intense for Airiella. "You called Stolas, didn't you?"

"I had to. You were in so much pain they were having a hard time working on you."

Onida figured that was the only reason Taklishim would have given in on that. "You are healed up. Try putting your wings away."

She heard the whoosh of the feathers as they retracted. "Thanks."

"Go pick your guys up off the floor and pull out the couch; it folds into a bed. Go and get some sleep. I'm not going anywhere."

"I'm fine right here. I'll sleep if you do."

Onida hated to admit it; the healing had taken quite a bit out of her, and the pain was getting intense. She felt the container being pressed back into her hand and gave in, rubbing the mixture onto her gums. "Thanks for saving us again, Raven."

"You are my family. I love you," Airiella said quickly. "Can I give you my blood? Will that heal you?"

"I don't know. If it saves these guys from draining themselves trying to heal me, I'm all for it." Onida already had that link with her from when she did it before; she didn't see how it could hurt to try.

"The cuts on your leg are still open, I can drip blood into one of them," Airiella offered.

"At the very worst, it doesn't work."

Onida heard Airiella shuffling around, and then she came into sight, her face tear-streaked, dirty and bruised. "I've got Jax's knife here I can use. Do you think it will matter that it has that anti-demon poison stuff on it?"

"No, I don't think that will matter," Onida said quietly. She hadn't realized how emotional Airiella had been. Degataga was right; it was humbling knowing someone cared enough about you to cry for you and stay by your side.

Airiella moved the blankets around, exposing Onida's legs. "I'm going to pick the ugliest one, give me a minute to be intrusive. Oh, I'm going to use this one, I hope my blood heals this at least."

"Airiella, wait. Look at my face, please," Onida requested. Once she saw Airiella and confirmed the tears she had in her voice were real. "I don't want you to do this because you think it's your fault, and you need to fix it."

The exhausted angel knelt and lay her head on the bed next to Onida's hand. "I do feel like this is my fault. You could have died. If I hadn't gotten so pissed off, I could have used more control to make sure no one was hurt. I almost lost you."

Onida heard the door open, "Siren?" Jax whispered.

"Come in, Jax. Maybe you can help me convince her that this isn't her fault." Onida slid her hands into Airiella's matted hair and massaged her scalp.

"She knows it's not her fault but will assume the blame anyway. It's because she loves you," Jax said softly, coming around the bed and into view. "Those legs aren't looking any better."

"She wants to use her blood to see if it will help." Onida felt tears sting her eyes.

"She's been pushing Degataga to do just that. But because he loves you, he wanted to be the one to fix you. He loses his reason when it comes to you. Baby, give me your hand. I'll open your finger."

"She's going to need more than what's from my finger." Onida heard her numb tone. "Slice my palm open."

Jax moved the chair and sat down in it, gently lifting Airiella to his lap and then scooted them close to the bed. Onida smelled the blood and felt the pressure of her hand on her leg. Onida didn't feel any pain thanks to the herbs that she rubbed on her gums.

It wasn't long before she felt the tingling sensations of nerves waking up and a painful burning fire started in her legs, spreading throughout her body. Something was happening; she just wasn't sure what it was yet. She was tempted to rub more of the herbal mix on herself, but held back, needing to see what happened.

"I need more, can you do the other hand too?" Airiella asked Jax quietly.

"Are you sure?"

"I am, that's what my raven is telling me," she answered, the exhaustion rolling off her alarming Onida.

"Hold still, siren." Onida smelled the coppery smell again. This time she could feel Airiella's hand sealing over the wound on her leg. She was also picking up on Airiella's emotions.

Onida let the tears fall. "Raven, these are words I rarely say so, please understand how hard this is for me."

Onida was able to move her head without pain now, and she turned to look at the disheveled angel, "I love you, too."

Jax held the crying angel while she let her blood flow freely from the wound in her hand. Onida felt the changes in her body as the rare angel blood did its work. "Did you fix her wings?" Jax asked.

"I did, it was the least I could do." Onida tested movement in her legs and found they felt normal. "I think I'm okay, Airiella."

"Not yet. The raven said to keep going still," she whispered as she had Jax squeeze down her arm, forcing more blood to seep out of her palm. After another five minutes, she pulled back, and Onida swung her legs over the side of the bed and stood with ease.

She took Airiella's palms in her hands and got to work healing them. "Jax, would it be okay if I help her take a bath?"

"It's fine with me, but that's up to her." He kissed her cheek tenderly.

"I can do it, I'm fine." She stood but wobbled.

"Let her help you, baby," Jax whispered in her ear. All she had the energy to do was nod.

"Stay close by in case I need your help," Onida commanded him. "Have Ronnie pull out the sofa bed because she is going to sleep after this, whether she wants to or not."

Jax stood and woke Ronnie up, then moved the chair back to where it was and sat down, leaning his head back on the back. Onida left the bathroom door open so she could see Degataga and Jax both. She ran the bathwater and added some of the soothing oils she had learned to make from Degataga that aided in muscle pain.

"Airiella, ask Jax to come and help me get you in the tub," she whispered.

"I can hear you," Jax walked in and lifted her while Onida pulled the dirty clothes off her and helped her settle in the tub.

"Any chance you have extra clothes in your car?" Onida was hopeful.

"Ronnie always carries a go-bag after seeing how many times Airiella had to pull from her pack. He's got extra shirts in there."

"He's bringing one up," she said, her head lolling around.

Onida took a closer look at the bruises marring the angel's skin and the various cuts and scrapes. It wasn't as bad as she thought it would be. Jax left the bathroom, and Onida cleaned the limp Airiella up and got her hair washed. It always made Onida feel better to be clean before going to sleep. She could do this for Airiella.

She could have let Airiella do it on her own, but the girl was close to passing out, the dark smudges under her eyes making her face look more bruised. Onida didn't want her to fall and hurt herself. She grabbed her brush and brushed in some leave-in conditioner to ease up the tangles and drained the tub.

"Jax," she called quietly. The large man walked back in and lifted Airiella out of the tub while Onida wrapped a towel around her body, then her hair. Jax sat down on the toilet, and together they got her dried off and in a t-shirt.

"I'll keep people out of the living room for you," Onida said, standing. "Or if you rather, we can put her on the exam table in the office."

"The bed is fine. Once Airiella's asleep, she'll be out

for a bit. It's usually loud thoughts from one of us that bring her out, not so much the noise around her."

Onida nodded. "Airiella, thank you for blessing my life with your presence." She hugged the weak girl to her, feeling the return hug lightened her heart immensely, no matter how faint. "Do you need help?"

"No, I've got her." Jax smiled gently. "Thanks for taking care of her."

Onida blushed. "It was her that saved us," she corrected him.

"Yes, but you didn't have to do what you did, and you did it anyway. That's the part that means the most to Airiella, not what she did." Onida glanced back at the now sleeping angel cradled against Jax's chest.

"She's remarkable and has truly changed my life." Onida touched her cheek gently. "Take care of her, Jax."

"Always. See you in a bit." He carried her out of the room, and she closed the door behind him.

She walked over to Degataga passed out cold on the bed, and she slowly started to work his dirty and blood-stained clothes off. Once she got that accomplished, she grabbed a clean washcloth and cleaned him up as best as she could without waking him up.

After she completed that, she sat down to look at the remaining wounds on her legs that the angel blood hadn't fixed. They weren't bad anymore, and most had scabbed up from the healing. The exception was the one Airiella had used to drip her blood in, and Onida understood why she picked that one. It looked to be the worst off and was still weeping even though she could see where it had healed up, at least half of it. She got it bandaged up and checked over the rest of her body, seeing where all the damage had taken place.

She looked back at Degataga and marveled that he hadn't completely burnt out. Onida was lucky to be alive. She quickly changed into a pair of shorts and a clean shirt and snuck out to check on Tama and Tak.

She popped open the guest room door and saw Taklishim looking every bit as wiped out as Degataga and her heart stuttered in her chest. "Oni?" Tama whispered.

"It's me, I just wanted to check on you." She silently moved across the floor to hug her sister.

"You are up!"

"Yes, Airiella gave me blood," Onida explained. "Dega is still asleep. I cleaned her up and sent her out with Jax to the sofa bed. So, if you guys go out there, be quiet."

"Jax let her do that?" Tama was shocked.

"She didn't ask him, and he offered to do the cutting for her." Onida looked confused. "Jax said it was Degataga that refused to use the blood."

"He did. Because Airiella was so depleted, he thought it would hurt her," Tama said carefully. "Tak agreed. She didn't tell you that part, did she?"

"No, she didn't." Onida wanted to get angry, but it wouldn't change anything. "I healed her wings up and the muscle damage."

"Well, at least that's done then. Is Airiella okay? Tak has been furious for two days because she refused to let anyone touch her."

"Two days?" Onida dropped to the bed, making Taklishim shift.

"She didn't tell you that either, I see. I've been keeping you out, and she rests for a couple of hours then gives her energy to Degataga and Taklishim so they could work on you."

Onida's eyes started to sting again, and she curled up next to Tama and cried. She let her sister hold her and soothe her. "Why would she do that?"

"She loves you, Oni. She protected Tak from damage with her wings and pumped energy into a shield around Ronnie, Jax, and Degataga. She couldn't see you to protect you. She found you and the boy after she made sure that Taklishim was okay and could heal any damage the others took. She told him to send Degataga that you needed help. She told Smitty here to send me."

Onida clutched at her sister's arms around her. "I was dying, wasn't I?"

"You were. Airiella got the tree off you, and Jax and Ronnie got you out from under it, but you had so much damage. I knocked you out, and she flat out refused to accept that you wouldn't make it. She had smeared a tiny amount of blood on your tongue and gave every bit of energy she had to Degataga, Taklishim, and me. Jax took the boy home while Ronnie held Airiella. Every time she passed out, Taklishim got a little more furious. Then she'd wake up, give more energy and pass out again. It was a cycle until Degataga got you to a point you were safe enough to move. Then she did the same thing here. She didn't leave your side. I'm incredibly grateful for it. I was so scared, Oni. Even Mom shifted back to human form."

"Oni, what are you doing here?" Taklishim's sleepy voice broke in.

"Airiella gave her blood," Tama answered before Onida could tell her not to.

"She did what?" His voice went from sleepy to angry in a split second.

"She's okay, Tak. I healed her, and she's sleeping on the sofa bed," Onida said through her tears.

"Are you crying?" His voice now sounded scared.

"She is, so maybe ease up a bit," Tama said gruffly.

Onida felt the bed shift, and Taklishim appeared in front of her. "Are you truly okay? Her blood worked?"

"It did." Onida's words slurred.

"I was scared, Oni," Taklishim admitted freely and slid his arms around both sisters. "Is Degataga okay?"

"He's still out cold. Airiella is too."

"She kept all of us alive," he whispered brokenly.

"Go back to sleep Tak, I'm going back to my room," Onida untangled herself from Tama after Taklishim released them. She kissed her sister's cheek, then Taklishim's. "Thank you for everything you all did."

She crept back to her room and slid under the covers into Degataga's side, where his arms wrapped around her, and she slipped into a deep sleep.

Chapter Fifteen

Degataga woke slowly thinking, he was dreaming that Onida was caressing him, and he didn't want it to end. He became aware that he had his arm around her, and Degataga bolted awake, panicked that he had jostled her in his sleep, and made it worse.

But as his eyes adjusted and he saw her worried gaze on him, her body sitting up, he thought he was dreaming again. "Oni?"

"I'm okay, calm down." She put her hand on his chest. Where had his clothes gone?

"What's happening? Is this a dream?"

"Sshh, no, it's not a dream. Lay down, please." Onida pushed against his chest and he gave in.

"Are you going to explain?" He looked at her closely, scanning her body and finding no damage at all.

"Airiella gave me blood," she answered, and shock registered in his brain.

"She wasn't well enough to do that." He started to sit up again.

"She's fine. I promise. I healed her injuries and got

her cleaned up. She's out sleeping on the sofa bed with Jax and Ronnie."

"Taklishim is going to be livid." Degataga sighed.

"He knows. I snuck in there to check on Tama, and he woke up."

"And you? No pain?" He resisted the urge to scan her again.

"I'm as well as I was before. Maybe even better. Please, relax," Onida coaxed him. "You are still wiped out."

"I am, I know. I'll be okay; I've gotten used to it the past couple of days. I thought I'd lost you."

"So I've heard. I'm sorry."

"You have nothing to be sorry for, a tree fell on you." The sight of her laying there, dying before his eyes, wasn't one he was likely to forget.

"Airiella blames herself."

"I know that too. I don't blame Airiella. No one else does either. We didn't know what would happen. She saw an opportunity to end it, and she took it. I would have done the same." Dega ran a hand over his face. "Did you undress me?"

"I did. I tried to clean you up too, but I didn't want to wake you up."

"Are you sure? No pain?" he asked again.

At her nod, he crushed her to him, burying his face in her hair and sobbed, letting the fear of the past couple of days go. "I meant what I said out there, Dega. I do love you," she whispered, and his heart broke wide open. "I know you saved me, too."

He shook his head, unable to speak. He just sobbed, happy to feel her in his arms, and responsive. She stroked his back and wrapped her legs around him. His body was weary, and his mind overwhelmed, but he wouldn't change any of it if it meant she was here, alive, and in his arms.

"I didn't save you, Oni, Airiella did." Degataga corrected her after he calmed down.

"She told me, so did Tama. It was you."

"If she hadn't given me a jump start by smearing blood on your tongue, I couldn't have done it. I couldn't have done it without the energy she gave me, or without Tak's help. As much as I want to be your hero, I know deep inside me, it wasn't me."

"I know deep inside *me;* it was your love that kept me alive. Regardless of who can claim to have saved my life, you are still my hero."

"God, Oni. You were so broken; I was terrified." He didn't want to let her go.

"It's over now."

"Jax didn't try to stop her, did he?" Degataga shifted so he could see her beautiful face.

"Not at all. Jax helped her do it."

"He's perfect for her. I need to shower, but I don't want to let you go." Degataga also wanted to bury himself in her body that she wrapped around him.

"I'll shower with you." She extricated herself and stood quickly, holding her hand out to him.

"She's truly okay?" He wanted to check on her to keep Taklishim from losing his mind.

"She is."

"There was significant damage to her wings," he remarked, standing and following her to the bathroom where he saw a pile of bloody clothes. "Are these hers?"

"Yes, I bathed her. She looked miserable."

"You are an amazing woman, Hawk-eye." He

climbed in the steaming shower and waited for her to join him. "You truly love me?"

"I do. It shouldn't have taken me dying to figure it out." She took the soap and gently washed him, her healing energy soaking into his tired body. When she slid her slick arms around him from behind, her body pressing into his back, he broke down again.

He turned in her arms and kissed her, holding nothing back. She willingly offered her body, and with her leaning against the shower wall, he took her, fast and desperate for the feel of her wrapped around him full of life and love.

He tried to go slow and gentle, but when she demanded more, he was helpless to resist and pounded into her mercilessly until they both shattered, her repaired limbs quaking and a smile gracing her lips. "I needed that," she said, her soft voice making him melt.

"So did I. Let me clean you up now," he said, slidding out of her body and tenderly washing the skin he'd spent hours trying to repair while Taklishim worked tirelessly, putting her bones back together. He kissed all over as he washed and rinsed, ending where he hadn't taken time to bring her to pleasure before roughly taking her.

He cleaned her up and then licked her clean her again, refocusing his efforts on the little bundle of nerves that drove her wild when he flicked it with his tongue. He didn't stop until she exploded on his tongue, her legs giving out as she sunk next to him, her breath coming out in gasps. "That was what I needed, Oni."

He turned off the shower, and they dried each other off and dressed quietly. Sneaking down into the kitchen to find Ronnie there working on his computer. "Good to see you up, Onida."

"How's she doing?" Degataga sat down in front of him.

"She had a few nightmares we had a hard time pulling her out of, but the past couple hours, she's been sleeping peacefully."

"Nightmares?" Onida grew still.

"I can't see them, but Jax could. Whatever happened took a toll on them both. I just checked them about five minutes ago, and they are both okay. Go and look if you want. I don't think they'll wake up unless you shake them."

"If Tama comes down and I'm not here, can you tell her that and have her take a look?"

"Sure," he drawled. "You think something is wrong?"

"I don't know, that's why I want Tama to take a look."

Degataga shot Onida a concerned look but didn't dwell on it because it seemed like she didn't want to worry Ronnie. "Want me to make us French toast?"

"Sure." Ronnie grinned. "I could eat that."

Onida chuckled. "I get to eat first, before you." She smiled and then pointed at Degataga, "him too."

"I'm just finishing up editing the footage we got," Ronnie explained, "then I'll help set the table."

"Were you able to film it all?" Onida was curious to see what had happened after she'd flown away.

"For the most part. The camera got jostled around some during those blasts, but I caught most of it. Did you want to see?"

"I do, but just from when I left. I remember the rest well enough," Onida said.

Degataga winced, remembering how Airiella was flung through the air like a rag doll right into Taklishim. He didn't argue with her; he just went about making breakfast, grateful that Mags had restocked the kitchen and kept them fed the past couple of days.

Ronnie pulled the raw footage up and let it play for her while he set the table around her. They saw how absorbed she was and the look of shock on her face. "How do I replay that?" she asked quietly. Ronnie showed her how to maneuver around the program and came to stand by Degataga.

"Why is she worried about the nightmares?"

"I'm not sure. Could be several reasons. Onida could be worried about brain damage that we didn't catch. It could be that Airiella was so emotionally traumatized it's triggering things from her past. Maybe it's because her energy was so low, she couldn't fight against the darkness that seems to go after her all the time. I'm only speculating. I wish I could give you a better answer." Degataga looked up and saw the worry on Ronnie's face.

"Whatever it was, it had Jax on edge. He wouldn't talk about it."

"Tama will look. Airiella is stronger than we all think she is," Degataga said calmly.

"You're wrong there. I know *exactly* how strong Airiella is. She sometimes forgets, and that's when things get tricky."

"Did you guys know she could do all that stuff she did?" Degataga was curious about that.

"Yes and no. Airiella did some of it at Franklin, but

there was a lot more control this time, as well as a lot more power. She practices with the water at home. She'll go out to the beach and work at it, Jax or I go with her. She's gotten better. Air and earth are as natural to her as breathing. She doesn't practice those much."

"Thank you, Ronnie," Onida said suddenly, standing.

"You're welcome." He went back and saved his work, closing down the computer.

"Can you send me a copy of the raw footage?" she asked, leaning on the counter.

"Sure, I'll make you a copy before we leave." Ronnie looked questioningly at Degataga, who only shrugged and plated up the first batch, handing it to Onida.

"No, you eat first, I'll cook the next the batch." She handed it back. "You need it more than I do."

Degataga didn't push back, simply took the plate and sat down to eat. He knew how low his energy still was. After two platefuls of food, he took over the cooking and made enough for Taklishim and Tama, who came down, Taklishim looking just as rough as he knew he did.

Onida asked Tama to check on Airiella, mentioning the nightmares, and silently Tama went into the living room while Taklishim frowned. "What do you think is going on?"

"Just a precaution," was all Onida said, eating slowly.

"I'm too tired to fight with you." He slumped back in the chair. "I'll check Airiella out myself."

"I knew you would. Eat."

Degataga set a plate in front of Taklishim and made one up for Tama, who came in a few minutes later. The twins had mastered the poker face. He couldn't read them when they pulled it out, and he wasn't sure what to think. Based on Taklishim's glowering face, he couldn't either.

"I'm going to make another batch and save it for when they wake up," Degataga announced to cut the silence down.

"Good idea, they'll wake soon," Tama said cryptically, digging into her food.

Taklishim huffed and stalked out of the room. "He's checking on her, isn't he?"

Tama and Onida both nodded. Ronnie just looked perplexed.

Chapter Sixteen

Would you tell me if there was something wrong?" Ronnie sat forward and boldly looked at Tama after a few minutes of silence.

"I would. I know what Airiella means to you," Tama answered gently.

"I know enough to realize you aren't saying something," he pushed.

"He's right, what aren't you saying," Taklishim demanded as he came back in and sat down, glaring at his wife.

Onida sighed. She knew Tama would keep quiet, and she didn't want her to fight with Taklishim. They were both too tired for this. "I think she gained a new ability when she killed that creature."

"What?" Taklishim hadn't been expecting that answer.

"The section of the brain that shows active for people that have pre-cog abilities lit up in her," Tama explained casually.

Degataga came up next to Onida and squatted

down. "You think her nightmares are something she sees in the future?"

"I do."

"That would explain why Jax didn't want to talk about it," Ronnie mused.

"Jax saw?" Tama stopped eating and waited for Ronnie to answer.

"He does when it's strong," Ronnie clarified.

"Out with it, Oni, I know there's more," Taklishim growled.

"Tak, stop being an ass." Tama shoved at him.

"I think that her energy was so low that her normal defenses couldn't hold up, and it allowed the pre-cog to come through. I sensed something different when I woke up. She had been picking up on all my thoughts. Everything. She normally can't do that with me."

"You're concerned that if she is picking up on thoughts that something else can get in." Degataga put the pieces together. Onida nodded.

"What if that is just a side effect from the blood?" Taklishim wondered.

"I hadn't had enough of her blood to do that. Degataga said she only smeared a small amount on my tongue."

"Can she pick up your thoughts, Ronnie?" Tama asked.

"Yes, but I also have a strong connection with her. She can read me, Smitty and Jax. Every once in a while, when Taklishim gets worked up about something, she'll catch a stray thought from him. She's never said anything about picking up on Onida's thoughts. Just that she could talk to her through the link."

"You think we need to test it then?" Degataga asked Onida.

"I do. With either Tama or you. See if she picks up on either of your thoughts."

"If she does, what does that mean?" Ronnie's worried tone broke through the jumble going through Onida's head.

"I'm not sure. When Airiella's energy replenishes, her normal defenses will go back up. If she's still getting the nightmares, then something changed. If they stop, then it's an ability she's had that her defenses block."

"Which means what?"

Taklishim shifted. "If it's new, then we aren't out of danger, and it's a skill she'll need in the immediate future," he said sullenly. "She seems to sprout these new things when things go sideways."

Onida nodded again, looking down at the table. "Don't broadcast your thoughts. Don't purposely think about it. She picks up on emotions directed at her, and it wouldn't be a true test. She told me that my thoughts were loud, and that was what woke her up."

"God damnit! Can't she ever catch a break?" Ronnie whispered angrily.

"That display of power showed she's more than capable of handling herself," Taklishim grudgingly admitted. "Not to mention her awareness when she's outside."

Ronnie finally laughed. "That shit was funny."

Onida slid her hand into Degataga's plotting out a good time to talk to him about what she saw on the footage. If she was right, they weren't out of danger, and Onida wasn't sure what they could do about it.

Jax and Airiella shuffled into the kitchen, looking like hell. Degataga scrambled up and got them the plates he'd made for them and brought them to the table. "I'm not hungry." Airiella tried to push it away.

"Raven, for once, don't argue and just eat," Taklishim implored, his tone pleading.

Onida was just as stunned as Airiella was, but she was happy to see that she ate. Slowly, but she ate it all. Degataga handed her a bottle of the yellow water Airiella called magic juice. She happily drank that down, and Onida didn't see that it made much of a difference.

"Can you tell me how you got her not to argue, please?" Ronnie asked. "That's a skill I could desperately learn."

Jax coughed to hide his laughter as Airiella glared at him. "Degataga, you need to go home. Your brother is sick," Airiella said, then her face morphed into shock as she realized what she'd said.

"Ells, what's going on?" Jax took her hand and gave Onida a look.

"Raven, look at me," Taklishim ordered. "Breathe slow, calm down. Focus on me. Put your walls up for me, please. Nod when you've done it."

Onida watched Airiella's pale face as she slowly gained her focus and nodded. "Jax, can you feel anything from her?" Onida looked to the worried man.

"No, she's closed up."

"Ronnie?" Onida glanced at him, and he shook his head.

"Stay focused on me, Raven. Can you pick up on any thoughts from Degataga or Tama? Don't look at them. Look only at me, focus on me," Taklishim guided her.

"He's wondering which brother. The younger one." She answered his unspoken question. Shock lined her face again. "Tak, what's happening?"

"What was your nightmare about?" Onida asked her, noticing Jax stiffen.

"Too much," Ronnie warned. "Her emotions are leaking through."

"That's enough." Jax stood, pulling Airiella with him. "Onida, can we use your room?"

"Yes, go on. Dega, go call home," Onida said, nodding towards her office.

"What was she leaking out, Ronnie?" Taklishim's tension was high.

"Fear. Sadness."

"Why did Jax pull her away?" Tama leaned forward to look at Ronnie.

"Because they were strong enough emotions to suck the energy out of her."

"We haven't replaced Fields yet on the council. I don't know who she can work with on pre-cog to learn how to harness it. The danger here is if she starts picking up on everything, it's going to constantly batter at her like the soul sight did." Taklishim rested his head on the table. "I'm sorry, Ronnie. I know this isn't easy on you guys."

Onida straightened. "I'll work with her on it. Dega and Tama can too."

"You think it's a new ability then? Meaning there's some sort of danger present?" Ronnie looked tired suddenly.

Onida couldn't lie, "I do."

Degataga walked back in, looking shaken. "My brother was diagnosed with the same form of cancer my father had. Early stages. I might be able to stop it. I've got to go back." He looked down at Onida.

"I'll come with you. Together, we are better." Onida stood, her decision firm.

"What about Airiella?" Ronnie looked lost.

"Taklishim will look after her." Onida knew that without even having to look. "She needs to recover her energy before we can do anything. With as low as she is, it will take at least a week until I am comfortable enough to start taxing her mentally."

"Here's what you can do in the meantime," Taklishim said wearily. Onida paused to listen. "You, Smitty or Jax stays with her all the time, don't leave her alone. If she has another vision or nightmare, whichever happens, someone writes it down. Keep track of them; note the time, the day, and where it happened. Look for patterns. Research them and see if you can find any matches; if so, note all that as well."

Onida thought about it all and agreed. "Also, have her work on her filters as she does with her walls," Onida added.

Ronnie wrote it all down and reviewed the directions with them before he was satisfied. "Are we staying here or going back home?"

"You can go home. Airiella's got her situational awareness down pat. If she feels immediate danger, she'll know before any of us do." Taklishim was back to weary.

"That's true, but if it's you in danger, she'll be unhappy that she isn't here," Ronnie pointed out.

Onida moved again, a restless feeling taking root. "Send Aedan and Mags back home, even Smitty, if he needs to go. You guys can stay here while I'm gone."

"I'm fine with that," Ronnie agreed.

Taklishim only shrugged. "I need to go home and get more rest."

Tama readily agreed with him and stood to embrace Onida. "Call me when you get there."

"You'll watch her?"

Tama winked, "Like a hawk."

Both Ronnie and Onida snorted out a laugh. Onida asked Ronnie to get a copy of the footage ready for her before leaving, and she went to pack a bag.

Chapter Seventeen

Degataga was lost in thought as the plane landed and taxied down the runway to their gate. He'd thankfully slept before they had to leave for their flight, and he rested on the plane. He wasn't quite where he needed to be to start a healing session, but Degataga would do what he could.

"One day won't change the outcome, Dega," Onida told him gently as if she'd read his mind. "We can start in the morning."

"If this is what it feels like to be Airiella, I don't envy her at all," Degataga mused.

"What do you mean?"

"Having to be facing impossible odds stacked against you constantly. One thing after the other pulled in so many directions."

"I guess I never really thought about it like that. Airiella just goes with it so well."

"Ronnie's reaction tells a different story. She might just be hiding the wear on her from us." Degataga wouldn't put it past her.

"I don't know if she ever worries about herself. If they didn't take care of her, she'd run herself right into the ground, trying to help everyone, I can see your point. If she's hiding it, she's hiding it well."

"Not as well as she'd like given the way Ronnie reacted. I was a little surprised that Jax pulled her away from the table." Degataga thought back to the morning.

"I'm not. Jax wouldn't have done it unless she wanted him to. That tells me she let him know she couldn't handle it." Onida tapped her nails against her teeth, waiting for the doors to open so they could get off the plane. "You might be on to something there."

"I think I am. Airiella visibly struggled after Bael. Even after Jax proposed."

"Her powers also got stronger after that creature threatened Ronnie and Jax." Onida stood, immediately moving back so Degataga could get out in front of her. She grabbed their bags down from the overhead bin and handed him his.

He took it and her hand. "It wasn't just Jax and Ronnie being threatened that pissed her off. It's her anger that made her stronger. When her emotions fuel her, her powers intensify." He kissed the back of her hand. "It's no different for me. Love for you pushed me harder and farther than I've ever gone before."

"She didn't protect them when she got flung back. I think that is confusing me."

"She did, you just couldn't see it. She fed so much energy into that ring around us that it went from blue to clear. I thought at first that it had died down until I was blown back against a solid wall I couldn't see."

"Her wings took the brunt of the fall, protecting

Taklishim," she pieced together.

"Right. It allowed Tak to heal me to come to you. I'm just wondering if that energy blast woke up the pre-cog in her. It's happened before." Degataga led them through the concourse. "My older brother should be here to pick us up."

"She's always had a form of it, I think, but I don't believe she considered it pre-cog. That touching thing she does, she shows people a future." Onida snapped her fingers. "Maybe it's not a new skill."

"That's right, I forgot about that. But it doesn't work with everyone. I remember Airiella saying that it only works when she does it for people that already have a connection. I don't think she could randomly walk up to two different strangers and do that. She also told me that sometimes it didn't work."

"Airiella is this mystery that we keep trying to unravel and only find more questions. It makes me remember when she said she didn't want to be a science experiment. Sometimes I feel like I am guilty of making her just that by trying to figure it all out. I pepper her with questions and study her in such a cold and detached manner," Onida explained, a distant look on her face.

"I don't believe she feels that you do that to her," Degataga consoled her.

"I do. I just realized it. I'm starting to realize a lot of things when it comes to her and all of us."

Degataga pulled his chirping phone from his pocket and sighed. "Let's rent a car; it'll be easier." He texted his brother back and led Onida to the area they could grab a car.

"Do you think she could fall? Like fall from grace, I

mean?" Onida looked at him carefully as they got in the rental car.

"No. Theoretically, yes, anyone could fall. Her? I don't believe it would ever happen. Do you know much of her past?" Degataga turned in his seat to look at Onida as they talked.

"Some. Airiella's told me bits and pieces, and I've overheard the guys talking about some things. Why?"

"Airiella's referenced her past, the bad things she's gotten through, and asked how she could be what we all claimed her to be when she's dealt with dark things. Aside from us, Kalisha and Father Roarke, I don't think the rest of the council put too much thought as to why she is here. Our little group has dedicated themselves to helping her. None of the others did. It's made me think a lot."

"What does this have to do with her falling?" Onida didn't see the path he was on.

"Give me a minute; I'll get there. We all assumed that Airiella was here to restore balance, and I do still believe that it is true. Think about this, though, what if she's here because of us?"

"What do you mean?" Onida still wasn't following.

"What if she is here because she's here to help us, not us help her?"

"Help us with what?"

"Think Oni. What does the council do?" Degataga wanted her to come to her conclusions and see if they matched his.

"We help when things of a mystical nature go bad." Onida's gaze had sharpened, and Dega knew she stumbled on something. He just wasn't sure if it matched his thoughts or not. "Okay. Hang on."

"Our council is the most powerful in the world, mainly because of us and Kalisha. Kalisha has passed on, but if Airiella joins the council, we *are* the most powerful one."

"*If* she joins, that is true. Give me a minute." Degataga knew she was spreading the pieces of information out in her head and putting them together like a puzzle. She had one of the sharpest minds he'd ever met. "Airiella is by far the most powerful person that fights for the light side. You think she's here to make our council better?"

"Yes and no. I think Airiella's here for us. She's changed all of us, made us all better. In our abilities, the way we see things, how we act personally and professionally. She's united us all, using love, which s is why I don't think she will fall. She's used love to pull herself out of her past. She's used love to pull us out of our pasts. She's used love to show us a common thread that binds us. She draws on her past and shows us she is no different than we are, that if she can accomplish something, then you can too."

"She's helping us while we are trying to help her?" Onida was back to the distant look he associated with her hawk. She was looking at things from a higher level.

"I know she's helping us. By that action alone, we take her help, what we've learned from simply being around her, and we spread it, restoring balance. We are her tools. She may out power us all, but individually, we are powerful on our own, and how we choose to use that power keeps us on the light side. Our council divided between light and dark. She exposed it. Unintentionally, maybe. Sorry, I'm off on a tangent. I don't think she will ever turn dark because she does everything out of love."

"Remember when she killed Bael, and she was bleeding out in front of us? We were trying to help her, and she insisted we help Jax?"

"That's not something I will likely ever forget, but go on." Degataga knew she had a point in there.

"Certainly, she was acting out of love there, but do you remember what she said when Taklishim said that the world needed her?" Onida's eyes were shining with tears.

"Yes," Degataga admitted quietly. "She said that without Jax, we don't have her."

"That tells me she can fall," Onida argued.

"I don't think so. It tells me that without love, she isn't her. It doesn't mean she will fall. It means her reason to fight has left. I don't believe she will fall. She can be broken just as easily as the rest of us. With Jax in her life, she has more reason. Losing him might mean we lose her for a little bit, but she'd be back. She still has the others, and she wouldn't turn away from them."

"Maybe. I think Airiella would have chosen death of herself over the death of him."

"Death is exactly what she chose. She explained it to Taklishim and Father Roarke. She told them both she has a better chance of coming back than the others do; they take priority. That's exactly why we wouldn't lose her for long. She'd realize she still has love to fight for."

"Wow, we got off-topic. Sorry about that."

"Don't be. I love that we can talk about random things, and after that conversation, I understand better why you think you are treating Airiella like a science experiment. We kind of just did in the way we analyzed her, her intentions, and why she's here."

"I think she's a hybrid," Onida blurted out.

Degataga thought about it. Raven, angel, goddess-like. "There's a legend about birds; I'm trying to remember it."

"They carry the souls of the dead and departed," Onida filled in, her eyes intense.

"That's the one. Oh. I see where you are going with this. Do you think Airiella carries the souls of all those that came before her?" The thought interested Degataga and made sense of some of the randomness they were facing.

"It crossed my mind the reason there has never been someone like Airiella before could be because she is an amalgamation of all those that came before her."

"That's brilliant, Oni. Her raven carries all the angels that have come before her. Angels wrapped up in a raven. With each new threat that arrives, her soul adapts." Degataga saw it much clearer now. "You are the most intelligent person I know."

"I'm torn between wanting to say that I hope that isn't true and being flattered that you think that." Onida looked slightly amused.

He took her hand, "Even if I weren't madly in love with you, I'd still respect and admire the intelligence and ability to piece things together to make a whole picture. Take it as a compliment."

"Did your brother request a copy of the pathology report?" Onida switched subjects, not entirely comfortable with the compliments. His declaration of love had given her butterflies in her stomach.

"He did." Degataga noticed the subject change and wondered if she still doubted his feelings for her. He decided to let it go for the moment, and he turned around and started to drive them to his house. "They want to have dinner with us tonight, but I've put that off until tomorrow. I figured tonight we could just do as you said, and rest up."

"Good, I think you still need it. Healing cancer is no easy task, even in its early stages. Tell me about your family. I didn't even know you had brothers."

"We hadn't gotten to that point in our relationship when I got called back. The oldest is one of twins, but the other died as a baby. He's serious, not much of a sense of humor, analytical, and comes off as cranky. The younger is the trouble maker, free spirit, and general prankster. I'm between the two of them."

"How is it you inherited the medicine man role?"

"Instead of my older brother?" Onida nodded.

"I was born different. I had an affinity for it. My dad saw it right away and took me under his wing. It was terrifying and exciting as a kid. Knowing you had these powers that not everyone else had, but also faced with the responsibility of protecting your tribe. I was in a constant battle with myself over running away and just accepting it. My mother was one that taught me the importance of staying put and being what the others needed me to be. My father was more inclined with me following my heart and doing what felt right to me. I longed to do what Tak did, and just leave. Travel the world helping where I could."

"Airiella told me something that's been rattling around in my head since she confronted me about you."

"She confronted you? About me?" Degataga wasn't sure how to take that.

"She recognized the pain in me and called me out on it. She was referencing her past and me telling her she needed to heal to move forward. She wasn't wrong. Anyway, she told me that love, death, and life were terrible beauty. It made sense on a certain level, but now, after being around you, the tree falling on me, Airiella practically killing herself to make sure I heal, it hits me on a deeper level. I understand the statement better."

"She knows far more than we give her credit for," Degataga said quietly. "I'm not sure I want to know everything she has been through to understand how she knows that."

"Your life was a terrible beauty," Onida mused. "My parents never forced me into anything. My mother chooses her animal form, and my dad lets her. He let Tama and I choose what we wanted to be. He didn't try to force a marriage on either of us, and he accepted Tak freely. I've been fortunate in that regard."

"You would have loved my dad." The thought that he would never get to introduce the love of his life to his father made him want to weep. "I do love being a medicine man, but I would have loved it more if I had been free to travel as I wish. It was only after getting to know you and understand the significance of a mate bond that it solidified in my mind that my home was wherever you were. They will always be my family, I will always love them, but I can live away from them. Living away from you ate at me in ways I didn't realize until I came back when Airiella showed up."

"I don't think your mother will accept me, will that be a problem for you?"

"She will. It might just take time, and no. I made my choice already. I don't regret it, or have doubts about it. Hawk-eye, with you, is where I belong." Degataga turned into a driveway. "Now, this is my house. I am willing to sell it, or we can keep it and use it as a vacation home."

"Let's cross that bridge later. We don't need to plan out our future right now."

"Are you worried that I am going to change my mind?" Degataga looked her face over carefully.

"Maybe? I'm not sure. I just know it scared me."

He accepted her answer and told himself to slow down. "As a warning, I've never really dated anyone before. So be prepared for a little heckling from my brothers."

Chapter Eighteen

Onida wandered the house while Degataga was on the phone; his confession was reeling in her mind. How was it possible that he hadn't dated anyone? She wanted to ask but was afraid of the answer.

She ran her fingers gently over the photos on the bookshelf of him, and who she guessed were his brothers. They all had the same smile, same dark hair, and brown skin. The evidence they had all spent a great deal of time outdoors. All very handsome men.

It was the photo of Dega with who she figured was his father that caught her breath. The respect, love, and admiration in Dega's eyes were arresting. His father had been proud of his son. Degataga had been right; she'd have loved his dad.

He had a kind and expressive face, deep dark eyes that smiled, and a head full of salt and pepper hair. It was how Degataga would look at that age. They had their arms around each other, and Onida felt the loss that Dega had to have been feeling for the man.

She hadn't heard him come up behind her and she

jumped a little at the sound of his voice. "That was after my first banishment of a spirit; he was so proud of me."

"It's a wonderful photo." She slipped her arm around his waist. "Everything okay?"

"It was Taklishim. The man is freaking out. I've never seen him like this."

"Tak doesn't freak out. Unless you mean, he's pissed about something Airiella has done that he didn't agree with."

"No, but she is the reason he is freaking out."

"We haven't even been gone a day, what could have happened?" Onida pulled her arm away and stepped back to see his face better.

"She had another vision while awake, and her reaction was bad. Tak said it was like someone had swung a sledgehammer into his gut. She's completely shut down and disappeared into the woods."

"She's missing?" That *would* make Taklishim freak out.

"Not missing, he could find her, but Jax told him to leave her alone. Taklishim said that Airiella was in pure panic mode, and Jax looked completely shaken. Tak said even Ronnie had been affected." Degataga laid it out for her.

"I'm guessing she won't tell anyone what she saw?" Onida tapped her teeth again, a habit she'd broken herself of years ago. What would set her off that bad?

"Maybe we should go back and just bring my brother with us?"

"Did Taklishim suggest that?" It didn't sound like her brother-in-law at all.

"No, that was my idea."

"She will tell me if she needs us back there. If Jax said to leave her alone, she needs space to deal with whatever she saw. Taklishim just needs to relax and let her do what she needs to do."

"That's what I told him; she's not a child. I asked what he meant by a bad reaction, and he said she screamed like she had when releasing that energy, the ground shook, and her wings came out."

"The scream before she died? Like that?" Onida was bothered by that. She could see why it upset both Ronnie and Jax, even Taklishim. Those screams were awful.

Degataga nodded and started to pace around the room, either an office or one he used as a library. A couple of books had writing on it she couldn't read, and she'd assumed they were in Cherokee. She moved out of his way so he could pace freely. She sat down in one of the armchairs and tried to use her thoughts to talk to Airiella.

Raven, can you hear me?

Yes.

Are you okay? Onida didn't want to push her.

Do these visions always come true?

I don't know. When I asked you about what you saw with Degataga and me, you said we made our own destiny. I would assume the answer would be the same. If what you are seeing is something you don't like, then figure out how to change it.

I'm afraid to sleep; now, I'm scared to be awake. Airiella sounded shattered.

I'll ask Degataga if there is something he can make that can help you sleep without visions. Would that help?

I don't know.

Where are you? Onida pressed on.

161

HAWK

I'm out in the area of woods that I destroyed.

Why would you go there? Onida was trying to figure out where Airiella was, mentally.

I'm trying to make things right; I'm blocking you out now. I want to be alone.

Onida felt only a void where she had felt Airiella before. What was she trying to fix? Should Onida tell Taklishim? No, she answered her question. He'd go out there, and she wouldn't get her alone time. The thought of her alone out there unsettled Onida, though.

She pulled out her phone and called Jax. "Hey," he answered, his voice strained and quiet.

"She's out where she killed that creature." Onida didn't waste any time in telling him.

"I know. I followed Airiella. I'm just letting her do her thing. She knows I'm near."

Onida breathed out a sigh of relief. "Okay. I was worried about her being out there alone."

"She's trying to fix it, Onida. She's breathing life back into it."

"Fix what?" For one heart-stopping moment, she thought he'd meant the creature.

"The land."

"She can do that?" Onida was amazed.

"Apparently," Jax answered softly. "The ground is green again."

"What does she see in those visions, Jax?" Onida didn't feel bad about pushing him, though she probably should have.

"My death. Taklishim's death."

Onida froze and shot a look at Degataga, who fixated on her. Two things she feared could change Airiella

162

in ways she didn't want to contemplate. "Then help her figure out how to alter them. Does Tama know?"

"No, she hasn't said a word about them to anyone. I saw both," Jax admitted.

"Maybe they aren't pre-cog, maybe it's a warning of what could happen. See if you can get Airiella to work through them and look for things that can be changed to alter the outcome," Onida suggested.

"I'll try."

"Reach out to Winnie; she had that ability. She might be able to help." It was the last suggestion she had.

"Alright. Thanks."

She hung up the phone and looked at it, fighting the impulse to call her sister. Degataga knelt before her and pulled the phone from her hand and set it on the table. "What did she see, Oni?"

Onida felt her eyes stinging again. "Jax's death, and Tak's death."

Degataga sucked in a sharp breath. "She won't fall, Hawk-eye. She won't let either of those men die either."

"Is there something you can make that would block the visions?"

Degataga hummed in thought. "I'm not sure. Is that even a good idea?"

Onida shrugged. She knew if she had to watch a vision of Degataga dying over and over, it would drive her insane. "Do you think that watching Jax die is going to be helpful for her overall mental state?"

"I have recipes for things that can bring on visions; I'm not sure I've ever had to make something to stop them before. I might have to ask Stolas that. Would he come if we called him?"

"I don't know. I'm glad that Taklishim doesn't know what the visions were about; I have no idea how he would react. Did you know she could bring life back?"

"What? I'm not sure I understand what you are asking me." Degataga's hand tightened around her own.

"Sorry. Not human life. She's bringing life back into that spot in the woods where everything got destroyed. She had said she was making things right."

"It doesn't surprise me with the way she can use energy around her. If anything, it makes her practice elemental skills."

"I'm assuming you have blessings around your house?" Onida changed the subject again.

"I do. If you want to call Stolas, we can head beyond the property line."

"Lead on, then. I want to be able to help Airiella somehow, and she needs sleep to recharge."

"Okay." He pulled her up and hugged her. "It's got you all over the place right now; I'm having a hard time keeping up."

"Sorry, I'm going in all different directions." She felt bad. Sometimes she thought that the dark forces working against them all were a step ahead, and they were scrambling to catch up.

She linked her arm through Degataga's and let him lead her through the property, wanting to feel him close. She couldn't imagine the darkness Airiella was fighting against, having seen two people she loved die. It also started to make sense to her why Airiella was out there at that spot, doing something to reassure herself that life was still there. The angel had resilience, but it also felt like it was cracking.

"He should be able to come here, we are past the property line." Degataga pointed out a painted stone he had placed to mark the spot.

"Stolas, I need your help." Onida projected her voice a little, letting the wind carry it to wherever it needed to go. She waited a few minutes and didn't get a response. Onida tried again. "Stolas, I need your help for Airiella," she clarified, still projecting her voice.

"I heard you the first time." She heard his rich voice but couldn't see him.

She didn't want to piss the demon off, but she also didn't want to play games. "It's serious. I need your help."

"Is it you that needs my favor, or is it Airiella?" She looked around, not seeing anything, but sensing his voice coming from the lone tree back here.

"Airiella does. Where are you?" she called out.

"Right here, doctor." He appeared to be leaning against the tree. "What does the lovely angel need? And why wouldn't she ask me herself?"

"She's a little preoccupied. She seems to have developed a strong pre-cog skill and is seeing things that are rather hard for her to take. She's afraid to sleep and is afraid to stay awake. Is there something you know of that can be made to block the visions, or aid them in showing her ways to avoid what she sees?"

"Those are two very different things. This skill is hurting Airiella?"

"She hasn't recovered her energy yet and needs sleep to do that. If these visions keep interrupting her sleep, she won't get her energy back. What she has seen so far is hurting her, yes. I think she's trying to cope with it as well as she can, but is having difficulty."

The demon was in love with Airiella, and she hoped to play on his sympathy for her. "These visions she has had are not upsetting to you?"

"I haven't seen them. I only know what Airiella has told me and what Jax has told me. It is upsetting to me in that it's hurting her, and I wish to help her through it."

"They are warnings; they're not something etched in stone. If Airiella saw her own death, that would be one she couldn't change. I will help her. Is she somewhere I can go?"

"Right now, she is. She is in the field where she killed that creature," Onida told him.

"I know the place. I will go to Airiella." Stolas gave a nod of his head.

"Thank you, Stolas, that is all I ask." Onida had hoped he would give a recipe to Degataga that he could use for the future, but she wasn't going to press her luck, nor put herself in a position to be in debt to the demon. He hadn't ever shown to be a danger to them and didn't come across as evil. But she knew him to be incredibly powerful in his own right.

"Taklishim is not with her, but Jax is nearby," Degataga told the demon.

"Thank you. Is that all?"

Onida studied the handsome demon, looking for signs of deceit. She hadn't ever found any before and didn't suspect him of it. "That was all."

"You don't want to ask of the danger?" His position against the tree hadn't changed, he still looked to be relaxed.

"If you want to share anything you know, we won't refuse, but we aren't asking," Degataga responded, his arm tensing up. Onida skimmed her fingers across his skin, hoping he would relax.

"Diplomatic answer. Nicely worded." Stolas righted himself but didn't move towards them. "There are legions below that long for vengeance against your angel for killing Bael; however, they are too afraid to make a move themselves. They are awakening the legends your native people have and setting them free to do their bidding."

"A demon released Spearfinger," Onida said carefully.

"Correct. Your people native to this land have a variety of interesting legends."

"A banshee isn't a legend of our people," Onida stated.

"A banshee showed itself?" Stolas was intrigued by that and took a step forward.

"She wasn't a harmful one; she was warning me."

"Then it wasn't sent by any of the armies below," Stolas replied. "She is perhaps a protector of your friend Winnie's family."

Stolas both interested Onida and caused her fear. She had no real idea what his powers were or what he was capable of doing. She only knew that he was capable of love and that Airiella had captured his attention. "I thank you again for your willingness to help Airiella."

"Don't call any others," he warned, stepping back to the tree. "There is always someone watching us come and go. I will protect Airiella how I can without revealing my allegiance."

With that, he disappeared, and Onida released a breath she hadn't known she'd been holding. "It went better than I thought it would. I'd also feel a lot better if we were back on protected land after hearing that."

They stepped back onto Degatata's property, and Onida turned to look back out where Stolas had been. She didn't see anything, but her hawk was telling her to stay alert. "Do you mind if I fly for a moment?" She looked at Degataga.

"Of course not. Are you sure you'll be safe?"

"I can't ever be sure of that, but Stolas won't harm me. That would hurt Airiella. In that, I trust him." She stripped out of her clothes, handing them to him and shifted to her hawk. She looked around with her hawk's vision, looking for things that didn't fit. Not seeing any from the ground, she took flight.

Chapter Nineteen

Degataga sat on his back porch, watching Onida circle high overhead. His thoughts had taken off going over the warning Stolas had given about native American legends. It certainly explained Spearfinger and her sudden appearance far from where she had reigned terror before.

There were so many different legends across the country's tribes that he didn't know what to expect. Several were utterly terrifying to think about, much less contemplate having to fight them. As a medicine man, he'd heard tales of practically every legend possible. There were a few that spanned numerous tribes.

Why would demons pick these legends to unleash? Did that mean they thought that Airiella wouldn't know how to defeat them or if she could? Or was it something more sinister? On a macabre level, he knew that he and the others would make easier targets than she would, and he also knew how much it would hurt Airiella if something happened to them.

They'd already lost Kalisha, and if Airiella was

having visions of Jax and Taklishim dying, it made sense to him that they'd come after them. Taking out the most powerful Native Americans would undoubtedly send a message that Airiella couldn't misconstrue, especially now that their combined power had split between locations. Logically that told him that he and Onida were the weaker links since Airiella wasn't there to back them up.

He scrubbed his hands over his face and looked up as Onida landed and shifted back to human. There was no shyness as she strode confidently towards him, naked and beautiful. For just a moment, everything else faded away, and he became lost in all that she represented to him.

Immediately following that thought was the realization of all that he stood to lose if something were to happen to her again. Fear crashed into him, and he shot to his feet as she approached, and he enveloped her in a giant hug, pulling her into the safety of his house.

"What's the matter?" she asked, concern coloring her voice.

"A moment of paranoia, at everything I can lose if something happens to you."

Her face softened, and she touched his cheek, her fingers trailing across the rough stubble that had grown. "We aren't helpless."

"No, we aren't. Doesn't change the fear I have of losing you."

"I take it that means you were dwelling on Stolas's warning about the legends?"

"I was. There are so many tales. It's overwhelming trying to think of what could come at us again." Degataga resisted the urge to shiver; he didn't want to give in it.

"It is. I've been thinking about it too while I looked

around. There's several about a raven as well, which I saw when flying around. I'm pretty sure what I saw was just a raven, but it put me on guard."

"Something we will need to continue to do. We are the weakest targets with no Airiella backing us up."

"Well, that's a pleasant thought. If the demons are after Airiella, they wouldn't be down here with us."

"They could, they know that we are attached to her and taking out powerful medicine men and women would be strategic, as well as a way to hurt her." Degataga hated saying it aloud, but he needed her to understand they weren't safe just because they weren't near her.

"There is a scary truth to that," she nodded, her eyes going vacant as she stared out the window. "I saw traces of something out there, though no real idea of what it was."

"We are relatively safe in the house and on my property." He handed her the clothes she had taken off, and she slipped her shirt and pants on. "I think I have stuff in the freezer we can use to make a soup for dinner," Degataga suggested.

"That's fine with me. I'd rather do that then go out. I think we need an early night anyway."

"As awful as it sounds to say, I hope we can do this quickly and get back," Degataga said over his shoulder as he walked into the kitchen and grabbed a few pots out. He dug through the freezer, finding a package of chicken and some frozen vegetables. It would do.

"It's not awful. I understand what you mean. I think we should re-bless your family's homes as well. Added precaution never hurts anything." She helped him make the soup, working comfortably with him.

They ate their soup, bouncing ideas off each other, and quickly cleaned up and headed for bed. Degataga was glad she didn't want to stay separate from him. "Were you serious about not having dated?"

His love life wasn't his favorite topic of conversation; it was one he was ribbed continuously about by his brothers. "I was serious. I didn't have a lot of time for dating. Besides, no one made me want to make time for it. I went out with girls, but never seriously. I think I became a challenge to most of them. They made competitions to see who could get me out for a second date, or a kiss. Losing my virginity became a major event among them."

He heard Onida laugh. "I'm sorry. Girls can be pretty terrible. I can't see it. I'd have been trailing after you like a lost puppy."

He tightened his hold on her, "If you had been here, I most likely would have made time to date. To be fair, I did have a few that followed me around, but I think it was because they wanted bragging rights."

"Too bad for them. I don't share well with others." Onida turned to face him. "I couldn't do what Airiella does. It seems like a lot of work."

"I'm sure it is a lot of work. They don't seem to suffer, and the love they all have is quite real. I couldn't do it either, the thought of you with someone else was enough to keep me awake most nights in agony. With that thought in mind, feel free not to share your past loves with me."

"I've only ever loved you. Sex is a different story, but I didn't love any of the men, it was just sex."

"Don't want to hear that either." He smiled and kissed her.

"You weren't a virgin when we met," she reminded him.

"No. I wasn't full of experience either. You had to have noticed that."

"I didn't. I was quite satisfied."

He wasn't as tired as he was before, after that comment, and he moved over her. "Maybe you bring it out in me. I should keep practicing to make sure you stay that way."

"That sounds like an excellent idea," she agreed.

He made tender love to her the way he wanted to the first time they got back together. He took his time and cherished every inch of her, and by the time they finished, they were both ready to sleep. He drifted off with his head on her belly and her fingers in his hair.

He woke, feeling well-rested, and alone. He heard the shower running and smiled at the feeling of domesticity settling over him. It was something he hadn't ever thought he would find. He sat up and stretched, his outlook this morning much improved over the previous day.

"Did I wake you up?" She walked in wrapped in a towel looking magnificent.

"No. You're beautiful." He crawled out of bed and crossed the room, wrapping his arms around her and lifting her to kiss her.

She hummed deep in her throat, "Good morning to you too."

"I can't tell you how much I want to keep doing this," he murmured into her neck.

"Me too. We can't. Let's go and see your brother and see what we can do for him. Maybe get a cup of coffee on the way."

"I do have coffee. Beans are in the freezer, the grinder's in the cupboard next to the sink," he told her as he walked into the bathroom.

"Perfect." He wanted to keep watching her. Every movement she made was graceful and smooth, like art in motion. If he kept staring while she got dressed, she wouldn't remain clothed for much longer.

He sighed and got in the shower, his thoughts of domestic bliss were interwoven with concern for his brother and worry over Onida meeting his mother. He knew she would eventually come around, but this first meeting was likely to be rough.

They got going after he grabbed a coffee and felt somewhat ready to deal with the day and all the potential issues it could be. Out of habit, he glanced at the sky as they pulled out of the driveway and saw storm clouds in the distance. He hoped it wasn't a sign of the way the day would go.

They pulled in to his brothers' driveway, and he noticed that his mother was already there. He'd been hoping she wouldn't be but should have known better. "I'm just going to apologize now for anything my mother may say."

"Don't worry about it. I've become desensitized from some things after working in a hospital and having to deliver bad news. Difficult people aren't anything new for me. With that, I'll apologize now for anything I may say."

Degataga laughed, "Don't. She will deserve it, I'm sure. In case I haven't said it, thank you for coming with me."

"You did. You're still welcome." She reached for his hand. "Come on. We can do this. It won't be so bad, and you also said she would like me."

"She will. Maybe not at first, but she will come around. I am sure of that." He kissed the back of her hand. "Time to work."

They walked up to the door, and it got thrown open before he could knock. His breath caught in his throat as he gazed upon his little brother; he looked so much like his dad that it almost hurt to look at him. "Waya," he said breathlessly. "You look more and more like father all the time."

"Dega, thanks for coming. I want to look at her though." Waya hugged him and pushed him out of the way. "My name is Waya; please tell me you are the one who finally hooked him."

Onida held out her hand, "I'm Onida. It's nice to meet you, Waya. I wish it were under better circumstances."

"If you aren't interested in him, I'm available." Waya grinned.

Onida laughed, a grin splitting her face. "I'll keep that in mind."

Degataga pulled her closer to him. "Back off. Let me in so I can see if you are worth saving. I may have changed my mind now."

"Degataga, shame on you for saying such a thing about your brother. Come, give me a hug, son," said Asgasga. She completely ignored Onida, and Degataga frowned.

"This is the woman I will marry, mother. I expect you to treat her as such," Degataga warned but leaned in to hug his mother. "Onida, this is my mother, Asgasga."

"Pleasure to meet you, ma'am." Onida held her

hand out and was again ignored.

"Pay no attention to her." Waya glared at his mother as he walked into the living room and grabbed a folder. "Here's the records they gave me that you asked for." He handed the information to Degataga, who promptly held it to Onida.

He watched as she read through the reports and scans, her eyes missing nothing. "What do you think?"

"I think we are lucky they caught this early. I expect everything will go smoothly, and we will get it taken care of," Onida answered with a smile.

"Who do you think you, are and what makes you think you are qualified to make such a statement?" Asgasga barked at Onida, her face a mask of fury.

Degataga saw red. Before he could lash out at his mother, Onida calmly said, "I am a medical doctor, graduated at the top of my class three years ahead of schedule from a very respected university. I specialize in epidemiology and also trained as a general surgeon. I did a residency in the emergency room, surgery, and infectious disease. I'm licensed to practice in both Washington and Oregon; I am also a trained medicine woman by four tribes in my home state. I think that makes me more than qualified. Anything else I can answer for you?"

Waya whooped and snatched her up in a hug. "I'm in love. Please marry me instead."

Degataga watched the exchange with a glower on his face. "Let her go, you imbecile. Mother, if you can't treat Onida with the respect she deserves, then leave."

"This isn't your house." She put her hands on her hips.

"No, it's mine, and I agree with him." Waya glared

at the woman. "Two medicine people are here to work on me, so I don't die. And she's a doctor to boot."

"She's not of our people," Asgasga said hotly. "She doesn't know of our ways."

"She's a native of this land as much as we are, that makes her our people," Waya interrupted before she could go any further. "Just because you didn't pick her out doesn't make her unsuited for Dega or to work on me. Onida, I for one and extremely happy you are here. This old bat can go home if she doesn't like it."

"She's worried about her sons, that I can understand. She doesn't need to leave if she can keep her mouth shut, and let us do what we need to do to ensure you are around to continue to torture Degataga. It's quite amusing," she said with a smile.

Degataga couldn't love her more than he did at that minute. He should have known not to worry about Onida. She was a strong woman, beyond intelligent, and she was his if he didn't scare her away by being a needy thorn in her side.

"Come back here. I have one of those portable massage tables back here I can lay on, so you aren't all hunched over me. I just assumed you'd want me to lay down with me being in a delicate state and all." Waya smirked.

Degataga laughed, "You aren't pregnant." He ignored his mother, took Onida's hand, and followed Waya down his hall to the extra room. He heard his mother spluttering behind them at their blatant display of dismissing her.

"Laying down is good. You may get tired and a little weak because your body will be fighting cancer as we direct it on what to do," Onida said gently.

"Beautiful and smart, tell me how you landed her and if there's another like her," Waya said, pulling his shirt off and laying on the blanketed massage table.

"She actually has a twin sister," Degataga said casually.

Waya practically jumped off the table, "Are you serious?"

Onida let out a delighted laugh, the best he'd ever heard. "He is serious, but she is also pregnant and married to his best friend. Who happens to be another medicine man as well as an Apache warrior."

"Nope. Not messing with that one." Waya lay back down, looking dejected. "The gray guy?"

"That's the one," Degataga confirmed. They put their hands on Waya and got to work. It wasn't long before Waya fell asleep, his body already exhausted from the work they were making it do. Hours later, Onida pulled her hands back, looking fatigued.

"Are you okay, Oni?"

"Yes. I think we got it."

"Really?" Degataga scanned his brother seeing she was right. "I think you carried that one more than I did."

"I'd like him to have a blood test and another imaging scan to make sure. He can call it a second opinion, and they will just question the pathology report. I'm pretty sure I got it all, though."

"I didn't see anything on the scan I just did," Degataga confirmed. "Hawk-eye, you are amazing."

"It wasn't just me, Dega. It was both of us." She smiled at him, her tone soft.

"You fixed my son?" Asgasga asked, standing in

the doorway.

"She did. She got rid of cancer. All I did was clean Waya's blood," Degataga said defensively, ready to put his mother in her place again.

Onida motioned him to stay silent, and she stood and faced the woman. "He will be fine."

Degataga saw the tears streaming down his mother's face then. He stood and walked over to her, hugging her tight. "He won't die from cancer, Mom."

"Your father would be so proud of you," she whispered in his ear.

"He'd also be proud of the woman I choose to love. You'd better get on board with that."

"She's not so bad," Asgasga admitted.

He looked back to see Onida waking Waya up and helping him put his shirt back on. He turned back to hear her telling him to rest for a while and to make an appointment for the second opinion. Love washed through him seeing the effortless way she was with his brother, how she handled his mother, and how she took over the heavy work of healing, so he didn't exhaust himself.

"She honestly did most of it?" Asgasga sounded skeptical.

"She did. Do you know why she specialized in epidemiology?" Degataga paused to make sure he had her attention. "She did it because so many Native American's become diagnosed with cancer, and she wanted to use her intelligence to figure out why. She wants to stop the deaths of this county's native people."

"You are right; your father would have loved her." High praise from his mother. "We will see you at dinner tonight?"

"Of course," Onida answered for him, coming up on his side. "I'm looking forward to it. Right now, I need a nap."

Degataga knew she had to be exhausted after that. And after they saw that Waya was resting peacefully in his bed, he ushered her out the door and drove home. She went straight to the bedroom and lay down. "Thank you, Oni."

She smiled, "You're welcome. I didn't do it alone."

Degataga lay beside her and watched as she drifted off to sleep. It felt good to have something go their way for once. Now she just needed to get through meeting his older brother, Wohali.

Chapter Twenty

Onida opened her eyes slowly, relishing the feel of the warm man behind her and his gentle snores that ruffled her hair. She wasn't sure why she woke up; she was still plenty tired. Then Onida heard it again, a soft buzzing sound that sounded like a large bee. She thought she was hallucinating and went back to sleep, not realizing it was her cell phone.

She woke a couple of hours later hearing the same sound, her brain was foggy with sleep though, and she was so relaxed next Degataga she didn't want to move. She drifted back off to sleep, but she dreamt of Airiella this time.

Something is here, Hawk-eye.

I can't believe you are calling me that.

Why? You are our very own Avenger. It's a pretty cool nickname. That's not why I'm here, though, Airiella told her seriously.

Where is here?

In the spirit world, I called you. Don't you remember? Are you okay?

I did a healing today, and I'm exhausted. I still have a dinner to get through too. I'm trying to get as much sleep as I can, so I don't sound like an idiot in front of Degataga's family. I don't think his mother likes me much.

Then she's crazy. Anyway, I think that's a mother-son thing. My mom did that to my brother, too. Thanks for sending Stolas, by the way.

I didn't send him quite as much as he took himself. I did talk with him. Have you slept at all? Onida thought to ask.

I did a little. I'm freaking everyone out. The visions won't stop, and now there's something here. It follows me from world to world. Sometimes I can see it, other times I can feel it.

What do you see? Stolas said the demons are waking up the Native American legends and sending them after us.

He told me that too. I don't know what I am seeing. Shit, I feel like I'm going crazy. When I'm awake, the visions are of Taklishim, Jax and Tama dying, or I seem them already dead. My reactions are awful, and they all freak out. I want to send them all away, somewhere far away. I know Stolas said they were warnings and could be changed, but I'm not seeing how it happens to figure out how to change them.

Have you tried to guide the visions? Lucid dreaming, Onida told Airiella.

No. The images are so damn awful that my brain freezes and I can't get past it. Winnie doesn't know what it is either, but Winnie said she's felt like she's hallucinating because she will see a shadow of something, then it's gone, but she feels the malice from it.

Can I ask you something, off-topic?

Uh, sure.

How do you know Jax loves you?

Yeah, that's pretty far off-topic. I just know. I can feel it coming from Jax, it's in the things he does, the words he says, his touch. He doesn't try to change me; he accepts my flaws, backs my decisions even when he doesn't like them. He will listen to my arguments if I don't agree with something, and he lets me do what I think is best. There's not just one thing. Why?

Dega says he loves me, and he's willing to do whatever he can to make us work. I still don't entirely trust that he won't walk away from me again. Onida felt like a child for it too.

Onida, sometimes you need to take a leap of faith and trust your gut. Love isn't straight forward.

Why did you choose Jax over Ronnie?

I didn't; they didn't put me in that position. Ronnie will branch off when he feels the time is right for him. If you are asking me how I know Jax is the right one, it's just my instinct. I'll tell you the same thing I said to both of them, loving Ronnie would be easy and fun for the rest of my life. It's never been easy with Jax, but the rewards are better. It feels different between the two of them. Jax lets me choose, and then does it with me. Ronnie will always try to protect me.

Clear as mud, isn't that what you say?

Airiella laughed, but it wasn't her carefree laugh, it sounded strained. *I do say that. Your instinct will match your heart; it's the brain that gets in the way.*

Okay, then, what does your instinct say about what you are feeling? Onida circled back to the reason

Airiella called her.

That's the fucking problem. I don't know. All I know is fear and danger.

Onida sighed. *Meditate. Clear your mind. When the visions happen, try to guide it. You need to shut the fear down and try to find out what it's genuinely warning you of and then find the solution.*

Onida jolted awake again. She didn't feel any more well-rested, but her brain wasn't as foggy, and Degataga was no longer behind her. Was the dream real or a combination of all the thoughts that were plaguing her?

"Oni, honey, you have nine missed calls from Tama. I think you should answer your phone." Degataga appeared in the doorway with her phone in his hand.

"That's what kept waking me up. It was my phone." She held out her hand, Degataga placed the phone gently in it and sat down next to her. "Tama?"

"Where have you been?" Tama shouted.

"Sleeping. We healed Dega's brother earlier. What's going on?"

"Sorry, Oni. Things have gone sideways. Airiella won't let anyone near her without threatening to blast them with lightning. She's lost about ten pounds in two days, she's not eating or sleeping, and she sits out in the damn field all day long."

"What? Slow down. Airiella wouldn't hurt any of you."

"None of us can get closer to her than what the blast radius was. She literally called lightning to her when I tried to get close. She blew Jax and Taklishim away. Ronnie is the only one who can get within five feet of her, and she won't let *him* get closer than that. She's burning through

184

energy she doesn't have."

"Why?" Onida didn't understand, and flashes of the dream came back to her. "The visions?"

"Yeah," Tama said quietly now. "She's seen all of us dead. Gruesome deaths. These visions are driving her insane."

"Didn't Stolas give her something to help her sleep?" Airiella had mentioned that she had talked to him.

"He did, but she won't take it. She's afraid if she takes it, something will happen to one of us, and she'll be asleep and unable to help."

"Hold on, Tama. I'm putting you on speakerphone." She switched it on and placed the phone on the bed. "Can you hear me?"

"Yeah. I need advice. Anything. Tak and Jax are about to lose their minds. She's not well. She doesn't come in when it rains; she just stays in that field."

Onida heard Degataga sigh. "Tak called me. It's true, Oni. She needs to sleep. Even if something does come, she won't be able to help due to the exhaustion."

"I don't know what I can do from here. What makes you think Airiella would listen to me anyway?" Onida was getting frustrated. She had very little information to go off of and she wasn't there. "Does anyone know what she thinks she sees?"

"What do you mean?" Tama asked.

"She came to me in a dream, told me that something is there, but she can't see it."

"Hold on; I'm finding Tak. He can't get anything out of her. He's even tried shifting to get close to her, and she keeps him out."

"She's scared, Tama. She told me all she keeps

seeing is you, Tak and Jax dead or dying. I can understand why she wants to keep you three away."

"What did she tell you about what she saw?" Degataga asked.

"She said she sees it in both worlds. She will see a shadow, but when she looks, it's gone. She said Winnie has seen it too and feels like she's hallucinating," Onida recalled.

"That doesn't tell us a lot," Tama said, repeating the information to Tak. "You're on speaker here now. Jax is with us."

"She sees a shadow?" Taklishim sounded gruff and entirely unlike himself.

"That was all I got from her. I think she said that is what Winnie saw."

"So what legends do we know of that have shadows?" Degataga asked.

"More than one," Taklishim answered. "I, myself, can look like a shadow if I need to."

"I'm assuming she isn't referring to you," Onida snapped.

"Hang on, at least she's talking to me," a very tired sounding Jax broke in. "She said sometimes she sees an animal and it has red eyes. Sometimes she sees the silhouette of a man."

"In the visions?" Degataga interrupted.

"No, with her eyes," Jax replied after a pause.

"Tak, you know what that sounds like?" Degataga sounded scared, and Onida gave him a startled look.

"Yeah. It doesn't matter how far away Airiella wants us to go and hide. If that's what it is, it will find us." Taklishim sounded just as scared, and Onida felt unease slide through her.

"Care to fill us in?" Tama asked angrily.

"Skinwalker," Taklishim said.

Onida shot to her feet, "Are you serious? Those are real?" She heard cussing in the background and now a very scared and tired Jax shouting.

"She needs to get out of the woods," Degataga said firmly.

"I've been trying," Taklishim fired back.

"Mom's out there watching her," Tama warned Onida.

"Then mom is in danger too."

"We will catch a flight out tomorrow," Degataga informed them. "I'm not proud of this suggestion, but find a way to play on her guilt, use it to get her out of there and back with you guys. Jax, research skinwalkers."

"I'll try to guilt her from my end," Onida said.

She hung up and stared wide-eyed at Degataga. "This is bad, Oni. I don't know how to kill them, or if she even can. They are very dangerous and brutal. If she sees those three dead, I can guarantee the death wasn't simple."

Onida nodded. "I've heard legends about them."

Degataga sat down and pulled his phone out. "I'm getting us flights."

Airiella, are you there?

I am. Airiella sounded awful.

You need to get back inside with everyone else. Don't argue with me. Just do it.

I can't, Onida. I need to keep watch.

You staying out there is putting the whole town in danger. How will you feel if something happens to Tama and those babies, and you aren't there to help her?

That's fucking low, Onida. Damn you, that was mean.

It's the truth. The land around my house is blessed, and the skinwalkers can't get on there.

Skinwalkers? Airiella sounded confused.

That's what we think is out there with you. My mom is in the woods watching over you. If something happens to her because you are stubborn, I'm not sure I can forgive that.

You just said the land was blessed, so as long as they stay on the property, they are safe, right?

Airiella! Stop arguing!

What if being around me is what is putting them in danger? Airiella argued.

Haven't we played the what-if game before? What if being away from you is what is putting them in danger? They all keep coming out there to check on you, which means they aren't on the protected land. If you go in, they stay with you. Use your head! Onida was shouting now.

Are you coming back?

Degataga is getting us flights back tomorrow.

Then I'll go in.

Now. Do it now! And tell my mom to go home!

Fine. You better be back tomorrow, or I'm going back outside.

We are going to have serious problems, you and I. Especially if you make me cry again because you end up hurt or my family does because of this asinine stubborn streak.

I'm going; there is one nearby. I can feel it.

Onida screamed in frustration. *Get moving!* The connection went quiet, and Onida frantically texted them all, saying Airiella was headed in and to tell her that she made it safely back; and that Airiella noted there was a skinwalker nearby.

Tama replied that Ronnie was with Airiella, and they were coming back and that Taklishim and Jax were threatening to put her in a cage. Onida almost laughed, but she remembered the conversation with Airiella about Jax and knew it was all words on his part. Taklishim, on the other hand, he very well could be upset enough to try to confine her.

She wrote back to Tama, saying not to let Taklishim confine her. It wouldn't end well for Taklishim if she were willing to strike him with lightning.

Degataga had left the room, and she found him packing a suitcase with books, most of which had the Cherokee writing on it that she couldn't read. She didn't interrupt and helped when he asked for things. His movements were tense and rushed.

"You had said you felt something here yesterday, do you think you could have felt a skinwalker?" he asked her.

"I've never felt one before, so maybe? I don't know. Aren't they invisible?"

"Sometimes. Sometimes, human, sometimes animal. Usually, a predatory animal, though they can take any form. I can honestly say, I don't know anyone who has survived an attack by a skinwalker."

"Well, then we will be the first," Onida decided. "Airiella is a formidable opponent." Onida believed Airiella could take one down; she just had to get over the fear first. "Stolas won't be much help to us with this one, will he?"

"Unlikely," Degataga agreed. "Do you want me to cancel dinner tonight?"

"No. Dinner with your family won't change any of this. Besides, I want to go over the blessings again in case I saw traces of a skinwalker. Leaving your family unprotected doesn't sit right with me." Onida met Degataga's eyes, assuring him she was okay. She sat down on the chair next to her and closed her eyes.

Degataga came up in front of her and kneeled before her, laying his head on her lap. "We'll get through this. Somehow, I'll find a way for you to trust me again."

Onida felt a pull in her chest, strong and unwavering. "I think what my heart is telling me is I already do. Unless the odd feeling in my chest is a heart attack," Onida mused.

"What does your brain say?" Degataga looked at her with a longing that made that feeling in her chest swell to gigantic proportions.

"Quiet disbelief and resignation." She threaded her fingers in his hair. "Jax knocked Airiella out on live TV, and she didn't bat an eye. You went to take care of your family. You went about it in a bad way, but I do trust you, Dega."

Chapter Twenty-One

egataga was on such a roller coaster of emotions he wasn't sure how he would get through the night. He'd read a few pages of some of the books he'd packed before Onida had come in. What he'd read had chilled his blood. Skinwalkers could bring on sickness in people.

His brother had never shown any indications before that he had any issues with his kidneys. Sure, some cancers could be genetic, but if what he had learned from Onida about it since then was right, neither he or his brother had any markers that would have given them a clue. Onida had checked him over thoroughly; she'd told him after hearing the news.

That meant that he was brought down here for a reason and that they were indeed targets. "Oni, maybe we shouldn't go to dinner."

"You think being there will make your family a target, don't you?" She nailed it right on the head.

"I do. I read a passage in one of those books," Degataga started to explain and was interrupted.

"You think it gave your brother cancer," she

finished for him, her tone matter of fact. "I've heard that legend. I've been thinking about it too."

She stunned him silent. He risked looking away from the road to glance at her. Her face was a careful mask of seriousness that made his fears all the more real. "I was hoping you would say it isn't possible."

"I can't. I also can't say that it's impossible either. Cancer happens. It happens a lot to our people, even those who have never been sick a day in their life. The timing of this is just too coincidental for me. I don't much like coincidences."

"I think we got separated from the others for a reason. Together, we are too powerful for something to take us. I'm not without fighting skills, but I am no Ronnie or Taklishim. I don't have an animal like you and the others. And I'm nowhere the level of lethal that Airiella is."

"I think we need to tell your family."

Almost speechless, he looked at her. "Tell them what, exactly?"

"Everything. As unbelievable as it sounds, your family needs to be in on it if they are to protect themselves."

"Even about Airiella? Taklishim will not be happy with that." He didn't even know if his family would believe half of it. Waya probably would; he'd seen more unexplainable things from his father than Wohali had.

"Taklishim will understand why. He knows you have family down here, and after we tell him about our suspicions about your brother's cancer, he will support our decision. I do think I need to ask Airiella for permission."

"Definitely. Or at least give Jax a heads up that you are spilling her secret."

"No, it needs to be Airiella, I tell. It's her life. If she doesn't want us to, we won't."

Degataga nodded. "If you think that's best. Are you going to call her?"

"In my head, I will. That way, if she doesn't want to explain it, she doesn't have to. She's more on edge than I'd like, and I don't want her to be reckless."

"Oni, just when I think you can't be more amazing than you already are, you prove me wrong."

She blushed and went silent. Degataga kept glancing at her as he drove to his mother's house on the very outskirts of town opposite his house. She'd be the one who would cast the most suspicion, though Wohali would be the most skeptical.

"She said to do it," Onida informed him a few minutes later. "She's going to tell Taklishim how it's going to be, she said. Might want to silence your phone."

Degataga laughed. "He'll wait until we are face to face to yell at me. I think right now, he will just be happy she is talking to him. The hard part will be confirming what she is without her being here."

"She said Jax would be texting me a picture, she thought of that too. Brought up her family at the funeral as an example." Her phone dinged, and she pulled up a photo that almost made her cry. "I'm glad we are going back tomorrow."

Degataga parked the car in his mother's driveway. "I am too. Why do you say that, though?"

She held her phone out to him, and Degataga looked at the displayed picture and felt his heart clench at the sight of the girl he had come to love like a little sister. Airiella's wings were on full display, and her knees bent in front of her; her arms crossed over her knees, her chin resting on her forearms. The dark circles under her eyes and gaunt look on her sad face hit him hard. She looked with despair out in front of her, almost at the camera; her gaze intent on something they couldn't see.

Even more surprising was the land around her that had been barren of life after Spearfinger, was teeming with life. Grass and wildflowers bloomed around her; the scorched earth now covered with green and what appeared to be little saplings.

The phone dinged again, and another picture came through. The angel in the same spot as she was in the other photo, but with no wings this time and sitting cross-legged, tears streaming down her face as she had her hands buried in the blackened earth willing life into it; a before and after set.

Degataga silently held the phone back out to Onida so she could see the second picture. He watched Onida bite her lip and try to hold back the emotions that the stark picture brought out. Even if you didn't know Airiella, the sight was a sucker punch to the heart in its candidness.

"Sometimes, I forget how hard this is for her. She's so strong and makes it look so easy. I forget how sensitive and emotional she is. How much she cares about others beneath that sarcasm and humor. This picture is a good reminder for me." Onida tucked her phone back in her pocket after texting Jax back a thank you.

"She's a lot like you in that regard, Hawk-eye." Degataga pulled her hand to him and kissed the back of it. "Maybe not the humor part, but the rest can describe you as well."

"I'm not emotional," she argued quietly. "Except

lately, but I blame you for that."

"Your emotions just show differently than hers; they are still there for anyone who cares to look hard enough."

She sighed and caressed his cheek, "Thank you for loving me, Dega."

He got out and went around the car to open her door. "Jax certainly has a way with a camera. Those pictures are remarkable. Like the one that he hung over their fireplace."

"I have a copy of that one on my phone, too." She stepped out and into his embrace. "She just told me Taklishim is okay with explaining to your family."

He nodded, grateful for that news, and held her hand as they made their way to the front door. "I'm going to tell them that I'm moving too. Might as well rip the Band-Aid off."

"No, don't do that. Let's tell your family that we will split our time between both places, you keep the one here, and I'll get licensed to practice here as well," she suggested.

He halted mid-stride. "Really? Are you sure?"

"I am. We can do a rotation. It doesn't feel right for you to move away from here."

"I love you so much." He swept her off her feet and swung her around in a circle. "I meant what I said, wherever you are is where I belong."

"I know. I can compromise with you. There are plenty of doctors at home, and Taklishim and Tama are both tribal medicine people. Dividing my time won't be hard."

The front door burst open, and Waya came barreling out, snatching Onida from Degataga. "Are you sure you don't want to marry me? I'm much better looking than him."

Onida's delighted laugh warmed Degataga's heart, even though his brother's preposterous proposal annoyed him. "I'm sure. I'm in love with him."

"Ouch! Rejected by a beautiful woman! Is that how it feels to be you, Dega?" Waya joked, putting Onida down.

"Funny. Get in the house. Onida and I are going to check the blessings and look for cracks. Let the others know we need to have a serious conversation before we leave tonight." Degataga scowled at his brother until he went back into the house, chuckling.

They checked the perimeter, Onida quickly getting undressed and shifted into hawk form to look from above and in the spirit world. He patiently waited until she finished her check, and after she dressed again, she pointed out a few weak spots. Together they reinforced the protection before rejoining his family.

"We'll do your older brother's house too before we go back," she confirmed. "Was Waya's okay? Never mind, we'll check his too."

They walked in, and Degataga saw the cautious look on his mother's face. "You're late."

"No, we aren't. We spent a little time going over the blessings on the property to make sure they were all still active and in place. You're welcome," Degataga told his mother with a glare.

She sniffed and cast a sidelong look at Onida. "Welcome to my home, doctor."

"Please call me Onida. My family calls me Oni. Whichever you prefer."

Degataga saw Wohali come around the corner.

"Wohali, good to see you. I'd like you to meet Onida. Onida, this is my older brother Wohali."

She shook his hand and smiled. "It's a pleasure to meet you."

"Waya speaks highly of you," Wohali granted her. "You are a doctor then, my mother said?"

"I am."

"Thank you for helping Waya." His voice softened as he looked at the younger man.

"It was an honor to be able to help."

Wohali studied her, and Degataga grew uncomfortable with the weight of his stare on her. "Let us come in," Degataga almost growled at his brother. "Where are your wife and the boys?"

"On their way to basketball practice," Wohali answered curtly.

Asgasga had said nothing the entire time, just watched the exchange with a cold expression. "Go sit. Dinner is ready," she finally said.

"Pay them no attention." Waya wrapped an arm around her waist, pulling her away from Degataga. "I'm going to convince you to leave Dega."

"You can try, but it won't work. I've grown rather attached to Dega."

"My heart is breaking," Waya playfully whined, holding a chair out for her.

Degataga smiled at his brother's antics and sat next to Onida, pushing Waya out of the way. "Find your own woman and stop trying to steal mine."

"It's not stealing if she comes willingly." Waya winked at Degataga, who guffawed.

"Boys, enough," Asgasga barked out.

Degataga passed plates of food to Onida, who tried some of everything. Wohali still studied her, "You are a medicine woman as well?"

"Correct. I trained with several of the tribes in my area. Both my sister and I did." Onida patiently answered all the questions thrown at her and snickered at the besotted look on Waya's face.

"I'm happy for you, Dega," Waya whispered to Degataga. "She's incredible. And super-hot."

Onida blushed again, and Degataga knew she'd heard him. "I know. I'm a lucky man."

The questions persisted throughout the dinner, and Degataga was getting more and more irritated by his brother. "What's with all the questions? Why are you interrogating her?"

"You've never brought a female home with you. Ever. I'm trying to learn about her." Wohali leaned back in his chair and crossed his arms.

"Well, if you are interested in my work, I've had several research papers published I've done about diseases and Native Americans, both in medical journals and tribal publications from a medical standpoint as well as spiritual. They are available online. If you are interested in my personal life, I'm afraid there isn't much to tell you. My work has kept me busy."

Degataga was proud of her; she hadn't been intimidated so far by his overbearing family. "Look her up, Wohali. I dare you."

Wohali shook his head at Degataga. "What about your family?"

"What about my family would you like to know? I am part of the Chinook tribe. But seeing as how our tribe never received a national status, we were swallowed up by others. My family and I, that is. We migrated away from the Columbia river basin and moved north. There are several tribes around us, and my sister and I are kept busy with medicine woman work. My father is considered chief for those of the Chinook that followed him."

"What tribes are around you?" Wohali asked curiously.

"Too many to name. The Makah, Quileute, Hoh, Chinook, Salish, Quinault, Chehalis, Twana, and S'Klallam are a few in my immediate area."

"Why does this matter?" Degataga leaned forward, resting his elbows on the table.

"Just getting to know her. What does your family do?" he continued.

"I told you, my sister is a medicine woman like I am. We are twins. My father is chief and runs the town council; he meets with other tribal leaders to work out issues. He is also a master craftsman with making canoes, and they are quite beautiful. My mother, she maintains her animal form most of the time. When she decides to join us, she is a renowned chef."

"Your mother has a spirit animal?" Both Waya and Wohali were interested now, and his mother narrowed her eyes.

"We all do. Yes." Her answer was blunt and straightforward. "We don't talk much about it outside our family or tribe, so consider that privileged information."

"Very privileged," Degataga added, his voice somewhat threatening.

"Hot damn. Onida's a doctor, a medicine woman with who knows what powers *and* has a spirit animal and beautiful to top it off. How in the hell did you wind up with her?" Waya looked incredulous at Degataga.

"Because he's my mate." Onida shifted closer to Degataga.

"What now?" Degataga's mother joined the conversation.

"We have a mate bond." Degataga challenged his mother to argue. She wisely chose not to.

"How is that possible if Dega doesn't have a spirit animal?" Wohali asked.

"I don't know, but it is. We both feel it." Degataga glared.

Onida put her hand on his thigh, calming him. "Can I ask what your animal is?" Waya was excited.

"I'm a hawk."

"She's a giant, red hawk, her feathers glowing like fire when she flies. Graceful and deadly," Degataga clarified.

"You are a messenger?" his mother asked quietly.

"I am. I can walk in both this world and the spirit world," Onida confirmed, her voice soft.

"Are all your family hawks?" Wohali asked, his tone a little more respectful now.

"No. My mother is a wolf, my father is a bear, and my sister is a cougar." Degataga knew this was information she never shared with anyone, and he was amazed she did so now.

"I repeat, this is privileged information," Degataga warned again.

"Your mom is a wolf?" Waya was excited. "Your dad, a bear?"

"She is a wolf, a huge one. She's so stealthy and

silent that you'd never see her if she didn't want you to. My father is also unusually large, and quiet for something his size. His strength and speed are unmatched among other bears in the area. If you were to see him, you'd better hope that it wasn't you that he was after," Onida said with a smile. "My sister, on the other hand, is downright scary. You don't see her until her claws or teeth sink into your skin. Her roar is deafening and she is larger than most cougars, her fur a beautiful tawny color. She has all the grace in the family. Don't make her angry."

Degataga laughed, remembering the cougar's fury on the live show. "Remember the internet footage of the live show I was on in Washington? The cougar? That was her sister."

"You're kidding me! I damn near shit myself when that animal popped on screen!" Waya exclaimed.

"Language, Waya," his mother scolded.

"Sorry, ma. Wow. Okay, yeah, she was scary. There wasn't a bear there, though. I did see some other things that went by too fast, was that you?"

"It was. It was me and my sister's husband, Taklishim."

"Your friend, Taklishim?" Wohali asked Degataga, who nodded. "He's an animal too?"

Onida shrugged at Degataga, "If we are going to be honest about everything, might as well," she whispered to him.

"He is. He's an eagle." Degataga shifted. "Let's clean up before we continue this talk."

Like a well-oiled machine, they all cleared the table, washed the dishes, and put the food away before sitting back down in the living room. Degataga looked at Onida and said softly so the others couldn't hear, "I could use Smitty's electronic savvy right about now."

"Why?" Onida looked surprised.

"They have a smart TV. I could mirror the images on your phone, so they would be large enough for all to see at once," he said.

"Hand me your phone. I'll call Smitty." Onida called, and Smitty walked her through the process, and they got it set up, the picture of Airiella crying on the screen was the first one.

"Who is that?" Waya asked, his face concerned. "She's gorgeous, but that's a heartbreaking picture."

"It's hard to look at," Wohali agreed, "at least without feeling something."

Degataga took a deep breath in, then started. "We need to talk to you openly about something that can't leave this room. I need your words before I even start."

"Is it to do with her?" Waya nodded at the screen, his eyes never leaving the angel. "You have my word. That picture makes me want to rush in and save her."

Onida choked back a laugh. "You wouldn't be the first that wanted that."

Degataga waited until his mother and Wohali agreed never to share the information. "Her name is Airiella, and she is the reason I got called away. Onida is the reason I stayed there." He met Wohali's eyes, "She's an angel."

"She looks like an angel," Waya agreed, still gazing at the picture.

"An actual angel," Onida corrected him and switched the picture to the one with her wings out to audible gasps from the others.

"That's not photoshop?" Waya whispered, standing

and moving closer to the screen.

"No, I assure you, it's quite real and very recent. Within the past twenty-four hours recent," Onida said, her eyes soft. "She's saved more lives than I have."

"Dega, have you been in danger?" his mother asked, her face pale.

"More than I care to admit."

"Isn't she the one who that show you advise for, that guy proposed to?" Waya stumbled out.

"She is. So no, she isn't available," Degataga announced, rolling his eyes.

Wohali still hadn't spoken, nor had he looked away from the image on the screen. Degataga tried to gauge his reaction, but his face was blank. Onida flipped the screen to the picture Jax had taken of her at the beach where the ocean spray outlined her wings.

"Wow," Waya breathed, his fingers tracing the screen softly.

"She's the most amazing person I have ever met." Onida gazed at the screen. "Her powers are unparalleled, and she willingly stands between danger and those she loves. Airiella is here to restore the balance of the earth."

Degataga took over from her as she choked up, "She literally killed a prince of Hell. She died for it too."

"Wait, she's dead?" Wohali finally spoke.

"No. Divine intervention and Onida brought her back. She's died more than once in her quest to save us all from demons taking over. Not only that, but she also gained favors from other demons who are more in the gray area than dark. She saved Onida's life a few days ago after she single-handedly beat and killed Spearfinger." Degataga watched his mother as he said that.

"Spearfinger?" she whispered, her hands fluttering over her mouth.

"That's not a myth?" Wohali butted in.

"Nope." Degataga used his phone and sent Jax a text asking for more photos to be sent to Onida's phone, specifically, if he had any from a few days ago and of her being what she was. Seconds later, Onida's phone started dinging, and she displayed the photos.

One that showed the leveled area first. "This dead area was the result of Airiella's power detonating Spearfinger. The crater is where the creature died, turned to nothing but fine ash. The blast leveled the forest, uprooting trees, earth, and rock. A tree fell on Onida, crushing her beneath it. Airiella lifted it off her, and the others helped heal her enough to get her back home."

The next picture showed Airiella, exhausted to the point of collapse sitting in the chair in Onida's room, Onida herself, still beneath the sheet. Degataga hadn't expected that one, and he held back the tears that threatened to fall. "She gave me her power every chance she got so that I could keep healing her. She shared with Tama and Taklishim. She's a pure soul with an endless amount of love."

Wohali cleared his throat, emotion rising in his eyes. "This is real? Spearfinger was there?"

"She was. I discovered her, and she almost sliced my wing off when I tried to hurt her to protect the child she was after. Dega healed me then too," Onida confirmed.

"The pictures are almost too artistic to be real," Wohali tried to argue.

"Jax has photography skills, but these all taken with his cell phone," Onida said.

"The reason we were checking the blessing here, will do so at your house Wohali, and also your house Waya; is we were told by the demon that befriended her, that other demons were waking up Native American legends and sending them here after her."

"What does that have to do with us?" His mother finally got her bearings.

"We believe the latest threat is skinwalkers," Degataga announced.

The room fell silent as they absorbed that information. "We don't know if Airiella can defeat them or not. Though, it is my personal belief that she can. We also believe that is why Waya got cancer, at least it's our suspicion. The demons are afraid to come after Airiella on their own. She has proven herself lethal against them, and they are scared. They also know that her weaknesses are those she loves. We figure that we were separated from the others to weaken us. By targeting us and hurting or killing us, she, in turn, is hurt. It's a loose argument, but one that has been proven true by the attack of Bael."

"Wait, Bael attacked?" Wohali shot to his feet.

"She killed Bael," Degataga clarified.

"She killed the right hand of the Devil?" Wohali whispered.

"You can't go back there, Dega. She is marked for death now," his mother pleaded.

"She was marked the second they learned of her," Onida muttered. "You don't understand how strong she is."

"Didn't you say she died because of it?" Wohali demanded.

"He gutted her," Degataga confirmed.

"So, you are telling us this, so we know why you will

die?" Wohali's voice raised.

"No, we are telling you this, so you understand that you are in danger because I am a target. We are telling you this, so you know to be careful, to watch your surroundings and trust nothing. Me leaving here should draw it away from you." Degataga snarled at his brother.

"A noble sacrifice then?" Wohali kept pushing.

"Degataga won't die. Airiella will make sure of that. She protected them all from Spearfinger. She took the damage herself to keep them safe." Onida stood, placing her hand in Degataga's. "Our intent with this is to educate you to keep you from harm."

Waya strolled over to Onida and hugged her tightly. "Thank you for the warning. The gravity of the situation won't fall on deaf ears. Just please keep my brother safe."

"I plan on it," she told him, releasing Degataga's hand to return the hug. "It's why we want to check both your houses. Also, I think you mixed up a couple of sayings there," Onida teased him.

"There's one other thing." Degataga looked out at his family. "I fully intend to marry Onida. She has graciously decided that we will split our time between here and there. She said she would get licensed here to practice as a doctor as well. I want you all to understand that this was her choice. I planned to move there to be with her."

"You were leaving?" His mother gasped.

"I was. I can't be without Onida."

Asgasga looked at Onida, "For this, I thank you."

Waya grinned, "I guess I get you as a sister, then."

Chapter Twenty-Two

Onida was uncomfortable after Degataga declared his intent to marry her. She had expected it, just not in that way. Wohali and Asgasga were stiff with her while Waya accepted her with open arms. "Please don't take the threat of skinwalkers lightly."

"Not at all," Waya announced.

"Will my boys be safe?" Wohali wiped his hand across his face and glanced back at the picture of Airiella exhausted.

"As long as she is alive, they will be." Degataga nodded at the screen. "If you feel safer, you can come up to Washington for a couple of weeks."

He hadn't checked with Onida on that, but she agreed with his offer. "You can use my house if you'd like."

"I don't think that will be necessary," Asgasga broke in. "If Dega thinks we will be safe here, that is good enough for me."

"I can't guarantee your safety, Mom. We will do our best to make sure you remain protected on your property."

Degataga's phone rang, and he looked down at it in surprise. "Jax?" He listened for a few moments, then put the phone on speakerphone. "Family, I'd like to introduce to you, Jax. Jax, my mother Asgasga is here, my younger brother Waya, the one that Onida just healed, and my older brother Wohali."

"Pleasure to speak with you all. My soon to be wife has angel ears, meaning that Onida must have been thinking about her or saying her name, and she tuned in because they have a connection between them. Airiella picked up that Onida offered to let you stay in her house so that you could feel safe. She talked with me quickly, and we decided to offer you the opportunity to stay at our house. We have four extra rooms there, as well as my brother and friend that lives on the property. There is also an indoor pool, and we are on the beach. It would be like a little vacation. The property is blessed and well protected. Airiella and I, along with our teammate Ronnie are currently up at Onida's house helping out."

Waya spoke up first. "This is Waya; I'm in. Will I get the opportunity to meet you and Airiella?"

"We can arrange that."

Degataga looked at Wohali, who looked like he was considering it, and over at his mother, who seemed resigned. "This is Wohali, and I have two boys, would that be an issue?"

"Not at all." Degataga heard Airiella's rich voice come through. "I'm Airiella, by the way. My friend also lives there, and she has three sons as well. They would have playmates."

Degataga smiled at the expression on Waya's face. "Remember, she's spoken for, brother."

"She's gorgeous, and she sounds like that?" Waya grinned. "I can't catch a break here!"

"We accept your offer," Wohali broke in with a glare. "I, too, would like to meet you both."

"I go where my sons go," Asgasga muttered.

"Perfect, we will meet you at the airport then and take you there. That way, you can meet us both," Jax said. "Dega, did you park at the airport?"

"We did."

"Then, Airiella and I can ride back with you, and we can leave the SUV for them to use."

"Sounds good, Jax. Thanks." Degataga looked over at Onida, who had just sat quietly with a little smile on her face. "This okay with you, Oni?"

"It is. There is nowhere safer for your family to be. You should arrange the flights before we take off to go check the blessings."

Degataga nodded and started searching for available seats on their flight back. He started booking them and almost laughed out loud at Waya's question to Onida.

"Is Jax going to kick my ass if I flirt with Airiella?"

"If you touch her without her consent, they probably all will. Jax isn't the possessive type and knows that Airiella would never step out. Ronnie, on the other hand, might crowd you a bit," Onida explained.

"Ronnie, he's the big one on the show, right?" Waya asked.

"He is. He is also very protective of Airiella. Don't cross any lines," Degataga warned.

"You said that a lot of people want to rush in and save her, or hug her, is Ronnie what you meant?" Waya sat back while his brother booked his flight.

"Being what she, their whole team is protective as

are Dega and me, my sister and Taklishim, and a priest that is on the council with us. There are also a few ghosts that watch over her as well as the demon. She tends to bring out that response in people. For a long time, she thought she was only an empath. A strong one, but nothing more."

"That's someone that deals with emotions, right?" Waya leaned closer.

"Yes, in a roundabout way. She can pull emotions from people or enhance something they are already feeling. That picture where she was crying, she had received several visions of those she loved dead. Nature is a potent tool for her, so instead of focusing on death, she went to where she inadvertently killed off the area and has been infusing life back into it with her own energy."

Degataga noticed that Onida even had the attention of Wohali now. "She can do that?"

"We are still learning what she can and can't do. She is too. I can tell you with a large degree of certainty, that if you are in her house, there isn't anything that will be able to get to you unless she allows it on her property. One of the ghosts that watch over her was a member of our council and an extremely powerful lady. With the help of the demon, she has made protective charms that are on the property. Not only that, but the priest also cleansed and blessed the land, as well as Taklishim, Tama, myself, and Degataga."

"Jax purposely bought a huge house so they would have privacy. And so that her large family would feel safe if they came to stay for a weekend. The whole team lives there. There are two houses aside from the main house on the property. Smitty and his fiancée live in one, and Aedan and his wife and children live in the other. Airiella's friend

Chrissie and her three boys use up two of the rooms. Ronnie has a room, and Airiella and Jax have their room," Degataga explained.

"Onida, if you are going to marry my son, do you think it would be possible for me to meet your family?" Asgasga asked, somewhat quietly.

"Of course. We will bring everyone down for dinner after you get settled in." Onida smiled.

"Okay, you all have flights on the same one we are on tomorrow morning. I suggest you get packed up. Onida and I are going to go by each house and do the blessing. Waya, please don't spy on her, she will have to shift, and she undresses for that." Degataga told the younger brother sternly.

Onida only laughed. "I'm not shy at all, most of us who shift strip down first, so we don't ruin clothes. We are used to being naked around people. I think it makes Dega more uncomfortable than it does me."

Degataga touched his nose and smiled. "Wohali, when are your kids back?"

"Probably within the next ten to fifteen minutes, why?"

"We'll go there first so that if they stumble on a naked lady, your wife doesn't freak out."

"Oh, yeah. That might be a good call. Okay then, let's go." Wohali stood and hugged his mother. "See you in the morning, Ma."

"Can I see your hawk?" Waya asked as he followed them out.

"You will." She promised.

She climbed in the car and waited until Degataga was in before she spoke. "Your mother doesn't seem to be happy about going."

"She's not. She doesn't like leaving home, but if both Waya and Wohali are going, then she will go too. Don't worry; she'll be fine."

"Wohali seems to struggle with what we told him."

"He is. Seeing will cement it all for him. Airiella will have him eating out of her hand. He will get along great with Smitty and Aedan too. Ronnie and Jax would be harder for him as they are more like Waya and open with their emotions."

"Smitty is more open now." Onida defended him.

"He is, but he's also an intellectual. Trust me; they will be fine. It will be Waya we need to watch out for; he's got an insatiable curiosity about everything. I often thought he would make a good medicine man."

"He would, I can see it in him." Onida thought briefly about starting some training for him. "I also sense a little power in him."

"You do?"

"I do. What if we were to start training Waya while we are down here next? He can help me with patients and get some hands-on medical experience, too, to back up what we train him," she thought out loud.

"That's a conversation we will need to have with him. You know Taklishim will cut him down if he fawns over Tama as he does you."

Onida laughed again. "I know. I might be looking forward to that the most."

Degataga barked out a laugh. "You *do* have a little mean streak running through you. I love it." He parked in Wohali's driveway behind his brother. "We are going to walk the property line first, and then she will shift."

Wohali nodded and followed behind. Onida pointed out a few spots that were easily breachable, and they worked together, blending their magic into the land. She let Degataga lead her around a hidden corner where she stripped down, handing him her clothes and shifted.

She flew out and sat on the hood of their rental, waiting for Wohali to notice her. "Wohali, this is Onida's hawk." The older brother approached slowly, fear evident on his face. She held out her wings slowly so he could touch them.

The touch was brief before he pulled back quickly, and seeing that the introduction was over, she launched and flew high, circling, looking through both worlds. She saw the same trace of something she had seen at Degataga's place and swooped down to get a closer look.

It wasn't on Wohali's property, but it was close. She quickly noted the areas that needed to be reinforced and flew back to the driveway, shifting as soon as she landed, paying no attention to the fact that she was naked in front of his brother.

"There's something out there," she said immediately, pulling her clothes on that Degataga handed her silently. "There are four more areas we need to reinforce. Wohali, stay inside once your family gets home, do not leave your house."

Onida noticed his eyes were round in shock, and he stood utterly still. "This is all real."

"Very real," Degataga added. "Call your wife and find out when she will be here. Do not leave your property."

Onida and Degataga took off at a run for the areas they needed to reinforce, their eyes open, and their senses on high alert. They made quick work of it, and Onida suggested they do a blessing on his car for when they left the next day. Liking the idea, they did that, and as they finished, Wohali's wife pulled in.

"Dega! It's good to see you!" A petite woman threw her arms around him, and two young boys jumped out, swarming around him.

"Storm, this is Onida. Onida, this is my brother's wife, Storm. My nephews, River, he's seven, and Rain, he's five."

"Pleasure to meet you."

"Storm, we have a lot to talk about, and they have to get going over to Waya's. Boys, inside now," Wohali said sharply, the fear bleeding out of his voice.

Storm narrowed her eyes but herded the boys inside. "We will be by here tomorrow morning, and we will follow each other to the airport. Don't go out. Stay in; there is definitely something out there, most likely following me," Degataga told his older brother. Wohali nodded and flew in the house.

"Well, that will be an interesting house tonight," Onida chuckled. "I get the feeling Storm doesn't like getting ordered around like that."

"Right you are. Storm's a little like you and Tama, though not quite as bad as Airiella. Aside from shifting in front of him, he was doing good up until that point. That kind of drove it all home for him."

Onida cringed, "Sorry. I didn't want to waste time with something being out there."

Degataga drove fast towards Waya's house, and they pulled in behind his car. "Let's do his car first. We'll have him pick up my mother tomorrow." They got to work on the car and then started walking the property line, finding several holes.

"This isn't good. We need to check over the house too and everything on it." Onida fidgeted. "Dega, I need to shift now. I can see better in hawk. Get Waya out here, so we know he's safe." She started pulling her clothes off as Degataga texted his brother, who came flying out the door.

"Cool!" he started, then stopped at the sight of Onida shifting. "Is something wrong?"

"You have large holes in your protection. Onida wants to see if she spots something already here. Stay close to me." Waya sensed the urgency in Degataga's voice and moved to his side, joking gone as he watched the hawk circle high overhead and then came in lower.

Onida swooped down on several spots, showing Degataga where the weaknesses were and then went back up high again and came to land on the front porch, looking at the door. Degataga came up and opened the door, and she hopped in, going from room to room and then back outside.

She shifted, "We have a lot of work to do," she said, pulling on her clothes again. "I can feel traces of something having been through here and in the house, though nothing is there right now. We need to get the property line fixed first."

Onida rushed over to the first spot, and they went from place to place, patching up the holes and reinforcing as they went. Waya was trailing behind them, observing, saying nothing. They went room by room in the house, blessing the corners, windows, and doorways as an added protection.

"Waya, do a cleansing in here after we leave. Burn sage and do the ritual," Degataga told him, Onida nodding.

"We blessed the car as well. You pick up Mom, tomorrow. We will meet you here, follow you there, and then we all go to get Wohali."

"Waya, do you mind if I scan you again while I am here?" Onida held out her hand.

"Are you worried something got to me?" Waya took her hand.

"Just a precaution." She smiled. She didn't find anything amiss and stepped aside so Degataga could do the same.

"All good, see you in the morning. Don't leave the house." Degataga led Onida back out to the car and climbed in.

"Seems more logical now to me that his cancer wasn't a naturally occurring cancer." Onida spoke quietly but with conviction. "Seeing the holes that were present and feeling the traces that it left, lead me to believe cancer was the result of something else. Whether that is a skinwalker or not, I can't say."

"I agree with you, and I'm also grateful for Jax and Airiella intervening and offering their house. Knowing they are safe is a huge relief on my mind."

"Yes, I may have to let her hug me now," Onida joked.

"We need to figure out how to kill these things before it's too late. The proximity was a little too close for comfort." Degataga pulled out his phone and called Taklishim, putting it on speaker and handing it to Onida while he drove home.

"Dega," Taklishim's voice came through.

"You are on speakerphone, we both are here," Degataga said.

"Onida, is everything okay? I'm assuming you shifted."

"I did. There is something at Dega's older brother's house I spotted. Not sure if it's following us or not. I also saw traces of it throughout his younger brother's house and found several holes in the protection around the house. If this is what you think, a skinwalker, how do we kill it?"

"I believe it's what caused my brother's cancer, Tak. It purposely separated us."

"Not good, Dega. I'm glad your family is coming back here with you. I've called Father Roarke as well and told him to stay in protected areas. I told him of the banshee too. He was excited about that part of it."

"He would be, being Irish and all," Onida mused. "Now tell us what we need to know. We aren't safe until we are back together."

"They are hard to kill, Oni. Much like medicine people, or shamans, are considered magic, we are considered white magic or good. Skinwalkers are our opposite, dark magic, dark witches. Most attempts to kill them have failed, and the skinwalker goes after that person with a vengeance. They have no kindness, no light to them. All I've been able to uncover are two ways to kill them. We have to find a way to direct their magic back to them, so their intent touches them, or we use bullets coated in white ash. The bullet has to hit in their neck, which is usually under something, either animal skins or bones. While shooting them might be easier, we can't exactly walk around with guns loaded with bullets coated in white ash, shooting suspicious characters in the neck. On our property or here on tribal land, it will be easier, but they can look like any animal or human they chose. They have necromancy skills, and upon locking eyes with someone, they can possess them, making the victim do and say anything they please."

"You're kidding," Onida breathed out. "How will we know who one is?"

"I'm hoping Airiella will be able to tell by using her soul sight."

"Is that Ronnie cussing in the background?" Degataga asked.

"Yes. Ronnie's not happy with putting her in direct danger again. Jax is less quiet about it, but he's on edge. Airiella keeps having visions, and she's not well. Tama has threatened to change into her animal and sit on her until she eats. Both men agreed with her."

"Have you ever seen one, Tak?" Onida wondered.

"Yes, when I was a child. Everyone who fought it died." They heard him sigh. "The last one managed something to mirror the magic back which killed it, but not before it killed the man as well."

"Bless Jax's SUV," Onida told him. "You guys stay on the property."

"I already did that. Ronnie will have them drop him off at home while they come to pick up Dega's family. He's not sure if he will stay there to help protect or come back. He's busy griping about it all right now. Tama and I are going to go with them to their house and double-check everything again. We will see you all there."

"Are my mom and dad safe?" Onida asked before he hung up.

"Yes. Your mom shifted and is in their house with your father."

"Thank you, Tak. Kiss Tama for me." She hung up

and looked at Degataga. "Do you have a gun and white ash at home?"

"I do. We can't take it on the plane, though. The ash we can. I'll pack it with the books."

"In the words of Airiella, shit just got real." Onida looked out the window as they drove, seeing if she could spot anything.

Chapter Twenty-Three

The flight back was quick for him, thankfully he wasn't sitting with his family, or it would have been worse. As it was, he sat there and held Onida's hand, both of then napping for most of the flight. Jax had texted, asking where Degataga had parked and said that he would meet them at their car.

It was a better option than trying to fight the traffic of picking up outside baggage claim. Degataga kept wondering all night if the lightning that Airiella summoned would be able to kill a skinwalker. If she hit it on the neck the same way a bullet would, would it work?

He'd fired off a text to Taklishim about it before they'd taken off, so he didn't forget. If that was an option, it gave them another layer of defense to at least try to get a mantra worked that would act as a mirror to reflect their magic back to them.

Even if she couldn't kill them, maybe the lightning would hold it off while they did what they had to do. Degataga hated to put her in the situation, especially after Spearfinger, but if she was going to be with them using her soul sight, it was better that she have a defensive tool.

Jax was going to end up hating them. Degataga knew he'd be furious if someone kept putting Onida in the firing line all the time, even if it was for the betterment of the world. They'd all vowed to help keep her safe, and Degataga intended to keep his promise.

The photos of Airiella that Jax had sent had hit Onida hard. Especially the one of Airiella in her bedroom watching over Onida. Whatever divine force was at work in that woman was the only thing keeping her upright. She'd ran herself ragged, and Taklishim had come unglued with her more than once.

Degataga had found Onida staring at the picture after he'd showered and come to bed. She'd been lost somewhere in her mind, her face clouded with worry and a sheen in her eyes that wasn't usually there. He hadn't known Jax had gotten a picture of it, but he shouldn't have been surprised by it.

The harder one for him had been the one in the field where she'd been crying. He did not doubt that Waya had fallen in love with her the moment he'd seen that picture. He had a soft spot in his heart for women in pain, and that picture spoke directly to it. He wasn't worried that Waya would interfere with the relationship she had with Jax, nor was he concerned that Jax would react to Waya's infatuation.

The plane touched down at the busy airport, and as they joined the droves of people headed to baggage claim, he couldn't help watching around him, his senses fine-tuned for something off. Onida had the same alertness to her own body. The demons were playing a dangerous game by doing this, putting hundreds if not thousands of innocents in mortal danger.

They collected their bags from the carousel and headed to the parking garage, his nephews wide-eyed and curious about the new place they found themselves. His brothers and mother were also cautious, while Storm looked somewhat interested like her children.

Degataga saw the SUV before the rest of them, and a smile lit his face knowing that with her, they would be safe. Then she was barreling towards them, a semi-grinning Jax behind her at the trunk of the SUV. She launched at Onida, forcing Onida to drop the bags she'd been carrying. Degataga stood behind her as a brace, so she didn't fall over.

"Hawk-eye, I'm so happy to see you!" Degataga was slightly alarmed at the gaunt look the angel had. Taklishim's worry had been justified and not exaggerated. Onida herself had tears in her eyes and hugged back just tightly as Airiella was holding on to her.

"Ells, let her breathe, baby." Degataga heard Jax's gentle tone.

"Jax, Airiella, let me introduce my family," Degataga said as they loaded up the back of Jax's SUV with their luggage. "This is my mother, Asgasga. My younger brother, Waya." Degataga waited while Waya openly stared at Airiella. "He's crushing, sorry, Jax."

Jax laughed, "No worries."

"This is my older brother Wohali and his wife Storm. Their boys River and Rain."

"Nice to meet you all, I'm Jax, and this lovely lady is my soon to be wife, Airiella."

"Hiya, kids. How was your flight?" Airiella stepped back another step from Onida, though Degataga could tell she didn't want to.

"It was fun. I like flying," River told her, beaming.

"Me too." Airiella held out her hand, "Let's get in and get going." Rain clutched at Airiella's hand, shocking Degataga. The younger kid had always been a bit shy but wasn't showing any of it right now.

Waya was still dumbstruck, staring. "Maybe Waya should ride with us," Degataga said, elbowing his brother.

"Nonsense, he's fine," Airiella said, climbing back out after getting the boys buckled in the back. She took his hand and pulled him into a hug. "It's nice to meet you. I'm glad they cured you."

Jax burst out laughing, "Now that's the look I recognize any time anyone meets her!"

Waya's face was a mix of rapture and joy as he hugged her back, finally finding his tongue, "You are real."

"Of course, she's real you dolt, let us get in the car." Wohali smacked his brother to move so Storm could climb in the car, him following.

Degataga helped his mother get in, and Waya finally followed. Airiella got in the front seat and leaned out her door, "Stay close."

"Do you feel something?" Onida asked quietly.

"I do. It's not close, but I feel it."

Degataga rushed Onida into the car and got in quickly after loading their bags. He waited for Jax to pull out and stuck close to his bumper. Once they finally got out of the cities and on to the quieter highway, he started to feel a little bit better.

"Airiella said something is close," Onida warned, her eyes roaming the road next to her. "She just said to protect your mind. Put walls up as she does."

"Do you see anything?" Degataga settled his mental

barriers in place. "Can she still talk to you if you block your mind?"

"Airiella closed herself off, so no. Before she did, she said she felt something probing at her mind, and she was working on telling the others how to envision blocking their minds off."

"Well, this will be the longest hour drive yet, waiting for something to happen." Degataga kept glancing around him, his nerves starting to tingle.

Onida pulled out her cell phone and texted, then returned to staring out her window. Her phone dinged, and she glanced down, then back outside. "Next to us, running through the woods as fast as we are driving is a dirty looking coyote. Airiella saw it and says the soul is dark. It's not the soul of an animal."

"Did you text Taklishim?" Degataga tried looking but couldn't spot the creature.

"I did. Tak said that it could change forms at will, not to trust that it will stay a coyote. He guesses that a coyote blends with this area, which is why that is what I see right now."

"We should be safe; I always keep my car protected. Oh no," Degataga groaned. "Is she doing what I think she is?"

"Looks like it. We are alone on the road at the moment, Airiella better get on with it." Onida's tone was curt, and she texted furiously.

Blue light shot out of the SUV window, and time slowed for Degataga enough for him to see she landed a direct hit on the ugliest coyote he had ever seen. It spun through the air, getting left behind as they drove on.

"Not dead," Onida said, turning back to face

forward. "Not even sure if she injured it."

"Well, everyone in that car just got a show." Degataga wondered how they took it.

"She said it was either that or her wings were about to sprout, and there isn't room in the car for them." Onida lightly laughed. "I wonder how excited Waya is right now."

Luckily the rest of the drive was uneventful, and they pulled into property behind Jax, hanging behind to make sure the gate closed before following Jax up the driveway. Chrissie, Ronnie, and her boys were outside to welcome the guests.

"Where's Tak and Tama?" Onida asked.

"Look up, honey." Degataga smiled at the giant eagle on the roof. "I'm guessing that means Tama is prowling around."

Sure enough, a cougar came trotting around the side of the house, sending Degataga's brothers and mother reeling in fright. He couldn't help the laugh that bubbled up from his mouth. He watched as Onida knelt and was tackled to the ground playfully by her sister, the large cougar licking her face as Onida tried to push her away.

"Go change before you make the kids scared," Onida whispered. "Never mind. They aren't scared."

All five of the boys were creeping up on the cougar slowly. He knew Tama could hear them, and she turned playfully and rolled over her tongue, lolling out the side of her mouth. "It's okay, she won't hurt you," Degataga encouraged them.

Chrissie's boys didn't hesitate at all, her oldest pouted, "We were hoping to scare her."

"Do you think it's a good idea to scare a big cat like that?" Chrissie called out.

Taklishim flew down silently, coming up behind him and grabbed his shirt in his talons, lifting the kid right off the ground with his mighty wings. He glanced back at Chrissie to see her laughing. "That'll teach you!"

She fit in just fine; Ronnie would be happy with her someday. Onida stood and looked at Taklishim as he came back, the cackling kid happy as could be. Degataga saw the look on her face and knew she was thinking about the babies Tama carried.

The eagle settled down next to Tama and looked back at Degataga, nodding his head to the front door. He saw the pile of clothes and headed to grab them. "Okay, everyone either turns around or go inside so they can change back," he called out. Shocked to see every one of them turn their backs and wait patiently.

Degataga dropped the clothes in front of the two and turned around, waiting for the signal. Hearing Taklishim clear his throat a few minutes later, "Waya, Wohali, it's good to see you both again; this is my wife, Tama, Onida's twin sister."

Degataga turned to see Waya grinning ear to ear. "Okay, Dega, you were right. That cougar made me almost wet my pants. Well, the eagle did too. I had no idea, Taklishim. It's good to see you too, brother."

Degataga introduced everyone, and Jax led them through the house, showing them around and telling them to consider it home. Airiella got them settled into rooms, and then they all waited downstairs for them to come back down.

"Did the lightning do anything?" Taklishim asked.

"Sent it flying through the air," Onida confirmed. "I couldn't tell if it was injured or not, and stopping to look didn't seem like a good idea."

"Airiella, you need to sleep," Degataga told her softly, her appearance startling, even more so now, that she used energy to blast out lightning.

"Can you guys give me an hour or so? Then we can do a little display that both your brothers want so much to see?" Her voice was worn thin, and Ronnie looked like he was about to combust.

"Two. Make it two hours," Taklishim growled out. "We can occupy them that long."

"Stop growling at me, Gandalf," she said and fire sparked in her eyes.

"Can I make a suggestion?" Degataga interrupted before they could start arguing.

"Sure." Jax put a calming hand on Airiella's arms.

"Gather up the rest of the connections and go with her. It will help immensely," Degataga said. "We can watch the babies."

Given the way that Airiella only nodded and didn't argue told him how bad off she was. Onida caught it too, standing and kneeling before her, taking her hands. He knew she was scanning the angel, and her frown told him she didn't like what she was seeing.

There was a look between Tama and Onida, and Tama came up behind Airiella and sunk her hands into her hair. Jax and Ronnie on either side of her stroked her arms, and soon she just collapsed. The sudden limpness of her alarming him.

Taklishim held his hand up, "Tama put her out; that's all."

Ronnie picked up Airiella, a sight that always left Taklishim feeling unsettled because it usually meant she wasn't well. "I'll bring her up, Jax. The others are all here, text them, give them the scoop that she needs us."

"On it." He stood, heading into the kitchen. "Make yourselves at home. There's a ton of menus in the drawer of places that will deliver here if you all are hungry, or Mags stocked up the fridge if you feel like cooking. Don't worry about noise waking her; she won't wake up if Tama put her out."

"Tama won't pull her out either unless it's been a minimum of two hours," Tama added with a smile. "I'll let him be bossy this time."

Smitty came running through the back door, "Is she finally asleep?" he asked breathlessly.

"With assistance," Jax mumbled. "She wouldn't have done it otherwise. Where's Jillian?"

"She's grabbing one of the babies to help. They'll be here in a minute. Mags said she needed a nap too," Smitty laughed, and Degataga smiled.

Soon the rest of the team filed in, ready to help their angel, and they all marched up the stairs, passing Degataga's family who was on their way down. "Where are they all going?" Waya whined.

"Airiella needs to sleep, she exhausted herself," Onida said softly, her tone worried.

"The boys want to play in the pool," Wohali said sheepishly.

"Perfect," Tama said with a smile, one of the babies cuddled up in her arms. "Tak has a suit here, and he can be the totem pole they climb on."

Degataga held out his arms for Onida to hand the baby over, while she took the one Taklishim was holding. "Which baby do I have?"

"That's Jackson," Onida said with a smile. "I have Ronan."

Chrissie ushered her boys up to their room to change into their suits. Degataga looked at his mother, who still hadn't spoken other than a few polite words. "Are you okay, Mom?"

"This is a lot to take in, Dega."

"It is. Here is the safest place for you to be, though," Degataga told her, noticing her eyes glued to the baby.

"Want to hold him?" he offered.

"If you don't mind." She sounded shy. Degataga handed the baby over who made little cooing noises at his mom, who immediately turned to mush.

Degataga turned to the kitchen to round up snacks for the adults and kids alike and followed the rest out to the pool. Despite the gruff exterior of the warrior, he was a natural with the kids, playing for over two hours.

At the three-hour mark, Tama handed off Angel to him and went to wake Airiella. He looked down at the beautiful sleeping baby in his arms and loved the way she felt there. He wanted to be a dad. He felt Onida watching him and looked up to see her soft smile.

Chapter Twenty-Four

O nida watched the way Taklishim herded the kids and found herself smiling at how good he was with them. He was going to be an excellent father. He got them all out of the pool, rinsed off and showered, and in dry clothes with no hassle.

Chrissie had been speechless. "That's never happened before." She stood up, "Ells needs to eat, is there anything, in particular, any of you want? I am going to get something ordered so it's here and she doesn't have a choice. Her favorite is Mexican," she told Dega's family.

Asgasga smiled kindly, "We are all good with that. Will she be okay?"

Degataga looked at his mom like she was crazy. "With sleep and food, she will be fine," he told her. "I'm shocked, you asked."

Chrissie looked questioningly at Onida, "Do you want me to order something other than Mexican?"

"No, it's fine with me. I just want Airiella to eat." Onida was blunt.

"Me too. I'm going to order a large variety. If I know Ells, it will be at least a half an hour before she comes downstairs." She headed out of the pool house. "Taklishim can take the boys into the TV room. There's a variety of movies in there they can watch."

Onida nodded and looked over, seeing that Tak had heard her, and he guided the noisy boys towards the house. Jillian, Degataga, and Onida followed the procession with the babies and the rest of his family in tow.

Onida herself was starting to become a little too comfortable with the baby in her arms, and she gladly handed him over to his mother as she came down the stairs beaming. "That was the best nap ever, even crammed into a bed with a bunch of smelly boys."

"How's she doing?" Onida wondered quietly.

"Better. Degataga was right; the connection helped a lot. Not only her, all of us. She looks almost human now. Tell me, are we in danger here?"

"Not on your property, you aren't. We will bless all the vehicles before we leave, and I'm sure they will talk about the danger later, too, if you want to sit in on it." Mags shook her head no. "Why not?"

"Now that I have kids, I'd rather not think about all the things that are out there trying to take them away from me. Sleep is already hard enough. I'm sure Aedan will listen and tell me whatever he thinks I need to know. Motherhood changes you in a lot of ways."

"Bad ways?" Onida thought about the things Tama would be facing.

"No, except for the lack of sleep part. Good ways. You'll see."

Chrissie was close on the time frame, and Airiella came down right as the food was delivering. She did look better and had color back in her face now. Tak, Tama,

Dega, and her surrounded Airiella, all of them putting their hands on her to scan her.

"Jeez, you guys, let a girl breathe," Airiella huffed.

"We are trying to make sure that keeps happening," Taklishim barked at her, his gaze full of concern.

Fascinated, Onida watched Airiella's face soften as she leaned into Taklishim, hugging him. It was new for Onida to see him give in to his emotions as much as he had lately. Taklishim rested his cheek on the top of her head and closed his eyes.

"Sorry, Gandalf. I know."

Even Tama was surprised. "If you aren't arguing with him and he's not arguing with you, there must be something wrong with both of you."

"It's good practice for him," Airiella quipped with a smile. "Those babies are going to wrap him around their fingers. I'm just softening him up for them."

Tama threw her head back and laughed. "Keep doing it then. I won't stand in your way."

"Where are Jax and Ronnie?" Degataga looked around.

Airiella blushed and didn't say anything. Onida blushed, knowing what that meant. "Leave her alone, guys," she interrupted, pulling Airiella away. "I need to talk to her."

"What's up, Hawk-eye?"

"Nothing, for future reference, that was me saving you from questions you don't need to answer."

Airiella grinned, "Gotcha. I smell tacos."

"Chrissie ordered some food for everyone. We all want you to eat." Onida used her doctor's voice.

"I won't argue. I'm hungry."

"It's about time you said that angel." Ronnie came up behind them and hugged her.

"Then let's get some food in her." Onida tugged at her. "We do need to talk about what's going on, and I think it's time you told us about the visions."

"Then you better let me eat first if that's your goal. I won't be able to if I talk about the visions first," Airiella warned, her body stiffening.

"Ells, think about what we just did." Onida heard Jax whisper to her and felt Airiella's arm relax at Jax's words.

Grateful he had that effect on her, Onida let go of her arm and wandered into the kitchen to see Chrissie setting everything up outside. Degataga's family was sitting around one of the tables talking easily with Smitty and Jillian.

"They want a demonstration later, Onida," Airiella told her quietly so they wouldn't overhear. "Am I okay enough to do one?"

"Yes. You are low on energy still, but not at dangerous levels like you were. Keep your connections around you while you can and draw from them. And tonight, you need actual sleep. Tama can put you out again to keep the visions away if you want."

"I could use what Stolas gave me for that." She looked around her backyard with a hint of a smile. "Now that we are all together, it feels better to me. I like Waya; he's full of life."

"He is. It's his mother and Wohali that seem to be the ones having difficulty."

"They'll come around. I'll have Chrissie drum into them how great you are at every opportunity. Mags will too." Airiella pulled her over to the food. "She's the best," she said, loading her plate and sending a look over to Chrissie. "Have you decided what you are going to do about Degataga?"

Onida felt a genuine smile light her face. "I'm going to let him ask me to marry him."

Airiella turned and studied Onida's face. "You aren't going to turn him down, are you? I'm not okay with that type of playing."

"No, Raven. I love him," Onida told her truthfully and scooped up some rice at the sound of her stomach rumbling.

"Good. Want to know something else?" Airiella had a strange look on her face.

"Do I?" Onida narrowed her eyes.

"I'm going to tell you anyway, because I like keeping you off your game." Airiella gave her an innocent smile. "Your sister isn't the only one pregnant."

Stunned, Onida looked around at the other women wondering which one it was, forgetting to move. She saw Airiella give her a look and laughed, the warm sound oddly making her heart feel lighter. Onida was missing something, based on the look on the angel's face.

It was only when Airiella slyly pointed right at Onida that she felt her heart thud in her chest. "No," she said out loud. "I'd know."

Would you? Airiella laughed again.

Are you joking right now? I honestly don't know.

No, Hawk-eye. I'm serious. You're pregnant. Twins if I'm right.

Onida felt the plate slipping out of her hand, her body flooding with shock. "Hey, Oni. Watch what you are doing, you almost dropped that," Taklishim said, catching her plate and stopping at the look on her face. "What's wrong?"

She tried to pull herself together, but she was shaking and couldn't form coherent thoughts much less string together a sentence. "Shit, I'm sorry, Onida. I thought you'd be happy." Airiella was in front of her, leading her to a chair. "Sit down with me, eat."

"How sure are you?" Onida whispered.

"Completely. I can see the babies," she said quietly, her voice too low for others to hear. "I honestly did think you would be happy."

Onida put a hand over her belly, Mags words about motherhood changing everything. She felt the protective instinct come over her. "I am, but right now, I am more scared than anything else," she heard herself admit, her voice sounding rough and harsh.

"Eat. If I have to, you have to," Airiella ordered.

Onida ate robotically, not tasting the food, her fears about her skills about being a mother rolling through her head, making her feel seasick. "I'm not good mother material," Onida whispered.

"That's utter bullshit," Airiella growled at her.

"No, it's not, I'm awful with people. Dega's mom doesn't even like me." Onida felt tears sting her eyes.

Airiella stood, holding Onida's plate. "Come with me, right now," she ordered, and Onida was too numb to argue. She let herself get led into the house and sat at the island in the kitchen. "Eat. All of it."

Onida did as told, some part of her brain realized that if she had babies in there, she needed the nourishment. She wasn't even aware of Degataga coming up behind her. "Oni? What's wrong? Airiella marched me in here and demanded that I make you eat and talk to you. She's all fired up."

"Oh, my God! I'm completely selfish and awful! I didn't even think about how this would affect your life!" The tears that stung her eyes earlier fell freely.

"I don't think you've ever been selfish a day in your life, but you've got me worried now, what's going on?" Degataga sat down next to her, his eyes full of love and concern.

"I'll tell you what's going on!" Airiella stormed into the kitchen, Jax hot on her heels. "She's under the completely wrong illusion that she is worthless as a mother! Total bullshit, by the way! I can hear your thoughts, so don't even try to argue with me!"

"Ells, maybe now's not the time to light into her." Jax tried to coax her away.

"Jax, stop, it's okay. She's right." Onida couldn't hide from Degataga's eyes. "I can't argue with her."

"Onida!" Airiella thundered, and the ground shook. "You've taken care of me, how many times now? Taken care of Jax, Mags, Ronnie, Smitty, and Aedan. Even those beautiful babies. Why the hell would you think that you wouldn't be a good mother? Who the fuck cares if you aren't a people person!"

Onida met Degataga's eyes and saw the moment he realized why Airiella was furious. "You're pregnant?" he whispered, reaching for her.

"Ells, he's got this, come with me." Jax forcibly moved the angry angel away and back outside.

"I am. Airiella just told me." Onida sniffled as he wiped the tears from her face. "I'm so sorry, Dega."

"Why would you be sorry about that?" He turned her chair to face him.

"Because it changes your life, and I didn't mean for that to happen. I don't want you to think I'm trapping you or forcing you to do something." Even as she said the words, she knew they didn't feel right; this was her fear talking.

"Oni, did you miss the part where I told you I wanted to marry you? That I was in love with you? What am I missing here? And why would you think you wouldn't make a good mother?"

"Dega, can I see you for a minute?" Onida heard Tama ask.

"Can it wait?" He turned to her sister.

"No."

Onida turned back to her food and finished eating, trying to force the fears that were swamping her away. She put her hand back over her belly and tried to feel the life Airiella told her was there. She was kidding herself; she was too strung out at the moment to feel anything.

Chapter Twenty-Five

He looked back inside at Onida, sitting there, making herself eat while she cried, and his heart raced. He was halfway heartbroken at whatever was bothering Onida and halfway elated that he was getting everything that he wanted. He looked impatiently at Tama. "What's so important?"

"Her," she said and pointed at her sister. "She's terrified right now, and Airiella just confronted her on all of it. While yes, it needed to be done, those two are both too blunt for their own good."

"Why is she terrified?" Degataga wanted to understand, so he knew how to approach her and get through to her.

"Because our mom preferred being an animal to being our mother most of the time. Oni has always thought that she would turn out like our mom, and she didn't want to do that to a child that needs love. You and I both know she isn't like that, but those fears are deep-seated in that genius's head. She told you she didn't want to trap you, didn't she?"

Degataga nodded. "I've already told my family I

wanted to marry her though, why would she think that?"

"Because throughout the years we've heard my mother telling my dad that she trapped him because she got pregnant and he felt like he had to marry her. It's not true; my dad loves my mom and accepts her as she is. But as a child, hearing that can cause damage, and it's damage I can see when I'm allowed to poke around in her head."

"Why is Airiella so mad right now?" Degataga understood what Tama was telling him, and it made sense in a way that hurt his heart to think about Onida feeling that way about herself.

"Airiella knows the thoughts that are flowing through my twins head. And because Airiella loves her so much, she's angry that Oni believes these things about herself. Airiella is still exhausted enough to have her filter off, and the raw emotion that tore through Onida knocked the girl flat." Tama wiped her hands over her face. "She's not unhappy that she's pregnant, she's scared. I can guarantee that my sister is stewing in every negative thought she's ever had in her head about herself."

"She's so much more than that," Degataga whispered.

"I know. My mother loves us in her way. If we had been wolves like her, she would have been present more in our lives. As it is, she was there, but in wolf form. It was my dad that took care of us and raised us while also trying to be chief and do all the other things he has to do. The maternal role was missing. Do you understand what I'm telling you?"

"I do. Can I go back in there now? Seeing her like this is doing something to me."

"That's the bond. Don't screw this up, or you are

going to be dealing with my cougar," Tama warned him as she shoved him back in the door. The ground rumbled again, and Onida lay her head down on the surface of the counter.

"Oni, look at me please," Degataga urged her, his hand on her thigh. She turned her tear-soaked face to him, her eyes turning red. "In no way, shape, or form do I feel trapped. Right now, seeing you hurt like this is making me hurt, and the other half wants to break out into song and dance because I am so happy that I get to be on this journey with you."

The ground rumbled violently, and her plate slid to the floor and broke. Degataga jumped up and picked up the large pieces so no kids would get cut and used his napkin to gather the shards into a pile. "I'm scared, Dega."

"Given the earthquakes, I figured as much. You might want to ease off the negative thoughts about yourself or Airiella is going to bring this house down." He sat back down and faced her. "The thought of caring for an innocent life *is* scary, Oni. You do it all the time. Every time you treat someone. It's what you do, Airiella wasn't wrong about that."

"Twins, Dega. There's two."

"Makes me twice as happy, Oni. Yes, I'm scared too, but it's normal. You are a natural nurturer. I may be slightly biased because I'm in love with you. But also, I'm thinking I'm not, based off the storm our temperamental friend out there is causing. You are one of the best people I know. Your heart is as pure as Airiella's. People skills have nothing to do with being a good parent, and besides, you do have them."

"I know nothing about being a mother, Dega. I

didn't have one."

"You do. Everyone has a different parenting style, and until you have children, you don't know anything about being a parent. How do you feel when you hold Aedan's babies?"

"In awe, in love, and peaceful," she admitted softly, the tears slowing.

"That should tell you everything you need to know right there, honey. You are going to be an amazing mother, and I can't wait to be their daddy." Degataga smiled at the woman he loved more than anything else.

"You are being honest with me?" she implored him.

"One hundred percent." He bent forward to kiss her.

"Airiella said the broom is in the closet by door and that she's sorry for yelling in front of everyone."

Degataga stood and got the broom, sweeping up the broken glass and tossing it in the garbage can. "Are you feeling better? Or is the earth going to shake again?"

"I feel better than I did."

"Regardless of having a maternal role model or not, that has nothing to do with you being a good parent."

"Logically, I know that. Fear isn't rational." She sat up and held his hands. "Will your mother ever like me?"

"She doesn't dislike you now. Ask Storm how it went for her at first. You'll see." Degataga squeezed her hands.

"That's not as comforting as you think," Onida said wryly.

"Right now, I think there is a slew of people out there that know our not so secret and want to congratulate us. Are you up to going back out there?"

She stood. "Did Tama threaten you with her cougar?"

"She sure did."

Onida laughed. "I'm ready."

He held her hand as they went through the door to the backyard, met a round of applause, and an angel that almost bowled Onida over. "I'm so sorry!" he heard Airiella crying into Onida's ear. "If I thought for one second you would be an awful parent, I wouldn't have told you like that. I was so sure you would be happy!"

"Ssshh, Airiella." Onida stepped away from the people and pulled Degataga with her. "I am happy. Between your blow up and Degataga's more gentle approach without the earthquakes, I feel better. You know better than anyone how strong fear is. That's all it was, fear."

Degataga bent to hug them both. "Airiella, I couldn't be happier than I am right now. Stop crying before Jax and Ronnie come over here; actually, I'm more afraid of Tama. Stop crying, so Tama doesn't change into a cougar and rip my throat out."

She snorted in laughter. "I'll give you that one, she is damn scary in that form. Okay, let me show you both, then." She took both of their hands in one of her and placed the other over Onida's belly.

In Degataga's mind, he saw the little sprouts floating in their temporary home, and the emotions overwhelmed him. He burst into tears and dropped to his knees, resting his head on Onida's stomach, sending messages of love to those little tiny lives growing.

"I'll hold them off a minute, but I'm not challenging Tama, so get your shit together," Airiella told them, stepping away, her tone light.

"Dega, stand up," he heard his mother call out. Onida pulled him up and kissed him.

"She better be your first stop," Onida whispered to him. "I'll head off the cougar."

He watched as she made a mad dash to Tama, and the twins clung to each other, a bond he hoped his children would have. His children. The thought threatened to take him down again. Airiella appeared back at his side. "Do you want me to ease the craziness inside you?"

"No. It's a good craziness. Your method of announcing it might be worse than mine on explaining why I left, but it's still good. Is there going to be an earthquake every time you get mad?"

"I hope not. I think it's because I'm so tired. I don't have much control when strong emotions like that hit."

"As hard as it was to hear you take her down like that, I'm also glad you did. Don't do it again. At least not without warning me first. Now, I better go see my mother before there is another emotional woman in the mix."

He left the snickering angel standing there and went to sit next to his mother. She had moved away from the others and sat close to the fire pit. "Maybe not the best way to learn that kind of news," she started.

"No, but regardless, it's welcome news. You'll be getting two more grandkids."

"Twins, then? Not surprising, they run in both our families." She fidgeted with her hands, looking down at her lap. "She's a strong woman, Dega."

"Yes, she is. And smart and funny in her own unique way. Independent and brave, and filled with so much love that she doesn't show."

"She shows it. It's in everything she does. In the quiet way that she walks, in her gentle touch, in the fire in her eyes and her smile. Not everyone shows their love in the same way, and hers is visible. I do like her. And I love her not only because she saved my son, but because she saved you too." She reached for her hand and placed a small wrapped package in it. "A mother always knows, Dega."

Silently he looked at the small bundle and unwrapped it to find his mother's wedding ring. "Mom?"

"Your father gave me that on our second date. Said he knew without a doubt that he was going to marry me and told me to hold on to it until I was sure. Only then was I to give it back to him so he could propose properly." Her eyes teared up. "I didn't tell him I knew then as well. I made him wait a year and a few months before I gave it back to him. I think it's time to pass the ring down; he would have wanted you to have it."

"Mom," Degataga choked up, "are you sure?"

"As sure as I was about marrying your father."

Degataga pulled her in and hugged her tight. "She thinks you hate her."

"I know. It keeps these strong women in line. I don't, Dega. I couldn't have picked better for you if I had tried."

"Thank you, Mom. I love you."

"Good. Remember that when you think of moving here permanently. Guilt will keep you close."

Degataga laughed. "She wants to split the time as she said. She told me not to sell my house."

"Does she know that you and your father built it?"

"Not yet, she doesn't. She will. Should I ask

her tonight?"

His mom scoffed. "You already knocked her up, and you want to wait?"

"No, I wanted to marry her the moment I saw her again when we met to interview Airiella."

"She's more than an angel, isn't she?" He saw her looking over at Airiella, who cozied up with Chrissie on one of the lounge chairs.

"Taklishim, before even meeting her, called her a raven."

"I can see that. Airiella's a mix of both. She's got power, that girl does. The damn ground shook with her anger!"

"A little startling when that happens. Airiella also zapped Taklishim with lighting too for bossing around Tama." Degataga laughed at the recent memory.

"She's got sass. I like her too. I hate to admit it, but you were right in bringing us here. Poor Wohali, he was pretty frightened when the earth shook. The demonstration she promised is going to shake the solid foundation of his pragmatic life. Your father always knew he couldn't carry on his torch. You, on the other hand, he knew the moment you were born. Those babies of yours are going to be special. Tama's too."

"I find myself suddenly nervous about proposing. I've thought about how I'd do it so many times, now that it's here, my brain is freezing."

"Ask the angel to make it splashy for you. Onida has no idea I gave you that. I grabbed it this morning before you got there. Go with your heart, Dega. I'm sorry I tried to force marriage on you, I see now how wrong it was."

Degataga felt the emotions rise in him again, which

also caught Airiella's attention. He tried to rein it back in, so he wasn't battering at her, but he motioned her over. "Hey, my mom had the idea that you could help me propose."

"Oooh, I'm in. What do you want me to do?"

"Make it splashy, that's what I told him. Catch Onida off guard. In a less earth-shaking way than your yelling at her did," Asgasga said bluntly.

He cringed at the guilty expression that stole over her face. "Any ideas?" He tried to ease the words of his mother.

"It's not quite splashy, but it's better than striking her with lightning. Here's what I think," she started, leaning towards them and lowering her voice.

Chapter Twenty-Six

O kay, folks, gather around. The party tricks are about to start so that we can hit the road and get rested up before we have to battle weird legends that want to kill me." Onida bit back a smile at the sarcasm Airiella was tossing out, but she agreed. Airiella still needed a lot of sleep.

"So, what are you going to show us?" Waya took a front-row seat, much to the amusement of Jax.

"What do you want to see?" she countered.

"Daddy said you have wings," Rain said, snuggling up in his uncle's lap. "I don't see wings."

"Okay, that one is easy." She smiled at the boy, and her wings came out in a rush. "Want to touch them?" She squatted down in front of him.

Onida sat down next to Chrissie, "Have your boys seen this?"

"They have. Airiella's upfront and honest with them and takes the time to answer their questions in the best way possible. The times they stump her, Ronnie steps in. They have a harder time with the things she's up against, understanding evil and what it means to the world than they do with any of her powers or what she is."

"Remarkable. Kids are resilient." Onida glanced at the row of kids now seated on the edge of the cement in front of Waya.

"It helps that Airiella is easy to be around. I think I was more surprised that they love Taklishim. Moth to a flame."

"Yes, that was unexpected. Good to see." She glanced over at Wohali, who was scowling and still skeptical despite seeing giant black wings right in front of him. "She's going to have a hard sell with that one."

"She wins them all over eventually, Onida." Chrissie laughed. "It's just who she is."

"Wohali, what can I do to help you understand my capabilities in keeping you and the rest of the world safe?" Onida heard the challenge in her voice.

"Wings aren't going to protect anyone," Wohali grumbled.

"That's not true, actually," Airiella argued. "It's my wings that kept Taklishim from being injured with Spearfinger."

"That's what you've said, but they are feathers."

"Would you like to attack me?" she suggested, raising her eyebrow. Onida saw Jax shift at that, and judging by the expression on his face, he didn't like that suggestion. He didn't stop her, but Ronnie stood.

"He hates it when she puts herself in danger," Chrissie whispered. "I have a hard time with it too. If I hadn't seen some of the stuff with my own eyes, I wouldn't believe it either."

"She explained to me a little in the ways the two men are different and what they mean to her." Onida recalled the conversation.

"She told me too. Said loving Ronnie was easy. For her, she's right. She doesn't always want to be protected. I'll say this, for me, Ronnie isn't easy. I love that he's protective. I also love that he wants to protect her and how he feels about her. It's a convoluted situation."

"I'm going to call Stolas," Airiella announced, and Taklishim bolted to his feet.

"Uh oh." Onida stood, ready to intervene. She didn't have the same fears about the demon that Taklishim did. She knew Stolas wouldn't hurt Airiella or any of them, but she wasn't sure how Wohali would feel in the presence of a demon. Though, it would solidify her story and claims.

"Sit down, Taklishim, or I'll make it so you can't move," she barked at him. She looked back at Wohali, "Would you like me to call my demon friend to the party to help me demonstrate?"

"No, I wouldn't like that at all." Wohali looked uncomfortable and a little scared.

"I've got it, Airy." Mags appeared with her bow and arrow. Onida saw Ronnie's jaw drop.

Chrissie walked over to her oldest son and had him stand with Airiella before sitting back down with Onida. "Having the kid there should make her point."

"You are one brave mama. I know he's safe, but I'd have a hard time watching that if it were my kid."

"Oh, the first time she did it, Mags was practicing, and the youngest wandered right into the path. Airiella moved so fast. The arrow shattered against her wings, and Ronnie had to catch me before I hit the ground."

Mags moved to the grass and took up position, aiming right for Chrissie's son. Airiella moved her wings, wrapping them both up, right as Mags let the arrow fly. True to word, it shattered on impact. Ronnie was halfway across the yard when she opened her wings to show the grinning boy.

Wohali said nothing. Tough crowd. Airiella sent the boy back to the rest and paced around. She picked up the pieces of the arrow and brought them to him for him to see it wasn't a fake arrow. He fingered the pieces but still hadn't said anything.

"Tak, shift and try to catch me off guard," she suggested.

"You aren't going to zap me again, are you?" He grumbled but stood and went inside to the sound of Tama laughing.

"Taklishim will help you see that my awareness of the surroundings makes it hard to surprise me." She pulled her earbuds out of her pocket. "He believed that me being in nature, looking for Spearfinger, while plugging my ears with noise as he called it, made me vulnerable. I was happy to prove him wrong."

She put the buds in her ears, and Onida laughed. The music was so loud that they could hear it. Taklishim would have been yelling at her, even knowing she was okay. "I swear she does this to set him off purposely."

Chrissie grinned, "Oh, she does. She enjoys it too. Ronnie loves it when she gets him going. Jax only gets amused."

"When they had this argument, I tried to catch her off guard. It was laughable how easy it was for her to keep me away."

"She practices all the time," Chrissie said seriously. "She doesn't take any of this lightly."

"I know. Taklishim knows as well. After seeing what she did with Spearfinger, there is little doubt among us that she can hold her own." Onida sensed movement above her, her hawk senses flaring to life. "He's here."

"How do you know? I can't see anything." Chrissie groused, searching the sky.

"Hawk, remember?"

Taklishim was a warrior. His skills were unmatched in this area, something not a lot of people knew. She saw Tama crossing the yard and kneel next to Wohali and knew she was explaining Taklishim's unique skill set by the intrigued look in his eyes.

A gust of wind appeared out of nowhere, and Onida heard the frantic flapping of wings as Taklishim righted himself, Airiella not having moved at all. She faced the ocean, her wings relaxed, her fingers tapping a rhythm against her leg.

Tama pointed to the roof behind them, and Onida saw Taklishim perched there observing Airiella. Wohali's expression became amazed. "The wind was her?"

"Sure was." Mags came up beside him and handed him the bow. "Shoot an arrow at her. I'll help you aim it."

"That doesn't seem fair to me." Wohali was back to looking uncomfortable.

"Trust me." She helped him aim. "Let it fly when you are ready."

Wohali took a deep breath and let the arrow go; the second he did, the wind carried it harmlessly away. "Okay, I'm a believer, and I am also shaking like crazy because I just fired an arrow at a person."

He believes you now, Onida sent to Airiella.

She turned around and smiled. "I see you, Tak." He

flew up and over the house out of sight. "Just like you saw in the car on the way here, Wohali, I'm well aware of what's around us, can sense danger, and protect those around me."

"I can see that. Yet you were still hurt fighting Spearfinger."

"I was, but the others weren't really. Tossed around a bit and had their ears ringing but no serious injuries to those around me. I can use the elements to help me. Watch the fire." She focused a bit, and the flames grew, shrunk to almost nothing, and went back to normal.

"So, if she is real, then that means that what we are facing and the danger it presents is real too." Degataga stepped in. "You felt the earth move when she was angry, that was her. Are you convinced to stick it out and learn as much as you can?"

Jax started laughing before he could answer and called out, "Waya, dude, she's engaged. Sorry man."

Onida looked at Waya and tried to hide her smile at his smitten face. Airiella trotted up to him and kissed him on the cheek, "It's true, sorry."

"One for the other side, too, please. After all, I had cancer yesterday." Waya tapped his other cheek.

Onida burst out laughing as Airiella kissed his other cheek and went back to Jax, curling up next to him. Degataga walked out to the grass and picked up the few pieces of the arrow that were missed and dropped them in the trash as he came up to Onida and held out his hand.

She took it. Degataga pulled her up and led her out to the grass in front of everyone. Confused, she just followed him, wondering if he was going to demonstrate something. Then all the lights in the backyard went out, the glow of the fire the only light she could see.

A ring of blue fire went up around them and made her jump slightly and panic, thinking danger was near. *No threat,* Airiella said in her head.

Onida looked around her and saw that she and Dega were illuminated perfectly with the blue light. It felt almost romantic except they were on display in front of his whole family, and trapped in a circle of blue fire.

Degataga knelt, and Onida felt both of them rise up in the air, a cushion of wind under her feet. "Oni, I don't have a lot of fancy words, but I do have access to an angel willing to put us on display in front of everyone shamelessly. My mom gave me this today; my father had given it to her, and with it, her blessing to pass it along to you in hopes that you will join our family. Will you marry me?"

Onida stared down at him, shocked. "You aren't doing this because you feel trapped?"

"Never. With you, my soul is as free as riding the currents of the air that carry you around."

She dropped to her knees in front of him, noting how weird it felt not to feel the ground under her in her human form. "Then, yes, I will marry you."

Bolts of lightning struck down over the ocean behind them in a fantastic display of light. Airiella lowered them both back to the ground and raised the flames of the blue ring around them higher, blocking them from view.

Onida wasn't going to waste the opportunity. She flung herself at Degataga, kissing him with all the passion he brought out in her, all the emotions she couldn't suppress around him and all the love Onida never thought she would have.

HAWK

When the flames started to lower, she broke away, her eyelashes wet with unshed tears. "I love you, Dega."

By the way, you are in trouble for using up so much energy for this, Onida sent to Airiella.

Can't say I'm terrified. Degataga's mom likes you, I heard it with my ears, so stop with that negative shit about yourself already. Or I'll use the rest of my energy to hold you in place while the ground shakes some sense into you.

Sometimes, I feel sorry for Jax. Airiella let out a sound that was half-snort and half-laugh.

Chapter Twenty-Seven

After the celebration dwindled, Jax opened his house to all who wished to stay instead of driving back. After some shuffling around with Jax and Airiella deciding to spend the night on the beach and Ronnie bunking with Chrissie, there were enough rooms.

Degataga was happy not to have to drive back in the dark. It also gave them a chance to discuss what to do about the skinwalker or however many of them there were. He went out to the car and dug a few of the books that he'd packed out, and a couple of bottles of white ash he had.

Most of the adults had gathered inside to talk about it. Storm and his mother had gone to bed. Aedan, Smitty, Ronnie, Jax, and Airiella were there. Ronnie and Smitty being excellent at research, was a big help. Waya, Wohali, Taklishim, Tama, Onida, and himself rounded out the group.

"Let's start with what exactly a skinwalker is," Ronnie began, looking at the books Degataga had sent down. "What language is this?"

"Cherokee," Degataga answered. "Spearfinger was a legend from my tribe. Skinwalkers, while they have legends among several tribes, I think, originated in the southwest.

So Taklishim probably knows more about them than I do."

"Much like ravens and angels, different tribes call them different things. Americans have legends of skinwalkers too. They've been called body snatchers by white people. Tribal people tend to be literal with their words, and a skinwalker is someone who walks in another's skin," Taklishim explained.

"Silence of the Lambs shit?" Ronnie asked.

"Not quite like that; most skinwalkers of tribal legends take the form of an animal, though they can take the form of a human." Taklishim started ticking off on his fingers: cannibalism, incest, murder, torment, and necrophilia. Grave robberies, mind-reading, necromancy, shifting, dark magic, causing diseases, and death are things they are capable of."

"Wow, is that all?" Airiella looked sickened.

"In southwestern tribes, magic is not paranormal; it's a way of life. I am considered a witch. So are skinwalkers. Medicine men use the magic for helping and healing, while skinwalkers use it for harm. They don't have to get close to you to kill you. They are by far the most dangerous of our legends. Their speed and strength are far more than yours as a human. They can go invisible and reappear, and they can scale cliffs with ease, race a speeding vehicle, as you saw earlier, and get inside your head."

"Wait, how is this different than a demon?" Jax asked.

"In white man terms, they would be very similar, though killing them is more on a level of killing Bael than killing a lower level demon. During the day, they walk the same way we do, blending in. It's when you lock eyes with them that you will be able to tell the difference. In daylight and the human form, they will have the eyes of an animal, in animal form, they will have the eyes of a human. Also, in direct light, their eyes will appear red."

"You are painting a bleak picture, Taklishim," Wohali said. "It doesn't seem like there is anything Waya or I could do to protect ourselves and our family against something like this."

"Taklishim failed to mention among the list of scary shit already voiced, that locking eyes with them allows them to possess you," Jax added. "He told us that yesterday."

"Taklishim and Ronnie are the two best fighters in this group," Tama pointed out. "Between the two of them we can come up with some moves to maybe expose their necks so that we can get at them."

"In the little that I've read, I have only ever seen that a shaman, in other words, us four," Degataga pointed to Taklishim, Tama, Onida and himself, "can kill one. I am skeptical about that because Airiella was able to kill Spearfinger, which was unheard of, too, not to mention Bael. Let's also not forget that she has skills and abilities that no one else on earth has combined in one little body."

"Hey! I'm not little," Airiella groused.

"You're smaller than me." Ronnie elbowed her gently. "And Jax, Aedan and Smitty."

"Don't make me separate you two," Smitty warned. "So the rest of us mere humans aren't effective against this, or are you saying we are going to have to get very creative?"

"That's it exactly. We have to get creative." Taklishim leaned forward, his face set in stone. "I won't accept any losses of this group."

HAWK

"Everyone still has the amulets that Kalisha made them, right?" Degataga asked, and the group nodded, except Waya and Wohali. "For starters, keep them on, and always be with someone if you are not on protected land."

"What will not being alone help? So, whoever is with you gets to watch you die?" Wohali asked, serious.

"It's backup, plain and simple," Ronnie answered. "For the time being, you and Waya have no real reason to leave the property here. The beach is protected along our property lines as well, and we have those marked. The food we can always have delivered, or one of us that has an amulet, goes with you."

"Please don't take this the wrong way, but how are you one of the best fighters in this group?" Wohali was struggling with all the information thrown at him, and it was easy for Degataga to see.

"I'm a trained fighter. Not in the magical, mysterious way that Taklishim is, but an actual fighter. Boxing, MMA. I work with my team on defensive skills and train them as I've trained so that we are ready for anything physical. I'd be happy to add you and Waya to our workouts if I am here."

"Count me in on that," Waya said. "Are you planning on leaving?"

"I haven't decided if I am going to stay or go back with Airiella and Jax. If I'm not here, Aedan or Smitty can lead you through the workouts and help you on the form." Waya nodded in acceptance. "Tak, what kind of moves are we going to need to work towards?"

"We will need to get the neck exposed. The only documented cases of kills that I am aware of in my legends are the skinwalker got killed by a medicine man mirroring the magic back at the skinwalker, essentially turning their magic on them, or a bullet coated in white ash to the neck."

"How do you make white ash?" Airiella questioned.

"Not ashes themselves," Degataga corrected her. "White ash refers to the tree."

"Well that makes even less sense, how do you coat a bullet in a tree?"

"We can use the ash of a white ash tree, or the sap from it, even crushing up the bark and leaves. In this, I question the legends. I don't think we need to use bullets. I think if we coat any blades, arrows, or other weapons in the white ash, it would have the same effect. What do you think, Taklishim?" Degataga looked over at the warrior.

"I agree with that. I do own a gun where the stock is from white ash, but the stock isn't going to kill a skinwalker. We could also fill hollow point bullets with the mixture, for when we are on protected land."

"Is that what these are?" Airiella picked up the two bottles Degataga had brought with him.

"It's the sap of white ash, yes. Those trees aren't native to this area, so it will be harder for us to find and replenish it easily. I do have contacts on the east coast that can send me more," Degataga added, pulling out his phone and making a note. "Preferably a living sample, it will be far more potent."

"We are taking this back to our land, right?" Onida finally spoke.

"I think it's better that we do," Taklishim answered. "It will keep those here safer, and we have far more protected land up there, making it easy to draw a line. They don't keep to the woods as Spearfinger did, they can be anywhere or anyone."

"Okay, so what makes it hard to get to their neck?" Jax asked while Smitty took copious notes.

"If they wear the bones of the animal they are, it makes them more powerful. Often there will be a necklace of teeth around their necks protecting them," Taklishim described.

"That means we need to throw them off balance somehow, so they use their arms to regain footing if they are in human form," Ronnie mused. "It's a natural instinct to throw your arms out when you fall, not protect your neck. Same with forcing them to strike out with their arms, it leaves vulnerable places. I'd think that with you three in your animal forms and Degataga trying to work whatever magic he can to mirror it back, it gives us a fighting chance. Especially with Airiella."

"I agree with Ronnie," Onida said, surprising all of them. "Taklishim is needed to fight, and in his animal form, it gives him and I the advantage of heights and moving silently. Tama, as a cougar, is downright lethal, and she's fast. Combined with Airiella, even if she can't kill it, she can distract it with lighting, earth-shaking, and air currents to help protect us. If we can find an incantation to mirror the magic back, Degataga can do that while we go at it from this angle."

"It also keeps the others out of the line of fire. Ronnie can stay in a protective circle with Degataga and point out weaknesses to Airiella through their connection, and Jax can assist Degataga," Tama added.

"How about we stay here another day and work with Waya and Wohali on ways they can improve fighting and forces that Waya can use before we head back?" Onida suggested.

"What do you mean forces that I can use?" Waya asked, confused.

"You have magic in you," Degataga told his brother bluntly. "Onida and I were going to talk to you about possibly training you in ways of a medicine man."

"Seriously? I'm in."

That left Wohali. "I'm not sure about any of this, but I will agree to not leaving the land and training with you guys. I don't like that we have no defenses as it is."

"You aren't defenseless here," Smitty took over. "Aedan and I are adept fighters, not at the skill level of Ronnie, but we are good. Mags is unparalleled in her skill with archery, and if we coat her arrows in the white ash, that gives us a longer range of defense. Aedan is skilled with a sword, and if we coat that, there is another layer of defense, and I am skilled with a dagger. Jillian knows martial arts, though she has never used it defensively, the skills are there."

"Not only that, but we are also on protected land. They might be able to see in, but they can't step foot on it, nor do I think their magic can penetrate through our protections. If Mags firing is arrows at them from within safety, it gives us added skills," Aedan thought out loud. "Taklishim, can their magic get through?"

"It shouldn't be able to. I'm going to check with Father Roarke to see if there is some kind of protection that Airiella can set with her energy and that of the light she carries in her. Their darkness can't beat out her light. She's proven that by killing Bael. This reason is why the demons are setting these legends loose; they can't beat her."

"I'm happy to try anything I can to add to the protection here," Airiella said, her energy rapidly fading once more. Degataga wanted to scan her again but held back, not wanting to draw attention to her. "This is our house; this is my family."

"You all are scared of my cougar; you should be scared of her. The earth moves for her," Tama said with a small laugh.

"After you rest up tomorrow, I want to do a practice session with all of us so we can see what all you can do. That last display with Spearfinger blew me away. You've been holding back on me," Taklishim challenged Airiella.

"Do you seriously want me to blast you with all I have? I can't; you'll die. That's why I hold back. I hold back when I practice by myself," she fired back at him hotly. Degataga held back a laugh, trying to change it to a cough.

She glared at him, and a gust of air hit him in the head. "Sorry, I was picturing you zapping yourself."

"Okay, that would be funny as hell." Ronnie chuckled. "I should shut up since I plan on camping outside with you in case you feel anything."

"You should be worried about feeling something," Onida fired off, to the shock of everyone at the table.

Airiella let out a delighted laugh. "I knew you had it in you!"

Jax looked at Degataga, then at Taklishim. "Let me recap. We are staying here another night, tomorrow we train physically, then you all with Airiella train with abilities. Degataga and maybe Ronnie and Smitty can help research ways to mirror magic back, and after another long exhausting day, Ronnie and I head back with you all and Airiella to your home to meet it on your turf?"

"It's a start," Degataga answered.

Onida threw out another suggestion, "Maybe we

stay tomorrow night too, so we aren't driving tired. We can take off in the morning. It gives us a little more time to train without worrying about when we have to leave."

"Better," Ronnie added.

"Jax, do you mind? I know you are out of rooms now," Degataga thought to ask.

"Mags and I have an extra one right now that can get utilized as well," Aedan offered.

"So do Jillian and I. No one has to camp outside. We can make it work. It's one of the reasons we all got such a big place. Once we knew what Airiella was all about, we figured that there would be more to come."

"I have no arguments," Tama said. "I am tired, though. Tak?"

"Reasonable plan. We'll make adjustments as we go. I'll train with you all in the morning as well."

"Me too," Degataga jumped in. "I, for sure, need some work on those skills."

"Great, then it's settled. Now, where are we sleeping? Airiella needs to sleep if we are going to turn around and wear her out again." Onida stood up.

"I'm still sleeping outside." Airiella slowly stood up. "I'll rest better connected to nature and get more energy. As well as be a warning signal for us all."

"I'm still with you, angel," Ronnie added, standing. "You all know wherever she is, Jax is. Guess that still leaves our two rooms open then."

Onida looked at Degataga, "Ronnie, we'll take your room. Tak and Tama can have Airiella's."

Chapter Twenty-Eight

What the hell, Gandalf?" Airiella yelled. Onida looked away from Jax for a split second and got knocked off balance by a sunstantial body shot.

"Shit, I'm sorry, Onida." Jax rushed over to help her up.

"Not your fault, your fiancée distracted me." Onida dusted herself off.

Onida looked back over to see Taklishim lying on the ground, laughing. "She's a better fighter than she gives herself credit for, Ronnie did well in training her. Airiella cleanly swept him when he tried a sneak attack," Jax explained, grinning brightly. "Even fighting against Ronnie, where she has to be completely tuned in, her instincts and danger awareness are active. Taklishim keeps learning that the hard way it looks like."

"Tama is certainly enjoying it." Onida absently rubbed her side as she watched her sister howling in laughter. "You pack a good punch too."

"I didn't hurt the babies, did I?" Jax looked worried.

"No, the human body does well absorbing impact and protecting life. It would take a lot more than that to disturb them at this stage. And if that is you holding back, then I'd guess he trained you pretty well too."

"He had to. Sometimes fighting was the only way to keep that darkness I used to have in me at bay. He'd work me until I passed out, literally. Do you know in all that time, all these years, the only time he ever really hit me was to protect Airiella? Even when we trained, all he did was correct my form and block my hits; he'd throw fake punches and kicks."

"How did he train so well then?" Onida had to admit to herself that she was curious about the large man.

"He would demonstrate on the bag, and guide my movements with his own. The only time he threw punches after he went straight, was on circuit fights. So many tried to recruit him to put him on the pro circuits. He's top-notch, so all credit for my skills go to him."

"Well, if it helps her take down a spirit warrior, then all the more credit to him. He's never going to live this down. Tama and Airiella both are going to remind him all the time, I can tell."

She got back in her fighter stance and resumed sparring. Even with her enhanced abilities, Jax proved to be challenging and kept her guessing on what he would do next. She landed very few blows against him, and even those she did land got partially deflected.

"Defensively speaking, your skills are average, you can hold your own. You'll need to work on the offensive though, it's not enough to just defend, you need to put your enemy on the defensive as well." Jax pointed out as they rested. "Switch partners!" Jax yelled.

"Who am I up against now," Onida asked him.

"Sorry. Ronnie. Remember the offensive part." Jax

winced. "He doesn't take it easy."

"How long do you guys do this for?" Onida was winded and sore.

"Look at this work of art and tell me how long you think we go?" Ronnie joked as he came up behind her. "I'm perfection."

"Your ego is certainly the largest part of you," Onida shot back. He was pleasing to look at, and she hoped that it didn't distract her. "You are finished beating up Airiella now and are moving on to other helpless females?"

"You've been around my angel too much; her attitude is rubbing off on you." Ronnie danced around her, his footwork light and effortless. "I've never beat up a girl unless you count Smitty. And you are certainly not a helpless female."

"I heard that asshole," Smitty growled from somewhere behind Onida.

"Okay. I saw you with Jax, you are passable at defense, but your attack is weak. So we are going to work on that. Use your animal strengths to predict my moves and counteract them. Even if you don't knock me over, get me off balance, even forcing a step I wouldn't ordinarily take is an advantage," he coached her.

"How do I counteract them?" Fighting wasn't her thing.

"If I punch here—" He aimed for her shoulder. "—you would want to move your body to the side, so my swing misses, but while moving, push your body weight to the other foot and let it propel you forward into an attack of your own. My hand is up, but this arm becomes extended and reaching out to you, leaving my body open here." He demonstrated in slow motion and without actually touching her.

"Okay, hold on. Let me think a moment. Can you demonstrate an attack on someone so I can see what your body is doing? I mean without me having to defend. I just need to watch a moment so my brain can piece it together." Onida couldn't figure out how to explain how her brain processed.

"Taklishim, no rest for you. Come over here," Ronnie called out. "After his sneak-attack on Airiella, I'm not truly worried about his fighting skills, so I'll use him to demonstrate." Taklishim walked up, and Onida fought back the urge to grin.

"Spar with me so Onida can watch the movements," Ronnie commanded the warrior. Onida saw just how much this was second nature to Ronnie and was impressed.

"Are you seriously going to fight me or just block my shots?" Taklishim put his gloves back on.

"Actual sparring, but I won't use force on my hits or kicks. I'm not trying to hurt you," Ronnie said calmly and confidently.

"I think it's funny you believe you can." Taklishim started trash-talking, and Onida did laugh.

"I just saw you flat on your back from Airiella, who was trained by him, and you honestly think he can't beat you?" Onida was bent over; she was laughing so hard. He glared at her. Onida stepped out of the way and stood with a proper viewing angle. "Please, by all means, Tak, show us your best. This demonstration is, after all, a learning opportunity for me."

Ronnie moved with precision and speed, landing each blow and kick he presented and dancing out of the way of the returned hits, cleanly evading Taklishim every time. Onida did want to learn what she could, but she also couldn't hide her glee at the warrior's loss.

Her brain was cataloging the way his body moved when he went to strikeout. He wasn't predictable; it wasn't until he was into the movement that she was able to see what was coming. It wouldn't leave her a lot of time to react, and she'd need to watch closely.

The longer the match went on, the easier it became for her to see the openings he was talking about in his form, and she began to formulate counterattacks. She was also able to see the many opportunities that Taklishim gave him, his overconfidence in his skills his downfall. She now understood what Ronnie was talking about by only being on the defensive, Tak didn't have much of an opportunity to strike back, and when he did, he timed it poorly.

"Okay, I got it now. Taklishim, you should go pick up your wounded pride and train with Airiella, she might be able to teach you a thing or two." Onida laughed at his expression.

"Ronnie, you are amazing," Taklishim admitted.

"Go away, it's my turn." Onida pushed him away. She turned back. "I saw what you were talking about, but I don't know that I will be fast enough to act on it."

"That's why we start slow." Ronnie danced around again, and Onida imitated his footwork at a slower pace until it started to feel more natural. "Good, now let's add upper body to that." He began twisting his body and throwing punches in the air.

Onida watched for a few seconds noting the twisting and punching and shifting weight of his feet and started to mimic his movements. He turned to her and began to throw punches at her, which threw her off at first until she realized he wasn't in reaching distance.

She watched Ronnie's movements for the clues that told her what was coming, and she was able to dodge almost all of the hits. He went through the same routine until she spotted the openings and hit back. She wasn't sure how many would have landed, but she felt more comfortable striking out than she did before.

"You learn fast and have natural grace. Fighting will be easy for you if you practice," Ronnie said, stopping and giving her a glove bump. He wasn't even winded and had hardly broken a sweat while she felt drenched. It wasn't easy; she didn't know what made him think it was.

"I'm going to switch over to Tama now, then Degataga. Either you can practice against someone and keep it going, or rest. I know you aren't used to this, and I don't want you unable to move." Ronnie handed her a bottle of water. "Drink up."

Onida opted to rest as Jax called out to switch partners again, Smitty came and sat next to her. "Ronnie wear you out?"

"Certainly did. Ronnie's quite impressive. I guess I always just took him for one of those over-muscled types that are all talk. He's truly not. I'm happy to say that, too."

"It's a mistake a lot of people make with him because he's such a jokester. There's no one I'd rather have at my back. Aside from Airiella."

"She's a whole different ballgame. I have to say; I loved seeing Taklishim taken down by both of them. When he's using his abilities, he's as good as Ronnie is. Don't tell him I said that."

Smitty laughed a deep rich laugh. "Your secret is safe with me. Finish drinking that, and let's do one round to see if you can use what you learned against someone that isn't a genius at fighting."

Onida downed the last of her water and slid the glove back on. "Okay. How much longer are we doing this?"

"He'll get through Degataga next, and then we will switch to drills with weapons against the dummies we've built. He wants to make sure that weapons are comfortable in everyone's hands. While we know that you guys won't be using them, he'll have you do it because it just enhances your skills," Smitty explained and started dancing around. His footwork was natural, but nothing like Ronnie's was.

Onida was able to spot his patterns and tells a lot quicker than she had with Ronnie and was happy that she finally landed a few hits against him. He got in quite a few more, but much like Ronnie, he didn't put any force into it when they got within touching range.

"Nice work. There are several times you would have gotten me off balance there, which is the goal. If you have to fight in your human form, I think you'll be okay. By the way, your sister is as natural at this as you are," Smitty complimented her.

"Feline grace. She's a stealthy cat. That doesn't surprise me."

"Ronnie is moving on to Degataga now. Rest this round, drink more water, and then on to weapons. Probably only an hour, then you all can break off and work on Airiella." Smitty drank down a bottle of his own.

"The endurance you all have is incredible," Onida remarked.

"This kind of training we are used to, at first, it was awful. To get to where we all are now, took years of hard work. Ronnie still exhausts us all the time, but with everything that we've dealt with, it's come in handy. He pushes Jax and Airiella the hardest. Honestly, Airiella is the only one he will truly throw punches at."

"Okay, that surprises me. Ronnie didn't throw any at me, and Jax said he doesn't with him either. So he doesn't with you and Aedan either?"

"No. After all the years that Ronnie watched his mother get abused, and then he, himself, got abused, it has made him not want to hit others. He does with her because she demanded it. He doesn't hit full force as he does in actual competitions, but he will hit. She argued for at least a month with him, daily, until he relented, then he cried when she got bruises."

"I can understand that. It's hard to be the reason someone you love gets hurts." Onida watched them all move in the violent dance.

"It works for her. She drastically improved once Ronnie started doing it, and she can even land hits against him now. With the rest of us, she can easily take us down. It's a little harder with Jax because Ronnie trained him so hard when he had that dark energy in him. Jax's skills are pretty high, as well. I'm not acting arrogantly by saying this, but we all are good at hand to hand combat, and now, even with weapons."

"That's not arrogant at all. I think it's great that you know your strengths and weaknesses. I believe this is beneficial to all of us, especially me, as I learned more about what to expect when I see certain body movements. Physically, I feel like I just ran two marathons, and Tak is going to have to heal me before I do anything else."

"Did we hurt you?" Smitty was immediately concerned.

"No, not how you are thinking. It's more muscle strain and stiffness than anything."

"They are changing again. Ronnie will be with Degataga, and Jax will be with Airiella. Those two are something to see." Smitty was smiling.

"Why is that?" Onida was curious to learn his answer.

"With them in each other's heads and being as close as they are, it's easy to predict the other's moves. So they block each other out. The problem that presents then is they are so attuned to each other's moves; they stand still. They don't do the footwork. It's fast and explosive moves, so they give no tells. They will circle each other, though."

Onida watched now, her attention diverted away from Degataga to watch Jax and Airiella. Judging by the sound of the blows, they weren't holding back either. "He's hitting her!" Onida exclaimed.

"Yeah. Airiella demanded that too. Once again, Jax was crying just like Ronnie was when the bruises showed up. She gives as good as she gets. With Degataga not having an animal, you might want to keep practicing with him so that his skills stay sharp. If he gets better, he will be a huge asset in a battle as a fighter and not just a healer."

"He does have battle skills," Onida defended him, "they just aren't physical ones. He can play with energy like Ariella can to a degree."

"That should make mirroring the magic back easier for him if he can do that," Smitty thought out loud. "He can redirect the energy in the magic sent out and reverse its course. Does he even need an incantation to do that?"

"I'm not sure. Are you and Ronnie working with him on that part after this?"

"That's our plan. Jax will probably be with us too. No, wait; if Airiella is outside, he will be where she is. One of us is always with her. Usually, Jax, Ronnie, or myself since we can communicate through our minds."

"How does that help if it's her that's hurt?" Onida was trying to understand the dynamic better.

"She tells us. If Jax is with her and sees something, he tells her. If she deems it necessary, one of us is always around the other, and she is the go-between. If she calls out to go on lockdown, whoever is inside does what needs doing to keep the rest safe."

"I understand. But again, what if Airiella's the one that's hurt?"

"Hasn't happened yet. Not in a way that renders her unable to communicate. In Franklin, we all saw what happened. Same with Northern State. In those situations, we are all together. It's just separate that we divide that way. I'm sure Jax or Ronnie told you guys that she practices on her own, right?" Smitty looked at her directly.

Onida confirmed they knew that. "When that happens, one of you is close by watching her, and the others are inside?"

"Or with the group. We try to keep one of us with Mags and Aedan in that way so that if we are all in our separate places, the line of communication gets through. When something urgent happens, she talks to all three of us at once."

"Has anything happened here?" Onida looked around at the expansive property.

"A few low-level demons got as close as they could to try and spy, but she felt them coming, and so did I."

"Am I going to be an awful parent?" Onida asked

him suddenly, shocking them both.

"Unlikely. You and your sister like to come off as aloof and distant, but we all see through that. If you truly believe you wouldn't be good at it, why do you practice as a doctor and take care of people?" Smitty reasoned.

Onida thought about that. Did she honestly believe in her heart that the babies she carried would suffer with her as a parent? Onida didn't believe it. Why it took Smitty to point out the obvious she didn't know. "Thank you."

"I'm Airiella's voice of reason, not a problem to add you to the mix." Smitty bumped into her shoulder with his. "Speak of the devil; I mean, angel."

Airiella grinned, sitting on Smitty's lap and leaning against him. "You were right the first time. Why were you talking about me?"

Onida didn't want her to know she still had doubts. "We were talking about how good you had gotten at this. Do I need to heal Jax now?"

Smitty hugged her, "Baby girl, I would pay good money to see you take down Taklishim like that again."

"That was pretty awesome, right? That's what he gets for trying to sneak-attack me."

"I have to admit, that was a big highlight for me, as well." Onida recalled seeing him laid flat and laughed again. "Let me scan you, please." Onida held out her hand, and Airiella grabbed hold of it. "Still a little low on energy, but I can feel it flowing from Smitty into you."

"I'm fine. Degataga is doing well out there," Airiella commented casually.

Onida looked over and saw how Ronnie was leading him how Jax had described to her. She fell silent and watched the two work, not realizing she still held Airiella's hand until Jax came up on the other side of Smitty and sat next to them.

When Jax took Airiella's other hand, a vision flashed across her eyes of Jax with his throat torn out, blood pooling underneath him into the dirt he lay on. She snatched her hand back from Airiella, who started trembling, resulting in the wind picking up and a slight tremble in the ground.

"Easy, baby girl, breathe." Smitty rocked her as Onida stared into her pale face. "It's not real."

"Was that one of the visions you've had or a new one?" Onida whispered the horror of it seared in her mind.

"One of the old ones," the visibly shaken woman answered.

"I'm right here, Ells, I'm fine." Jax moved closer to Smitty as tears fell silently down her cheeks.

Onida stood up, her mind shaken at the image she had seen. She searched for Taklishim and found him sitting with Aedan. Waya and Wohali were sparring with each other in front of them as they called out tips; both men red-faced and dripping sweat.

"Take a break, guys," Onida called out to them. Taklishim stood up fast at the expression on her face. "Aedan, can you go sit with Airiella?"

Concern flashed across his face, and he jogged over the yard to crouch in front of her. She looked at Taklishim. "I saw one of her visions, the one about Jax. Tak, his throat was torn out. Not cut, but torn. It was a brief image, but to me, it looked like a bear or wolf."

Taklishim paced, "We can't heal that."

"No, we can't. That means we need to prevent it. If that's what we are facing, the skinwalker is going to imitate my mother or father. For as brief as it was, I can see why it shook her. His throat ripped out to his spine," Onida choked up and shook her head, hoping the vision of the gruesome sight would fade and knowing it wouldn't. "If that's how she saw you and my sister as well, I'm surprised she's sleeping at all."

"How did you see it?" Taklishim rubbed at his face.

"When Jax touched her, I was holding her hand." Onida dropped her voice. "We need to warn my father."

Chapter Twenty-Nine

Ronnie was distracted by something with Airiella, and Onida looked like something had scared her. Their training match came to a screeching halt as they both looked at the women. Onida was deep in conversation with Taklishim, and Aedan, Smitty, and Jax surrounded Airiella.

"Something is going on," Degataga said unnecessarily.

"One of her visions got inadvertently shared with Onida through touch." Ronnie had full-on turned around and faced away from Degataga. "Take a break," he said as he fled to her. Degataga watched as he moved in next to Aedan, and they all had their hands on her.

Degataga moved over to Taklishim, Tama, having joined them. "What happened?"

"I saw the vision of Jax she had. It's bad, Dega. If we had been hoping to be able to heal him or save him, we can't. His throat got torn out," Onida spilled, her hands shaking.

"Torn out?" Degataga grabbed her hands and held them between his.

"She thinks a bear or wolf based on what she saw," Taklishim said in a low tone.

"My mother or father," Tama added, understanding what Onida was referring to, instantly. "Well, not them, but the skinwalker acting like them."

"If it can possess them, it could very well be them," Taklishim warned, his voice strained. "We need to plan for this."

The horror of the situation dawned on Degataga. They might have to fight against Onida's parents. He saw that possibility snake across the twins' faces, and the fear took root that they might have to kill a parent or both of them. Onida's hands turned icy on his own.

"Oni, what are the chances if she touches Tak or Tama with you holding her other hand, that you would see the other visions?" Degataga asked quietly.

"I don't know. Mentally, I think it's going to knock Airiella flat. It has the power to knock me flat mentally too. Seeing Jax like that was bad enough. Why do you want me to see them?"

"If the wounds are different, it would be a tell," Degataga explained.

"You seriously want me to do this?" She looked at them all. "I think you will be able to see what she sees too if we are all touching. Do you want that memory in your head?"

Tama rubbed her belly, stepping closer to Taklishim. "Tak, I don't think I could kill one of my parents, even knowing they were possessed."

"We have to find a way to stop that then," he said

gently to her. "Are you willing to see your death? Is that something you can tolerate?"

"If I need to," she said as Onida wrapped her arms around her sister.

"Then let's do this while they are all still around her to give her comfort. It's not fair to her for us to voluntarily make her do something that has caused so much distress. You both saw the state she was in; you are going to ask her to go there again?" Onida warned, her protective instinct on high.

"I'll do it, Onida." Airiella's weak voice came from behind her. "If it means we can figure out a way to stop these from happening, I'll do it. It never crossed my mind that it could be your parents that you would have to kill, and I'll do anything to keep that from happening."

Degataga looked with admiration in his eyes at the brave angel standing before them. Her connections stood around her like a wall of support. "Are they all going to be touching at the same time?"

Ronnie nodded, "Except Mags. If we all see, we all know."

"Can you direct the memories that way?" Onida turned, Degataga now at her back, supporting her.

"I think I can. It's worth a shot anyway." Airiella's voice was glum and her eyes shiny with fear, but her face was a mask of determination.

"This could be why you were having the visions, to begin with." Degataga softened his tone. "To warn us that the Chief and his wife were in danger."

"I know that now. At least now that Smitty pointed it out after Onida's thoughts leaked all over my head. Let's do it, it's not going to get any easier if we wait longer, and

I'd rather get it out of the way before playing with weapons."

"On the patio please, that way you can lay in a chair, no risk of falling." Jax led her to the patio and flattened out a chaise lounge, him and Ronnie immediately sitting on either end of it. Airiella climbed on between them and lay with her head in Jax's lap, his fingers in her hair on her scalp, her feet in Ronnie's lap where he pulled off her shoes and socks and started rubbing her feet.

Aedan and Smitty pulled up chairs next to her legs and put their hands on her bare skin. "Please only one of you at a time. I'd rather not have Tama see Taklishim's dead body, and vice versa. The emotions from that will overwhelm me."

"So, how do you want to do it then?" Onida asked, picking up one of Airiella's hands.

"I need the doctor Onida to come out, not the emotional one." Airiella turned her head to look at Onida. "Do you know what I'm saying?"

"I understand. Can you do Jax first again, I let go too fast first time to get a good look." Onida made her request and tried to distance herself as much as possible. "Dega, hold her arm here so you can be my backup eyes."

"Raven, can we both join in to see Jax?" Tama pulled up a chair and sat down as Taklishim asked for permission. She just nodded numbly, tears already slipping out of her eyes as she held out her hand.

Degataga braced himself as Waya and Wohali sat down quietly, taking it all in. There was nothing he could have done to prepare for the picture that appeared in his mind. He heard Tama gasp and Taklishim swear at the same time. He fought his own feelings of fear back and tried to catalog the injuries.

It was more than just the torn-out throat. There were defensive marks on the limp arms where it looked like Jax had tried to fend off the attack. He took note of it all, and the longer the picture stayed there, the more it seared into his memory.

"Enough, angel, that's long enough," he heard Ronnie tell her, and thankfully the image faded.

Degataga opened his eyes to see the petrified ones of the rest of the group. Ronnie was a mess and trying to hold it together. Jax was the only one not shocked as he'd seen it before. Tama was shaking, and Taklishim was still, the warrior side of him trying to take control as his essence flickered. Aedan and Smitty both had horror written on their faces.

"I'll squeeze your hand Airiella; when you feel that, let go of the image, okay?" Onida stroked her face softly, waiting for the confirmation. Once she had it, she told her, "Tama next."

Tama looked like she didn't want to pick Airiella's hand back up. The moment she did, Degataga was thrust right into another image, of Tama this time. Her belly shredded, her body naked, deep teeth marks on her shoulder and right leg, and again, the throat ripped open, claw marks along the side of her head where her scalp had ripped away from the skull. She lay half on cement and half on grass, blood staining the ground.

It could have easily been Onida laying there, and Degataga fought for control of his emotions and had to let go of Airiella's arm. He opened his eyes to see Tama drop her hand and run to the patio's edge and throw up. She pushed Taklishim away and heard her tell him to get it over with; that she was okay.

He reluctantly put his hand back on Airiella's arm. He didn't want to see his best friend dead. True to his warrior self, Tak walked up, ready to face death, and boldly took her hand. Once again, Degataga became transported to another scene of slaughter.

Taklishim was naked as well, with a spear through his chest, pinning him to a tree. Claw marks down his torso; the skin flayed open. Several puncture wounds marred his arms and legs, his long gray hair matted with blood, and his throat ripped open.

Degataga tried to look away from the body to see if he could spot the location of the tree. To him, it appeared to be in a yard, one that was manicured to some degree, the lower part of his legs was on grass, and he spotted a few flowers.

He couldn't take anymore, and he let go. Feeling just as sick as Tama, he stepped back and looked at the stoic warrior who refused to let go. The guys around Airiella all looked as horrified and sick as Degataga felt. Onida had let go of Airiella's hand, and he moved back to her, resting his hand on her shoulder.

Taklishim still held her hand as she openly sobbed into Jax's leg. "Raven, we are going to change this. It's not going to happen." His voice was the gentlest he had ever heard the warrior use with her. "Open those angel eyes and look at me, please," Taklishim asked her.

Degataga noticed not one of the guys had moved their hands away from her, and he hoped that she was drawing comfort from them. He couldn't imagine having those visions night after night, even during the day. Airiella finally turned her head and looked at Taklishim with swollen eyes.

"There she is." He put her hand against his face. "It's because of you that we will beat this and keep that from happening. I need you to trust me on this, sweetheart."

Airiella sprung from the chair and wrapped her arms around Taklishim. Degataga had to turn away, or he would lose whatever thin thread of control he had over his emotions. The heartbreaking sobs that tore through her were too much.

Onida stood up and turned into Degataga, burying her face in his chest as she shook with her own silent tears. He held her tight and pressed kisses to her temple. If what he had seen was a warning of what was to come, they were dealing with more than one skinwalker.

From the wounds he saw, he had surmised that Onida was right. They were looking at a wolf and a bear. The coincidence was too large for it to be anyone other than her parents. It was a very cold and calculating move designed to destroy those not killed, rendering them useless after seeing their loved ones murdered and having to kill her parents. Or even worse, him having to do it and Onida turning away from him for having done it for her.

"Oni, love. Call your dad, have them both come here first thing in the morning. Insist on it," Degataga whispered in her ear. He waited for her to pull away and gather herself enough to make the call.

Airiella was still clutching Taklishim, so Degataga pulled Jax aside. "I asked Onida to call her folks and have them come here first thing in the morning. If they stay here with Smitty and Aedan, Airiella will know they are safe through the connection, right?"

"Yeah, Smitty will be able to watch them both. What are you thinking?" Jax positioned himself so he could watch Airiella.

"If they are here, whatever we face won't be them. Both sisters will know it and will be able to fight, knowing they aren't fighting their parents. It also gives those here another advantage having two animals on-site that are skilled in fighting. Even if they appear as her parents, Airiella can confirm that both are here and unharmed," Degataga thought out loud.

Degataga saw Onida nod her confirmation at him, telling him her father agreed, and she walked over to Tama. Jax interrupted his train of thought. "Why take out Tama and Taklishim though?"

"My best guess would be they consider them to be the biggest threats and Oni and me as the weaker links. With you, because you are her fiancée and ultimately because they are trying to hurt her. Isn't that the demon's endgame? She's already told us all that without you, we don't have her."

"This is so many levels of fucked up." Jax ran his hands nervously through his hair. "Taklishim has *never* used the word sweetheart with her before, or a tone that soft. I've never seen Tama lose it like that either. Losing any of you would shake her enough to cause damage."

Degataga saw Taklishim hand Airiella off to Ronnie and the other two guys, and they all crowded around her while Taklishim went and pulled Tama to him, the two soul mates clinging to each other. "I'll say this; they aren't very bright if they assume that Oni and I are the weak links. Those two may have better fighting skills than us, but she's a damn genius."

"Go, Dega. Be with Onida for a bit before we resume. I need to be with Ells right now. She needs to get this out." Jax pushed him in Onida's direction. "And Onida needs you."

Chapter Thirty

Degataga settled in with Aedan, Smitty, and Ronnie to start researching mirroring spells. Aedan called Father Roarke and filled them in while Ronnie and Smitty went to work on their laptops, and Degataga began to go through the books he had brought with him. Waya and Wohali helping and marking pages they thought looked promising.

Onida stood outside on the beach with Tama and Taklishim in a triangle formation with Airiella in the middle. Their emotional morning had taken a toll on them all, but it had also given them a fit of driving anger to succeed. Jax sat back at a distance between them and the house.

"Raven, do you still trust me?" Taklishim called out.

Onida watched her, a wary look crossing her face as she nodded. She knew what was coming, and she also knew without hesitation that Airiella was not going to like it. She hadn't let Jax in on it knowing that Airiella would be able to see and feel his fears, as she must be doing now based on her tentative looks towards Jax.

"You know I do." Her voice was unwavering.

"Then you are going to fight my warrior," Taklishim calmly announced.

Onida prepared for the ground to move, or the air to gust. She didn't prepare for the swell of a wave crashing to the beach right behind her. "No, I am not. Taklishim that isn't safe. How many times do I need to prove to you I can take you down?"

"It's not about that, Airiella," Tama responded. "It's so we can see what you can do when not holding back in fear of hurting us."

"Damn it! Onida and Taklishim both know what I can do! They saw it when I leveled the forest!" she screamed at them.

Onida didn't know what made her turn around, but as she did, she caught the entire ocean in front of her swelling like the fabled rogue waves that have wiped out cruise ships. She almost shifted on the spot but turned her back to the sight that made her blood run cold and tried to reach Airiella.

"Let the water be, Airiella. No one will be hurt. Tak, she has power over the ocean; this might not be such a good idea. She's not wrong, and we do have a good idea of what she is capable of doing. Making tsunami sirens go off wouldn't help us," Onida tried, fighting the panic that was trying to take hold of her. Drowning had always been a fear of hers. She didn't want Taklishim to follow through on his plan now.

"I wouldn't let anyone drown." Airiella sighed in frustration. "I honestly didn't know that I was doing that."

"Is your control with the water as good as it is with earth and air?" Taklishim stepped closer to Airiella.

"Almost. Sometimes I lose sight of it and get lost in

the sensation that comes over me with it. I can get it to respond to my call quickly, but sometimes the strength of what I ask it to do gets out of hand."

Onida saw the shadows start to come out of him and tried to calm her breathing down. When backed against a wall, Airiella accomplished amazing things, but threatening Jax could have disastrous consequences. Onida also realized that Airiella has never seen this part of Taklishim. Each of the times it had come out around her, she'd been out cold.

Much like what happened in Franklin, things happened simultaneously. A wave of panic that tore from Airiella slammed into them, and an instant later, she turned electric blue, and her wings flew out of her as she was in motion faster than Onida had ever seen her. Before Taklishim's shadow could get halfway across the beach, Airiella was in front of it.

A gust of wind ripped through, and the earth trembled, while a massive wave grew out of the corner of Onida's eye. Taklishim froze in place, Tama was lifted straight into the air, and rings of fire appeared around Onida and Jax. Onida found she couldn't move and gaped in astonishment as the ground pulled Taklishim's feet into it at the same moment his shadow slammed into Airiella.

Hold your breath; she heard in her head, the same instant she heard cries of alarm coming from the house. The shadow slammed and pinned Airiella to the ground as a huge wave slammed into the fire around Onida, the roar deafening, and she saw Taklishim get swallowed up by the water.

The fear of drowning thundered through her, and she shifted, her animal trying to flee the danger. All sound washed from her. All she could hear was the water, the saltwater burning her hawk's eyes as the sky lit up blue, and a blast of energy sent her tumbling around inside her protective ring, causing her to shift back to human.

As the water receded, she first saw Tama still suspended in the air, but now in her cougar form and absolutely panicked. Then, all of Onida's energy got pulled from her. From the way Taklishim went limp and was coughing up water, she knew he had too. Tama's as well, as she shifted back to human. Airiella was still flat on the ground.

In the span of the longest thirty seconds of Onida's life, Airiella had rendered them all useless while Taklishim's shadows tore through the angel unable to get at Jax. The others were all at the beach entrance, behind a wall of blue fire that kept them safe.

Onida saw Airiella sit up, her eyes glowing in a way she hadn't seen before, and she felt her energy flowing back into her. Onida got unsteadily to her feet and waited to be released. Tama was lowered to the ground and rushed over to check on Taklishim.

Airiella did something, and a gust of warm wind circled them all, drying them off. As Jax reached Airiella, the ring of fire around Onida and the wall holding the guys back disappeared. She feared they had pushed her too far.

Onida went to take a step forward and found herself too afraid to move closer to check on Airiella. *Please don't hate us,* Onida pleaded. Her heart began feeling cold when she got no response.

Degataga had gotten to Airiella and was checking her over, having seen the shadow hit her. Taklishim's shadows had a way of tearing through souls that made it feel like you were breaking apart from the inside out. When confronted with evil, those shadows could rip parts of the soul out of the body. He wouldn't have sent that at Airiella, but he didn't know what those shadows would do when faced with a power like hers.

Degataga stood and went over to Taklishim, where Tama had her hands on him, and Onida finally felt herself propelled forward to make sure he was okay. "He's fine," Tama told her, her voice shaking. "She wouldn't hurt him. I told Dega to let him cough the water up, on his own; he deserves it after that. I knew that would backfire."

Onida had too. She'd have reacted no differently if she had sensed danger coming at Degataga. That had been Tama's argument from the beginning. Taklishim insisted that if they wanted to see what kind of control she had, they would have to do something extreme.

"What brought all you out here?" she asked Degataga, who was sitting back on his heels looking shell shocked.

"The panic that washed through her hit those guys like a runaway train," Degataga said softly. "They moved as one, and fast. What the hell were you thinking, Taklishim? You sent a shadow at her?"

"No. I sent it at Jax," Taklishim admitted. "Is she okay?"

"Physically, as far as I could tell. Airiella only let me touch her for a few seconds, though."

Onida gasped as Taklishim rose in the air, her control so precise that Onida hadn't even felt the air stir around her. To his credit, Tak didn't fight her and looked sorry for what he had done.

"Raven, I'm sorry," he rasped out like he had

no oxygen.

"That was fucking stupid, man," Ronnie growled out. Tama nodded in agreement.

Airiella released Taklishim with no warning causing him to thud down onto the sand. Degataga pulled off his shirt and handed it to Onida, while Smitty came over with his for Tama. "What would that thing have done to Jax?" he asked Taklishim softly so the others couldn't hear.

"Knocked him over," Taklishim told him. "Nothing more. I gave it clear intentions."

"It did more than that to her," Smitty told him. "She said it acted like that darkness that was in Jax but without the evil intent. It fought her."

"Is she hurt?" Onida saw the shine in Taklishim's eyes and understood that the warrior was deeply unsettled by it all.

"It hurt her mentally. Every one of us felt it. Logically, I get why you did it, but don't do it again," Smitty warned and stood, his posture slightly aggressive. "She absorbed that shit."

Onida broke down in tears and allowed Degataga to gather her up to him and cradle her. This test had been a spectacular failure, and she could have gotten seriously hurt. The shame she felt swamped her.

Stop it. I know none of you meant to hurt me, take your sister, and get dressed. I can't take any more emotions right now.

Onida pushed away from Degataga and grabbed Tama's hand. "Come on, let's go get dressed."

Chapter Thirty-One

Degataga looked at Onida in confusion as she walked away; he understood a moment later when he saw Airiella's face. She had told her to go, tThe others too. All that remained on the beach was Ronnie, who hadn't let her go, Jax, himself, and Taklishim.

Her eyes were a strange color, reminiscent of when she killed Spearfinger, and he felt a tremor of fear run through him. They needed her on their side, and Taklishim may have gone too far with this. To his complete surprise, Ronnie put her down, and both Jax and he left.

"That can't be good," Taklishim muttered, his voice still hoarse from coughing up all the water that had filled his lungs.

"She's not unreasonable, explain your intentions, Tak," Degataga advised him.

"Why hasn't she moved?" Taklishim grew worried.

Degataga stood and offered his hand to Taklishim to help him up. "Let's go find out," he answered as Taklishim stood somewhat shakily.

"Raven, can we join you?" Tak asked meekly.

She simply nodded, still not speaking. "Will you let

me scan you now?"

"Not yet. I'm vibrating with high voltage and connected to a power that's flowing through me, and I don't know if it will seep into you or not," Airiella said quietly. Degataga noted her eyes still had that glow to them. "It doesn't feel safe."

"Is this like what happened after Spearfinger? Is that why you sent Ronnie and Jax away?" He sat down and crossed his legs in front of him.

"Kind of, I sent them away because I can't take any more of these emotions battering at me. Lifting the tree and my fear for Onida made the energy dissipate last time. Right now, I think anger is fueling it."

"Raven, I'm very sorry."

"What the fuck was that Tak?" Her voice had an eerily calm quality that put Degataga's nerves on edge as she switched her focus to Taklishim.

"I call them shadows. They are like lost spirits that fall into a gray area looking for something to do. I call them neutral as they aren't bad or good; they just are. They all have a certain quality that allows me to use them. Some can rip parts of souls right out of people, and some can shred parts of souls and others I just use to hold people in place until I can get to them. They act on my intent and do precisely what I ask them to. Never have they fought before or not listened to me."

"I'm not dumb, and I know you wouldn't have sent something to hurt Jax. I don't believe you intended to hurt me either. I'm aware you wanted to see my reaction times, and how much I was capable of pulling off at the same time. I've already told you that what you saw with Spearfinger should have given you a good idea of what I can do. You asked me to trust you, and I did. But Tak, that trust needs to go both ways," she said flatly. Degataga still felt uncomfortable with her tone, it was carefully even and low-pitched conveying a calm that wasn't there. It was like the eye of a hurricane.

"It was a calculated risk, and I'm willing to pay the price for it." The warrior infused strength into his words. "I should have trusted your word more; I'll give you that. There's no one to blame for that but me. It's my fear of the skinwalkers that brought me to that decision. It's my fear for your safety that I needed to test you. I may be a hardened warrior, but I have a soft spot for you that leads me to make irrational decisions. Regardless of how many times you have proven yourself."

Degataga watched silently, as Taklishim stripped away the layers he kept himself behind and showed Airiella the emotions that boiled under the surface. It didn't faze her. "Why do you continue to think that I can't see what you try to hide? Empath, remember? All that shit is white noise. It may work with others, but it doesn't work with me. I can see right through all of you."

Degataga cleared his throat, "I should leave you two to talk this out." He went to stand up and found himself forcibly pushed back down with a feeling of heavy gravity.

"Sit still. You need to stay because I don't think I'm okay enough to get back to the house by myself, and he isn't in any shape to help me," she told him simply.

Surprised by her candor, he stayed put, and the gravitational pull he had been feeling eased up. The glow was still in her eyes, so he didn't ask to scan her again. "What was that flash of blue light that forced Oni and Tama to shift?" Degataga asked her.

"My energy as I absorbed whatever that shadow was. It wasn't neutral; I can tell you that. It fought me pretty good. Whatever intention you gave it, it wasn't what you had intended. It would have hurt Jax, and that is what made me react. If it had been neutral, I wouldn't have sensed the danger the moment it came to the surface."

"That's not possible," Taklishim murmured, his face forlorn.

"Where do you pull them from, Tak?" Degataga asked him gently.

"The spirit world. I can use them here or there."

"Is it possible they became tainted by something?" Degataga didn't know a whole lot about his warrior skills, just that he was deadly.

"Anything is possible now," Airiella broke in. "I'd suggest next time you decide to test me, maybe you don't go after the person I can't live without."

"If I'd had any idea that it was even remotely dark, I never would have done it, Airiella." Takishim's eyes shone again. "I shouldn't even be able to pull anything dark. The dark reacts with me; it's why I don't like Stolas coming around. I know he means none of us harm, but my soul reacts."

Degataga was picking up an odd vibe from Airiella, and he wasn't sure what was happening, but she was gritting her teeth, and her fists clenched. The air around her felt vibrating, and before he could ask, another energy blast tore through her, knocking both Taklishim and him flat to the ground, the air pushed out of his lungs.

Slowly Degataga pushed himself back up and saw the glow had faded from her eyes. She was shaking violently, tears falling down her cheeks. The thud of heavy footfalls sounded, and Degataga looked back as Jax ran into view.

"I've got you, baby," he said softly, dropping to the ground behind her. "I'm okay; they are all okay." He pulled her into him.

Degataga leaned forward and did another scan of Taklishim. "Airiella, what was that?"

"It was that power leaving her," Jax told him as she cried. "It took down her walls, and I felt it. It wasn't painless."

"What kind of power is it?" Degataga asked as Taklishim came to and struggled to get back up. He patiently waited while she tried to calm herself down, Jax slowly rocking back and forth as he held her.

"I don't know," she finally said. "It feels like when my body tried to purify that energy I pulled from Jax. It's not dark. It's more like every emotion shoved into one tiny grain of sand that can't possibly contain it all, and it bursts."

"It's every emotion?" Degataga struggled to understand.

"It would be hard for someone, not an empath, to get what she means. Imagine how you felt when you proposed to Onida," Jax started, "then combine it with how you felt seeing her trapped under the tree, then how you felt seeing she was okay. That's not all emotions, but it can kind of give you an idea of the power of what she's trying to say. Now imagine trying to describe all those emotions with only one word."

"Impossible," Taklishim said numbly. "That's the word I would use. You can't fit all that into one thing. The pressure inside you just builds until it explodes out of you, all the little pieces trying to grab on to keep hold of what they can't hold on to so you feel like you are ripping apart."

Stunned, Degataga stared at Taklishim, the picture he painted making sense of what just bowled him over. "Airiella, is that right?" Degataga could only whisper. "It's everything. Every emotion that battered at you today. That's why you sent them all away."

Jax nodded for her, his eyes clouded as he kissed her temple. He slowly let Airiella go, "Are you sure?" he asked, and she just nodded. She weakly crawled over to Taklishim and sat in front of him.

Knowing how strong of an empath she was, Degataga inwardly cringed at what she must have been feeling based off how he felt when that energy released through him. She continuously surprised him, and with as open as she'd been with them about everything, he realized she'd sheltered them from the truth Airiella didn't want to burden them with; she bore it instead.

Taklishim, it seemed, understood that. At least now. The remorse on his face was genuine as they stared at each other. Airiella was still shaking, Degataga could only guess at the silent communication happening between the two of them.

Taklishim held his arms out in an invitation, and she leaned into him, the silent and heartfelt apology accepted. Jax breathed a sigh of relief. "Siren, please let Degataga scan you."

She pulled back from Taklishim and in a weary voice, "Do you understand my capabilities now?"

Degataga huffed out a silent laugh and waited until she was ready before reaching for her hand.

"Better than you think, Raven." Taklishim shifted

and tried to stand again but couldn't.

Degataga didn't see anything wrong, but Jax pointed to her chest when her eyes were closed, mouthing that she had pain. Degataga scanned again, slower this time, and found a tiny fracture in one of her ribs. His palms heated as he healed it. She needed energy too.

Jax helped her stand and turned her towards him, lifting her shirt and muttering. "Have any more of that stuff that helps with bruising?" he asked Degataga.

"May I?" Degataga asked quietly. Jax turned her around exposing the colossal bruise spreading across her sternum. It traveled down her torso and up over the top of her bra along her chest bone. "Is this from the shadow?"

She pulled her shirt down and nodded slightly, not wanting Taklishim to see. "I'm fine."

Degataga didn't reply to that and helped Taklishim up, sliding under his arm to help support his weight for the walk back to the house. Airiella climbed on Jax's back, and they slowly made their way back.

"How bad is the bruise?" Taklishim asked in a low tone; his guilt was evident. "It shouldn't have been able to do that."

"It's ugly. I'll have Oni ask her dad to bring more of it down with him; there's a container of it on her nightstand." Degataga tried to keep his tone light, but Tak's admission that it shouldn't have been able to do that bothered him. He might have to call for Stolas again.

Chapter Thirty-Two

Onida hung up the phone and looked at her sister. "They made the switch. Let's just hope it worked."

"Who did they use?" Tama asked, her voice desolate.

"Another bear and wolf, he said. They will go outside in animal form and spend a few moments out there and then go back in. He did confirm someone was watching the house, but it's three skinwalkers, not two." Onida understood Airiella's obsession with wearing Ronnie and Jax's shirts. It was comforting. She had pulled her face up under the collar and breathed Degataga's scent in.

"Are we going to survive this, Oni?" Tama rested her head on Onida's lap.

"I believe we will. That little unintentional display was just as impressive as what Airiella showed with Spearfinger."

"Why would she lift me above it and leave you to get soaked? Especially now that she knows you are pregnant?" Tama turned to look up at her sister.

"She protected us both. Airiella lifted you because there is a greater risk of something happening to you at this stage. For me, that ring around me was powerful, even if it wasn't, the babies in me aren't at risk as yours are, my body insulates and protects them at this stage. She protected everyone behind her too."

"Okay, but if she knew Taklishim wouldn't hurt her or Jax, why did she lock him down like that? Not that he didn't deserve it, but he took the brunt of that," Tama asked, slightly confused.

"I don't know. I can speculate, but it's only that. We'll have to wait until the others come back inside to find out answers. Something about that whole situation felt off." Onida didn't want to play a guessing game. "My gut is telling me there had to have been danger there for her to react as she did."

"I think so too." Tama's tone was low. "If she was just angry, I think she would have just zapped him."

"You aren't worried she will hurt Tak, are you? She knows the importance of mate bonds and how they affect each other."

"No, but that was the exact reason I told Tak not to do this. Not with Jax. He could have used Aedan. If someone had done that to me, he would have reacted the same way." Tama turned back on her side. "Oni, my stomach feels weird."

Absently, Onida put her hands on Tama and scanned her. "I think it's emotional fallout, Tama. Babies are fine."

"I think I recognized the spot I die in," she told Onida in a hushed voice. "Outside the recreation center."

Onida nodded; she had thought the same thing after she got over the horror of it. Jax's had looked like the backyard of her father's house, and Taklishim's had looked

---

like the woods behind her house. Three deaths, three locations, three different skinwalkers. They were going to try to separate them.

She grabbed her phone that was sitting next to her on the bed and called her dad. "Can you activate your phone tree and tell people to stay inside tomorrow, no one at the recreation center at all, or near your house, or mine?"

"I told them all to stay inside, but I will call again and say the center is closed tomorrow due to a dangerous situation. Anything else?"

"Tell him that if people see us, to stay away, we are actively hunting the danger," Tama said.

"I heard her. I'll take care of it. We are leaving here before the sun rises, we will be in someone else's car," Chief Tyee said.

"Did you tell the people posing as you and mom that they are in danger?" Onida asked as an afterthought.

"I did. Neither will leave the property."

"Just hurry up and get here so we can see with our own eyes that you are you and are safe," Onida demanded.

"We can come now if that will make you feel better," her father suggested.

"It'd make me feel better," Tama said loud enough for her dad to hear.

"Then we will leave now, let our kind hosts know please."

Onida hung up the phone. *My parents are on their way now; I hope that is okay.*

It's fine. I told Jax. We'll have Smitty get his room ready, Airiella replied.

There are three of them. Three skinwalkers.

Are you sure? Airiella asked.

Yes. Tama and I recognize the locations, and my father said someone was watching them.

Onida didn't hear anything back and figured she was telling the others. She lay back on the bed, Airiella's bed, since that's where she had stayed the night before. Tama curled up in front of her, "What do we do, Oni?"

"We fight, we win, we live. There're no other options here. There isn't one person that it would be acceptable for us to lose. Don't even entertain the thought."

"She's going to always be in danger, isn't she?" Tama's eyes searched her sister's face for the answer.

"Most likely. For me, it means I always will be too, since I choose to fight with Airiella."

"Tak too. Though he needs to start trusting her more, her life is hard enough as it is. Is she angry with us?" Tama asked.

"I don't think so. I think there's more to the story than we know. We'll get told everything when Tak and Dega are back. How did you feel when the energy got pulled from you?" Onida put her hand on her sisters' belly. She wanted to feel the pulse of life.

"It was weird. I didn't know what was happening at first; my emotions just went blank, my energy sagged, and I shifted back to human. Then my energy came back, and my emotions returned as relieved."

"Relieved?" Onida wasn't sure if that was the feeling that came back to her.

"Yes. Relief that it was over and we all survived."

The bedroom door opened, and Degataga came in with a barely walking Taklishim. Tama and Onida both sprang up as Degataga put him down on the bed. "What's wrong with him?" Onida asked carefully.

"No energy, a little bruised from the tumbles. It probably feels like his soul has been sucker-punched repeatedly," Degataga answered. "Do you have any of that bruise mix I had been using on you?"

"I do. I grabbed it as an afterthought." Onida ran to her purse and dug through it until she found it and held it out to Degataga.

"No, can you use it on Airiella?" he told her quietly.

"She's bruised? From what?" Onida hadn't seen anything impact her.

"The shadow," Taklishim answered. "It wasn't neutral. She said it was tainted with dark, that's why she reacted so strongly."

"The shadow physically hit her?" Onida was shocked. "That's never happened before."

"Tak, how was it dark? You can't pull dark." Tama had her hands on him and was scanning him for injuries.

"I don't know. But it hurt Airiella. I hurt her." Taklishim's eyes glistened, and his throat thickened up.

Airiella, come here please, I'm in your room.

A few minutes later, Jax walked in with Airiella on his back, her body limp, face pale, and occasional tremors running through her. "Put her on the bed next to Tak, please, so I can check her."

"Dega scanned me already," she argued, her voice small-sounding.

"I don't care, I want to do it myself." Onida stood firm until Jax gently set her down.

"It's her chest," Jax said quietly so only Onida could hear him.

Onida nodded, so he knew she heard him and

gently lifted Airiella's shirt, barely holding back the gasp that came up. Bellybutton, to her neck, was a livid bruise. "This is from the shadow hitting you?"

Airiella's eyes were closed, but she answered. "That's the only impact I got. It fought me, tried to get inside me like Jax's dark energy used to do."

"So, instead of fighting it, you absorbed it?" Onida was trying to figure out how this could happen. Tak's shadows weren't corporeal. She unscrewed the lid from the container and started spreading the mixture over her skin and rubbing it in lightly.

I'm going to have to reach under your bra, Onida warned her.

It's fine. Have Jax pull it off if you want. I'm beyond caring right now. Airiella pushed herself up on her elbows, and Jax reached behind her to unhook the bra, moving it out of the way. Tama and Degataga both gasped, seeing the extent of the bruising reaching halfway up each breast.

Taklishim pushed himself up, and his eyes bulged out. "That shouldn't be possible!"

"I've found that everything with her shouldn't be possible, yet it happens anyway," Jax grumbled, his eyes dark with worry.

Onida continued to liberally spread the mix over the bruise and took the time to scan while she was touching Airiella. The obvious was she was energy-deficient again, and she remembered the comment Airiella made earlier about how she couldn't take any more emotions.

"Is it hard on your right now all of our emotions are running on high?" Onida didn't stop rubbing the lotion mix into her.

"It is. It's bleeding energy from me," Airiella admitted quietly. "You all are normally calm and keep stuff contained, but not so much today."

"Will it help if I take Tak into Ronnie's room?" Tama wondered.

"Yes. Put your walls up, Taklishim," Airiella murmured.

"I'll come to check on him in a minute, Tama." Onida looked over at her sister.

"No need, he's okay. Degataga took care of him earlier."

"I'll help you, Tama," Degataga offered, and got Taklishim up off the bed, supporting most of his weight. "He needs to eat, too."

"Food and sleep," Onida repeated. "What happened when you absorbed it?"

"It fought me pretty hard, but I turned my lightning on myself, and that's what that first big blast was."

"You've got to stop being reckless with yourself like that," Onida chided her.

"She's not reckless." Jax jumped in to defend her. "She may step into danger more than we'd like, but she's not reckless with herself."

"I wasn't criticizing her, Jax," Onida corrected him. "I'm worried." Onida gently pulled Airiella's pushed up shirt back down over her chest. "Do you think Stolas would come if you called him?"

"He would. Why do you want me to?"

"To try and understand how something dark got through Taklishim. And how it could happen without him knowing." Onida was thinking out loud.

"If Taklishim reacts to him, is it really such a good

311

idea to call Stolas with Taklishim as weakened as he is right now?" she pointed out.

"Maybe not. I'm not sure how to get the information though." Onida didn't know what else to do. "If he has to use his warrior form to fight the skinwalkers, there's a chance something else dark could come through and go after you guys again."

"Try talking to Winnie," Airiella suggested. "If anything, she can get a message to Stolas to try and find the information out for you."

"I should have thought of that, sorry, Airiella. Same advice to you, eat and sleep. Don't wash this stuff off until tomorrow morning, that bruise is deep. I'll speak to Winnie as well. Do you want your room back?"

"No. I want to sit out on the patio. Don't worry about me." She pushed herself up and slipped the bra off from under her shirt, which Jax threw in the clothes hamper in the bathroom. He handed her one of his sweatshirts that she slipped on and stood up, a little wobbly still. "I have my raven watching for your parents."

"Maybe you should hang out with your connections a little bit." Onida wanted to order her to do it though she knew it wouldn't get her anywhere.

"They are already out there waiting for me." Airiella smiled. "I can't be effective without energy; they will boost me."

Onida watched her walk out of the room, feeling proud of how far she'd come. She was a bit subdued right now, but today had been trying and emotional for all of them. She washed off her hands and sat on the edge of the bed as Degataga came back in.

"I think I need to get in touch with Stolas," Dega

said as he sat next to her.

"I told her the same thing, but she pointed out that since it's hard for Tak to be around the demon that it might not be the best time to do that with him weakened. She suggested I talk to Winnie instead."

"Can you ask Winnie to have Kalisha come through?" Degataga requested.

"You need Kalisha?" Onida found herself surprised by that.

"There's a hoodoo spell that can mirror magic back. If she knows it, she might be able to teach me," Degataga explained. "Ronnie stumbled upon it, the mention of it anyway. Not the specific spell or how to work it. We were about to start looking for it when we went running out there."

"Are they still looking for it?"

Degataga laughed. "Not exactly. Look." He stood and went to the window.

Onida joined him and looked down to see a sizeable fluffy blanket on the ground with Airiella in the middle of it sandwiched between Jax and Ronnie with Smitty at her head, and Aedan and Mags at her feet. Jillian and the babies off to the side. "Well, she needs the recharge."

"She expended a tremendous amount of energy when she absorbed that shadow. The rest left her when her emotions got too much for her to handle." Degataga remembered the second blast that flattened him and Taklishim.

"Is that what that second one was?" Onida remembered feeling it.

"Yeah. That's how Airiella described it. Said it was like trying to contain every emotion in a grain of sand."

"Sounds a bit overwhelming, especially for an empath." She backed away from the window. "Is Taklishim okay?"

"I healed him earlier; right now, it's just mental and low energy. He feels understandably guilty for what went down. Between being worried about him and checking him, Tama kept on him about how stupid it was."

"She hurt Taklishim enough for him to need healing?" Onida was stunned by that.

"No, I think the out of control wave that slammed into him and her dropping him back on the ground beat him up. It's inadvertently because of her, but she did warn him that she sometimes lost control of the water element."

She *had* warned them; this entire thing had been preventable if they had only listened to her. "My parents switched out themselves with another bear and wolf and left in their car. They are on their way down here, should be here shortly."

"I heard. Jillian said the room was ready for them." Degataga pulled her to him. "I'm pretty sure that Airiella could kill anything she encountered."

"Probably. At what cost though?" That was what worried Onida. She pushed away from Degataga. "I'm going to rest lightly and try talking with Winnie."

He kissed her forehead. "I'll go downstairs and wait for your parents."

Chapter Thirty-Three

"Dega, you wanted to see me?" Kalisha appeared before him, startling him so severely he almost dropped his water.

"Kalisha, still as beautiful as ever." Degataga smiled at her. "I need your help with a mirroring spell."

"Can you be more specific than that?"

"Skinwalkers can attack using dark magic. It's how they possess too. If I can mirror back to them what they cast, legend says that it can defeat them," Degataga explained. "We stumbled across a reference that there is a hoodoo spell that mirrors magical intent back on the caster."

"Ah, yes. There is. I don't think you will be able to cast it. I might be able to make you a magical mirror that I can imbue the spell into; by sending your energy and intent into it, it should activate and have your desired result. How soon do you need it?"

"Before we leave for home in the morning," he said apologetically.

Her musical laugh sounded sweet to his ears and made a wave of nostalgia wash through him for his departed friend. "It's always urgent, is it not? I will get it done for you. I'll tell Winnie to have Stolas bring it to you."

"That's fine; I'll warn Tak. We've missed you, Kalisha. It's not the same without you."

"Of course not, I'm the only me. You *are* aware that this is probably unnecessary and that our angel can probably handle this on her own?"

"Yes. Onida is worried about what it will cost her. The last few times have drained her so badly we weren't sure she would recover fully." Degataga remembered the picture of her by the bed with Onida. "It was scary."

"It was noticed on the other side. Both Stolas and Winnie were nervous. With good reason. When something is going on with her, Stolas seems to hover around Winnie. There are dark forces at work to infiltrate every avenue to her they can. When drained like that, they are finding opportunity."

"Is Stolas handling the changes well?" Degataga didn't want to lose him as an ally. He had an incredible knowledge about plants that had saved them numerous times. He also wasn't such a bad guy.

"Winnie said he's been working hard to gather as many of the lighter demons on his side as he can from what she has observed. I heard that he thinks that if there is a balance there, it will help her restore the balance here."

"He's not wrong. Airiella wouldn't want him to put himself at risk. She's fond of him."

"As he is of her, that much is plain to see." Kalisha smiled a brilliant smile. "I must get to work on this as soon as possible if you need this by tomorrow. I might have to learn to be nicer to Stolas; I don't interact much with him."

"Oh, yes, sorry. We will be leaving here in the

morning, headed back to Onida and Tama's homes. We hope to fight them on home turf."

"It's a good idea. Keep the blessed land close by; Winnie also said that whatever you guys did to Airiella not too long ago, not to do it again. A shockwave tore through there."

Degataga stared aghast. "I-It did?" he stuttered.

"Yes. Use caution, my friend." Kalisha popped out, and he heard the charm that someone was at the front gate. He scurried over to the camera screen and saw an unfamiliar car.

"Yes?" he spoke through the speaker.

"It's Chief Tyee," came the disembodied voice.

Degataga opened the gate, and once the car was through, he closed it again, watching the entire time to make sure nothing else came through. He waited for a few seconds more, then headed outside to meet them. Thirty seconds later, Onida came out the front door.

"Airiella told me they were here," Onida responded to his questioning look. "Figured it was better to tell him about the babies and us in person, rather than a slip up from one of the others."

"Will you allow me to ask him for his blessing formally?" Degataga knew she was independent and didn't need her father's blessing to marry him, but it was a sign of respect. One that Degataga had every intention of showing.

"I don't mind. Dad will love it. You know it's not necessary." Onida's cheeks were flushed.

"I know. I also know that Taklishim asked him. We are perhaps doing this a little backward, but my intent is the same." She slipped her hand into his and leaned against him. "He'll also get to meet my family."

"Let's hope our mothers aren't at each other's throats." Onida shifted her stance as their car came into sight. "Rather, let's just hope that my mother is human long enough for her to meet your family."

Degataga remained silent as Onida squeezed his hand tight until the car door opened, and her father stepped out. She tightened her grip when her mother got out in human form and kept it going until they got close, and the light on the porch Onida had turned on shone on their eyes.

He saw her studying them carefully in the light, they both had human eyes, and Onida relaxed her grip and threw her arms around her father's neck. "Dad! I was so worried." She moved to her mother and gave her a less exuberant hug. "Mom, it's good to see you."

"Chief Tyee, ma'am." Degataga shook their hands. "Before we go in, I'd like to ask your permission to marry your daughter. I asked her last night, and she agreed."

"Certainly, you have my permission. You know that goes without saying." Chief Tyee pulled Degataga in for a hug.

"There's one other thing you should know, Dad." Onida's voice took on a shy tone he wasn't used to hearing from her. "I'm pregnant, with twins."

Chief Tyee swung Onida up into his arms and spun around with her while whooping. "Finally!"

Degataga loved hearing Onida laugh like that. He looked at Onida's mother, "Any objections from you, ma'am?"

"Oh, no. Not a one. Onida will be a wonderful mother," she said, tears in her eyes.

"So, you will be moving up here then?" Chief Tyee

put his daughter back down as Onida hugged her mother tight.

"That was my plan. Onida decided that we will split our time between here and there. She wants to get her license to practice in Wyoming and help my village that way. I'm fine with it since my family will be there. My home is with her, wherever that may be."

"I still have no objections." Chief Tyee clapped him on the back. "We didn't encounter anything on the way down here," he switched subjects rapidly, "but at home, there were three spotted by a member of my tribe that can see things others can't."

"Onida guessed at three as well," Degataga confirmed. "My family is staying here as well until we can get this cleared up, so you will get a chance to meet them. Come with me."

Onida grabbed their bags from the backseat and followed them in the house. "Bit of a full house at the moment, but this is where Jax, Ronnie, Aedan, Smitty, and Airiella live," Onida explained.

Smitty stepped in the back door. "Chief Tyee, it's a pleasure to see you again, sir. You'll be staying in my extra room, so I'll take your bags for you while they show you around."

"Thank you, son. Allow me to introduce my wife, Beth."

"Pleasure to meet you, ma'am." Smitty shook her hand then took the bags from Onida.

"Okay." Degataga showed them around the downstairs, the TV room, kitchen, and bathrooms before leading them outside. "Guys, I'd like you to meet my future in-laws. My mother Asgasga is here, my older brother

Wohali and his wife Storm, their two boys, River and Rain. This one here is my younger brother Waya. Guys, this is Onida's parents, Chief Tyee and his wife, Beth."

Handshakes all around, and then Degataga introduced them to Mags and her babies. "You remember Jillian and Aedan?"

"I do. Thank you for having us in your home." Chief Tyee smiled brightly.

"The pool is right over there," Airiella told them, "and the house next to it is where you'll be staying with Smitty and Jillian. We figured you'd have more quiet there."

Jax, who was still sitting behind Airiella, said, "The property is clearly marked, and this little path heads directly to the beach. The land is all protected, and you are safe to shift if you need to. Security cameras are at the front gate, and the corners of the property facing out to see if anyone gets close."

Onida saw Chrissie coming outside. "This is Chrissie; she lives here as well. She has three little boys too."

"Hello. I can't introduce the rascals right now, they are all asleep, thankfully."

"This is my parents, Chief Tyee, and my mom, Beth." Onida gave a side look to her mother, "Please stay in that form."

"Nice to meet you both." Chrissie shook their hands and took a seat next to Airiella. "Ells and I have been friends since junior high school."

"And if we shift, are you and your boys going to be okay with that?" Chief Tyee asked Chrissie.

"Of course, they love Taklishim and Tama. They

think Tama's cougar is the best animal ever."

"I am a bear, and my wife is a wolf. When they wake up, if it's all right with all of you, we will shift, and you can meet our animals." Onida flinched a little at that and felt Degataga squeeze her hand.

They all agreed, and Degataga brought them to Smitty's so that they could show him their room and let them get settled in. Degataga went back out as Chrissie and Airiella were discussing dinner. They decided to order a diverse spread from a local barbecue restaurant that the guys all swore by.

Taklishim and Tama weren't down yet, and Degataga wanted to let them be. Taklishim had been pretty exhausted. "Were you able to find anything out from Winnie?" Degataga pulled Onida close to his side, wanting to feel her against him.

"A little bit. Winnie thinks that a demon was influencing some of the pool that Taklishim pulls from for his shadows. She thinks it's a low-level demon planting seeds of vengeance wherever they can. Maybe what Taklishim pulled wasn't dark when he pulled it, but those seeds planted took root for whatever reason after he released it."

Degataga sighed and leaned his head on hers. "Anything is possible at this point. It feels like we are constantly a step behind and scrambling."

"We are. All we can do is react. Winnie said that Stolas is putting together an early warning team, so to speak, so he can warn us when things are starting; to try and give us advanced notice. He's doing what he can, and honestly, I can't say that I ever expected to have a demon going to bat for us. He truly doesn't want us, or Airiella hurt. His intentions might be selfish where she is concerned, but he's fully on her team."

"Winnie thinks we should trust him more than we do?" Degataga was reading between the lines.

"She does. She agrees that Stolas can be arrogant and smug at times, but she also sees how much it bothers him when he finds out that things are after us again. Not just her, but all of us. He accepts that someone coming after us hurts her." Onida studied her fingernails. "You are right, with what you aren't saying, it's hard to trust a demon. Oddly enough, I find myself in that situation. I think if we were in mortal danger and he knew it, he would intervene somehow."

"I agree, with all of it. Stolas has been more than helpful and has shared knowledge with me freely. I'm hesitant to ask too much because I don't want to owe him, and I know how wrong that sounds."

"I think whatever debt that could be seen as us owing him, Airiella has paid. She freely gives him love. Did Kalisha come to talk to you?" Onida fiddled with the ring on her finger.

"She did. Seeing her was both good and bad. Brought up how much I miss her and how much of a loss she is to our group. She still has her magical laugh and that smile that lights up her face." Degataga rubbed his face. "She knew of the spell I was talking about; she doesn't believe I would be able to cast it. She's going to put the spell in a mirror that I can push my energy into and tell it my intent to send back to the caster."

Onida laced her fingers through his. "I miss her too. Does she think it will work?"

"That I can't answer. It's only a guess on our part

that sending the magic back will work. Her magic will work, of that, I have no doubt. Whether or not it will kill the skinwalkers, we will just have to see what happens. She did tell me that the shock wave of Airiella absorbing that shadow got felt on her side."

"Winnie told me that too. She was furious with me for not warning her. Winnie said it hurt. We could have caused damage to her or Jax," Onida whispered.

"It wasn't intentional, Oni." Degataga tipped her chin up and kissed her lightly. "She knows that. And she wouldn't have let it happen. She *didn't* let it happen. Let's just enjoy our night before jumping right into the fire again tomorrow. Your parents are here; they are safe, that's one less thing for you to worry about."

Chapter Thirty-Four

Airiella says we aren't alone," Ronnie relayed, his eyes roving across the heavily wooded landscape as they drove north.

"Danger?" Degataga asked.

"Yep. Airiella says it's currently a low buzz, constant. She thinks something is pacing us like before." Onida turned and saw Ronnie looking behind them at the car with Airiella and Jax in it. Taklishim driving as close as possible.

"You could have ridden with them, Ronnie. I can talk to her the same way." Onida felt terrible, he was clearly worried about her.

"It was *my* choice; she didn't make me ride here. I'm a good fighter and would rather be where I'm most needed. I'm just looking to see if she's blue or not. If she were, that would mean it's pretty close to us," Ronnie explained, facing forward again.

"I wonder if that means that two are back on your lands, and this one is a tracker?" Degataga thought out loud.

"I can shift and go out the window, try to see where

it's at," Onida suggested.

Both of them yelled out no at the same time. Onida fought the urge to roll her eyes. "We don't have a way to protect you from magic if you are spotted." Degataga tried to rationalize their response.

"I get it. It was just a suggestion." Onida purposely kept her tone bland.

"We are close, probably another fifteen minutes from here. Then we need to figure out where to call Stolas from to see if he has the mirror ready." Degataga watched around them nervously, his unease apparent.

"I've been thinking." Ronnie shifted sideways in the seat a little, "those visions all happened in different places, meaning that at some point each of them went different ways. We need to stick together, no going off alone."

"Correct. Only go separate ways on the protected property," Onida agreed. "No leaving the property though, not without all of us together. I want to alter the visions, but not replace who is dying in them."

"How will we meet Stolas then if it bothers Taklishim to be around him, and he can't come on the protected lands?"

"We will have to pick a spot where we can easily move on to protected lands. Like at Onida's house, we can go out to where the blessing ends while we all remain on the protected portion of the land, and Airiella can stand two feet in front of us," Degataga mapped it out.

"The sacrificial lamb?" Ronnie's tone was sarcastic.

"Her idea, not mine." Degataga pointed out carefully. He understood how Ronnie felt. "She told us it would be safest for us if she did it because she has more defenses than we do."

"I'm aware. I didn't intend it to come out that way," Ronnie said apologetically, his voice a low rumble.

"If it makes you feel better, go with her." Onida turned again to look at him. "She won't like it, but that's between the two of you."

"I already had this argument with her, and it didn't do me any good."

"I don't like it either, Ronnie," Onida said truthfully. "I even suggested we all go as one and stand in her ring of fire."

Ronnie's abundant laughter filled the car. "She didn't tell you her plan then!" He laughed again. "No wonder she's riding in that car! She wants to make sure Taklishim didn't find out!"

"Care to fill me in?" Onida snapped out; she was sure she wasn't going to like whatever he had to say.

"Might as well, she can't zap me from there." Ronnie shrugged. "She's going to put a ring around us, and ask Stolas to fling some dark magic at her while she stands on her own, to see if the ring protects against magic."

Degataga cursed quietly. "I should have known. She was asking me all those questions about what happened while I was in the ring when Spearfinger was attacking."

"That's why you called her the sacrificial lamb," Onida mused, her anger rising. "Damn it."

"Oni, did magic come through while you were in the ring?" Degataga glanced at her.

"No, not really. The energy did, but Airiella wasn't using dark magic either. What about you?"

"No. We got tossed around a bit, but the ring filtered out that part of it if there was dark magic. I'm sure she will be fine." Degataga tried to sound convincing.

Ronnie barked in laughter, "Yeah, she'll be fine. Sure, let's go with that. The fucking woman is going to be the death of me. Onida, you may have to write me a prescription for valium or something."

"Can't she hear your thoughts?" she asked him gently.

"Yep. Airiella's pissed at me, but she's stuck in a car with Taklishim, who she said was in a fragile state after last night, and Airiella can't get mad without him knowing she was up to something."

"Well, telling Taklishim he's in a fragile state will certainly take care of the fragile state," Degataga stated. "Straight to your house, Oni?"

"Yes." She glanced worriedly back at Ronnie.

"I'm fine, Onida. Just frustrated." Ronnie sighed, "She tells me all the time I don't need to protect her, but it's instinct to want to protect those you love. Right now, I feel split between needing to be here with her and back at home with Chrissie and the boys. Chrissie tells me to come here and take care of Airiella that she will be fine, and Airiella tells me to stay home and watch over Chrissie." He threw his hands up in the air, "I don't know what to do. I fucking hate watching her walk right up to death and laughing in his face. I have no idea how Jax isn't insane from this shit."

Stunned, Onida didn't know how to respond to the rant. Even Degataga was silent. "What does your heart tell you, Ronnie?" Degataga asked in a soft tone.

"That she needs to do what she needs to do, and I should stop trying to interfere. She's told us all several times before that she needs us, but she doesn't. Airiella said that it's the aftermath that she struggles with; the fear, pain, and emotions that happen after it's all said and done crash down on her, and she feels like she's drowning. She falls apart then, curls up so sweetly into me that I fall in love with her all over again. She spends time with each of us until she feels back on solid ground. Part of me wonders if that's who I want her to be, this softer side of her that melts into me. Then I feel like a huge jackass because I know that's not all she is. It's for sure a part of her, but so is this other part."

Onida felt tears sting her eyes at the words he let spill out. It was easy to see how much Ronnie loved Airiella, and it became a little clearer to Onida why Jax was the right choice for Airiella. "How do you feel with Chrissie?" Onida asked, not turning around to look at him.

"Like a savior. I know she's the one for me, I'm just struggling with letting go of Airiella. Those times I think I'm ready to do it, I try to say the words and my heart breaks, and it hurts so bad I can't go through with it. I'm still that much in love with her. I can't be Jax. I can't hate what she's doing and not say anything. He doesn't like it either, but he doesn't stop her."

"Can I make an observation?" Degataga looked at Ronnie in the rearview mirror. "It doesn't seem like anything has changed with Smitty and Airiella."

"It hasn't really. Only the physical part."

"He was holding her yesterday," Onida said, not catching on.

"Not that physical part, the sex," Ronnie clarified.

Blushing, Onida nodded, finally understanding. "And that is the part you don't want to let go of?"

"Makes me sound like an asshole, but it's part of it."

"You don't think you will find that with Chrissie?" Degataga broke in again.

"I don't know. What if I don't?"

"Then she isn't the one for you." Onida said it simply. "When the right one is in the picture, they fill all the spots in you."

"She's going to love you always, Ronnie. She will always need you. Those moments that mean so much to you, they won't go away," Degataga assured him. They pulled up to Onida's house, and Degataga parked the car. "It took me leaving Oni to figure it out. Not something I plan on doing again."

Onida climbed out slowly, her brain trying to process everything that Ronnie admitted, and it was clear that he was hurting. She saw him get out, and just as quickly she saw Airiella launching herself at him, tears streaming down her face.

Onida moved to stand next to Degataga, Taklishim, and Tama, hanging back at their car with Jax, letting them have their moment. Onida saw both sides of Airiella, the soft one that Ronnie craved so much, and the fierce one she was more often than not lately.

Now that she knew more about Ronnie's past, she understood on a deeper level why he needed a woman that he could feel like he was protecting and not just picking up the pieces. The connection he had with Airiella was undeniable. Like Degataga had said, it wouldn't change whether he was with Airiella or Chrissie. His heart just wouldn't be so troubled.

Onida looked over at Degataga, "I don't make you feel unneeded, do I?"

"What?" Degataga looked down at her. "Why would you even think that?"

Onida gestured to Ronnie and Airiella. "I can see it

a little more plainly now."

"No, Oni. You fill all the spots in me perfectly. Their love is great, but I also see the love between Jax and Airiella, and that is closer to what we have."

"Give them a minute, let's go in." She nodded her head at her sister, and they filed around the two and followed them inside.

"Sorry about that," Jax apologized. "I didn't realize that Ronnie was having a hard time."

"Don't apologize." Onida lay her hand on his arm. "He's torn."

"He should have talked to me about it." Jax was shaken up.

"I think he feels that he would interfere with what you and Airiella have." Degataga came up alongside them. "Give him time. He's holding on out of fear."

"Speaking of fear, Taklishim." Jax took a deep breath. "Airiella is going to call Stolas to hand over the mirror for Degataga to use. She's also going to test herself. This test is her choice, on her terms."

Onida saw the resigned look on Taklishim's face. Yesterday's disaster had taken an emotional toll on him. "What kind of test?"

"She's going to ask him to hit her with dark magic."

Fury crossed the warrior's face for a moment, "What about the rest of us?"

"She'll have us in a circle. She will be in one too. She wants to make sure that the circle filters out the dark magic," Jax explained. "She's not doing this to piss you off; she's doing it to understand the limitations of what she can do."

Onida saw Airiella and Ronnie starting to head

towards them. *Your secret is out,* she warned.

I figured as much. Please trust me on this. It's on my terms, and I'll keep the rest of you safe.

I think the part that you are missing is the rest of us have to sit and watch someone we all love purposely get hurt while we do nothing. That's not easy for any of us. This upset from Ronnie should have made that a little clearer.

Airiella didn't respond but had paused in her forward momentum. Ronnie moved around front of her and blocked her from view while they talked again. Onida glanced over at Jax's face to see if she could understand what was happening.

"She shut me out," Jax told her. "What did you say to her?"

"That it's hard on those who love her to watch her do things like this to herself while we couldn't do anything about it," Onida repeated.

Jax sighed. "You aren't wrong. It is hard, but it's not much different than what you guys did to her yesterday. You planned an all-out attack on me to get her to respond. Maybe you all should work on your communication skills, work together, as a team, instead of her against everyone else. She feels just as isolated as you do. This idea at least was a plan she came up with that puts no one else in danger to test herself."

Degataga cleared his throat. "Jax is right. We all want to know what she can do and her limitations, but we aren't working with Airiella. It struck me the other day how much Airiella shields from us. On the surface, she's open and telling us everything we *need* to know, and keeping the stuff that would impact our decisions locked away. By that,

I mean the emotional aspect of it all. The kind of toll this takes on her, not as an angel, but as our friend. We have every right to worry about her because we love her, but that doesn't give us the right to burden her further than she is. The person in this world that is closest to her is doing exactly what we all should be doing, letting her decide what she thinks is best. If she's right, great, if she's wrong, we all learn. Lois Lane didn't hold Superman back, she sent him off into danger, with her love and support. She knew he would do what he needed to do, and it was okay to worry. Families of police and soldiers do it every day. Why should we be any different?"

Onida was speechless. She wrapped her arms around Degataga's waist and buried her face in his shoulder. He was right. They treated her with kid gloves when they should have been including her in the discussions. They hadn't taken the things she'd told them into much consideration and acted as they knew better than she did.

"I'm sorry, Jax," Taklishim said contritely. "I'm more aware now of how our decisions impact her, and it shouldn't have taken me this long to figure it out. She's all but told me on several occasions, and I bulldoze right over her anyway."

"Do you understand why Ronnie's connection is so strong and important to her?" Jax sat on the arm of the couch. No one answered him, so he went on. "He's her emotional support. Her connection to him is pure emotion. Do you understand why he's so nervous all the time? He catches all the emotions of what is happening. Before, during, and after. He feels what she does. If what you feel watching her go through something is bad, imagine what it feels like for him, who has his own emotions and hers on top of it. It's the same for me, but on a deeper level. Seeing any of us, including all you, hurt, causes such deep emotions in her that it bleeds out to all of us. She makes her own decisions based on what she thinks is best for everyone, and that is why. It's yet another layer of protection. Include her."

Taklishim looked chagrined. "I'm truly sorry. I'll tell her that."

"You want her on your council, but so far you haven't proven to her that you will even listen to what she has to say. Do you even know that what she wants most is a chance at a normal life?" Jax's eyes had taken on a sheen. "The words from her that impacted me the most, out of everything she's ever said were as I came up on her outside the first time we really talked. She told me she had been hoping for someone that thought she was worthy of saving instead of always being the one that had to save everyone, but that she didn't think that would be me."

"But that's what we are trying to do," Taklishim started.

"No. You are caging her. Think about that statement." Jax looked at him hard.

"She doesn't feel worthy," Tama said sadly. "She wanted someone to care enough about her, not what she can do for them."

Jax pointed at her, "Bingo." He rubbed the heels of his hands in his eyes. "Since that day, I have done everything I can to show Airiella how worthy she is, and when she told me that she needed me after the fact, that's when she felt weakest, I decided to be exactly what she needed. She has the fighting part down; she practices her control; she works on situational awareness and multitasking. She has yet to figure out just how important she is to everyone, not because of those things, but because of what she brings to our hearts."

Onida felt herself breaking down. She was guilty of precisely what Jax had pointed out. They all were, except maybe Degataga. "We *do* treat her like a science experiment."

Taklishim looked the worst out of all of them, Jax's words making an impact. "She doesn't know we love her?"

"She knows," Jax assured him. "She just doesn't know why. Tak, Airiella lost her mind when she had the vision of you dead. She was inconsolable. Ronnie and I weren't enough to soothe that pain. Airiella so badly wants your approval and acceptance; she idolizes you. Having to show you what she saw without infusing her own emotions into it almost broke her. She's not detached when it comes to any of you. Onida, I sent you the picture of her by your bed for a reason. I wanted you to see how it affected her. She *is* love."

Degataga tightened his arm around Onida. "She's coming in now."

"I know," Jax said. "She can feel the emotions bleeding off you all. Suck it up and try to be what she needs if you value her as a person. If her only value to you is as an angel, continue as you have been."

Jax stood and walked out the front door to stop her from coming in, giving them a moment to gather themselves after that bombshell. Onida held tight to Degataga but turned her head to face Taklishim and Tama. "Everything he said is spot on, we've been so wrong."

"Her instincts take over when danger is near, we

haven't trusted her to do what comes naturally, and we try to intervene. Each time she has stopped us and finished the battle on her own," Degataga told them. "Jax has insight into her that we don't have. If she needs us to help with the aftermath, then that is what we do. Pay attention to the clues she leaves us. Looking back, I can see them now after what Jax has said. She is an angel, raven, whatever you choose to call her, but to me, she is Airiella first. That incredible empath who sees and feels so much more than we can ever know and who made us all feel the depth of love she has in her."

"She was saving us before she even knew she could." Onida looked at Tama.

"And now she's going to do it again, but we made her feel bad about it by doubting her," Tama finished.

Taklishim swore and looked like he was going to have a nervous breakdown. "Onida, call her in here, please," he said roughly. Onida nodded, and Airiella walked in a moment later, looking about the same as Taklishim.

"Let's not do this now," she replied wearily and leaned heavily against Jax who was behind her, Ronnie came on up on her side and clutched her hand.

Taklishim ignored her. "Remember yesterday when we both broke down?" He stepped closer to her. She nodded for him to keep going, her eyes guarded. "It wasn't because I died and saw it, nor was it because Tama died, or even Jax."

Confused, Airiella raised her eyebrows. "I'll bite. Why then?"

"Because of what it did to you. I broke down because of how much it hurt you. I know I'm hard on you, not just because I know you are capable of so much more.

I'm hard on you because I can't stand the thought of something else happening to you. I'm awful about telling people how much they mean to me. I grew up that way. Tama is the other half of me the way Jax is the other half of you. I'm sorry, Raven. I never stopped to consider how all this made you feel at your human level, in your heart. If it helps, I'd be this hard on you even if you weren't an angel or raven. I'd feel the same way about you if you were nothing more than Airiella, empath extraordinaire. I promise to do better at working *with* you instead of telling you what to do without listening to you."

Onida saw her tear up. "No more emotions, please!"

"They don't make you weak, Airiella. They make you strong," Tama told her gently.

"This is what you hold back from us," Onida couldn't help but say. "This part of you right here is what we need to see to understand. Degataga saw it, maybe that's why he was always pushing us not to do what we did. Regardless, we can't help if we can't see what we, ourselves, are doing. Yes, we need to be better at communicating with you, but it's a two-way street."

"If you truly want to know what I'm feeling, then everyone hold hands," she said quietly. "This is an onetime offer. I don't let people in easily as I am sure you are all aware." Jax and Ronnie let go of her and stepped away. Onida caught the flash of fear that crossed her face.

"Are you afraid of us?" She halted in her steps.

"No, just of letting people in," came the quiet response. "They are already in, they know."

Onida stepped forward and boldly grabbed her hand, Taklishim took the other and Degataga and Tama completed the circle. There was a buzz of energy that flew through them all in a loop. "Raven, I don't feel anything."

"Give me a minute," she growled, "this isn't easy for me."

The first feeling that slammed into them when she dropped her walls was love. It filled Onida with wonder, then the second wave of everything that she hid from them was underneath. Onida felt her knees start to buckle and found Ronnie behind her holding her and Degataga up, Jax behind Taklishim and Tama doing the same.

Tama was sobbing, Taklishim was struggling, though tears still fell. Degataga was not crying, but his face betrayed him in a way that tore at Onida. She, herself, felt the tears streaming from her eyes as she tried to name all that was running through her. Insecurity, failure, pain, sadness, embarrassment, fear, anger, hope, and even farther beneath that was another layer of love.

She saw flashbacks in her mind of Airiella at different stages of her life, flashbacks of her own life as well. With a start, she realized that while a good portion of those emotions that were ripping her apart was Airiella's, she was also feeling the feelings of everyone around her as Airiella took them on, relieving others of their burdens.

She dropped Airiella's hands and covered her mouth. "Every day is like this?" She whispered the question, afraid of the answer.

"Yes." She tried to pull her hand back from Taklishim, but he held it tight, let go of Tama's hand, and picked up the one that Onida had just let go of, holding both of Airiella's hands.

"Help me be a better man so that I may be a better parent," he told her brokenly.

It was like the energy in the room was suddenly cut

off as Airiella slammed her walls back up. "Tak, you are going to be an amazing father. Never compare yourself to your parents or any others."

Onida felt a change in the energy and found that her fear was gone; her strength and confidence now boosted. She guessed the same happened to the others because their faces reflected it. "Did you just take my fear?"

"I did. I took it from all of you. Don't face these things with fear. Leave no room for doubt. Give me a moment, please, I need to step outside and let go of this," Airiella said calmly, a mask that belied none of her genuine emotions, firmly in place.

Onida watched her walk back outside, Jax looking after her while Ronnie looked at each of them with a pointed look on his face. "Do you understand now? She's come a long way from when you first met her, and there's no doubt she's stronger than any of us. It doesn't mean she can't be hurt." Ronnie tapped his chest, "In here. The scars you don't see unless she lets you."

Chapter Thirty-Five

Degataga gathered himself while Airiella let go of all that she took on. What he had felt had shaken him, just as it had the first time she had let him in. He risked a look at Taklishim and saw he was doing no better than the rest of them.

"Head in the game, Tak. Bring out the warrior," Degataga reminded him. "You too, Tama. It's fight time as soon as we step off this property." Curt nods were his only answer as they finally slid into the mode they needed to be in to survive this.

He turned to Onida and saw she was ready. "That's my girl," he whispered to her. "Hawk-eye time. I love you, honey."

Airiella stepped back in, her gaze cool and her energy radiating strength. "From here on out, no one is alone. You all stay together, no matter what. Please don't argue with me." She met each of their eyes, "Gandalf, Catwoman, Hawk-eye, Dr. Strange," she called, using her sentimental nicknames for each of them.

"We will follow your lead," Degataga answered for all of them, laughing inwardly at the nickname she'd given him.

She turned and headed back out the door rounding the house to the back of Onida's property. The second she crossed the property line, a dominating line of blue fire encircled them all. She didn't lock them in place, but the barrier around them was palpable.

Degataga let the energy of everything flow through him until he was sure he could identify each source. A raven flew up to Airiella and shifted into Stolas. The demon's expression was somewhat stormy. "I don't like this, love."

Ronnie bristled next to him at the term of endearment. "Calm down. He's no threat to her," Jax reminded him.

"I know. Airiella's not his love, though."

"It's okay, man. I know he loves her. Everyone here loves her." Jax put a calming hand on his friend. "Besides, this barrier doesn't hold me as it does the rest of you. If I thought he was making a move on her, I'd walk over there."

Degataga saw the mirror getting handed off, and Airiella walked it over to Degataga, reaching through the fire like it wasn't there. "I hope you know what to do with this." He took it and stared down at the magical mirror, feeling for the spell that was in it. It was potent, Kalisha was good.

She walked back to Stolas, and a ring appeared around herself. "Wallop me."

Stolas was not happy with the demand, and Degataga was able to feel dark energy swirling, its strength was frightening to him. The energy was strong enough to cause Taklishim's warrior to surge to the surface, Tama immediately shifting. It was unquestionably the power of someone strong enough to be a prince of Hell.

The blast that smacked into them was just energy that fueled them, no darkness. But it knocked each of them around quite a bit. Degataga got back to his feet and saw that Airiella's wings were out, and she was down on one knee but otherwise unharmed from what he could tell without scanning her.

"Thank you. That was just what I needed to see," Airiella said, a little breathlessly. She walked up to him and took his hand. Degataga felt the flow of energy change again.

"What's she doing?" he wondered, aware he thought aloud.

"Giving him love," Jax answered. "Watch his face."

Sure enough, the demon's face softened, the light that made her unique fill his eyes. "Does it help him?"

"Not really, she says it makes his soul a little less muddy, but it's something he craves. The feeling of love and she has plenty to give," Jax said with a soft smile, watching as Stolas gave her a gentle kiss on the cheek then disappeared.

The ring of fire around them blinked out. "Did anyone get hurt by that?" she asked.

"No angel, it just knocked us around," Ronnie said, looking around. "Are we alone?"

"Nope. They are closer now. Come out across the line but stay close enough to jump back over it as a group," she cautioned, turning her back to them as they came closer to her.

"Are you going to let me use the mirror?" Degataga asked.

"Yep. I'm pulling a play from Ronnie here. You guys

will take the lead, and I will watch to see what they do and see if I can learn anything from them before joining. I'll keep you protected. If their magic feels anything like what it did with Stolas, I'll be able to feel it gathering. Stay together."

"Did his dark magic get through your ring?" Onida asked.

"A trickle, but my lightning burned it off. What's important is that none got through yours, which was a lot more powerful than the one around me." Airiella suddenly spun, dropping into a squat with her wings spread wide as a giant wall of blue flames surrounded them.

Onida stepped into the spirit world for a moment only and felt the same thing as she did in the living world. The air was dead silent and still, the glow of Airiella lighting the area surrounding them. She saw no spirit movement, but Onida did feel the energy build, and she stepped back.

It looked like the ring around them was gone, and Onida went to step forward, but Degataga stopped her. "It's just invisible now, but very much still around us. I don't think it will hurt you if you touch it, but let's not test that," Degataga whispered to her. "I think she wants them to think we are unprotected."

"Form a circle facing outwards," Ronnie suggested, and they dropped into a formation so that all directions of vision were covered. Degataga had seen that he had pulled out his throwing stars and that Jax had a knife.

"Can you feel that?" he whispered to Onida.

"The dark energy? Yes, it's getting closer, but I can't see it."

"They can remain invisible," Taklishim reminded.

In front of me to my left are three dark souls using the trees for cover, Onida heard Airiella say.

"Did the rest of you get that message?" Onida asked, getting quiet grunts of acknowledgment. She saw three shadows dart towards the trees Airiella mentioned and knew Taklishim was going on the offensive. Her sister's cougar was completely still watching for a sign of movement.

An inhuman cry echoed in the air, and one of the Skinwalkers appeared. Its eyes were a glowing red, a skull resting atop its head with leather straps holding the jaw bone in place over its jaw; an animal pelt of some sort wrapped around its shoulders and a choker of teeth around its neck, effectively hiding the kill spot.

A chill ripped through Onida, and she knew without a doubt there wasn't anything she could do against this creature. Beside her, Degataga shifted his stance and aimed the mirror at the visible creature at the same time Airiella wrapped her wings around her and dove to the side. The earth trembled and opened up beneath the skinwalker, swallowing its feet and holding it in place. A force slammed into the invisible wall around them, a dark substance oozing down its sides. Onida flinched.

"It stinks of sickness," Taklishim said of the substance.

Ronnie's movements were subtle, but he was moving slowly, then Onida saw a star flying towards the creature that Airiella had rooted in place. It landed, but it wasn't a killing blow, it only made it angrier. The air was heavy, with a dark feeling that kept pressing against the barrier that was keeping them safe.

"Touch the wall Degataga; it will power you. Same

with you, Tak," Airiella advised softly, on the move again.

"What the fuck?" Ronnie practically shouted, then lowered his voice. "Where'd she go?"

Good question. Onida couldn't see her. *Where are you?*

Spirit world. Tell Ronnie I'm fine. I'm going to pop back out behind this trapped one.

"She's fine, Ronnie," Onida whispered as a bolt of lightning slammed into the one they could see and branched out to the other two who now became visible. The other two didn't have a skull or pelt on; they were in the bear and wolf form already and looked identical in animal form to how her mother and father did.

Chills racked through her, and Tama growled low in her throat as they stared at the now smoking figures. Two more blasts of lightning hit them, and their howls of pain filled the air, but it didn't kill them, and now all three of them were turned towards Airiella.

Degataga swore, and Taklishim sent a series of shadows while Ronnie threw two more stars at the animal's necks. "I can't mirror anything back at them if they aren't sending it our way."

"The wall around us is down, she's distracting them so we can get at their necks," Jax said as he started to move.

Taklishim blurred, moving like a shadow and silent. Tama was marking the wolf as her first prey and set off after him. Ronnie paused to survey the area. "What are you doing?" Onida asked him.

"Looking for a good vantage point," he said softly.

"She wants us together, we need to follow Tama and Taklishim," Degataga told him. "And Jax. They won't stay distracted with her while being openly attacked by the rest of us."

Onida lost track of the one in human form. "The one went invisible again," Onida warned, and the three of them stepped closer together and moved as a group.

"What strikes me as odd right now, is the three she had visions about are the three separated from us," Ronnie said, his tone cold.

Onida gasped as Airiella dove at Tama winding her wings around them both as something unseen sent them both flying backward, Airiella slamming into the trunk of a large tree. As soon as she got her feet under her, she must have said something to Tama because the cougar grabbed Jax and hauled him back to the group.

A wall appeared around them again, and Jax looked down at his bloody arm. "That stings," he said, his voice shaking, "and I lost my knife."

Onida grabbed his arm and quickly healed him. "Taklishim is still out there," Onida whispered, Tama bumping against her legs. Onida spotted the knife Jax lost and told Airiella where it was, wanting to give her another weapon to use.

Degataga had his eyes closed and palms facing the ground, playing with the energy that he could when another blast of magic slammed into the barrier around them, this time knocking them all off balance. Onida felt the flow change, alarm ringing through her as she understood it was coming from inside with them.

Degataga's eyes flew open, and they had an odd glow to them. "It worked." He smiled menacingly.

"What worked?" Onida took a step away from him, Ronnie pulling her behind him. Tama roared. "No, no, no, no, no," Onida muttered. Not her mate. Sick dread welled up inside her.

Before the horror of what was happening could sink in fully, Ronnie lashed out with a series of punches, and Jax went for the legs, knocking his feet out from under him. Tama leaped on his prone form and went for the throat.

Pressure around them built, stealing the oxygen from Onida's lungs as Ronnie delivered another swift punch to Degataga's head, knocking him out. *Help!* She sent out before she dropped to the ground.

Chapter Thirty-Six

He felt the invasion the moment it happened. He felt the blows rained down on him by Jax and Ronnie. Tama's claws were digging into his chest, but he couldn't do anything. His body wasn't under his control. The skinwalker had him, but it didn't have his mind.

It was trying to take over his spirit; the darkness spreading faster than Degataga wanted to think about or admit. It was going to use him to kill the others, and he couldn't let that happen. Between the moments of blacking out and coming to Degataga used the powers he had perfected over the years of healing and learning about the body and fought back. There was no way he was about to hurt the woman who held his soul.

He heard Airiella's voice thunder out a scream of fury and a blast of pure light energy tore through him, fire burning his veins as her light pulsed against the darkness. She was giving him her power! He latched on to it and pushed as hard as he could, the thought of Onida needing him fueling his magic.

One of Taklishim's shadows tore through him, the pain was unbearable as it felt like his soul split in two, but combined with Airiella's energy and his will, the split part of him remained light and came back under his control. He heard his voice groaning in pain.

"Dega, can you hear me?" Airiella demanded.

"Yes," he croaked out, a victory in itself. "Need to figure out how to fight my own soul," he rasped.

A scream tore through the air as it dawned on Airiella what had happened, and Degataga grew to understand just what it felt like for Jax to have to fight himself for control. The feeling was sickening, and his body only listened to half the commands he gave it.

An angry tear-soaked face appeared in his line of sight, Airiella sounded like she was far away, but she was right there saying something, he only caught part of it, something about helping him after they killed the others. The scent of blood filled his nose and distracted him.

He should be fighting something, but his mind was losing focus, and in a moment of sharp clarity, he felt the swelling of dark magic, and he fought against the disgust that rose in him as he realized it was coming from himself. With a struggle, he held the mirror up to his face and pushed as much of his energy into it he could.

"No!" he heard Onida yell, and the mirror was ripped from his hands, but not before it worked. Vile sickness swept through him, and he retched violently, rough hands rolling him over, so he spewed all over the ground. "Not happening, not happening," Onida was repeating, and the warmth of her hands was a welcome feel. "Stay with me, Dega. I love you."

The untainted part of him knew there wasn't anything she could do, but he never got a chance to get the words out. Spasms and cramping hit his body hard as waves of pain attacked his every cell, and all that came out was an agonized moan, he knew he was dying.

He heard Airiella call out for Stolas, saying she might need him to help bring her back and her sending Taklishim and Tama back into Onida's house to heal each other. Then the owner of that voice appeared in front of his blurry eyes in a vision he was sure would haunt him forever.

She was coated in blood, her glow beneath giving her a demonic look, her eyes a bright amber color that signaled she was on emotional overload. Her wings broken and battered, dripping blood and a knife clutched in her fist, her face set in stone. "Listen up, you evil fucker, you are leaving this body either willingly, or I will pull you out," she growled. "I am not losing my friend to you."

Another wave of severe pain shot through him, making him arch off the ground, his silent scream loud in his head as he fought back with everything he had in him. "I love you, Dega," Onida cried.

"Degataga, I know you can hear me, you are not dying today, so get ready for this." Airiella's voice penetrated the pain.

Distantly he was aware of what she was about to do, and he wanted to tell her not to do it, but he couldn't. The pain was relentless and on the verge of breaking his mind. He saw Ronnie dumping water over her hand and cleaning it off only to helplessly watch as she tore her palm open with the knife and dripped the blood into his mouth.

I know you can hear me now, so you fucking fight, do you understand me? Live for your babies. Live for Onida. Losing you will kill her.

It sounded like Airiella, but he had to be

hallucinating, he didn't know what was real or not anymore. He fought the pain anyway, fought the feeling of sickness swamping him, and thought of the life he would have with Onida, of watching her belly grow with his babies. He had to get through this to make that happen.

Then a tearing pain like no other he had felt started like she was ripping his soul out of his body only it wasn't his, it was the Skinwalker. She was pulling it from him; fear hit his mind at what could happen to her.

Stop it. Don't think about it. Fight. Help me.

Sobs tore through his chest, and his mind filled with the sound of rage-induced howling, and he felt the unique energy of Airiella pouring into him, giving him power. He latched on to it and pushed through the pain, separating the dark magic from his soul and willing it away, calling on the energy of everything around him to pull it out of him.

You have to kill it now, Dega. I don't have anything left in me.

With a violent scream, the skinwalker was torn from his body as Airiella's blood filled his mouth. He instinctively swallowed not wanting to choke, and the burst of power and emotions that filled him pinned him down for a moment right before a blinding flash of light and energy held him in place with a stunning display of blue fire.

Chapter Thirty-Seven

Onida was thrown backward by an explosive blast of energy that rippled the air, cutting her off from Degataga and Airiella with the biggest and most vivid ring of blue fire she had ever seen. Dazed, she tried to get her bearings and saw Stolas, Jax, and Ronnie struggling to get to their feet fifty yards away.

She watched in fascinated horror as the skinwalker slowly stood and kicked out at Airiella, causing the angel to crumple to the ground, weakened from the energy loss she suffered by ripping it out of him. She saw Airiella slide the knife into Degataga's hand as she tried to pull herself up.

Ronnie, Jax, and Stolas came running towards her. Ronnie picked her up off the ground, checking her over while trying to watch Airiella. Jax attempted to go through the ring but couldn't. She had effectively locked them all out, and Stolas was pacing rapidly, his movements agitated and aggressive. But he didn't get within twenty feet of the circle.

"She's hurt pretty badly," Jax whispered, his eyes flooded with worry.

There wasn't anything Onida could do for either of

them. "You can't get it in at all?"

"No, I can't even get closer than five feet away," Jax confirmed.

"That means the skinwalker can't get out either," Ronnie pointed out.

"Which was probably her intention all along," Onida completed the thought.

Degataga had gotten to his feet and was drunkenly swaying, looking like he was talking to himself. Onida had no idea what was going on with him or if he was hurt, but he had Airiella's blue glow. "She gave him her energy!"

"And she's dying for it!" Stolas snapped.

"What?" Onida cried.

"She's dying. Her life is fading, and I don't know if I can bring her back. Her light is turning various shades of gray. She took on the energy of that creature," Stolas spit out.

"Degataga, kill it!" Ronnie screamed frantically.

Jax paled, but said, "I can still feel her, she's still with us."

Onida kept her eyes glued on Degataga, Airiella's life force flowing through him. "Come on, Dega," she muttered quietly, "use the power and kill it." She didn't hear Taklishim come up behind her, didn't recognize the grinding of his teeth, didn't feel her sister take her hand. She didn't notice when they walked away.

She watched Degataga go through the motions that Ronnie had taught them all, his body stiff and not fluid like it usually was. She wondered if the possession had hurt him, or if getting it out of him had hurt him. She held her breath as Dega went to strike out at the creature's throat and missed. The skinwalker quickly disarmed him.

Ronnie fell silent next to her as they waited to see what would happen. Onida thought for sure she was about to lose the only man she'd ever loved. Despair flooded her body, though her pores. She didn't believe any of them expected the skinwalker to turn to Airiella instead and stab the knife into her chest.

Screams went up around Onida from everyone, and she dropped to the ground, her mind not understanding how this could be happening. Stolas screamed out for Seir and sent the other demon out for a list of things he needed, and Onida prayed. For the first time in a long time, she prayed to every god that was out there to spare the lives of these two individuals that she loved so much.

The shock of seeing Airiella stabbed seemed to knock Degataga out of his stupor, and he flew into motion doing everything he could to shove the skinwalker into that wall of fire around them. Each time the skinwalker touched it, it burned him. He kept at it until the creature dropped the knife.

Degataga moved to grab the knife at the same time that Airiella's hand wrapped around the leg of the skinwalker and shoved lightning into it. Degataga sliced cleanly through the throat, blood spraying across his face and body, down over Airiella and soaking into the ground.

Onida burst into tears as the skinwalker seemed to fold in on itself and crumple down at Degataga's feet. Degataga slumped down and checked Airiella, putting his hand on the barrier around them. Onida wasn't sure what he was doing, but he started to glow, and she guessed he was taking power from it.

"Jax! I think he's taking power from the ring, try to get through!" Onida choked out as Jax ran at them only to get repelled back as he got close.

She could see Degataga holding his hand on Airiella and talking to her quietly, his other hand on the wall around them. Whatever he said worked because the ring came down, and Taklishim barreled into the ring to pull out the skinwalker and throw it on the fire he had started.

Stolas got to Airiella before Jax did, but she was already in Degataga's arms. "Home. Take her home," she heard Degataga tell him as Seir came back and the both of them disappeared, to the alarm of everyone standing there.

"Wait, Ronnie, wait," Onida cried. Seir popped back in and grabbed Stolas and Onida, both of them appearing in the driveway of Airiella's house, as far as Seir could bring them. Degataga was in the process of changing the blessing on the property to allow Stolas and Seir access, the power in his body radiating out waves of the energy she always associated with Airiella.

Seir disappeared and returned with Ronnie and Jax, who opened the gate and verbally gave permission for Stolas and Seir to come on to the property. He told them both where her room was. Seir disappearing with Degataga and Airiella once again as the rest of them ran up the driveway to the house.

"Shall I get the other two for you, my lady?" Seir asked Onida.

"What other two?" She was out of breath, her brain panicked at everything that was happening.

"No," Jax answered for her. "Taklishim said they would drive down. They needed to finish burning the bodies to make sure they couldn't come back."

Onida's steps faltered, and Ronnie caught her, "I've got you. Degataga is okay." He slowed down and helped her as the reality of the situation struck. "I need you to stay level-headed; they might need your skills as a healer and a doctor. Stay with me, Onida."

She turned her head and focused on Ronnie; they needed her. She had to get it together. She didn't know the state of either Degataga or Airiella. "I might need Taklishim," she managed to get out.

"For now, we only have you, so stay with me, Onida," Ronnie repeated. "Fight the panic." His calm voice got through, and she let him lead her. His touch soothing, and when her steps faltered again, he just picked her up and carried her.

As they neared the house, Ronnie handed her off to Jax and bellowed for Smitty and Chrissie. Chrissie came flying through the front door; her face was a wild mess of tears and panic. "Get me water for Onida and Degataga, clean towels and any extra men's clothes you can find, please," he asked her kindly.

She nodded, and Ronnie and Jax brought Onida up the stairs and stopped outside the bedroom door, waiting for Chrissie. Ronnie made her drink some of the water before going in, which she had to admit helped clear her mind.

Jax had to lean against the wall he was shaking so badly, and Onida reached out and touched his arm, scanning him, finding a few injuries, she quickly healed them and did the same to Ronnie. "Will she be okay?" Chrissie whispered to Ronnie, who couldn't answer. But the fear in his eyes gave away his thoughts.

"Believe in her, Chrissie." Onida kept her tone kind and soft.

She opened the bedroom door and fought back the

urge to cringe at the sight of Airiella's bed, covered in blood. Degataga was leaning over Airiella, his hands on her, his bloody face streaked with his tears, eyes closed, and a look of total concentration on his face.

Stolas was leaning over the other side of the bed, applying a paste of some sort to the knife wound, the demon himself crying quietly, shaking his head. "What does that mean?" Jax asked him. "Why are you shaking your head?"

"She's gone, I'm sorry. I don't know if she will come back or not." Stolas choked back a sob.

"I can still feel her," Jax whispered, "she's not gone."

"Bath," Ronnie said unevenly, "let's get her cleaned up. If that blood all over her is diseased, it won't help. Someone go get Smitty, Aedan, and Mags up here."

"I'm on it." Chrissie ran out of the room.

Degataga and Stolas stood back. "I gave her some of the mixtures that will keep her from feeling pain, and one that will give her some energy. The mix on the wound will help heal it and stop any internal bleeding for a bit." Stolas looked at Onida as he said this. "She has no pulse."

"She's had no pulse before," Onida said bravely. "If Jax can still feel her, she's not entirely gone. Never give up hope on her."

Stolas gave her another container, "Use this on him; it will kill the disease the skinwalker inflicted on him. Also, have him clean up, they are right about the blood."

Onida took it, and as Ronnie lifted Airiella from the bed, she moved to strip the bed of all the bloody blankets and sheets and handed them off to Stolas. "Can you take these out back and burn them?" He nodded at her and then watched as the rest of Airiella's connections tore into the room to a chorus of gasps of horror.

"Fucking hell, this doesn't look good." Mags bit her lip.

"Chrissie, can you go with Stolas, so the others don't assume demon is attacking us?" Onida asked the frazzled woman gently. "I think Degataga's family might be able to tell what he is. Stolas, are you going to stick around a bit?"

"Do you mind if I do?" he asked, looking at Jax and Ronnie.

"No, you are welcome here," Jax said firmly. "I'm aware you love her. If she's going to come back to us, that's what she needs to feel is love."

"She chose well in you. I thank you for your graciousness." Stolas looked back at Onida and handed her a little bag of herbs. "Put it in your water and drink it. It will help with your energy. You'll be needing the boost."

Onida took it from him, gratefully, "Should I take it now?"

"No, wait until you feel low, then take it. I'll take care of these." Stolas nodded to the bloody linens at his feet.

"Ronnie, can we use your bathroom so I can get him cleaned up?" Onida retook charge.

"Of course. We'll all be in here, come back whenever you are ready." Ronnie held the limp form of Airiella close to his chest while Mags ran the bathwater.

"Are you all getting in with her?" Onida thought to ask as she pulled Degataga to the door.

"We will," Jax answered. "It's a giant soaking tub. I figure if we are all touching her, it will help."

"You are right about that," Degataga said,

woodenly, his body sagging in Onida's arms.

"Come on, let's get you cleaned up." Onida tugged on him gently, grabbing the extra clothes Chrissie had brought in and some towels. Being detached wasn't easy, and inside she was a quivering mess of worry and anxiety, but without Taklishim here to direct, she needed to step up.

Chapter Thirty-Eight

Degataga allowed himself to get led around. He was terrified for Airiella, for himself and Onida, and at what he had witnessed and done. He broke down in tears again as she undressed him, the clothes a harsh reminder of what their day had been. Skinwalker blood, his blood, Airiella's blood, all smeared all over his skin and that ruined pile of clothes.

To his surprise, Onida stripped down with him and pulled him under the steaming hot spray of water to stand with her. She didn't speak with her mouth, but her eyes and gentle touch told him volumes about how she felt, and how much she understood what he was going through.

She rinsed him clean, the bottom of the shower pink with all the blood that had washed off him. She kissed his chest and wrapped her arms around him, just holding him under the water. He shuddered, remembering how he thought that he wouldn't get to feel her like this again and tried to pull her even closer, his arms clenched tight around her body.

He felt the warmth of her healing abilities and let it spread throughout his body as he cried into her neck, his fears seeping out of him as her love washed him clean. She took care of him the way he'd always craved in the moments of need where his heart was too heavy for him to carry alone.

She pulled away and gave him a soulful kiss and started to wash him with soap, her fingers kneading the muscles that were tight and gentle where bruises marred his skin, a reminder to him that he had been the danger to them at one point.

When they finished, she dried him off and rubbed the minty smelling mix Stolas had given her into his skin, covering every inch of his body. After it soaked in, she did it again, a sign to him that she was worried. Stolas had never steered them wrong on one of his mixes; he didn't doubt that it would do just what he said it would do.

Once she was satisfied, she helped him get dressed, her own body still blessedly naked as her only thought had been to take care of him. She pushed him down into a chair and crawled on to his lap and curled into his chest and let go, silently crying. Her slim shoulders were shaking violently under his arms.

Chrissie snuck into the room and laid a set of clothes on the bed for Onida and took away the bloody ones, silently asking him if he wanted them burned too. He gave her a slight nod, and she crept back out of the room.

A few minutes later, the demon walked in as if he were walking on air, not making a sound. He handed Degataga a bottle of water and motioned for him to drink it and left just as silently. He opened the bottle and chugged it down quickly; the herbal taste not awful and had a hint of spice to it. The pain in his body began to dissipate, and a sense of calm came over him.

He slowly stood up and carried Onida to the bed and set her down, pulling on the clothes Chrissie had left for her. "I almost lost you," she told him, her eyes puffy and red.

"Yes, you did. Almost. Airiella wasn't going to let that happen. And I can't tell you how glad I am that Ronnie and Jax beat me down. I couldn't fight it off, and it would have killed all of you."

"It did something to me inside to see them hurt you like that. Another part of me knew why Ronnie and Jax were doing what they could to put you down without causing serious harm. For a moment, I thought Tama was going to kill you. How did it get to you?" she whispered hoarsely.

"Through the energy that I was using trying to cut off its source, it followed it back to me. It was the most sickening feeling I've ever felt. It took over the use of my body, invaded my soul, but my mind remained me. I think it wanted me to know it was going to make me kill all of you." Degataga shuddered again. "I understand now how Jax felt. Not having control over his body, knowing he was doing things that hurt others. Feeling the dark sickness inside that starts to kill you off."

"I'm so sorry, Dega." She trailed her fingers over his cheek, her eyes sad.

"If Tak hadn't hit me with a shadow, I'm almost sure you would have been the first target. My mind was screaming, my thoughts dark. The pain of my soul tearing like that, it had a clearing effect in a way that it kept my thoughts my own." He sighed, thinking of how many this had affected. "I hope that no one feels guilty for doing what they did. I harbor no resentment for it."

"Ronnie may have a few lingering issues. He had made it clear to me that the only time he struck people was when he was in a controlled fight. He stuck pretty close to Jax after that." She held tightly to his hand, and he felt the warmth of her scanning him again. "It's working," was all she said.

"Airiella saved me, Oni. Not only by pulling that thing out of me, but she also saved my soul with her blood, her words saved my mind. Her powers saved my physical body; her energy saved us all. She told me to live for my babies to live for you." He pressed his hand against her belly. "What she didn't know was that your love saved my heart."

"She knew. She always knows. She sees right through us all, and she does whatever she can to make sure that our hearts are protected, even giving up her own life. Should we see if we can help now? It's been over an hour."

"I couldn't say it then, but I love you, Oni. Always." He stood up, pulling her up with him. "Let's try to repay the favor she grants us all the time. Did you know she told me to kill it, that she couldn't?"

Onida shook her head as she walked out of Ronnie's room. "What do you mean?"

"She knew I needed to kill it, for what it wanted to make me do before I knew it. She gave me everything she had to help me too. I wouldn't have wanted to live if I had killed any of you. Even if it wasn't me doing it, it still was, if that makes sense."

"That's why Ronnie knocked you out," Onida said gently, then changed the subject. "Taklishim and Tama will probably be on their way soon."

They walked back into Airiella's room as a variety of wet bodies were holding Airiella while Ronnie pulled one of his shirts over her head. Chrissie and Stolas had brought in chairs for everyone to sit in as well. "Any change?" Degataga softened his voice.

"Still no pulse, but I still feel her," Jax answered. "Sorry for the beating, Dega. It was all we could think of to do."

"You did the right thing," Degataga told them, looking first at Jax then carefully at Ronnie. Onida had been right; he was struggling with the memory of it. "Ronnie, if you hadn't done what you did, I'd have killed my unborn children and the woman I love. Followed by the rest of you. You helped save everyone."

Jax walked up behind his friend, dropping an arm over his shoulder as he buried his face in Airiella's limp form. Degataga heard his muffled thank you and saw Jax's grateful look. Stolas hovered on the fringes of the group, his face forlorn as his eyes followed wherever they took Airiella.

Ronnie carried her over to the freshly made bed and kissed Chrissie on the cheek as he walked by her. Jax sat down first, Ronnie handing over the angel and then helped Jax settle her between them and trying to arrange her wings in the best way possible, the rest filling in so that they all would be able to touch her.

"May we?" Degataga asked them.

"Please." Despite Jax's belief that she was still there, his face held the agony of what she had endured. The worry about her fate, and the fear he would lose his love.

Onida and Degataga stepped closer, each of them

laying their hands on the lifeless form. Degataga didn't know what Onida felt, but as Stolas had said, he felt no life in her. Keeping his face relaxed, Degataga scanned the rest of her noting the injuries and damage she had sustained. He pulled back the same time Onida did.

He glanced at her and saw the deeply etched worry that lined her face. "Jax is right, I can feel her, but barely. I don't think she has the energy to come back, as we have seen before. While I can feel the energy you all are giving her, it's not enough. She gave it all away."

"What does that mean?" Ronnie's voice was raw with emotion.

Degataga cleared his throat, trying to keep it from thickening up. "That we have a lot of work to do. Maybe if we heal the other injuries, her body will be able to do whatever it needs to, for her to come back. What do you think, Oni?"

She nodded at him, grateful he had stepped in. "It's a start. Maybe by the time Tama and Taklishim get here, they will be able to help."

"Keep touching her," Degataga advised them.

Stolas stood up, "Now would be a good time for you to drink that drink, Doctor."

Degataga handed her the little bag of herbs he'd seen sitting on the bathroom counter and picked up. Chrissie handed her a bottle of water. He waited while she mixed it up and drank it as quickly as she could. She gave him a nod and put her hands back on Airiella, and he followed.

They didn't need to talk; he could see what she was doing to fix the internal injuries, so he started on her wings, pouring everything he could into it. It took them several hours, and by the time they did all that they could, it was dark out.

Tama walked into the room as they sat back and put her hands on Airiella's head, scanning her as they had done. "Did we miss anything?" Degataga asked her quietly so as not to wake Mags and Aedan, who had fallen asleep, Chrissie as well.

"No. Airiella's in there, though." Tama sounded relieved and sad.

"Where's Tak?" Onida asked.

"With the kids. Chrissie's boys are a little worried; they saw Airiella when she came in. He's trying to get them to eat."

At varying times, people drifted in and out of the room; they fell asleep for short periods, and Onida opened the window at some point. "She likes the feel of the air on her."

Degataga remembered one of his father's stories from when he was young about the wind and the ocean. "My father told me once that the wind and the ocean know everything. The air traveled over the whole world, carrying wishes, dreams, whispered prayers, depositing them where they needed to go. The ocean carried all the tears cried, the knowledge of the earth and humans and all other creatures."

Jax and Ronnie looked over at him, waiting for him to continue. Taklishim leaned in the doorway, Tama nestled against him. Stolas simply nodded. Onida stroked the back of his hand, and he took a breath before continuing.

"He said that since time began, it's been the same water, the same air, so as things came and went, they just collected knowledge. The storms that happened were a result of their anger and injustice over the wrongs done throughout time. He told me that if I whispered my wishes to it, they would hear me. And if my heart were true, they'd help deliver the messages to where they needed to go."

As if on cue and breeze blew through the window, caressing his face. "I remember this story now because of what has happened over the past week. I think of how many wishes and hopes I've sent out over all of this. The wishes my mind keeps sending out right now in hopes that the wind is listening and finds my heart pure."

"Is this a Cherokee legend?" Mags asked, Degataga not knowing she had been awake.

"No, not that I'm aware of; I think it was a story of hope my father told me using his wisdom of the universe and how it works."

"It was, he told me the same story," he heard Wohali say. "Sorry for intruding, I just wanted to make sure all was okay. Waya is here too, but I think he's asleep." Degataga looked around and saw them propped up against the wall on the far side of the room.

"Go on," Onida said in his ear.

"Well, as I sit here, wishing and hoping for a sign, I can't help but wonder what happens when the night doesn't answer your cries? What happens when the air is still and unresponsive? Do my wishes and hopes fall flat?" Degataga went silent for a moment as that thought sunk in the group. "I've had that thought more than once this week. This month even. Seeing Spearfinger, seeing Onida crushed by a tree. Watching as Airiella kept vigil over her, forsaking her own health." Degataga's voice thickened up slightly.

"Watching as we trample over the one individual

who speaks to the wind as if it's part of her. It occurred to me a few minutes ago that as the raven, she is a messenger. As an angel, she is the same. The wind carries her and her intent where she needs to be. The wind speaks to her, listens to her. So, if the air is still, is she dead? Have we all lost everything?"

"No," Waya spoke up. "It's when the air is still that it's absorbing everything. When the night is silent, it's taking it all in. Listening."

"Because after it is all said and done, it will carry that message to where it needs to go," Wohali finished. "The air is never still for long."

Degataga felt his eyes well up with tears. "My brothers are right. What we see here, playing out before us, the wind already knew. We all wish the same thing for the same outcome, and no matter how horrible what happened was, the wind already told her."

"It's a fancier way of saying not to lose hope," Wohali explained in case anyone didn't get it.

"It's easy to see only a body lying there with no pulse and believe the worst. It's so much harder to say that you feel Airiella, that she's still there when every sign is telling you she isn't." Waya's voice held a pearl of wisdom reminiscent of his father and Degataga's heart swelled with pride for his brother.

Degataga felt the energy shift in the room, from one of desolation to one of love. Even stranger was yet another breeze that blew through felt by them all and carrying the scent of jasmine. "See? She's here."

The sound of the ocean waves crashing outside grew loud, and an explosion of blue light engulfed the bedroom bathing them all in the loving energy they knew as Airiella.

The soft sound of cries reached Degataga's ears, and he opened his senses to feel the spirit.

He felt the love flowing freely through Airiella's connections, the relief from Jax seeing the light they knew signified life. Ronnie's energy bouncing between happiness and worry. Mags, Smitty, and Aedan overcome with gratitude. Chrissie was bordering on disbelief. Taklishim and Tama still held fear, but love was there too.

Waya and Wohali were utterly amazed, and beside him, Onida radiated life. As the light dimmed, Degataga took in the room on a visual level. The only ones with dry eyes being Waya, Wohali and Onida.

Stolas was on his knees, shaking, his mouth opened in a silent cry that Degataga couldn't try to understand. Taklishim was also on his knees, prostrate, with Tama crouching beside him. On the bed, all of Airiella's connections clutched at her, Chrissie having joined them.

Waya and Wohali, while not crying, were sitting stock-still, their faces were shocked, and their eyes were brimming with emotion. Onida had her eyes closed, her face peaceful, and a soft smile on her lips.

Degataga himself was crying quietly as he now felt in his soul, the breaths she was taking on her own, her pulse resounding in his ears, the promise of life back in the room as the wind answered all their prayers once more.

Degataga stood up, "Let's go rest. Let them be," he said quietly, holding his hand out to Onida and nodding at his brothers.

Chrissie looked over at them, "You can use my room, Ronnie's too. I don't think any of us are leaving here."

Stolas slowly stood, kissed his fingers, and pressed

them lightly to Airiella's head. "Please tell her I was here." He then disappeared.

Degataga looked over at Onida, "Can I just hold you for a while?"

Chapter Thirty-Nine

A month had passed since that awful day. It had brought them all closer together, and Onida was grateful for that. Degataga had sent his family home and promised to be down next month, and Onida's parents were safe and back in their home.

Tama and Taklishim scanned Degataga every day, looking for signs of disease, damage to his soul, or mental well-being from anything that had happened. He was perfect, though. He'd had a few rough nights where he woke with bad nightmares, his terror a living thing in the room with them.

Amazingly, Airiella had spoken to him as he woke, their mental connection not a figment of his imagination like he had thought. Onida was so grateful for it too because her nightmares over it woke her up in a less chaotic way, and she couldn't figure out how to soothe them both.

She needn't have worried. Airiella was present and taking care of them all quietly in that unique way she had. Sometimes with brutal honesty, sometimes with gentle sarcasm and humor, and others with nothing more than pure love.

Onida moved her shirt and spread the gel on her belly while she waited for Degataga to come into the office. She smiled when his presence walked through the doorway, the way he carried himself washing over her. The smooth stride full of confidence at his place in the world. His smile back at her one of the private ones he only used when he was with her.

"Is it okay that I'm nervous?" He sat next to her on the exam table.

"Yes. We've already heard the babies through Airiella. You hold the wand, press it into me firmly, but not hard, and move it like this," she showed him.

Degataga did as she instructed, taking care to be gentle, and soon the sound of the little heartbeats filled the room. Onida pulled the machine closer and freezing the screen to get pictures she hit the print button. As the printer spit out the images, she held them out for Degataga to see.

"This is baby number one, right here, and this one is baby number two," she said as she pointed them out.

"This is us, our love," Degataga said breathlessly, his eyes bright with wonder. "We created little lives."

"We did." Onida laughed. "Are you happy?"

"I'm deliriously happy. I'm also terrified because we created two little lives that are part of each of us, and they are going to be ten times smarter than we are."

"I'm happy too, Dega. These little ones are going to be so lucky to have you as a father."

Onida heard the door crash open, her sister displaying none of her usual feline grace. "Let me see, Oni!"

Degataga held out the pictures to Tama, his eyes

never leaving Onida's face. "Marry me next week."

Onida felt her breath catch in her throat, and she fought back the urge to ask if it was because of the babies. She nodded her head, afraid to speak, to ruin the moment with her doubts. Tama screeched with happiness. "Can we do it at Airiella's? Oh! On the ocean?"

"Tama, you can't offer up Airiella's house like that," Onida chastised her sister.

"Why can't she?" Airiella snuck in the office, her face a giant smile. "My timing is perfect, I see."

"Airiella, I'm sorry. I totally forgot about our appointment." Onida stood quickly, wiping the gel off her belly. "Let me clean up."

"Hawk-eye, don't rush. Let me see the pictures." She slid next to Degataga and Tama.

Onida was sure there was a goofy smile on her face as Degataga proudly pointed out the tiny babies. Probably the same smile that was on his face. She pushed the ultrasound machine out of the way and fixed her clothes.

"We get to be aunties at almost the same time." Tama came up next to her. "How cool is that?"

"I think it's pretty great," Onida admitted. "I've always hoped that our kids would be as close as we are."

"They will be. Are you going to do the mate bond as well?" Tama whispered.

"We haven't talked about it yet. Do you think I shouldn't bring it up?" Onida risked a glance at Dega, who was in a deep conversation with Airiella about something.

"I think he'd be insulted if you didn't," Tama pointed out. "Besides the fact that Airiella is probably ratting you out to him as we speak."

Onida let out a bark of laughter, knowing her sister

was probably right. "Side note, since I have this out, want me to do another picture of yours for you?" She gestured at Tama's rapidly growing belly.

"Yes, please."

"Go ahead, Dega, and I are planning your wedding," Airiella informed them, a smirk on her face.

Onida blushed and took care of her sister quickly. "Oh, want to know the sex?" she asked Tama, a smile blooming on her face.

"You know? You know!" Tama shouted excitedly. She studied the picture carefully. "I can't tell. Does that make me a bad mom?"

All Onida could do was laugh. She stood there and waited, knowing Tama had asked Taklishim if he wanted to know. The sound of her door thudding open let her know that the warrior had arrived. "She knows?" He ignored everyone in the room and looked only at Tama.

"Oni knows, she hasn't shared yet, though." Tama narrowed her eyes, trying to read her sister.

"What are you hoping for, Gandalf?" Airiella poked at him with her finger.

Onida had never seen Taklishim look so suddenly shy. "If you laugh at me, Raven, we are going to have some big problems," he warned her.

"That's not something I would laugh at Taklishim." She grew serious. "Matters of the heart aren't funny."

"I want girls," he said so quietly Onida wasn't sure she heard him.

"Because of your sister?" the angel stood next to him, Tama holding his hand.

He nodded slowly. "I'd name one after my sister, hoping that she would be happy wherever she is."

Airiella's face crinkled up, and her chin wobbled as she fought back the tears. "She's proud of you, Gandalf."

Onida stepped over to Airiella, not sure what was going on with the angel. She looked at both Tama and Taklishim, "I can keep it a secret if you want to be surprised."

Tama and Taklishim gazed at each other for a moment. "Tell us," Tama said softly.

"Taklishim gets his wish," Onida replied, pulling Airiella and Degataga out of the room to leave them alone for a moment. "You knew, didn't you?"

"I did," Airiella confirmed quietly. "Just as I know you will do the right thing and talk to this man about the bond you are afraid to mention."

Put on the spot, Onida didn't know what to say. Degataga took the matters out of her hand. "I'm not sure why you think I wouldn't want to do that, but I do. Tell me what is required."

"Blood," Onida said carefully. "An oath said under the moon."

Degataga pulled out his phone, "Perfect. There's a full moon next Wednesday. Beach wedding under the moon it is."

Airiella squealed. "Yes!"

"You are a meddlesome angel," Onida retorted at her. "Let me scan you."

"I'm fine, Oni. Dr. Strange already scanned me." She danced out of reach. "Better get ready. Jax said he'd grill up dinner for the reception afterward."

Onida let herself get lost in the shuffle of trying to prepare for a wedding. She went with Degataga to get a wedding license, let Tama sweep her off to countless stores looking for the perfect dress while Degataga worked on getting his family up here for the ceremony.

She contacted Father Roarke and asked him to come up and do the honors for them, and let Airiella and Jax handle the rest. Her body was starting to recognize that it was pregnant, and morning sickness started to set in.

Degataga did his best to help ease the symptoms, and she started to wonder if it was just stress over the whole wedding thing, not pregnancy. She still had that lingering doubt in her mind that Degataga was only doing this because of the lives growing inside her.

Two days before the wedding, she did her best to tamp down that voice inside her and take the bull by the horns. "Are you sure you want to do this?"

Degataga froze and turned to look at her slowly. "Are you having second thoughts?" He set the cup he had been drying down gently and schooled his face to remain impassive.

"No. I'm fighting the fear inside me that's telling me you are doing this because I'm pregnant."

At her words, his body relaxed, and he reached for her. "With or without children, I want this. We both have gotten brought back from death's door all too recently, and it just made me move faster. I think you are the only thing in my life that I have never been more sure of wanting."

Onida sighed, her heart hammering against her ribs. "Sometimes this insecurity thing is inconvenient," she whispered, her lips brushing his.

"It's my fault, and I'll make it up to you." His arms tightened around her. "I was worried for a second there that you were going to call it all off."

"That never even crossed my mind. I knew from the

first moment you walked into that council room. Well, my hawk knew. It took me a couple of dates."

"Did you find a dress?" Degataga leaned his forehead down, resting it on hers, their eyes locked in a deep gaze.

"Tama did. She said it was perfect, so I'll trust her. I'm not really a type of person, and she's more into fashion than I am." Onida smiled at the thought of her sister. "She loves this."

Degataga slid his hands down her back and cupped her butt, lifting her, so her knees parted, and she straddled his hips. He turned, setting her gently on the counter. "I can't wait to marry you. To lay claim to you in a ceremony that bonds us for eternity."

"Sitting like this, I think I want to get claimed." She reached between them and unbuttoned his jeans, her hands sliding down, stroking him.

"I should make you wait until after we are married, but I'm not strong enough to hold back when you touch me like that." He pulled her closer, balancing her on the edge of the counter.

She stroked him harder, eliciting a deep groan from his lips. "I guess it's a good thing I'm stronger than you then." She pushed him back and buttoned his pants back up.

"That's just cruel." He shifted, trying to get more comfortable with a lot less room in his pants.

"I'm just teasing." She hopped off the counter and took his hand. "Come on, time for you to make it up to me."

Chapter Forty

Onida looked in the mirror and frowned. "I don't look like me," she told Tama. "I look like you."

"Well, we are identical twins, so that makes sense." Tama laughed.

Onida met her mother's eyes in the mirror. "Mom, what do you think?"

"I think you are beautiful and that you do look like you. Tama's dress was a lot showier than this one," she pointed out.

Onida glanced down at the simple gown her sister had picked out. It landed just above her ankles and flowed with her body movements while hugging her gentle curves, making her feel more feminine than she was used to feeling. The dress was sleeveless and had a V-neck that ended between her small breasts.

"Airiella said to stay barefoot," Tama advised as she fastened an exquisite turquoise necklace around her neck.

Onida's hair was swept up off her neck and in a simple chignon and had a few turquoise pins strategically placed. The makeup was simple, but again, more than Onida was used to seeing. She had to admit that she looked beautiful and elegant.

There was a soft knock at the door, and Onida's mother opened it slightly to peek out, then wider as Asgasga walked in, trailed by Jax. "Is everything okay?" she asked him nervously.

"Yes. I'm your official photographer, just came to get a few shots." His smile was genuine and warm. "You look stunning, Onida."

She blushed and looked down, Tama reaching forward and tipping her chin up. "None of that. Thank the man."

"Thank you, Jax," Onida replied promptly.

"Go about finishing up," he instructed her, sitting out of the way. "I like my shots to be candid."

Asgasga stepped forward, "He's right, you are stunning. I was hoping you would do the honors and use the blankets that my husband and I used for our wedding." Asgasga held out a blue blanket to Onida. "In Cherokee weddings, each person wears a blue blanket, then when the ceremony is complete, you are draped in a white one that symbolizes the one life you share."

"It would be an honor." Onida held the blanket close to her chest.

Asgasga reached out her hand and stroked Onida's cheek, "It's an honor to have you as a part of my family."

Tama gently took the blanket from her and draped it over Onida's shoulders, "Like this?" Tama asked Asgasga, who nodded in reply, her eyes shining with unshed tears. The blue of the blanket complimented Onida's skin tone and was an excellent accent for the blue of the necklace and pins in her hair.

Jax posed them for a few party photos and then left

declaring the ceremony ready to begin, escorting Tama and Asgasga back down, leaving Onida standing there with her mother. "You are going to be a great wife and mother, Oni. Much better than I have ever been. Let that fear right out of your head. You aren't like me."

The simple words overcame Onida, and she didn't know what to say. Her mom took Onida's arm, and gracefully went from the room to where her father was waiting. At the sight of her, Chief Tyee broke out into sobs. "Oni, you are so beautiful. I'm so proud of you."

"Dad, don't cry. If my makeup gets ruined, Tama is going to make me sit still so she can do it again," Onida pleaded with her father. Secretly she was thrilled with his words of praise.

"I'm your dad, it's allowed." He smiled through his tears. "I'm so happy right now."

Once he was back under control, he took Onida's other arm and walked her out of the house, through the backyard and down to the little path that led to the beach. From what Onida could see, Airiella had outdone herself. She smelled the cedar wood of the benches they'd had made as a wedding gift and saw the people closest to her sitting there waiting for her to make her entrance.

Soft flute music was playing as they stepped forward down to the beach, and her eyes fastened immediately on the man she was marrying. An identical blue blanket around his shoulders and a simple black tuxedo covered his body, and her breath caught at how incredibly beautiful this man was, standing in front of a gently burning fire.

Their very existence bringing them together as they were supposed to be; that voice of doubt that had been plaguing her disappeared the second their eyes met. Degataga's eyes were shining with love and admiration. She could only hope that he saw the same in her own eyes. She was a lucky woman.

His eyes held the promise she needed to hear. His smile held the love that kept her going. His body held the protection her soul craved, and he was the part of her she had been missing. She was whole with him; she didn't feel lacking.

"Oni, you are the most beautiful thing I have ever laid eyes on," he whispered as she approached.

"Ditto." She smiled softly at him.

The sun started to set, and Taklishim and Tama said blessings over the ceremony, the guests, and the land on which they were declaring their union. Father Roarke led them in a simple wedding ceremony and then pulled out a piece of paper.

"Now, I will read a tribal prayer for the couple," he said.

"God in heaven above, please protect the ones we love. We honor all you created as we pledge our hearts and lives together. We honor mother—earth—and ask for our marriage to be abundant and grow stronger through the seasons;" the earth rumbled in response, startling Onida. "We honor fire—and ask that our union be warm and glowing with love in our hearts;" the flames behind Father Roarke grew. "We honor wind—and ask that we sail through life safe and calm as in our father's arms;" the wind swirled around them. "We honor water—to clean and soothe our relationship—that it may never thirst for love;" the water rushed towards them, trickling over their feet. "With all the forces of the universe you created, we pray for harmony and true happiness as we forever grow young together. Amen."

At that moment, lightning flashed through the sky in acknowledgment of their union, and Father Roarke lifted the blue blankets from them and placed a white one that covered both of them. "I now pronounce you, husband and wife. Go on now, kiss her." Father Roarke smiled at Degataga.

As he settled his soft lips over hers, their family broke out in cheers and clapping. The sun had set, and the moon rose in its place, it was time for their mate ceremony. Taklishim stepped forward and handed Onida a small silver knife inlaid with beautiful turquoise in the shape of a hawk.

She took a deep breath in and gripped the one-sided blade in her palm, the sharpness of the blade separating her skin with ease, and she held her now bleeding hand over the open fire and handed the knife to Degataga who did the same. Their blood dripping into flames, Onida started.

"My animal chooses you to complete her soul. She vows to protect you, provide for you, and honor you in all she does. She opens her soul to you, her chosen mate. She offers you her blood that flows through her veins so that her life is tied forever to yours. With the moon as my witness, I make this sacred vow and take you as my mate, a bond that can never be break."

Onida felt the bond come to life at her words, and she looked at Degataga, the man now her husband. He repeated her vows, his voice steady. "My heart chooses you and your animal to complete his soul. I vow to protect you and your animal, provide for you and your animal and

honor you and your animal in all that I do. I open my soul
to you and your animal, my chosen mate. I offer you my
blood that flows through my veins so that my life is tied
forever to you and your animal. With the moon as my
witness, I make this sacred vow and take you as my mate, a
bond that can never break."

She held her bleeding palm out to him, and
Degataga grasped it with his own, their blood mingling
between them as that mate bond snapped into place,
energy and power flowing freely between them in the most
intimate way. Their souls merging and minds were opening
with the magic that was theirs alone.

Oni, you are my life.

As you are mine, Dega.

Bolts of lightning lit the night sky in a way that
fireworks never could, and they both felt the love of Airiella
flooding their bodies with her happiness. Waves crashed up
on the beach, over their bare feet, and into the fire, putting
it out. The smoke swirling it's wisps up into the air and to
the moon, sealing their bond.

Tama was the first to congratulate them, taking
their hands in hers, she healed up the wounds and kissed
them both. "Time to party!"

Onida still held Degataga's hand and they led the
way back up to the backyard where Jax fired up his grill
and cooked them a feast. Their hands still clutching each
other's they ate, laughed, and danced until they were the
last ones still standing under the moonlit sky.

"Whatever comes next, I can handle knowing you'll
be there with me." Degataga smiled and kissed her slowly.

"I think what happens next is a whole lot of just
married sex where we don't have to worry about getting

pregnant because it's already happened," Onida joked.

"Home, then?" Degataga grinned, ready for that part to begin.

"Yes, home. Tama made me put on some incredibly exotic lingerie under this dress, and I'm anxious to see what it feels like when you take it off me," Onida told him with heat in her eyes.

"I guess that means I'm going to be speeding then," Degataga told her as he pulled her to their car.

"I love you, Dega."

"I love you, Oni."

Michelle Lee on the Web

Michelle on Facebook at
tiny.cc/MichelleLeeWrites

or write to
MichelleLeeWrites@gmail.com

Also by Michelle Lee

The Raven's Journey
Book 1: See Me
Book 2: See Me Revealed
Book 3: See Me Go
Book 4: See Me Believe
Book 5: See Me Overcome
Book 6: Hawk
Book 7: Ronan
Book 8: Stolas

I S.P.I.
Supernatural Paranormal Investigations
Book 1: Surf & Turf
Book 2: The Doxy Proxy
Book 3: You're the T*ts
Book 4: Cop Out

Made in United States
Troutdale, OR
06/09/2024

20360178R00216